SNOOTY BARONET

SNOOTY BARONET

by

WYNDHAM LEWIS

AUTHOR OF "TARR," "THE WILD BODY,"
"THE APES OF GOD," ETC.

HASKELL HOUSE PUBLISHERS LTD.
Publishers of Scarce Scholarly Books
NEW YORK. N. Y. 10012
1971

First Published 1932

HASKELL HOUSE PUBLISHERS LTD.
Publishers of Scarce Scholarly Books
280 LAFAYETTE STREET
NEW YORK, N. Y. 10012

Library of Congress Catalog Card Number: 77-176492

Standard Book Number 8383-1359-0

Printed in the United States of America

CONTENTS

		PAGE
I	New York	1
II	Val	6
III	Humph	57
IV	Mithras	89

V	Lily	108
VI	The Hatter's Automaton	132
VII	A Lord of Language and his Boat	165
VIII	Bull-fight—Bouches du Rhône	199
IX	The Universe of Absence: postscript to bull-fight—bouches du rhône	231
X	Persia	234
XI	Bandit-Host	299
XII	Snooty's S.O.S.	307

SNOOTY BARONET

NEW YORK

NOT A BAD face, flat and white, broad and weighty: in the daylight, the worse for much wear—stained, a grim surface, rained upon and stared at by the sun at its haughtiest, yet pallid still: with a cropped blondish moustache of dirty lemon, of toothbrush texture: the left eye somewhat closed up—this was a sullen eye. The right eye was more open and looked bright; it sat undisturbed under its rolled-up wide-awake rounded lid. The right side of the face had held out best!—The nose upon the face indicated strength of character if anything—the mouth, which did not slit it or crumple it, but burst out of it (like an escaped plush lining of rich pink), that spelled sensitiveness if anything, of an inferior order. The brows and temples were up in a fawn-saffron "Derby". The "Derby" was the ordinary transatlantic "Derby"—the sort men are careful religiously to remove when they enter the public hall of an hotel, particularly west of Nantucket, to show that they are educated. (There may be ladies there!)

The face was on-the-lookout behind the window-glass of the taxicab. The left eye kept a sullen watch: it was counting. Numbers clicked-up in its counting-box, back of the retina, in a vigesimal check-off. When it had counted up to a thousand and forty—starting however at four hundred and eighty (a *fifteen-cent-tariff* yellow knickerbocker, as luck would have it) the taxi stopped. The face drew back. The door opened. Grasping the forward jamb, a large man thrust out one leg, which was straight and stiff. Pointing the rigid leg downwards, implacably on to the sidewalk, the big man swung outward, until the leg hit terra-firma. The whole bag-of-tricks thus stood a second crouched in the door of the vehicle. Then stealthily there issued from its door, erect and with a certain brag in his carriage, a black-suited six-footer, a dollar-bill between his teeth, drawing off large driving gauntlets.

The face was mine. I must apologize for arriving as it were incognito upon the scene. No murder has been committed at No. 1040 Livingston Avenue—I can't help it if this has opened as if it were a gunman best-seller.—The fact is I am a writer : and the writer has so much the habit of the anonymous, that he is apt to experience the same compunction about opening a book in the First Person Singular (caps. for the First Person Singular) as an educated man must feel about commencing a letter with an " I ". But my very infirmity suggested such a method. I could hardly say : " The taxi stopped. I crawled out. I have a wooden leg ! " Tactically, that would be hopelessly bad. You would simply say to yourself, " This must be a dull book. The hero has a wooden leg. Is the War not over yet ? " and throw the thing down in a very bad temper, cursing your Lending Library.

I was leaving the States next day. This was New York. And I had driven to this up-town address to collect my mail—a month's arrears of it, for I had been moving about constantly. Here was the office of my american agent, 1040 Livingston Avenue.

Having told you my profession (in the Passport sense) I must do what is called in more pompous treatises, to issue a caveat. I am not a narrative writer. As to being a " fiction " writer, I could not bring myself to write down that I am not *that*. I may never I hope be called upon to repudiate an imputation of that order. But the art of narrative, that is a different matter to " fiction ". To Defoe I take off my hat. Then there was Goldsmith. I should prefer to make it clear at once at all events that I occupy myself only with scientific research. Such claim as I may have to be a man-of-letters, reposes only upon the fact that my investigations into the nature of the human being have led me to employ the arts of the myth-maker, in order the better to present (for the purposes of popular study) my human specimens. Henri Fabre dramatized his insects in that way. I have sometimes thought that had I a mind to, I could write narrative with unexampled success. But I remember the retort of Elia when William Wordsworth (like William Windham and his master Burke, no great friend of the *Tricoteuse*, having had a bastard by one, in point of fact) had asserted that he could write as good a play as Hamlet *if he had a mind to*—namely, " But you see, he h-h-h-h-h-hadn't ! " Also, it may be that I only believe so much in the certainty of my triumph in that line, because most contemporary " fiction " is so wearisome, not satisfying, as I find it, my perhaps-too-exacting demand for scrupulous analysis. The shortcomings of the scientific training, if you like ! But so I feel it to be.

I get out of the taxi, then, as you have seen, I enter the large swing-doors—always an uneasy operation with me in America, where their glass wings are apt to be dashed round with the velocity of a top, and often I have met with minor accidents, on account of my leg. Ten minutes later, the doors ever-turning—it is a big busy business block—there I am again ! Under my arm is a parcel. That is the *mail* which I had come to fetch at my agent's.

How clumsy this opening is after all I have just been saying, you are certain to say to yourself !—for here is a hero, with a mechanical leg, upon the sidewalks of New York, a parcel beneath his arm—containing, you have been informed, a month's arrears of mail, and (as who cannot at once divine?) an important communication. And it is perfectly obvious that he cannot open it there and then, jostled by the american crowd, and tear open the letter or cable in question.—He could, it is true, be knocked down—Mr. Churchill has conferred upon that device an air of probability. This could happen in Fifth Avenue, or better still the corner of East Forty-ninth Street and Park Avenue—the guilty driver hitting the high spots as he sped off to the shelter of the Bronx—the packet would naturally burst, and be violently broadcast by the charging machines. The essential document could be picked up by a traffic-cop and sent on to the hospital. All that I see. But this shall not happen. No, you shall on the contrary have the satisfaction of observing me belie my boast. Painfully, or at least slowly, I shall remove myself for you from in front of the revolving door ventilating the lift-hall of the concrete tower where my agent has his office. Yawning I shall take you past the Empire State Building—upon the other side of the street, so that you may look up into the summer sky and admire Al Smith's Last Erection: and compel you to wait for the red traffic-light, take you deliberately across Fifth Avenue, and in due course of time you shall enter with me the second of the large spinning four-fold doors, which admit a promiscuous public to the hall of my hotel. Only when we reach my small room upon the twentieth floor of the Schuyler Hotel can we get at the cable. It is a cable.

The cable reads:

When do you sail important HUMPH.

All I have to do now is to pick up the telephone at the side of my bed and reply, to the woman clerk at the Telegram Counter in the hotel hall:

Sailing tomorrow *Europa*.

Thus we swiftly connect with Humph. And Humph is the hero of this story, not me at all. Our next stop will be London, England. Will you pass over the Atlantic with me as quickly as possible, please?

VAL

I HATE ARRIVING in London and won't bore you with that. I was met of course with posters, the intervening stations between Southampton and London were plastered thick with them. They were one and all of the usual admonitory order. A welcoming Ballyhoo—to bring us up-to-date! In a democracy the business of State is conducted upon an oily pulpit note. (Thus " Service " is the keynote of the american continent. But are we much better?) SEE YOUR OWN COUNTRY FIRST: how often has that stopped me from taking a ticket to Cornwall?—or BUY BRITISH spoilt my appetite for Cheddar? And now it is BE MANLY! BE BRITISH! DRINK BEER! (In every pub. this obscenity hangs over the bar.) So many stern and unexpected duties crowded upon the returning traveller! BUYERS ARE BUILDERS! exclaimed one placard at Winchester.—But this was very bad! I pulled down the side-blind—I buried my face in a copy of a sadly diminished British Sunday Newspaper. All the week's nonsense was compressed into a handful of pages no bigger than the Stock and Share Supplement for the New York Sunday omnibus-newspaper. MORE SERVICE! I became acquainted with the latest forms of prayer prescribed for the British Churches. Such items as (I quote from memory) " From lording and bossing it over other people, such as Bengalees, Kafirs, Black Boys, etc., instead of submitting as good Christians to other people who desire to lord and boss over us—GOOD LORD DELIVER US!"—" For all our sins as a nation, of early and misguided Individualism—FORGIVE US IN THY MERCY O LORD!" Then I read the latest literary-sermon, upon the literary-page. This was very bad indeed. The officiating goodman-critic, from his week-end pulpit faced his congregation, the Well-to-do who read a book a day, telling them how to lay out the money they still enjoy at the expense of Miners, Stokers and other riff-raff. The Old Ladies of Land's End and the Worthy Widows of Caithness, pencil-in-hand to jot down his list of those authors "to be watched", were assured that "literature was not something that could be taught" (nothing *scientific—he* could not teach them at least): it was an affair of the *heart*. It "was something to be *loved*". Oh dear! At that I gnashed my great white teeth and tapped my mouth (there were ladies present), "gaped" in my throat awhile, with fearful side-long grimaces of politeness, and fell flat asleep. I woke up at Waterloo mildly refreshed. I do not much like sleeping upright but sometimes there is nothing for it.

Had I considered what Humph might have to say to me upon my return, while I chugged across, boxed up with a hull-full of morons, stupefied in the see-saw of the Atlantic-routine? Why no, I can't say I had. I have tried just now to remember—I suppose once or twice, while shovelling discuses about the top deck (for the most part shooting short, into Minus Ten, on account of my clockwork limb) I must have repeated to myself "Important", once perhaps and then dismissed it. Nothing conceived in the brain of Humph could by any possibility be *important*. But when I reached my rooms—two basement rooms and a closet with a basin and tap—my landlady indicated a large pile of letters upon my work-table. Two letters marked URGENT were revealed, as I ran through the pile, and one was from Humph. I opened it therefore, I gave it priority over the other urgent one (the other smelled—

"women and children last!"). And this is what I read, yawning yet glad to be back.

MY DEAR SNOOTY,

Thanks for cable. I see the *Europa* gets in on Sunday. Please give me a ring first thing Monday morning. Don't fail to do this. I shall be in all the morning. I have something to put up to you, the best yet. You know what we've talked over so often. It's what we've been looking for. I can't tell you till we meet. Ring up early.

HUMPH.

This put a different complexion on it I confess. I said to myself, yawning still, that I would telephone as this Dunmow Flitch suggested, bad luck to him. There was something there that he had up his sleeve perhaps that might be worth looking into. Anything for money now. I had been hit by the dollar, still on its gold-standard. Anyway I should have to see him—I sat right down and began to tear open the envelopes: some had been so carelessly steamed open and stuck up again that they just peeled up before I got my finger inside. Half were bills. The other *Urgent* letter was from Valerie.

You have been wondering, I expect, how I manage to get about. We all have the minds of Income Tax Inspectors these days. It is a fault. But I sympathize with you—I simply can't read a book myself when the fellow doesn't tell me right away how it is he is able to go to the South Seas or for that matter have a new Morris-Oxford, or dine at the Savoy. If I didn't make haste to enlighten you we shouldn't be comfortable, I know. I understand. So here goes.

Have I got a silver spoon in my mouth? That is the gist of the matter, isn't it? So *Were you born with a silver spoon in your mouth?* then. *No, but I have a silver plate on my head* is the answer to that. *And* I have a nickel nether limb, fitted with clockwork!

My pension for all that is my fortune, sir, she said. That puts that straight, doesn't it—now we can go ahead! My pen makes me a little too. So I move round in my crippled state more easily than when I had my two legs.

I opened the letter from Valerie, yawning my head off.

What Valerie said in the letter, what she *said*, that is perfectly immaterial. Old Valerie always got under my skin. (I am apt to employ the idiom of those I suppose I am addressing, you understand me?) I go to see her in her maisonnette. Always I go with reluctance, as if I were going to have out a very cushy tooth, soft and easy, but still a pang. And then that dentist's manner! To continue the simile. What a repulsive technique! Old Val's revolts me.

She is nothing if not shoppy, the old harlot. (But picture to yourself a dentist who giggled all the time while he was yanking your tooth out!)—Still I go for more! I go regularly. I go with irritation. I go with a subtle confusion. I even go with shame, but I go regularly: sniggering (I catch the trick) I succumb: and old Val whisks my leg off quicker than any woman I know. (I only know two as a matter of fact, with whom my relations are such as to provoke or suggest that act of drastic amputation in the natural course of things, at a certain point in the interview—where it recommends itself as being if not necessary at least more practical.)

Whenever therefore I took up a letter of Valerie's I did not see the words at all, luckily. No syllable was visible upon the wordy pages. This was a distinct advantage of course. I only heard the voice. But one might go further and say that fortunately the voice itself did not come through at all distinctly—since it must be confessed that it was not a very attractive one. I just had sensations of sight, a few tactile vibrations, corresponding to a certain number of obscurely pleasant past occurrences. Nothing more.

From all this you will gather, and you will be right, that I am for old Val every time, or was. I suppose I was keen on the old girl, or she'd " got me in the bed " to use her customary expression. Well let us leave it at that. Val was in the enviable position of a siren at that time domiciled in my blood-stream. The *words* in consequence of her song, anyway, *they* meant less than nothing. And a sickly old sex-dirge it generally was, which she propelled through the post in coffin-shaped envelopes.

Besides (I think I said that just now), many of Val's expressions were quite unprintable, except in de luxe editions privately printed in Paris or Milan—here it would be out of the question to undertake a literal transcription of old Val's mother-tongue. We should all be in quod—I for writing it, you for reading it, and the poor devil of a printer's devil for setting up the stuff—about the publisher I shouldn't mind (he probably ought to be there anyway).

I rang up old Valerie at once. She was there of course. She was always there ! Of late her one or two earlier boy-friends fought shy of the old girl (because she's got into hot water with a group of " Gossip-Stars "—gilded young girl-bachelors and middle-aged monocled martinets, one especially named Venetia—on account of literary indiscretions). She just sat there near her bed-telephone all day long, hoping against hope that she'd get a call. Scarcely had one pushed the pennies into the automatic machine (I always used a public-box in a pub. and I believe she had come to know the sound and time-interval for its rusty wheel) then *there* was the old girl's voice, bright and expectant. Indeed hers was the quality of patience that is not strained, of a first-class mouser—all sense of time apparently lost in an uncanny concentration, crouched above an alas ! very-little-frequented mouse-hole !

And all that over the tell-tale wires was conveyed to you the moment you called her up. In her careful business-like voice as she snatched the receiver down, it was all there and more. You dreaded to think how long she had sat there. And then she possessed such a terribly finished telephone-personality. Her telephone-voice was that of the stage-impersonation of telephoning, with a dummy-telephone. And then, oh, the shattering gaiety of the mayfairish high-life drama, as arranged for the suburbs (once a day, a matinée, perhaps, and once, or perhaps two, a night). Such impeccable technique, for what of late had become such a lonely little part!

"*Hull*-o Snoots! I've been wondering when you'd get back——"

"Here I am!" swelling in the telephone-box. "I am right here."

"I *am* glad! Have you had a good time? When did you get back?"

That is what happened on this occasion.

I made a few aimless remarks.

"Been going out a lot lately Val, been going out a lot or not?" I enquired. "Any parties—any nice parties?"

"Parties! No-o-o-o! No parties *at all* Snooty! I know you don't believe me!"

"Yes I do!"

"You *don't*!"

"Oh yes."

"You always imagine me Snoots living in the midst of a wild orgy of petting-parties—picnics—balls—routs!"

"Routs?" I roared forth, causing the pub.-cabin to thunder, stamping upon the concertina floor, while Val tittered hysterically at the other extremity of the wires in Chelsea—"parties!"

"Yes-s-s-ss!" back she buzzed in the bass, at the top

of her telephone-form. " If you only *knew* Snoots how *few*——! ! "

" Ah ! " I did then faintly exclaim, with due incredulity.

" But it's a *fact* Snoots—it's the *truth* ! " she screamed into the receiver. " Only two—no *three*—last week ! "

" You don't say so ! " I knew from experience of Val, though she was far from crediting me with such tremendous powers of observation, that " party " meant one or two thankless jaunts to some semi-suburb. Some little bohemian *ménage*—present, that is the " party ", two harassed artists, hangers-on of the party-gang bosses—a dish of cod hotted-up and stuck in a gritty scallop-shell, a glass of oatmeal stout, tinned pears, and Craven A, cork tipped.

I knew she longed to see me. Not quite for the same reasons that I desired to see her : but her need, more complex, was greater than mine. I liked the old girl. The pathos of her depressed me nevertheless and here was the first touch of it. Frankly I had to fight against that sad feeling each time I wanted to see her. I now said in what is for me a cordial even caressing voice :

" Shall we meet !—Shall I come round Val and when—how about tomorrow night ? I will come to dinner, what do you say ? I will come about nine.—Nine o'clock."

I deliberately took rather long over this. That would give Val time to think up an excuse for being able to see me the next night. It was my humane intention to save her face, for my own sake if for nothing else. It would depress me so terribly should she grow cowed all of a sudden at having to say simply " Yes Snoots—I have nothing to do. Come tomorrow night," I could not bear it. I should not go.

But even as it was it had been a shade sudden. *Tomorrow night !* The assurance of my proposal, however disguised, or slowed-down, threatened to undermine for the moment the cherished rôle—that of the so-much-sought-after-girl-of-fashion. I awaited the result with anxiety. I did hope she would not just say *yes*. But it was all right. The poor old girl, through much rough usage, was never at a loss—though the fizz, the *mousse*, when she answered, had gone out of her phone-tones.

"Tomorrow!" A short sharp pause. "I think that will be all right. Let me see." A much shorter pause—she was afraid I was about to suggest a more distant evening! "If you don't mind holding on just a moment Snoots—just hold on will you and I will look at my engagement-book—I'm sure it will be all right though!"

I was positive it would be too: I picked my teeth and tapped my foot, while she pretended to look in her book. There was quite a good pause this time, before the instrument rattled and gasped and again opened up.

"Yes Snooty that will be all right. That will be lovely! At nine then! At nine did you say?"

"Nine, yes."

"All right nine. I'll expect you. That will be lovely."

"Good-bye Val."

"Good-bye Snooty-darling, till tomorrow."

"Till tomorrow."

I always sleep as though I never would wake again my first night in Old England and about eleven o'clock next day and when the pub. opened, I telephoned Humph. But Humph's secretary said she was sorry, Humph had just got through from Cornwall where he had gone two days before on Saturday. He could not possibly get back till the afternoon as he had been detained, and would I please ring up at four-thirty? That would be impossible I said. The pub. was shut at that hour. But over that inelegant fact I threw the pompous word *impossible*. Next morning I would telephone I told her, as now I was doing: and Humph's office-wench good-bayed.

That night at nine I was before Val's railings, I pressed the button on her doorpost, the window as it lumbered up gave out its harsh protesting rattle (a heavy old window, perhaps as old as Adam, Robert and James that hated to be disturbed) and from the first floor flat immediately above the front-steps, there was the girlish old head of Mistress Val the Chelsea Enchantress, *model* 1930 (great reduction in price). It was poked out for her to make certain it was the right man of course—there were so many—one couldn't be too careful could one!

"Hullo Snoots!" came her soft roguish snort, as she coyly prolonged her scrutiny, at gaze upside down for a picturesque second or two and me looking up at her, smiling-cheeked, my big teeth in evidence (my pack of visiting-cards). But the head shot back into the room pronto—I heard her coming down the unlighted staircase, hurrying. No time to be lost—*I might go away!* When she reached the door I might no longer be there, if she did not put her best foot forward. I prayed she might not break her neck.

Standing clipped in under the waist, in my rug-like tweed portmanteau-overcoat, of reefer finish—as if it had been sucked in where the parting of the legs began, in an inelegant sartorial crevasse—softly I stroked, through the hefty pouch of its side-pocket, my mechanical thigh. I steadied my countenance for this confrontation. Everyone was banished from my face, I banished even myself. In their place I put Butler. I will explain this however. I have to make you acquainted with all of my habits, one by one.

As I came along I had been thinking, as very often I did at that time, of Samuel Butler's very odd habits with women. It was how for instance he visited, for ten solid years, a particular woman—regularly every Saturday it was I think he did it, except during summer vacations (Alps and Sanctuaries need I remind you) and the woman never during all that decade knew so much as his name. That was a record I think in incognito. Perhaps he may have said " I'm Sam." But I should doubt it.

When that strange visitant ceased abruptly to put in an appearance, what then? Was the woman superstitious about his stopping? I expect so—a friendly element had suddenly given her the cold shoulder. She had been given the bird. The bird had been given her by the Anonymous Man. Presage of the sere and yellow leaf. This swallow had quitted her mellow furrows. Had she known however that that swallow was Genius (that is something abstract) too, what a shiver would have gone through her mortal marrow! Woman, an abstraction to him, and he as Anonymous Man—as becomes Genius, abstract and nameless. There was a fine situation I said to myself—and I wished I could be " Snooty "—an abstraction, a mere quality—not have as was the case a clumsy tribal cognomen, of the house of Imrie, and of the house of Kell.

But how much did Butler leave upon the sage plush victorian mantelshelf (while the corsetless wasp-waisted Abstraction, with its mane of golden hair, affected to look the other way) when he left the Pimlico bed-sitting-room? He was a liberal person. (We have the testimony of his upkeep for forty years of a master-sponger of his own sex.) I now remembered a pound I had borrowed from Valerie and I put my hand in my note-pocket. She opened the door upon me as I was fingering a paper pound-sterling.

" Snoots! " she panted, in her best arch coax.

" Val! " cried I, and I grinned in the face of as much of my fate as Val represented—turning up like a bad penny. Or was it *I* who turned up, as Einstein would have it: or is it really impossible to say which? Had this front-door and myself been forever approaching each other, and which had run quickest through intervening time, to run to meet the other? Certainly it, not I! Yes, most unquestionably, and all this ponderous Chelsea mansion, its heavy porch, had been brought up to me bodily, with old Val reeling in its doorway with her beady eyes and beckoning me inside. That was my account of the transaction. Einstein had supplied me with just the subjective physical framework that suited me.

She stepped back and I raised my artificial foot and entered the hall as she retreated. As it were sadly, as it were wistfully, she beat her slow retreat. She was being shy and silent, she was being girlish. I for my part was being Samuel Butler!

There is scarcely anything I enjoy so much as imagining myself for a short while other people. I do not mind if they are quite unimportant. But for preference I take up a man with a name, that is only natural. According to the classical canons of acting I suppose I should be rather second-rate. For there are only a few parts that suit me. No one knows better than myself that for that profession at least I have too much personality. This does not prevent me from acting however.

I have often impersonated Samuel Butler. He is distinctly one of my favourite rôles. I can pick him up quite easily, though in physique we must be as different as chalk from cheese. I am a very fine man indeed—once you have seen me you would hardly forget me; whereas Butler was an ill-shaped fellow according to his own account. But that makes no difference.

If you knew me you would be familiar with a particular smile which often visits, but does not belong upon, my face. That is my *Butler smile!* Old Val has remarked it over and over again. She has not the least suspicion of its origin, but she dislikes it extremely. All my friends dislike it extremely. I have not brought it to its fullest perfection yet : but when I have, I am confident that it will have an even more painful effect.

I often do Butler when I visit Val. I even have a Butler laugh. It goes with the smile. But for some reason it has never been so effective. I have closely studied its effects : but I have not so far been able to account for its miscarriage, and comparative ineffectiveness. I believe it is something to do with my teeth.

That night I stopped Butler quite some time. I even paid back the pound. And I am bound to say I had a very agreeable butlerish time of it, tucked up in the lion's skin of the famous author of " The Way of All Flesh ".

In the hall I tapped old Val about a little just to show I esteemed her back as much as her front. We thumped up the stairs making a great deal of noise, Val saying, with her prim white-collared masculine manner " Don't Snoots ! " and I being a little fresher than usual just to flatter her up. She was tickled to death of course and squirmed so much at the bend of the stairs we nearly tumbled.

My God I had forgotten. I suppose I have to describe her for you. That is a bore. I had forgotten about it. There is really nothing much to describe, however. Her eyes are too close together, her forehead too narrow, which makes her best in profile. But in profile there's her chin. That's a little too " double "—she's always talking about it. Her hair is thin, and it is fairish. Her face has a swarthy massaged flush. (If you look too close, it is full of pits : under the make-up it is a field of gaping pores—her nose is worst in this respect : some day it will disintegrate, for all practical purposes.) She screws up her eyes and giggles nearly all the time. Then she will quickly stop, as if offended suddenly, straighten her face out, sniff very slightly, and pull her upper lip down like a latch over the under one, and look over her left shoulder hard at the floor for awhile, prim-lipped and frowning. But her figure is *good.* It is really a good one, if you don't mind an extra pound of flesh, in the right place. Then as to her general appearance, that is not bad. She intends it to be mayfairish and mannish: she really is not too bad getting into a taxi or going into an hotel. She passes all the mirror-tests of the Lounges and cloak-room passages. I could take her to Claridge's without shocking the *sommelier.*

As for her age, I have no reliable method for women's ages, but Val conceals hers *somewhere* between thirty and forty, that is as near as I can get. She might be a very blowsy thirty or so, or a pretty good thirty-eight.

When we came into her sitting-room, she turned round and faced me as though she had a bone to pick. A habit of hers. She put down her head, depressed the flexible centre of her upper lip in a cat-like prudish *moue* and looked up, in an arch pause, for a brief moment. What would Butler have done I thought? I had not the least idea. I was at a loss to imagine, so I sat down upon the settee in my portmanteau-overcoat and stuck out my leg.

She wheeled slowly.

" Snoots " she said " how are you ? "

How still the room was—you could have heard a pin drop in the street outside. I looked up at her and yawned.

" You look well Snoots ! "

It was really just as though we'd had a row—a very intelligent row. But not a cross word had ever passed between us. As to high words it was unthinkable. *High words* would be out of the question, as between old Val and Yours Truly.

I rose from what an American would undoubtedly describe as a davenport—and if you are an American that is what it was. I crossed the room and sat down at the table, where I saw a salad and some slices of bread.

" Shall we have supper at once ? " Val asked, curt prim

and distant, watching my movements as if they had been those of a rude and incalculable enemy.

" Sure ! " I said.

She left the room. She had gone to the kitchen to hot up the *pot-au-feu*, made out of threepennyworth of dog-bones and yesterday's vegetable scraps, plus a toasted crust. I uncorked a bottle of Château Neuf du Pape—she thought the name would take me in as it does the general run of London off-licence customers—and I placed it near the coal-fire, in the grate. At least I would have the stuff *hot*. I might have had it *boiling* with advantage, as I discovered. Then I removed my overcoat and fell back upon the settee.

When she came in with the *pot-au-feu* in the earthenware saucepan I got up, I went across to the table. Neither of us spoke, the meal started in silence. We were an old married couple, sat down at the table—brooding and eating. I'm bound to say I felt very *Butlerish!* Several times I had broken into the Butler smile and Val had remarked it and shied away or tossed her head. She was playing up fine. It was almost as if she hadn't known my name, and as if we had done this together for a decade. We were like a stage-version of " an old married couple ", by a pair of victorian lawbreakers, painfully " under the rose ".

I got up and fetched the Château Neuf du Pape.

" Well happy days " I muttered.

Fixing me with a severe offended eye, she drank and then, pricking up one eyebrow expressively, transferred her gaze deliberately to her plate.

" When I was in China " I said.

" Have you been in China ? " I was interrupted at once.

" Oh yes."

" You might have sent me a postcard."

" A postcard ? "

" Yes a postcard."

" Would a postcard have conveyed anything about China ! "

" Perhaps not. But still. It was you not China."

" Oh ah ! " I yawned—I was absolutely certain that Butler would have said *Oh ah*. He must have said *Oh ah*. He couldn't have gone on like that for ten years without often saying *Oh ah*.

But this was very bad ! What was coming to the old girl ! For a moment I looked at her with suspicion, in exactly the way Butler would have scrutinized Jenny, if she had heaved a certain sort of melodious sigh—one in short that blew up from unprofessional horizons and whispered sadly of a Little Grey Home in the West, with Butler paying the rent.

This was very bad indeed. Was it possible that a certain objectionable rite had substituted itself in Val's feeble mind for the more honourable sentiments of a bohemian high-brow " bit " (which was her favourite word for tart) ? Perish that thought ! This is the point at which I drew out the pound. I put my hand in my note-pocket and, drawing out the pound, put it down between us on the table, continuing of course to eat anything I could find, which was not much.

" What is this ? " she asked.

I waved my hand.

" Don't be absurd Snoots ! What is this for ? "

I waved my hand. My mouth was full.

" You are ridiculous you know."

She pushed the pound over, till it passed under the spoon by the side of my plate.

" You don't owe me anything Snoots. Don't be *silly*. Put this away. Please don't be *stupid* Snoots."

Reaching out my hand, I dropped it upon the further edge of the table.

" I owe you—leave it there. So."

" But you *don't* Snoots."

I was really rather angry with her, for she was pretending there were so many pounds of this sort between us that she had lost count and never expected to see them again. I knew her so well. Val was always trying to force money on me to get me in her power she thought, and I, I was not going to stand it. Let old Val get her money as she liked was what I thought. But let her keep it to have her skin improved, *not* hint to me that if she hadn't had much luck, for a month or two, it was because she hadn't been able to afford a face-massage because I'd taken her last shilling! I'd heard her talk about other people! If I did live in a basement-flat, that didn't say she could treat me as if she kept me.—What would Butler have done in such a situation?

" You seem very flush Snoots ! " Val said, eyeing me as if I were a pickpocket. This is what it is to be poor ! " Have you been making a lot ? I thought you were away a long time."

I wiped my mouth and eyed her a little severely.

" Tell me Val " I said " how are you fixed ? Have you sublet ? "

" Not yet. Didn't you get my last letter but one ? I don't suppose you read them anyhow. I've not sublet because I didn't want to, for the moment."

Very high and mighty, thought I. She's going to give herself airs now. The Bradbury overshadowed the supper-table.

" Is Mortimer still paying the rent ? "

She nodded. But she saw from my tone I guess, that I was in no mood for more fiscal high-hatting. And the old girl melted up quickly all that sort of stuff. I guess she knew that it wouldn't take much for me to snatch up my hat and say " Well, I must be going."

" You know Snoots what Mort's like. He doesn't know

what he wants. That's all over really. He can't make up his mind—he's very cross."

" Isn't he paying then ? "

" Oh yes he's *paying* it ! "

" That's the main thing."

We eat a few more dismal mouthfuls and I swallowed the *Pape.*

" Mort's cheque came yesterday. He hasn't been up for weeks now, not since May-day."

" That's not long."

" I don't know why he sends it at all ! After all why should he ? Why should Mort pay my rent at all ? I can see no reason why he should. It's not easy to find people who are ready to pay regularly your rent, especially now."

" I suppose not."

" But is it ? I don't know many who would."

" I expect that's true."

" Well isn't it ? "

" Damn it yes, it must be ! "

" Very well. That's just what I think."

I'd got the old girl onto one of her favourite topics. What I wanted was to get her to tell me how Mortimer expected her to dress up in her black velvet dress. That always tickled me.

" I think he *ought* to pay " I exclaimed in a rather argumentative vein. " He gets what he bargained for. What more does he want ! "

" I know."

" He always *has* paid."

" Certainly, I know. But now it's not the same."

" I don't see that."

" Mort can't make up his mind to stop seeing me."

" Well then ! "

" Yes Snoots I agree. *I know I've got him in the bed !* "

I burst out laughing.

The shining points of her eyes had almost disappeared in the screwed-up flesh, and they were so near together that it looked as if they squinted, as she sat (a little more flushed than before with the papish liquid) transfixed by my sudden laugh, peering intently at me.

"You laugh Snoots, but that is true!" She was up on her hobby-horse and no mere laugh would unseat this hobby-horsewoman. She saw herself "in the Bed"—the mad pedant-of-THE-BED that she was in the wild ascendant. The boastfulness of the gifted amateur, thrilled with this shoppiness (of which the true professional is so notoriously shy), injected her head with blood, and a vein stood out in her temple.

"*I've got him in the bed,* Snoots—like that!"

The almost insanely bright points of her eyes sparkled like the paste in a property-tiara, in the crevices of grease-painted fat beneath her plucked eyebrows. She demonstrated with a spasm of her ten wriggling fingers, which she strengthlessly snapped to upon an imaginary Mort, *how she had him in the bed.*

Fascinated (for the hundredth time, for if I had heard this once I had heard it far more than that) I saw the convulsive shadow of Mort—I saw this wraith (I had never met him) struggling in THE BED—clutched with ten fluttering tentacles, of muscleless flesh, remorselessly closing in upon his impalpable substance—writhing in a delicious constriction. I heard the muffled panting of this fat shadow (for Mort was somewhat fat and short of breath) as he gave up the ghost. I felt the limp weight of his subsequent corpse, drained of its blood: and as she loosened her fingers, as they came airily apart, waggling dreamily away from each other, as her right hand separated itself from her left, I could almost perceive the dead weight, of the extinct Mort, sink down to the floor, like a stricken sausage-balloon, beneath the bullets of the

Richthofen Circus.—I heaved a long sigh at this harrowing spectacle.

" Well ! " I said. " You've got him in the bed ! "

She giggled hysterically, rapidly nodding assent, her eyes sparkling, closer than ever together, tickled to death with her prowess.

" Absolutely ! " she exclaimed : " and a great deal of hard work it has meant too Snoots ! You may believe me as to *that*. I'm sure no other woman could have done what I have done ! He's the most difficult man I've ever had to deal with, which is saying a lot."

" I know, you've told me he's difficult."

" Difficult ! He was *hopeless* to start with Snoots ! He had an inferiority-complex that he never expected *himself* to get over—I've never met such a difficult man. It took me sometimes at first a *whole night*—I was worn out in the morning, absolutely worn out Snoots ! It's funny I know ! But I did make poor old Mort into a new man. I have really Snoots."

I laughed till my sides ached at the picture of the distasteful operation. But when I thought of the bringing to life of this flabby phantom and reflected a moment upon the immense complexity of the enchained system—image behind image, sensation within sensation perhaps back to the Flood and before—which it had been necessary to revive and to set in motion, I became suddenly grave.

Val was watching me, without relaxing, her eyes with their insane pin-point sparkle fixed upon my face.

" What are you thinking about Snoots ? " she asked.

We had moved to the side of the fire. I had taken my wineglass over with me, and had been sitting bolt upright upon the edge of the settee holding it upon my mechanical knee. Val had curled up cat-like I suppose she would figure it, warming a hand now and then at the by-this-time positively roaring coal-fire—it made so much noise that it sometimes drowned our voices, with its discharges. Great Britain in July!

"I was thinking about Mort."

"What were you thinking about Mort?"

"Only what you were saying."

"Why did you look so serious all of a sudden?"

"Did I do that? I was wondering if he ever missed the bus when you giggled in his ear if you want to know."

She straightened out her flushed and excited mask, pressed into service the prim *prunes-and-prisms* 'college-girl' make-up, and turning towards the fire, stared at the bellicose coals.

"Does he?"

"Do I giggle a great deal Snooty? I suppose I do."

"What I meant was that he might think you were laughing at him."

"He wouldn't mind *that*" she said—she hated leaving the subject, she looked back at once.

"He still does acquit himself?"

"But of *course*!" she screamed, fixing me with her beady eyes screwed-up afresh for the fray. "Does he! Why he's quite *good* now—no really he is Snoots! Really he would pass in a crowd. He was a C.3 lover when I met him, if that—he was *nothing*. Now he's a—oh a B.6."

"How marvellous."

"*No one* except me would ever have had the *patience*!"

"Of course not."

"No one! He knows that. Now he's quite the he-man. No, it's a fact. He's started an affair with a 'little piece' in his office. There's no holding him now! He rolls her about on the top of his desk."

"His roll-top! Well!"

"I know, it does hardly sound credible, does it, but I happen to know it's true. He's shown me the girl's letters."

" That only goes to show that what they say in America is true."

" What's that Snoots ? "

" Oh as to the change in the behaviour of their fairies."

" Oh what's that ? "

" They say that a few years ago if you said a harsh word to a fairy he would go aside into a corner and sob, but that now if you're snooty with him he knocks you down and telephones for the nearest ambulance. They say they can't account for this change in their fairies. They don't know what's come over them all of a sudden. I think the fairies haven't changed much probably, but the *others* have. I think that's it."

" You think they have ! "

" *Minderwertigkeitsgefühl !*—The day of the Great White Male is done—you know the idea."

" I don't believe it's that."

" You think it's a new and brighter type of woman that has brought this change over the face of things, I suppose. She has just pumped her pep into the worm, and the worm has turned ! "

Giggling she savagely dug the great blocks of rumbustious carbon until they burst into a deafening conflagration. Cold as the weather was, it became a trifle warm.

" But I don't know whether Mort has ever been a So. I'm pretty sure he has. He hates So's, of course that means nothing."

" That's a bad sign."

" I think so too. I always thought Mort was a So, when I first knew him."

" He is a So."

" His tastes are very soish if he's not one." She kept on poking the fire, as if she had forgotten to leave off : not so much to 'betray her abstraction ', as to aggravate Mr Butler.

" It used to amuse me very much at first " she brightly confided " when he used to get so *angry*—if I hadn't put on that black velvet frock he made me buy he was *furious* ! He designed it himself, you remember I told you."

" I remember distinctly."

At last, the Black Velvet Frock !

" When he was coming to see me I always had to put it on."

" Really ! "

" Yes. Always—he'd even write to remind me—*be sure* you put it on ! I wore nothing under the black velvet."

" How indecent."

" Mort insisted. Well it was all *the black velvet* did it, he's crazy about velvet. But I've made more of a study of Mort than I have of any man. There's one thing I know—Mort'll never find anybody else who will be so good for him as *me*. Of that I'm certain."

" No."

" Never ! "

" It's unlikely."

" It's impossible ! "

" He must know that."

" He does in a way—let him try his little bits for a while and see ! I know what will happen—he'll be back again where he was in a year's time. He'll slip back very quickly he'll find without me ! You see if he doesn't. But he'll not pay the rent much longer, I don't think at least. That's been difficult for some time—he's sick of it."

" Sick of it."

" I don't mind if he doesn't."

" There are more fish in the sea."

(Out of which Aphrodite resplendently ascended—especially with such a fine line of talk as Val's.)

" No I mean I think I shall be all right."

" Of course."

(Nature pensions off her old girls, her veteran gang-women. Nature never forgets her Bed Companions—*good old Nature!*)

" If my next book does as well as Rothbein believes it will—I had a letter this morning—then I shall be all right Snoots. I shall be all right. It will do well I'm certain, it is a *good* book. No really."

" What book ? "

(How was I to keep track of her erotic autobioffalry in a thousand and one *stinkfein* octavos ? For Jesus' sake !)

" The ' chap ' book."

" The Chap Book ? "

" The ' chap ' book yes, you know the one I started before you left Snoots."

(The *one* ! There were ten I could swear.)

" It is *really* much better Snoots. Of its kind—you know as a rule I don't think much of—I'm not an *author* ! "

" An author ?—*not an author ?* "

" Snoots, don't be *sill-ly* !—I've put Mort into this one. I think it is the best I have written."

" Oh ah " I yawned, and as I did so I banged my mouth about, as if I were my own sparring-partner. " You've put Mort into it you say ? "

" He doesn't like it. He's seen it, I showed him the rough-draft. He says I shouldn't have described him as being impotent."

" That's absurd."

" That's what I told him ! He said he thought I ought to have left the Bed out of it."

" Leave out the BED ! "

" I know ! But it was what *happened* in it ! "

" It's narrow-minded to object to being described as impotent. It's senile almost."

" No but Snoots I don't see why he should mind do

you! And I made him get better at the end of the book. I made him get quite good.—It's not *that* he minds really."

"I should hope not."

"It's not that. He said I'd made him mean about money. He says he's *not* mean about money, he thinks I ought to have left that out it's caddish."

"What, to be close-fisted?"

"To say he is, to *say* he is."

"I should take him out altogether and have done with it if he had much more to say about it."

"I can't do that. He's the principal character."

"That makes no difference."

"No but he's practically the *only* character."

"Suppress him!"

"But the book!"

"Be ruthless!"

"No Snoots listen!"

"Yes."

"There is one thing that Mort's very ashamed of."

"I'm glad to hear that."

"No it's very bad."

"What is it?"

"He thinks I know nothing about it."

"Oh."

"Mort would *hate* my putting *that* in."

"What is it?"

"It doesn't matter what it is. But *I've got him with that!*"

Val had been sitting, elegant and prim, within kicking-distance beneath me, but now she was leaning forward, in a half-crouch—a most beady-eyed self-appointed confederate, squinting up into my face. How could I shake the old girl off? She had compressed one hand into the fist of a superwoman—a gesture that was a readily identifiable relative of the celebrated *I've got him in the Bed* one.

But it was a more wide-awake and belligerent Mort that she had got shut-up in this latter fist-prison.

I stared heavily at Val. I directed down at her a mournful and vacant look. What an old goose this girl was! With her loosely-hung tongue she would do herself some mischief before she was through! If anything, more loose-hung yet was her *pen*. Would not this sister-instrument —this double of her foolish tongue (merely an auxiliary, a duplicate Unruly Member in fact)—would not this incontinent pen demonstrate its ability to bring greater trouble in the wake of its wagging, than even its fleshly counterpart?

The pen is the tongue of man, is it not? Just as (for tradition) in their gossip-sagas women (primitive women, Betsy Prigs) compose countless *feuilletons* with their unceasing tongues.—The pen, for women, has always proved a treacherous instrument. It eludes them, with its more cold-blooded techniques—for all those emotional purposes at least, to further which they commonly take it up. Nor is the pen in fact a thing of improvisation, not at its best in the market-place. The pen is not really a tongue at all!

But old Val was a portent: she cannot, it is a pity, be disqualified for that position on the ground of her petty station in the world, or slender powers, or her slight beauty. To pretend that she can, is to have little sense of the present age—an age of battalions, not of single spies. It is the age of Numbers!

Would it be better if women were not taught to read and write at all? A utopian enquiry, that is self-evident, but it may not be amiss to take it up. It could, for instance, be argued as follows:—Since they are so liable to confuse *tongue* and *pen*—become such inveterate scribblers upon the slightest provocation—might it not be best if women could be denied all instruction in letters at all?

But consider how easily this could be turned round upon

men! We must I think agree that the above proposition would betray great superficiality in the person advancing it. Once you recognize a danger—similar to that of locusts in the tropics—in the growing abuse of mere human speech (*Language Habit*, as nicknamed by my chief master) then you are confronted by a problem that goes far deeper than gender. No, gentlemen! The very existence of art and of formal and symbolic expression is involved I am afraid —*may be said to be at stake*—in this.

Still Sex has its place—single-handed almost it provides this full-fledged portent, Val or another. Undeniably the woman has a monopoly of those rudiments of expansive emotion which constitute the beginnings of art.—It is seriously to be doubted as to old Val (to pass from the general to the particular) if any longer she realized what she was *saying*, so accustomed had she become to *write* it: it is most questionable if she recognized at all clearly what she was *writing*, so inordinately had her inkslinging stimulated her tongue. It sufficed for her to look out of the window, or to chat with her char-girl—she now scarcely could see or hear *anything* without incontinently rushing to her inkpot, in an instantaneous diarrhœa of words. Or thundering all day at her Remington, she was threatened surely with the same pulmonary decay, ensuing upon private indisciplines, as the factory-seamstresses surprised by Ellis, lost-to-the-wide in the erotic nepenthe of the sewing-pedal.—But as we know, there are great sub-hosts of moonstruck women in the same condition. The almost anonymous mass, nameless as far as any significant name goes, of *Novels of the Year* (communist if by that you understand common and not individual, the sub-activities of crowds, not persons) may at any time assume the proportions of a biblical Plague, upon the same footing with locust or with rat.

But upon this I grew very depressed indeed. It was

always the same in this house, she could not hold her tongue, and I swore this should be my last visit. Poor old Val was a melancholy case. The closer her eyes crowded together in her head, the more insanely they glittered, the more recklessly her tongue wagged, in a hide-bound pedantry of essential-sex, a torrent of giggles to keep the words company, the more evident it became to me that here would be a case for the clinic. Three or four years at most would remove this woman out of the age-class beneath the immediate patronage of Venus. Then she would just do nothing but gibber—and probably write a five-hundred-page novel a day!

So I settled down very gloomily to listen for a while longer. I had to humour her as we are counselled to indulge the 'mental', I took on the seductive mannerisms of what I supposed to be the Male Nurse. But she still was enough master of her controls to respond to appropriate stimulus: perhaps, I argued, I might, at the right moment, plunge her back into silence.—But she was off again, and I followed with growing alarm.

"*I've got him in the bed Snoots!*" she was exclaiming. "I've got him like that—the reason he does not come here is nothing to do with that!"

"I should think not!" I hastened to assure her.

"It is all Audrey's doing, *she* is the cause of it all! Audrey is a *cad*. She has been making mischief all round, but *especially* with Mort. Not that I care! It isn't that. But I think Audrey's behaved in such a perfectly *beastly* way about me. Mort believes everything she says."

"But what can she possibly say?"

"Oh I can guess what she says!"

"It couldn't be anything that Mort really minded could it?"

"Well she might say I had talked about him, you know, in a horrid way."

" That is impossible."

" But Audrey is a perfect liar ! "

" Would he believe her though ? I'm sure he wouldn't —he would know she was lying."

" You don't know Mort—he'd believe anybody."

I burst out into nervous laughter and this relieved the tension a little bit. She seized the tongs and adjusting their griffin-clawed callipers to a large block of coal, wielding her fire-irons like a slinger she discharged this jet-black bolt plump upon the orange crest of the fire, into which it sank majestically.

It had been my Butler laugh I had given.

Now this unimportant humble hanger-on of the big Chelsea 'Party'-bosses and mandarins of the high-brow-racket-for-the-rich, she was in disgrace. She had given proof of bad party discipline—she had thrown away the few poor little trumps she had somehow or other trumped-up. But this was not because of any lack of the most slavish conformity to all manners and tricks of speech at the moment obtaining—no one in that respect could have outdone her.

When first I (as too hearty and low-bred a stranger arriving from the african Veldt) came among this glittering crowd—Val's Youngers and Betters (those way-up of course—rich, with the iron of Lesbos and of Sodom in the soul from birth—not brought in, in upstart fashion, later in life) there was one thing that used to astonish me. It was this.—Something disobliging *said* about them in conversation would enrage, I discovered—whereas the same things to the letter, *written* about them in a book, that would cause them the keenest satisfaction ! But how was this ? It puzzled me at the start extremely.

Before long I found out, however, that there was a perfectly sound explanation, if you cared to look for it. They were so inordinately vain, or loved publicity with such a startling passion, that there was literally nothing you might not write about them in a book or newspaper. That was the fact of the matter. Afterwards I made the fullest use of this paradoxical *carte blanche*.

So where at first I had hesitated to avail myself of the living model, for my specimen cases (in connection with my field-work in animal psychology) later on I freely drew upon conspicuous people. And I must say I have invariably found them grateful and highly flattered, whatever it might be my painful duty to say about them. They would be disappointed, even, if you depicted them in an agreeable light, for they know only too well that then no one would read the book.—My field-work luckily has never detained me for long among these particular english herds, however. American aggregates for instance are much more interesting in my line of work.

But Val I could see had pulled herself up short. She intended to pass on to more general topics. I knew of course from experience what that meant. We should find ourselves upon the spot wandering in a forest of tall Christian Names—far too good to be true in fact, for no body of parents, however adequately equipped, could possibly have possessed so felicitous a taste in names, so rare a baptismal technique, as many of these implied. Upon its more commonplace outskirts we should be amongst the Raymonds and the Adrians, truly and in very fact in a *fairy* woodland: but the female nomenclature would be of a stately victorian simplicity, out of the pages of Mrs Gaskell or Miss Austen: and Valerie (*Valerie* was good my word!) heartiest of old underdog snobs, would mouth them all with the same unction with which formerly Servants Hall or Suburb turned over greedily upon its title-loving tongue the names, and reported wise-cracks, of marquises and dukes.

" Raymond and Alice " said she and, very suitably grave, I nodded encouragement " were here last week."

I had not the faintest idea who they were (I knew at least fifty Raymonds—a favourite name—and two dozen Alices) but I looked very grave indeed—as if she had said *The Great Mogul !* (and indeed they were that for her, these fantastic nobodies, only a few rungs up from herself, most probably)—I looked properly impressed and a model of gravity, and with a glow she softly proceeded—

" They wanted me to go to a party at Jane's."

(*Now that was nice of them wasn't it !* I showed plainly in my expressive looks.)

" I wouldn't go " she snapped, and looked away, to confirm the splendid refusal.

(*No of course you wouldn't !* my glances conveyed—it was not an *important* enough party in all probability.)

" I am sick of parties " she snapped again : " and I hate Jane anyway ! "

And, by the beatitude I conjured into my shining eyes I informed her forthwith how lovely I thought it must be for her to be a picker and chooser—to pick " Jane " up and drop " Jane " down—to like her one minute and hate her the next—and then from an absolute surfeit of such exclusive delights, to come to hate parties too, for the time being : in fact, to sit at home all day long *quite alone*, just doing nothing—except once a week, going out to eat an Irish Stew and Chips with a nice quiet homely little suburban artist-couple. That anyway would be the life for me, if I was a girl like Val !—All this I plainly showed and more.

But she did not go on, to my surprise, except to say :

" Jane is awfully rich—she's one of the *chaps*. I don't like her though."

She stopped dead now, and I found her looking at me, then turning her head abruptly away, with the *moue* that went with the ghost of a sniff. So we sat for some seconds. What had I done? thought I. What had I left undone? Then suddenly it dawned upon me and I laughed at my density. Recapturing my gravity at once, I coughed and she looked up and then stared over at me.

"Who is Jane?" I softly enquired, with a puzzled expression.

The life and light came back into her face.

"Jane?" in a tone of instant surprise she loudly echoed: and she pulled her upper lip down, settling her face into what she considered the well-bred mayfairish prim-lipped mask of ingénue-débutante false-decorum—a trick contracted at the same time as the mannish starched shirt-waist and Radcliffe Hall neck-wear, stiff and male to a fault. "Oh, she is Jane Crewe. The Crewes are very rich—they have just taken a big house in Cremorne Square, they give big parties to all the Olivia-Margery-Joyce-Hughie and Julian set."

Energetically I nodded at each of these names—one, two, three, four, five nods and a final salaam, and the old girl was in the best of fine fettle and rattled along for quite ten minutes about all those bright nebulous mononominal patrons, of Gossip-column-class—on to the hem of whose garment she had clung like grim death—but who had all shaken her off, of one accord, and by common consent, about a year since, when she had pooped in their faces.

And now a very alarming thing happened.—The telephone-bell rang!

I positively jumped. I had forgotten that there was such a thing in the world as *the telephone*. I was totally unprepared. It was unnerving suddenly to hear this excited signal, in the isolated home of this bawdy hermit-crab.

For all her training in a hard-slogging school and good-class dissimulation, Val was not quick enough for her reflexes—*she too* started slightly.

It took all her sang-froid, but she threw on the spot a look of deep unconcern into her face. Thereupon a most fascinating conflict of forces developed. There was the impulse to leap to her feet and seize the telephone—that must in the first moment have been overmastering. Yet at all costs it must be nipped in the bud: there must be nothing of that sort at all!—Languidly she must rise to her feet, negligently she must remove the receiver. But not *too* languidly—not *too* negligently! For (*Hope springs eternal*) who might not be at the other end! *Anybody* might be there at that very moment, haughtily tapping a well-turned sapphic toe, and exclaiming grandly to herself—"*When* is the bitch going to answer I should like to know! I suppose she's got some beastly *man* there—as usual!"—Why, "Jane", even, might have gone mad and might suddenly have taken it into her head to call up Val (whom she had only seen once, for ten minutes) might she not! And her access of acute dementia might only last a few seconds! She might come to her senses, once the telephone was in her hand!—So HURRY! every nerve in poor old Val's body shouted! Time and Tide wait for no man, but there are other things too that are impatient and inexorable. Oh fling yourself upon that telephone, her whole nature must have been shrilly bellowing in her ear.

I admired her in these breathless moments more than I can say. Many firm-lipped stolid skippers upon wave-swept bridges, in the climax of a shipwreck, deserve our admiration less. I felt that I had wasted my amazement upon many self-collected and imperturbable heroes of the history-book. They had the guns thundering about them—they had been stupified by some mammoth storm-at-sea. To go down in parade-order, with bands playing, is all very well—*there* you are only one cell among many, in a contagion of sacrifice. This one small adventuress was the entire crew of *her* cockle-shell ! Oh good old Val !—I sent up a tenuous *Bravo !*

As she slowly got to her feet the suspense, for me the onlooker, became intolerable. Perhaps she would burst a blood-vessel ! It was quite likely. But she reached the instrument at the end of a series of quasi slow-movements which had been as near the ideal of Leisure as these cramping provisos permitted. Then, as her hand was about to grasp it (and I jumped this time fairly out of my skin) the infernal thing began ringing again suddenly like a fire-alarm !

As (white to the lips by this time) she picked it up (and the abominable clangour was abruptly shut off as she did so) fragments of a cross voice broke weakly and scrappily about my ear : then I turned my head instantly away, not to overhear more of these dull secrets. (I make it a rule, even in the high paroxysm of eager field-work, never to put my eye or ear to a keyhole, however great the temptation. *Noblesse oblige* is a device that secures one from cracking one's head inopportunely, in the dark, against the mangy poll of some fellow-eavesdropper.)

" This is about you Snoots " Val said, and with her hand pressed down upon the mouth-piece, she stood, archly at gaze, looking at me just over the receptacle for the message that she was waiting to convey when I should have given expression to my wishes.

" Oh for me " I said, turning round, as I struggled upright. " Who is it ? "

" Well.—You don't want to go, do you, to *Douglases* tomorrow night, I'm sure you don't ! "

" Who is Douglas ? "

" To Douglas Montague's."

" Not particularly, why ? "

" No, I didn't think you would. I'll tell him so. I happened to say to him that I might be seeing you tonight.

He's just rung up to know if we could come round tomorrow evening to dinner. Bessie Ritchie is going to be there and Blumenfeld—you know: Raymond."

"Oh yes, Raymond, of course. Tomorrow evening, I am afraid that will be impossible" I said.

"No of course not—I was sure you couldn't."

"It's the night of the Highland Ball," I said. "It's the Highland Ball."

"Is it? Yes of course it is!"

She took her hand off the mouth of the telephone: I could hear her telling Douglas that tomorrow was the night of the Highland Ball—we could not come: the Highland Ball. (*We* I observed).

The next night was not the night of the Highland Ball, or of any other Ball as far as I knew. I don't know why I said the Highland Ball. From what I could gather, the excuse went down all right with the Montague with the scottish front-name. Upon further proposals, on the part of this uncommonly hospitable person, I could hear that Val was throwing cold water, or humming and haing. It was indicated that for the present that disposed of the matter—that I was present, that I could think of nothing but the Highland Ball at the moment (one thing at a time) but that perhaps he might be calling her again in the morning.

She stuck down the telephone quickly—carrying her eyes over to me, as she did so, her lips opening to speak (picking the beastly thing up and putting it down again, all day, these gestures of course were a second nature). But she stamped down its heavy base upon the butter-dish, and the butter evidently supposed it to be a butter-stamper and spread out accordingly to receive an embossed picture of a cow, or a pattern of noughts and crosses.

She dragged the telephone off the butter frowning, while I gave way to a fit of justifiable laughter.

" What are you laughing at ! " she snarled at her work.

" The telephone " said I. " What do the Telephone Company give you for advertising them on your butter-pats ? "

She laid it down upon its side and wiped its base with a piece of paper.

" Are you going to the Highland Ball tomorrow night, Snoots ? " she said.

" I don't know " I replied. Evidently she knew there was no Highland Ball. She must have a scottish friend—one of those typical " Scots " to be met with at that function !

" Oh that reminds me—I suppose you didn't see *this* Snoots " she said, and putting her hand into a half-open drawer of her desk, pulled out a newspaper cutting.

I took the cutting. It was a long Gossip par., and it was headed BARONET GOES SAMURAI.

I frowned heavily upon this cutting, and put it down unread upon my mechanical knee.

" When did this appear ? " I asked angrily.

If there is one thing I particularly dislike. it is that ' baronet ' business. I live in a basement flat for which I pay eighty pounds a year. I have not had a club for years now, as I cannot afford it—any money I've got I need for other things. And *Samurai*—that was Humph, who else would think of it ?

However I must read it I suppose, I thought, and with a scowl at Val, I took up the cutting again.

Sir Michael Kell-Imrie, seventeenth baronet, known to his friends as " Snooty ", is at present in Japan, where he is studying the psychology of the Samurai caste, we hear. This should yield interesting results. " Snooty " is a bit of a philosopher, and already has published more than one book. Temperamentally something of a swashbuckler himself, of the red-blood school, he should find much in common with the warlike traditions of the Samurai. It may be recalled that in 1920 or thereabouts Sir Michael, or Mr Kell-Imrie as he then was, got into hot water, the fieriness of his highland nature getting the better of him as he noticed a woman beating her husband outside a public-house. Rushing into the fray with the battle-cry of the Kell-Imries upon his lips, he quickly delivered his fellow-man, with a well-directed left to the woman's jaw. For this he spent a night in the cells. Subsequently when the case came up for hearing, the injured woman was unable to make good her claim, namely that as a result of the baronet's knock-out to the jaw she had sustained permanent injury, which prevented her from acquitting herself as before of her duties as char. Her jaw (so her husband assured the court) was as strong as ever. Further it was shown, that, in consequence of war-wounds, " Snooty " might not be so competent as formerly to exercise a fine discrimination ; and even it was possible (so his counsel contended) that he may have reverted to one of his more characteristic gaelic ancestors : in the heat of the moment, suddenly hearing the cries of distress of the unfortunate husband, he may have mistaken the woman's exiguous skirt for a highland kilt, and in fact imagined himself in the presence of some tribal foeman, claymore in hand.—Having regard to his distinguished war record (Sir Michael Kell-Imrie was five times wounded and has an artificial leg) he was warned by the magistrate, and fined ten pounds and costs.

It is all very well being " a bit of a philosopher ". But such stuff as this, when first brought to one's notice gives one a nasty cut. I put the thing down upon the settee beside me. I did not utter a word of course. Words are not my medium and that's a fact, with persons of the sort stood for by this Gossip-guy. My brow must have been pretty black. I can imagine that, upon running through the cutting, I lost a little of my charm. Old Val certainly had checkmated me with her cutting.

I will explain in a moment the reason for my sitting down to write this book. It's out of my line, as I guess you can see. But at the moment, having put this newspaper-cutting under your eyes, for your information, it is necessary to say a few words about what that par. treats of. (And it was best to put forward the cutting, verbatim.)

When just now I spoke of the club to which I formerly belonged, I did not tell you, but perhaps I ought, that following upon the scandal disclosed in the above par. (there were two other silly affairs as well, both the result of sudden weakness, caused by my head-wound) thanks to that publicity I am not by any means popular with other members. If I were rich that would not matter.

As to the affair outside the *Load of Hay*. To-day I see things more clearly. Now I should not take action, in that way. (I should walk off and think no more about it.) I allowed myself to be led away by my chivalrous impulses on that occasion, that certainly is true enough. I did do what they say I did. Observing a woman beating in the most cruel manner a cowering wretch of my own sex, I did interfere. And, if I struck this enraged bitch on the jaw, it was not more than she merited.—But to-day I would not meddle in such a matter. The man, I now can see quite well, should have had the enterprise to run away. I would not act the cop for him. As to the woman—I am amused at myself when I think what I did! Since I have made, recently, a careful study of californian introversion, I realize that the situation may have contained more complexities than I at the time supposed. Equality within the frontiers of a single sex I now know to be impossible. I might even have gone up and congratulated the woman.

But let us sink all this for the moment. It must be taken up again—it is an authentic fragment of something thrown off the central Me. I recognize it, but must pass on. Val was well pleased I could see with the nip given me by her cutting. (She may have heard who was its author.)

I beat down her inquisitive glittering pin-points, as she waited for me to speak, with a mighty scottish frown. When she saw there would be no discussion, she prinked down her mealy and pitted countenance again, and gave the coals the benefit of her reverie. I bottled up the bad blood the cutting had made. When Val next looked my way, I was grinning at her : but she sustained my grin no more than my black-as-thunder expression. Honours were even, and I threw my pre-war leg on top of the timber article.

The papal Château Neuf was finished. Val got up and said :

" Would you like some brandy Snoots ? I have a little."

" What is it ? "

" Oh it's Three Star I think. Don't you like Three Star ? "

" No but give it me."

She stepped quickly out of the room, frowning, one eyebrow on high, and returned with the bottle of brandy, which she placed upon the supper-table.

It may have occurred to you that I show myself a little remiss as a lover, I do not know. But should that be the case, I will try to correct that impression. I told you that, in the hall, in a casual way it is true, I showed appreciation of my hostess's person right away. But I *did* not say—and that I must now go into I suppose in order to make the foregoing scenes intelligible (I have put it off as long as possible) I did not I am aware tell you one thing : namely that I *never kiss*.

I now got up, however, and approaching Val, as she stood anticipating some move on my part, I gave her a wooden peck on the neck. She pecked me back, upon my chin. (I considered that she deliberately missed my mouth.)

If I do not kiss—and that I never do under any circumstances (excepting when in " the Bed ")—I do nevertheless bestow an accolade, upon those occasions when it seems called for, or if circumstances imperatively demand it. The exact moment cannot be decided in advance. This time

I had put it off rather long. (It was Butler who was responsible for that.)

Now of course a good deal of Val's manner that you may have noticed is undoubtedly accounted for by that fact. My not-kissing is displeasing to her. Why shouldn't he kiss? is what she says to herself I suppose. "*I've got him in the Bed!*" beyond any question she would say (she must say it to herself, seeing that she says it so repeatedly to other people). "Then why shouldn't he be more civil and touch-tongues when we meet, after a long and bitter separation?" That is the idea, I think.

It is quite unnecessary for me to explain all these points to you in detail, as they crop up. If you want to know, I refrain from clipping and kissing out of bed mainly because of the furniture. Then, I prefer to go into action all together and all of a piece. A further reason. If I have to converse for a stated time with such a giggling fantoche as old Val, before we get down to business, I find it best, more rational, not to begin with a juicy close-up of the specimen I shall be compelled, in spite of myself, to do a bit of field-work on, while she is blowing off steam, and depressing me with a mannikin-parade of all her poshest social attitudes and a whole wardrobe of complexes. So much for that, I think.

I poured myself out a stiff glass of Three Star—it was better, Martell or not, than synthetic rye-whisky, that much one may allow.

"Happy days" I said and carried the glass to my lips.

Old Val stood a pace or two off from where I was. She drank a little Three Star. Then she put down the glass, pushing it on to the table, and stood with downcast eyes—she was white-collared, stiff, shut up in a 'mutinous silence', parading the archaic reserve of the Children's Nursery. My old imitation-Society-'piece'—modelled on the best Late Mayfair (Peter Pan Model) was out to perform before me (a Command Performance, I don't think !) the chidden aproned Miss. She was a damask-cheeked Miss of fourteen or fifteen Springs (say in a mid-victorian Boarding Establishment). Sullenly she awaited the executioner's pleasure, with neck-bent, and a well-whipped sanctimonious 'poke' thrust of the pentathletic head. She was in the presence of *The Principal* : he (with all his rods in pickle) was about—so old Val would interpret it—to up with her dimity frock and administer a well-deserved *fessée*. But (overcome by the luscious contacts) destined to follow this up with extremely improper advances.

"Lonely nights ! " she gave the correct Music-hall response, piling on the demureness in chrismatic clots, out-cloying Devon (her lips succeeding in becoming the ripest of prime hothouse strawberries) but with as much of the sly as became a wronged woman—or a victorian flapper-minx-in-the-wrong, her B.T.M. already smarting in antici-pation. So we stood, face to face.

Replacing my glass upon the table empty, I leered at her again, and this time she leered back. She dropped the School Miss overboard, and ran up with a will the Jolly Roger.

"Come Valley ! " I muttered cordially.

She grappled with me at once, before the words were well out of my mouth, with the self-conscious gusto of a Chatterly-taught expert. But as I spoke I went to meet her—as I started my mechanical leg giving out an ominous creak (I had omitted to oil it, like watches and clocks these things require lubrication). I seized her stiffly round the body. All of her still passably lissom person—on the slight side—gave. It was the human willow, more or less. It fled into the hard argument of my muscular pressures. Her waist broke off and vanished into me as I took her over in waspish segments, an upper and nether. The bosoms and head settled like a trio of hefty birds upon the upper slopes of my militant trunk: a headless nautilus on the other hand settled upon my middle, and attacked my hams with its horrid tentacles—I could feel the monster of the slimy submarine-bottoms grinding away beneath, headless and ravenous.

"Oh Listerine!" I sighed, as I compressed the bellows of her rib-box, squeezing it in and out—it crushed up to a quite handy compass—expanding, and then expelling her bad breath. I put my face down beside her ear (I wished I'd brought her a bottle from the States as a useful present).

I was well away, I left much behind me I give you my word in those first spasms of peach-fed contact. Squatted upon the extremity of the supper-table, with my live leg (still laden with hearty muscles) I attacked the nether half of my aggressive adversary, and wound it cleverly round her reintegrating fork. (We were now both suspended upon my mechanical limb.)

"Valley" I said (I always called her Valley when I was showing her my affection) "Valley" I said "I've often thought of this little Valley!"

"You are a liar Snoots" she whispered in hoarse tones.

"I've often thought of this pleasant Valley!"

That was the signal for us to go towards the folding-doors. The double-doors lead directly into the chamber where old Val keeps her Bed—as the dentist keeps his dentist's-chair in his operating apartment. (I should not be surprised to hear that some especially zealous dentists sleep in their dentists'-chairs.) It was there she had "got" Mort, there she had "put on the spot" according to her own grim saga, a whole gallery of introverts. With her post-victorian muscle-stuff she had melted their shot-guns like wax (arsenals of such) in her laboratory-brazier.

I entered, lisping heavily.

"Put the pail outside."

I pushed old Valley in. She went in with one brooding stagger, then another after the first, and so on, of wanton bottom-lagging sham reluctance—as I propelled her from behind in successive pushes, 'low blows'. When both of us had passed fully inside, into the bedridden cabinet, already frockless she appeared again in the doorway, without me, just where a moment past my back had been (as I had been translating her from room No. 1 to room No. 2). She shoved outside (placed first just within the sitting-room) a gilt-flowered, emerald slop-vessel. Quickly she withdrew once more, that done—might I not change my mind if she were gone too long? Stranger things had happened. You can bring a stallion to the river-bed but you cannot always make him sip. Swiftly in view of this the folding-doors met together with a determined click. —She had got me safely inside—I sat upon the Bed in the unlighted apartment. I awaited her to assist with my mechanical limb.

The room where we had been eating and conversing was empty at last, except for the robust solus behaviour of the coal-fire. That still discharged an occasional round for luck (and to prove it was there still and independent of our consciousness) at the high georgian ceiling, or sent up a flickering violet flare. (How well I understand the unique position of the carbon atom in our *Mysterious Universe!*)

Owing to that unaccountable feminine aversion for all that is direct (perhaps a hall-mark of our time) I am reluctantly compelled at this point to break off my narrative. But it is only necessary to skip a matter of ten minutes, perhaps a quarter of an hour. No very long time at all had elapsed certainly, when the folding-doors once more came violently open, pulled from the inside on this occasion. A one-legged man hopped out. He was as naked as God ushered him into the world and as the Grave will take him back. Sitting down upon the end of the settee, and bending over the gilt-flowered slop-vessel, this man proceeded to be ill. For the best part of a further quarter of an hour he continued to be ill. Eventually he sank into an arm-chair, whose big square hollow shelf fronted the fireplace. Repeatedly he carried his hand to that part of his skull where there was a silver plate.

That one-legged naked man in the sumptuous second-hand Chelsea arm-chair—carrying his hand, as if in pain, to a spot upon the rear portion of his skull—within his abundant corn-yellow crest-lines—was me. (Upon my opening page I had to introduce myself, as you will recall. This time again I have to perform that office, as you might otherwise not have recognized me unclothed.)

* * *

The next morning came, or the time when one wakes, and rises (one's own private sun, rising in one's own private calendar). And there in the half-light were still the stars of overnight the insanely glittering pin-points of Val's two eyes were fixed upon my face, as if they had never been extinguished. I woke up painfully, I gave her a dull glare. We were horizontal, both our heads were upon the same billow of swan's-down—in fine, we were lying side by side in The Bed, where she had got me—where she *got* me, and I had *done her wrong*.

My head ached very much. It was a powerful ache from ear to ear. First I had fallen asleep, I suppose I was exhausted by my sickness, near the pail. When I was woken by the cold, as the fire got low in the grate, I went in to my Valley. Her soft snore, drifting in from the next room, had apprised me of the fact that she was sleeping the sleep of the Just. She did not wake up as I slung myself into the bed, and soon I was asleep as well.

"How do you feel Snoots?" Val asked me now.

" Rotten " I said, and I took a death-mask of my face with the palm of my hand, plastic above each eye, attempting to drive the blood out of the skin.

So I was not at all well. My head always gives me trouble at the moment of the climax under the silver plate. *That* always lays me out. But generally by the time morning has come round everything is once more O.K. I am sick and then I sleep.

This was very bad ! Old Val had been a V.A.D.—she converted The Bed into a hospital pallet for the occasion. (The sex-appeal of The Nurse is well established.) At first I would not hear of it. Not the Bed—I was very apologetic. Out of delicacy I suggested *the settee.* Why not the settee ? But she said *No no ! The Bed—!* So be it said I. And so The Bed it was.

After a little nursing I was all right. By noon I was ready to dress. I felt as right as rain. I leered at her again, even, to reward her. But great as the temptation must have been, she did not take me at my word. I was glad enough, as you may imagine ! Anyway, my head was still ringing a little. I am not a good life and that's a fact.

After what I have said I know it will surprise you—it surprised me ! But Val had a letter by the first post. The Char brought it in upon a plate. (Both of us were astonished, and the Char-girl seemed to be too. But nobody said anything.)

It was a real, sealed, and properly-stamped letter (there was nothing to pay on it). It was not an unstuck-down one, with a green halfpenny stamp. It had been franked in London, England, and some one had paid threehalfpence for it. In short it was a real letter.

Upon reading the letter (she did not of course open it at once and read it but put it down upon the breakfast-tray) Val gave a kittenish bound into the air (she was sitting by the side of the bed, where I lay with my head massively poulticed, only one eye free to gaze out upon the world and keep watch) and she squealed, flourishing the letter at me:

"Oh, look at *theeeeece*! Read thaaaat Snoots! Some one wants the flat—yes, the *flaaaat*! Yes, *this* one!"

I was of course unmoved. Frankly I did not care if they wanted it or not, though I could not believe that anyone in their senses, at the price asked by Val, should wish to rent it. I yawned, and as I did so my one uncovered eye went up under the bandage and was lost to view. I kept it there as long as possible, leaving my mouth wide open—I occasionally tapped it, stretched and unstretched it slightly, in bored spasms.

"But don't you think it's *thrilling* Snoots—Snoots! aren't you *pleased*! Snooty!"

"Not particularly!" I yawned. (This question had annoyed me, I scarcely knew why.)

"I know but Snoots, just think, she accepts my terms—the woman accepts my terms!"

"She must be crazy." I brought my eye out and looked at her a little severely.

"No, but Snoots darling think of the *money* I shall have!"

"Well!"

I did not like this *money*. The old girl was always referring to money.

"Well—I shall be able to do something for you Snoots—you mustn't live in that basement flat it will kill you. I shall be able——"

I fixed the old girl with my eye. I said nothing. This was very bad! (This was what came of allowing oneself to be too familiar with a demi-rep—it was the *demi* that did it—she was neither fish nor fowl and was resolved to treat me as if she had been one of the rich women she imitated and who now snorted at her name.)

" And your *work* Snoots—think what a difference it would make, if you could give all your time to scientific work. I know you don't like my talking about it, but your psychological—the research—work is of great importance. No I'm not humbugging Snooty. I know you don't think I understand. I do understand its importance."

This was very bad! I could not stand much more of this. (I knew as sure as I lay there that this woman would end by saying she kept me.)

" Valerie! " I said very sharply.

" What? "

" Have you a telephone? "

She did not understand at first. Had she *a telephone*? But I kept up an incessant fire from my single eye. I was determined she should understand! She should not pass on before she had understood that I was not the dupe. Yes, *telephone*, my eye said! Are you a telephone subscriber? Oh, are you really! I shouldn't have thought you needed one enough! I do not hear it ringing very often!—My single eye spoke volumes in short, about *the telephone*: and at last she understood—she knew that I knew!—We understood each other.

An injured look instantly came into her face, raising a mild storm in her chest—a heave or two, nothing more—in its passage: it was with a great deal of almost open reproach in her manner that she replied:

" You know I have a telephone Snoots."

" Very well. May I use it? "

I was going to put the old girl through it. Once and for all we should have done with *money* as a subject! No more cash-chats!—I would press my advantage.

" Do you mind if I use it? I suppose it's still in working order! "

There was nothing ugly in Val—I should not have stood her a minute if there had been. But now she darted me an extremely injured look—a little sickly, I thought, like the sallowness of autumn, reproach and sadness mixed.

"I think so. Try for yourself however."

Her chest gave an isolated and rather sudden heave and just for a moment no more it occurred to me that she might be going to resort to tears, but it passed off at once—she may have read something really *decisive* in my eye, as to the feasibility of weeping. She rose extremely loftily—raised up into the air, as it were, by the emotional afflatus in her surging lungs. This pneumatic heave, say a big noiseless sigh, having carried her to what seemed to me an unusual height, she paused there. She looked down upon me for a long second perhaps, without expression (except that she was looking *down* and that there was *no* expression). Then she passed into the other room.

I gave my Butler laugh—that of Butler as invalid.

Dragging the table-phone in at the end of a long cord, she gave it to me, it just reached the centre of the bed. I placed it upon my stomach. Then I lay with it standing up starkly upon my swaddled trunk, while I put my memory system into operation to recall the number. Val sat down again in the arm-chair at the side of the bed.

A fire-proof curtain had been run down between us by what I had done. Nothing I could have thought of could have been more superbly effective. Of course I knew I had gone up in her estimation.

These masterly results (so easily obtained) gratified me, I confess, to such a degree that I showed myself magnanimous.

"So you think you've sublet your flat" I said.

"I've told you what the woman says."

"That is capital. The studio as well of course."

"Yes the whole thing."

"The whole thing as it stands—furniture, fittings—*telephone!* Everything."

She nodded.

" For when is that ? "

" At once—as soon as I am ready."

" Ah ha ! That is good. You will accept of course, and get out."

She nodded heavily.

Very negligently I took up the telephone. Still engaging her in conversation (" Did she have to do up the place or not—how long was her lease for ? " and so forth, of course you see the idea) I gave Humph's number to the exchange. I gave the number sandwiched in between two languid sentences, as a sort of lofty stage-aside. I handled the instrument so much *en maître* in fact that I very nearly lost my connection. The telephone for me it was clear was an *absolutely* secondary matter—though what I was saying to Val was scarcely occupying more than a fraction of my attention. The *telephone* was a fraction of a fraction therefore—and a contemptible fraction at that. I yawned so much I nearly swallowed the receiver ! Tapping my mouth, in a bored bellow to Humph's clerk I announced my intention of looking in about three o'clock. " About three ? Let me see——! "—" Yes about three ! "—and with that, without waiting for what she might have to say as to Humph's precious movements or the probable length of his luncheon engagements, I hung the thing up—with the crash of an autocrat. Three was *my* hour—THREE. That settled the matter.

Val was very quiet. She was very subdued. But she was *too* quiet I considered. She was watching me I thought too closely. It was with a novel interest I knew, and of course *respect*. There was great respect, that went without saying.

I was unprepared I confess, under these circumstances, for what she next said.

" I shall have three hundred pounds if I get this, Snoots."

I could scarcely believe my ears but this was undoubtedly what the woman was saying. What disgusting resilience —*how* could I stop her? "*about* three hundred counting Mort's rent-cheque. There are one or two other things —if Rothbein coughs up as he promised—it might be *four*! Nearly four. Not quite."

This was very bad! She took my breath away. There was now every indication that there was worse to come. I felt it in my bones. From the significant manner in which she was pinning me down with her beady headlights and attacking me (frontally this time!) with her beastly money-confidences—seeking as usual only more so to involve me in an undesirable *complicity* as it were, there remained little doubt but that bad as this was so far, there was far worse to come. She referred to the letting of her flat as if it were an illegal operation: it was just as though she had been proposing to me the cracking of a crib (instead of informing me of the subletting of an apartment —at a criminal rate it is true, but otherwise an orthodox transaction).

But her eyes grew narrower yet, and I instinctively shrank into the Bed as I saw some blow coming. I yawned violently—it was all I could think of at the moment— and ran my unblinkered eye up under cover. Thus, with my mouth wide open, and all the rest of my face out of sight, I awaited the attack—I heard her begin again, and as I did so produced a sort of yawning *yell*. I *would* not listen! But I could hear her pull up and then she made a fresh start.

"Hermione wants to let me her villa—I heard from her yesterday." (I knew this was a lie, for that would have made *three* letters that she had received yesterday, *which is impossible*—as Euclid, with far less secure grounds for such robust confidence than I possessed, would have said.) "It is not far from Toulon—it is a very quiet place, there is absolutely nobody there at all as a matter of fact." (This meant it was swarming with people of course—but it was not *that* that mattered—it was what she was going to say next—I felt like plunging my head under the clothes—*where* should I flee, to escape from this strong-minded old discredited Party-hack!) " William and Julian went over there this winter and said it was absolutely deserted, there's a good plage, quite small, they breed donkeys—there's absolutely nothing else, there's absolutely not a cat—except a gipsy encampment. Julian said it was what the Riviera must have been like at the time of *Smollett*! Rather lovely it sounded." (It must of course be stiff with people by this time even if a year ago it was comparatively free of the art-tourist and Gossip-column stinkpots—but *that* did not matter! It was not that at all!) " Shall I take it—I am half a mind to write off and accept Snoots. I want a rest. No, I am bored with London, I'm sick of the Party-crowd, she wants to let it for six months. *Shall* I take it Snoots! If I wrote and said I'd take it, would you come down there and work. Not for long of course if you didn't want to. Six months if you liked—or a week. If I thought you would I'd write off and accept now."

I knew it! She had it all mapped out.

" You could do just what you liked of course—you need never see me if you didn't want to. And it would cost you nothing—don't be angry Snoots. You are so absurd about money. You are too proud—that's where it is *Sir Michael*! I know I've put my foot in it—but if I like to spend my three or four hundred pounds in that way why shouldn't I—you'd come and stay with me if I were *rich* and not ask to pay for your bed and breakfast, would you! Why shouldn't you with *me*! I *am* rich at the moment —or I *shall* be. Why not—it's snobbish of you!"

This was certainly very bad. I closed my mouth up

tight, I brought my eye out. To say I frowned at her would give a poor idea of the black reproval that met each fresh sentence that now was falling from her lips.

" I don't mind how much you frown, so long as you do what I ask, Snoots. You are not well—you know that, I suppose! *Well* then!" (It was the Nurse speaking—I began undoing the knots of my bandage, and unwinding it from my head.) " You're so beastly proud—if it wasn't for your silly old title you'd act differently, you know you would! Isn't that *good psychology*, Snoots darling?"

I eyed her with some curiosity. Could it be possible—was old Val after all by way of toying with the thought? Would Lady Kell-Imrie sound better than Valerie Ritter? My face slowly relaxed. My large teeth crept out—my hideous show-window of whiteguard tusks came out of my mouth in parade-order. There was a spasm inside my body. Next thing the whole apartment echoed with my Butler laugh.

" I'm glad to see you're better!" she sneered lightly. " Snoots, you haven't answered. Why don't you say you'll come down——"

" I've said nothing have I—did I say I wouldn't?"

Her eyes opened wide, and then the sparkling pin-points almost disappeared as she screwed them up as tight as fists and screamed—

" *Will* you Snoots? No do you mean it—will you *really* come?"

I put my good leg out, moved to the edge of the bed, and so sat a moment looking at her, my foot pressed upon the floor.

" Yes I'll come" I said.

" You *will*!!!"

" When a Kell-Imrie says *yes* he means yes!"

HUMPH

WHEN I LOOK at Humph's chin I am reminded of a strong-box. The chap is all chin. I hate this face more than I hate my own, which is saying a good deal. I disliked it from the start, a long time ago.

As a box, supposing the thing were that, it would as a matter of course be fitted with a false bottom. It is not a straightforward chin. If you opened it up (touching a spring, and removing the lower jaw, with its snow-white, well-stocked dentistry and well-upholstered coral gums) you would detect that the spacious cavity did not represent *all* of the chin. The box would not be as deep as you had expected, that is not *quite* so deep. There would be a half-inch of draughtage missing, to be accounted for somehow. The hollow would be short weight.

If faces were made of wood (Humph's is a sculptured figurehead with best pouter gardee-bust, protruded forward at the attention, at the wooden salute) then the spring-worked *cache* at the bottom would be used by this idiot for carrying dispatches, of that I'd stake my life. Hip and thigh smitten with military discipline (I saw him at it) he was right through—*We were all King's Men*, but Master Humph is a born King's Messenger. None would go more woodenly into a reserved compartment of the Orient Express, bearer of a state-document between His Gracious Majesty of Britain and his omnipotence the Sultan-that-was—accredited to the Sublime Porte, that is what I mean. And a pre-war penny-a-liner, concocting a crime-yarn for the upkeep of his frowsy brood, would pop Humph in as he stands, and have him throttle the thugs in the pay of "a Foreign Power", as they fell upon him as he dozed in the corner.

As for chins, I confess I am in no position to talk. I have enough and to spare myself of that. My life-long I have suffered on account of it. My teeth are so substantial, that is the fact, that the chin to go with them has to be of a solid make. But I am not in Humph's class.

Humph's head is an outsize article altogether—he is a lad that must give the hatter some mad moments, first and last. But that is nothing, what is important is that Humph is absolutely like a big carnival doll—all costard and trunk, no legs to speak of. With a portentous wooden head-piece, varnished a ruddy military pink-and-tan (Brigade of Guards), the fellow trots in. Standing to attention, he stares out blankly at you: to command or to receive orders. He has been given a pair of brown eyes, why I don't know. His brow is one of those meaningless expanses of tanned wood, it slopes back a little, *brownly* flushed (he flushes *tan*).

Captain Humphrey Cooper Carter enters a room with his sturdy little legs flexed at the knees, under the weight of his torso and block. But the animal moves quickly! He covers the ground there's no mistake—almost at a scuttle. Then he draws himself up short, with a military jerk. How well I see him, in my mind's eye—halted, or set in motion, with a pointless suddenness. Lousy little automaton! I stomach the chap with difficulty really! Little low-down knees bending with *a taken-short look* that he has—how I object to that well-drilled, semi-legless body. He is just Doctor Fell—except that I know to a nicety *why*.

So I ask you to picture my literary-agent—he hurries here and there in a spate of unnecessary rushes—a put-on-impulsiveness in fact—catching his face up as he whisks round as a dog does its tail—fixing you full-face, half about-turning, with parade-ground precision: or out of his dog-eyes of desolate blank brown he looks at you as if to say—"Yes I know I am not real!" Of course he is not. HUMPH is not real. I may not myself be very real (I have been told I am not, especially after that blackguard Howglen put me in that book of his, name and all), but Humph is twice as bad. The truth may as well be told at once—let us get it over. This man is a puppet. And, of all odd chances, this man is my agent—he attends to my publicity, and is my go-between for my books, with those old ruffians the publishers. How that has come to pass I will tell you. We are old friends, Humph and I fought for Scotland during the Great War. He is English but I of course am Scotch (my name must tell you that). We went out to the Western Front in the same draught of the Scots Guards. We were both gassed at the same moment and lay side by side more or less at Etaples. After that I lost sight of him. By pulling wires he got some job at the base, whereas I went back to my regiment, to be wounded two dozen times at least. I lost my leg happily, and got a beauty in my head. Hence the rather large way in which I live, as I have explained just now.

To cut a long story short, ten years ago I caught an amazingly large fish. It was that tipped the scales. It is strange what small things do—and there you are before you know it upon a perfectly new track. It was an accident. I had intended to catch a great fish, but not such a huge one. It fought under the glassy sea like a winged bullock. I saw this immense shadow I was trapping but when we dragged it up into the stark daylight, dead, I was amazed. At the time I was coasting, for that purpose, off Madagascar. I was in a launch I had chartered. (Afterwards I bought it.) My wooden leg had proved a certain handicap in that healthy life of killing and eating primarily, which my physique and experiences had bred in the bone. But I discovered that for most of the operations of large-scale fishing it was peculiarly suited—for harpooning, hauling upon deep-sea tackle, pulling up nets and so forth. It gave me a purchase. I did a bit of big-game hunting first (my rifle was cracking away amongst the last remnants of the wild beasts not to be wiped out, south of the Soudan, before the last shot was fired in anger between the Tommies and Fritzes, or almost so). But as it turned out it tired my other leg. Once I had practically to hop two miles in the tropics, after a fast lion. That proved conclusively for me how useless it was to go after anything *with legs!* So, in a word, I gave that up.—I took to the sea.

Sedentary occupations I frankly detest—unless you call seagoing sedentary, I except that. (I am a sort of caged beast myself. I have been *winged.*) But I am very introspective. Consequently, I contracted the habit of keeping a diary. (All this is how my life as a writer started.) From that I passed, almost imperceptibly, to enlarging, in the form of newspaper articles, any experience of interest in scottish sports magazines. From that it was but a step, I suppose, to making up into a book such matters as I considered might be of scientific value. My first book dealt with the Big Game of the Great Deeps. I was purely a naturalist.

For reading I have no great turn. But when I was on my back for months together I read, and enjoyed to do so. At the time in question I had read " Moby Dick ". The book had a great vogue after the war, because it was violent I think (certainly not its beauty). It was an epic of a great ' Kill '. That must have been it. I read it at once, I forget exactly when. Herman Melville gave me my clue.

The transcendentals of Leviathan! At that moment that was just about my mark, I was a typical ignoramus.

I knew nothing. I had been trained as an engineer. Reading about *Dick* gave me my first leg up.

I volunteered for polar exploration, but the doctors would never pass me. I thundered against my disability, at the Admiralty I threatened to fit out a ship. After that I succeeded to my title. I received a small sum in cash along with it: that and my blood-money still unspent (I am a Scot) put me in possession of funds. This was a little later.

In the case of " Moby Dick ", I was astonished at what I read. It passed into me—I scarcely can be said to *read*, like other people. For some time I could think of nothing else but its dark meanings. I attempted to penetrate them, with my clumsy imperfectly-trained intellect. I have never fathomed that book even now (it is my Magnetic Pole)—it is deep water, it is cold, it is mysterious. My mind encountered some barrier beneath the surface of the words. That was like a barrier-reef—yes if you wish, the walls of a tank (what is the sea but that?) that was a *sensorium*, cut out of the surface of a star. These were the limits where two universes met, element above element—atmosphere above the watery plane. But I (as the ideal Mystacocetus) I was born for both! What then? All the while I felt strong and free. Yet I knew henceforth I had been in some strange manner entrapped.

What exactly did I experience can you tell me? It was I think an understanding of my anger that it gave me, as I read on. All I can say for certain is that as far as I was concerned I gradually became conscious of the fact—I felt like the hunted fish. *I felt like the Whale,* in a word. I was, as I read, upon the side of that monster. It was *I* the Leviathan. (This upset me very much when I first found it out.) The more I read the book, the more I understood (darkly, and at first with misgiving) that in this mystical battle I was *not* upon the side of Man. I experienced from the start a secret animosity for Captain Ahab, which I was at first at a loss to explain.

Now I have told you in what manner I was influenced by this extraordinary book. This it was that finally caused me to throw up my deep-sea-fishing. I disposed of my boat. Then I took up my present work.—I am however anticipating—as I believe it is correct for an author to say when he has outrun himself as it were, in the appointed conduct of his narrative, as I notice I have just done.

With my first publisher I really had no luck. It was after I had caught the great Skid and was something of a hero. I will draw a veil over what happened between that shrewd man-of-affairs and myself. I blush when I think of it. It is sufficient to say that on that occasion it was I who was caught: this gave me a great dislike for all such people, once caught being not twice but forever shy. So I looked round for a middleman who might act for me, in any future ventures of that sort. After a few enquiries, I was told of a man who had just started agenting, who was a very able man, it seemed. What was more important from my point of view, he was a gentleman, my informant told me that he was reputed, even, to have a good deal of money. *Less motive to steal!* I reflected (though that is I know a thoroughly unsound deduction). Imagine my great surprise, upon entering his office, to find myself confronted with Humph! *Well I'm damned!* we both of us said heartily together. And since that time, much as I disliked him, Humph had been my agent—he was the first person I saw upon my returns to London, the last person I saw before I again started out upon some scientific expedition.

As I must now take up the business of this visit, and give an account of what transpired at my agent's, it will be necessary to explain what I do, that I should require an agent at all. This is not quite easy, it will demand a page or two. But for that purpose I will return to Herman Melville. With him my enlightenment began.

I have made the statement, namely that I sided with the fish. Stupid as I expect that must sound, this spoilt my fishing for me. That was the next step. I had intended to specialize in the biology of the ocean, but I went off that and returned to terra firma. (And to think that first the ivory leg of Captain Ahab had drawn me towards that powerful myth! It was the patron-saint, in our English Letters, of the One-legged, after all. Only *gradually* I turned away from Man.)

But then I came to have a strange notion about all this. —Here was this vast beast upon the one hand, and then, a minnow by comparison, there was the figure known as Ahab upon the other (upon an ivory stool, a tripod of tusks, smoking the pipe of peace which he cast away, the fire of which hissed in the waters). But I saw Captain A. as the spear-head of the Herd. He stood for Numbers. It was *he*, in fact, who was the giant! As I saw it, it was the great solitary floating colossus that was the private soul, of any creature. Wherever met, that was, in whatever universe, the One over against the Many. And it occurred to me that I might do worse than this: To—on behalf of that great lonely wandering animal, but really in the interests of that great principle—to seek to reverse the position, to the best of my powers. I was *another* Ahab, but of opposite sign.

I thought over this for some months. What I suppose I was doing was to hatch a plot against Mankind, a plot that had only one plotter: for I rapidly discovered that I was alone, with my hard vision, and there was no one alive I could trust. But I kept my own counsel. I never opened my mouth.—Returning to the earth (I, like that great amphibian, could only drag myself from spot to spot, I had been wounded, I had been unlimbed) I might hunt down the fool-hunters, one by one—lying in wait for them in unexpected places—picking off a few at least.—Their only strength lies in their great numbers. I would never attack, upon that point I was firmly decided, any man I could respect, for he would be in the same case as myself. Even if he were bad and treacherous, I would not raise my hand against him: I would mark down and pursue, selected for the purpose, members of those ape-like congeries—gangs, sets, ant-armies, forces of Lilliput, number-brave coteries, militant sheep-clans—fraternities, rotaries and crews.

To this end I cast round me for a plan of operations. Once my eyes were opened, then I saw distinctly enough upon all hands, all the transfigured Ahabs, as safe as houses, armed to the teeth with deadly rockets, and chattering machines that gushed a hail of lead, who had thrown off all restraint. Everywhere they were engaged in an exultant carnival of overthrow, to commemorate the destruction of the last of the generation of the giants (for which I read, for my part, Manhood and Genius): and I observed them strutting in every direction, drunken with their unexampled success.

I have got used to it by now, and so have they of course —I no longer watch it. But at first I was struck dumb at the sight. I was deeply astonished.—Of course I did not say to any living person all that I had seen. Stealthily I observed this saturnalia, and then I turned aside, to take counsel with myself how I might most effectively bring it to nought. And at first, as you may imagine, I did nothing. I thought a great deal about it, and that is as far as it went. What could I do single-handed?

Man, the little rogue, was compacting with the insects! I saw him, he was plainly resolved to sweep away all the noble values: it was his purpose to exterminate all those creatures of his own kind who seemed destined to advance to a higher perfection of living, or who had Infinity in their glances. It was sufficient to be suspected of dreaming at night, to be called an " idealist ". It was enough to betray some restlessness at the recital of a schoolboy obscenity, of coal-heaver wit, to be denounced as a spitter-upon-the-Flesh, as being anti-body, a disgusting *ascetic* !—It was very bad indeed. Everywhere it was as bad as it could be.

I could not at this point, in sufficiently few words, for the path is intricate, demonstrate all the stages that have led me to the particular line of work by which I am known. Since my *fish* book, two books of mine have been published. In these I have taken up the study of Man upon exactly the same footing as ape or insect. The regular anthropologist has done that, it is true, but only with a " backward " race, or an " inferior " class. I on the other hand make no distinctions. My victims are ' progressive ', popular, even ' fashionable ' persons, of topdog race and showy class—not prominent politicians of course, Mayors, Crowned Heads, etc. (because they are only lifeless puppets, they have no power or significance at all). I select always the popular *outsider*, for preference.

First I trotted out, in volume number one, a couple of officers who had been known to me, they were in my regiment. I dissected them like a pair of lice. They were in fact no better, *esprit de corps* apart. Why not say so? They both would have betrayed their regiment for a consideration (a handsome one): they had no honour. *Human* is a silly word no more: all the so-called ' human ' values depend upon (1) training: or (2) the agency of the civilizing intellects of ' sports ' (exceptional men). There is nothing else but the animal welter.—I am a ' sport ' of course.

Those who have submitted to elaborate training or enjoyed its advantages, or those rare figures possessed of original intellect, those I never touch.

For the purposes of these in part mock-researches, I have invented a new literary technique. Into this it is not necessary to go very deeply. It is sufficient to say that I do not simply measure, catalogue and plot out graphs and statistics. Mine is a picturesque method. I show my exhibit *in action*. I select a case of typical behavior. This is of course how it comes about that my pitch marches with that of the narrative writers. But it is quite distinct.

Accepted as a sort of disciple of Watson, I attracted to myself a modicum of limelight. I had a measure of success. " How Science can be almost more entertaining than Fiction "—you know the sort of idea. " People Behaving " the first of these two books was called. This gave the critic of the silly season (it is always the silly season in the " Book Pages ") his opportunity, as indeed I had calculated it would. " People Misbehaving " the cheerful ruffian called it, with great satisfaction. This did a lot of good.

Some of my specimen *people-behaving* (or ' misbehaving ') have been treated as if they were characters in a novel. For instance my Miss X. Three (my people have numbers, not names) has been compared to Miss Desmoulins, the Bayswater Adventuress, in " The Last Chronicles of Barset ". An English ' Pécuchet ' another was called. I have had a good success with my two books.

It is important for me to supply in more detail the technique of the success of these two books. Recently a book called " Babbitville " was written—that vaguely was upon my lines. The author went and settled in a Middle West town, exactly as if it had been a settlement of the Pueblo Indians. He compiled an account of the lives and habits of the inhabitants as if he had been studying a tribe of backward Indians.—But I am different to that. I do put up a good show for your money. *My* exhibits have adventures. They marry and are given in marriage. As

I have said, I display their 'behavior' in a suitable situation—adapted of course to bring out the most full-blooded response of which they are capable.

But suddenly I was side-tracked. These behaviorist specimens of mine were compared by a very eminent literary critic to pictures by Rousseau the Douanier: he compared my methods to theirs, and the results of my methods too. This comparison took on, it went well. The ruffian had evidently had a brain-wave. Others took it up. The naïf outlook—they saw it at once! Of course!—the freshness and stiffness of the primitive, or the child-artist. That was it! *Sapristi!* I could have shot him! Yes they all cried at once in chorus: *These are really Works of Art!* They are wooden—or rather metallic.—I was for this scribbling pack-in-full-cry constructing Frankensteins—it was the *Tales of Hoffmann* over again. As *science* these books of mine were preposterous (like a picture devoid of perspective). From the standpoint of psychology they were quite ridiculous. But *that* was not, it seemed, the way to regard them at all! No. *They should be looked upon purely as art.* Oh they were little primitive masterpieces! And "*what* an odd fish this Mr Kell-Imrie must be!" What a simpleton—yet what a charming, what a gifted simpleton! The perfect naïf.

This of course was very bad! Between them they had succeeded in making a legend for me which did not at all suit my book. I knew, better than they could tell me, all my shortcomings. I was only too aware that I was in some respects preternaturally obtuse. If you like, a kind of inspired moron. I could have told him *that*. (I have to bore holes in my head before I can get an idea into it. I am a dullard, with some cunning, that is all.) But it was most inopportune that they should have hit upon this inspired french painting moron to club me with. By transforming into mere *art* all my mock-science, they had made me a present of something I had no use for at all. An *artist* was the last thing I have ever desired to be (and certainly not a sort of pavement artist, like the beastly " Custom House Officer " they gave me for a double !).

But of course everyone repeated this tag about *Rousseau.* The book-critic is always far too busy keeping his end up socially ever to have time to read a book. He is particularly grateful therefore when some formula is discovered, the use of which will give him all the appearance of having penetrated to its heart without in fact ever having opened its pages. So I became simply " the *Douanier* " for these people.

I am freely described as " a genius ". You can imagine how much *that* impresses me ! Considering that no book-critic would keep his job for a moment if he did not employ the term " genius " at least about six times every week (the exact number of times is fixed by the number of authors put forward that week as " geniuses " by the publishers—if seven publishers *each* have a new genius that week—or if Messrs. Gollywogs and Ogpu have three and the rest four between them—then *seven* is the number of times the epithet has to be made use of).

But one of the brightest of these squinting puff-merchants had a bad brain-wave : he substituted *Policeman* for *Douanier*. This was of course not bad, in one sense. For my portraits do partake of the criminal dossier. I *am* forced to do a good deal of detective work before I get my model to come to life, and to *behave* as it should, without hitch. I *am* slightly policemanesque !

It would be a great thing for me, I know, if I could smash the *Douanier* legend. But as a matter of fact it came to an end in the most simple and unexpected fashion—yet not a very satisfactory one for me, I am afraid.

The title-page of my second book, although I had at that time succeeded to the baronetcy, upon the death of my cousin, in no way indicated that fact. But as a kind of mild celebrity began to attach to me (not one of the six or seven " fiery portents on the horizon " as Mr Bennett always called it, but a quiet little *also ran*, who got a patronizing pat at the foot of a column—a " we must not forget to mention "—) and people grew (very languidly) inquisitive, it became known that I was in fact Sir Michael Kell-Imrie. Strange as it may sound (though it would not seem at all peculiar if you knew the book-critic as well as I do) " the Baronet " gave the death-blow to " the *Douanier* ! "

Scarcely a week had elapsed since the broadcasting of this item of information (I suspect by Humph) when somebody gossiped to the following effect: " Sir Michael Kell-Imrie, whose literary interests—as witness his curious and rather sinister experiment in *Behaviorism*, ' People Behaving ' (called by one of our critical wits ' People Misbehaving ')—do not prevent him from being a keen sportsman. It will be recalled that some years ago Sir Michael (or Mr Kell-Imrie as he then was) landed a fish of such dimensions that it required a crane to lift it into the upper museum gallery where it now is to be seen, suspended from the ceiling. Sir Michael is the seventeenth baronet. His grandmother was the famous Elvina, Countess of Taliesin, who was considered one of the greatest beauties of her time."—This was very bad.

Subsequent to this, my legend became an entirely different one. I became a rather ' sinister ', even macabre, *Baronet*. But I was no longer a ' genius '. A Baronet cannot be a genius. (It would not be seemly for him to be a genius.) Nor of course can a Baronet be a simpleton. That would be equally incompatible. The eminent book-critic who first called me a " Custom House Officer " was rather ashamed of himself. All the monthly and weekly Reviews, especially any founded over fifty years, solicited an article from my pen. So matters stood more or less at the time of which I am writing.

I of course was only too glad to see the back of ' the *Douanier* '. But I confess that the ' Baronet ' who had taken his place was if anything more of a problem. Now for some time I had had in preparation a *third* book, mainly designed to knock out the ' Baronet ' (without of course reinstating the ' *Douanier* '). I had been compelled to alter my technique somewhat. A conference with Humph was at the present juncture perhaps due. The ' Snooty ' cutting shown me by Val, much as I disliked it, might serve even a useful purpose. That is how my affairs stood when I entered the office of Humph and as usual ran up against his chin.—I had been looking at this chin now, off and on, for a decade and a half. And every time I saw it I experienced the same *congestion* in my brain, if you can understand me. It entered my consciousness as an impenetrable lump. Nothing could break it up or mollify it. It made the lower part of my face uncomfortable to look at it. It made me tongue-tied. It gave me lock-jaw! I turned my head away. But there it was like a great wooden shoe clamped upon my jaw.—I had to put up with it however. So grinning from ear to ear, and showing every tooth in my head, I entered into a grim struggle with my *stream-of-consciousness* (obstructed by this irreducible *object*) as a stammerer must be with his stammer.

* * *

There were three or four authors in Humph's room as I had expected. His large private reception-' den ' (distinct from the offices where the staff rapped out his idiotic messages, packed and dispatched hundreds of fiction-novels to London and New York publishers) very clubbish, very posh, with portrait-prints of literary giants, a framed letter from Swinburne to Humph's great-aunt, and a really enormous enlargement from a Leike negative, of a horrible hunting-group in Kenya—Humph's chin throwing everything else into the shade, even the african sun, as it swelled out from under a seemingly dwarf *puggaree*. It was suggestive altogether of a mushroom suffering from some very unusual disease—a growth that had swallowed up its stalk and had spread out fanwise upon the earth beneath.—The whole of a lion's family, including the well-grown sisters and a patriarchal brother, lay in a dark heap beside Humph. He had evidently wiped them all out. So at least his chin said and there was no one there who was man enough to contradict it.

The authors all knew how rich Humph was and he never had less than three or four in his room at a time. They all hoped Humph would so fall head-over-ears—or shall we say head-over-chin—in love with their last manuscripts, that he would buy them outright without troubling to send them round to the publishers. But it wasn't *that* the Chin meant, stupid as it made him look. Humph had never yet parted with a penny in that way, as I could have told them if they'd have asked me. It required the soft hand of a woman to do the sesame-business with old Humph's purse-strings. But even then the girl had to tickle him to death before she could get at the treasure.

"*Hal*-lo!" he exclaimed hurriedly and shortly under his breath, meeting me at the door, staring at me in a great wooden unsmiling blankness, grasping my right hand just as it was escaping into a pocket. "I say, I hope you don't mind I've got *some*."

He'd *got some*—he'd got *some tea*—he'd got some sardines—he got *some* at all events—his wide-open eye fixed itself blankly upon my face, as he stopped at his *some*.

"I hope you don't *mind* I've got *some*"—again he stopped, at what he had got—he allowed his voice to tail away at 'some', to sink with discouragement until it was lost at our feet. Then cautiously he looked back over his shoulder, into the room, with puzzled hesitation. " I've got some people ! "—All I've got is *pee*-ple, in mournful surprise he told me, dropping his voice still lower at *people.* " I've got some *peeeep*-ple here ! " he whispered rapidly. Then he added hastily, " But they won't be here *long.* Do you mind ? I'll get rid of them at once ! Do you mind ? "

The authors surveyed me, as I came down the room, with varying degrees and blends of animosity. I was a rival penman—they of course took it for granted that I was another author. But noticing that I only had one leg, matters improved. They seemed to mind less. The social handicap involved in lameness, if it did not soften their hearts, set their minds at rest. Such an unquestionable handicap in the drawing-room and dining-room carried almost as much weight with them—in depressing the scales in my direction, their end rising, with relief, into the air above me—as if they had detected the existence, beneath my rather commonplace externals, of a first-class mind. (Such a discovery as the latter would of course have made them almost *friendly.*)

" Sir Michael Kell-Imrie " Humph introduced me. I 'met' the lot, and immediately a new atmosphere was created. As " Sir Michael " I became a new person. My game-leg became an aristocratic embellishment, my authorship became a harmless joke.

I turned my back upon the company and looking out of the large semi-fogbound windows, considered the swollen Thames, which ran beneath. I followed with my eyes the tugs or whatever they were, flattening themselves out by leaning their funnels back upon their decks, to scrape under the really hideous bridges. And I computed, a natural association of ideas, how much water had flowed under the bridges of the Thames since last I looked out of that window. And I wondered how much more of this dirty fluid tape would have to be dragged seaward before the authors back of me would pass out of the door, reluctantly, one by one, and I should be left alone with Humph, to talk things over. The muddy tape of water was at present being dragged past Putney, too, and there at Putney was my Lilly! I decided after Humph that I would send a telegram to Lilly. At this I started humming—it was her favourite tune—" Nobody loves a poor fat girl, But ah how a fat girl can love! ", and I heard Humph say—

" I say Kettleworth I am most awfully sorry but I'm afraid I shall have to——"

" Not at all—I must be going as a matter of fact! What is the time? "

" You understand old chap don't you! You do understand old man."

" I'd forgotten—how late it is! "

" It is rather. Mind you ring me up old boy."

" Yes of course! Well good-bye old chap! "

" Good-bye—er—Kettleworth! "

I heard the last footfall of the last author, the door closed, and then I turned round.

It was a large old square apartment, made for the English that are dead and gone, under the early Georges, very solid and spacious, with room for the ceremonious movements of persons, modelled upon The Quality, if not of it. Humph stood in the silence, up by the massive door, in the further corner, eyeing me, but ' under his brows ' as it were. In his hands he held his pipe and his oilskin tobacco-pouch. The pipe had its snout in the pouch, he was filling it with his head lowered over it. But his rich brown eyes all the time were fixed upon me, as a couple of his stout fingers waggled inside the transparent oilcloth, pulled automatically at the damp particles of leaf. Humph was acting somebody, one of his best-seller heroes doubtless. I looked at him and slowly yawned.—As a rule this would have brought him out of his corner. But he remained where he was.

I laughed, to clear the atmosphere. I did not wish this super-chinned lump of melodrama to spell-bind himself for too long a period near his door. Already he had taken a goodish time to drive out the authors.

"Well!" I exclaimed.

But Humph did not move. This was unusual. He went on filling his pipe. I yawned again. The fact had to be faced—this was a dramatic moment in the perpetual *dime-novel* in the midst of which old Humph lived and had his being. We were at the point in the tale upon which everything hinges—I mean the creaky old door with which Humph was accustomed to lock up his chamber of horrors—his *plot* in other words—for Humph of course, like Val, was an author (we all are authors to-day) apart from the fact that all his life was spent among authors.

"Did you have a good time Snooty?" he enquired in what he regarded as a quiet and serious tone—I could write his books for him, I knew his *hero* so well! "What was the crossing like? Lovely I expect."

"Smooth—perfectly smooth" I said. "Absolutely smooth." His chin had begun to get me down, and now that he had called into play his strong silent manner, it was more prominent than ever. It was of course the manner that went with the chin. The chin was now so much to the fore that we were both practically inside a chin, rather than inside a room. He had *got me in his Chin*, to parody old Val.

He folded up his oilskin pouch, put his pipe between his lips, seized it between his teeth, thrust his pouch in his pocket, and advanced towards me. As he approached me, fixing me with his eyes of faithful brown, he said—

"What do you know about *Mithras* Snooty!"

Wild horses could not have dragged a word out of me at that moment. My brain was simply choked with *chin*. I could do nothing but move my lips up and down. I could not utter a syllable.

In a lower voice, as one soliciting a confidence, he said—

" What do you know about *Mithras*. You know the mithraditic cult."

I stared at him stupidly.

" Mithras " I lisped at last.

" Mithras ! " he replied with energy.

I sat down, in my portmanteau-overcoat, and stuck out my leg. I did not wish him to see that I was tongue-tied. He might guess that it was the power of his chin. I frowned—I affected to be reviewing my store of knowledge, regarding Mithras, and the bull-cult. This gave me a breathing space.

" What do you know of the Bakhtiaris Snooty ! "

The intensity of the gaze of this man of action became unendurable. When you consider the immense earthwork of prognathous vacuity above which he was compelled to level his glances at anybody who was then *before the fort* so to speak—in an extremely exposed position—this should not be a subject for surprise but the contrary.

I knew absolutely *nothing* about the people in question. But I knit my brows—it was all I could do under the circumstances—and I affected to brush up in my head my fund of knowledge, dealing with the Bakhtiari whoever they might be. He stood over me, and pulled hard for a short while at his pipe—it evidently would not light, which, so busy had he been acting—and seeing how full in consequence he had stuffed it with tobacco—was not to be wondered at.

" Snooty " he said impressively, taking his pipe out of his mouth. " Will you come with me to Persia ? "

I shook my head emphatically at this. As to that I

could give him a yes or a no. It was a *no*. I had no wish whatever to visit the empire of the ex-Shah. And if that was where the Bakhtiari were, they could stay there for all I cared. But what on earth had he got in his great wooden head that caused him to wish me to go to *Persia* of all places—seemingly at a moment's notice! Could it have been the *Persian Exhibition* at Burlington House? It must have been that, of course. Was it this his cable was about? Indeed, again, this must be it!—I felt a shade of annoyance with my agent. I regretted my dollar bill for the Night Letter.

But Humph came down to earth: in fact he sat down instead of standing over me. Smoke began tranquilly to rise up into the air from the crater of his pipe. He fixed his soft brown eyes a little severely upon me. The business man, the man of common sense, peeped heavily forth. He stepped out, sat down, and took control. (Humphrey-the-Dreamer had always to be checked in this fashion by a bustling hard-headed business double. I don't know which I hated most.) A kind of *business lecture* was the upshot. When I saw what I was in for I resorted to prolonged yawning. This I found, in the long run (rather to my surprise), loosened my tongue.

"What are your plans for *work* Snooty!" Humph enquired in a rather heavy, a rich and fruity, business undertone. He was eyeing me all over suspiciously as he asked this question. It was as if (from the strictly business angle) I had been concealing the signs of some flagrant economic heresy about my person. "People are asking when you are going to do another travel book—*scientific* you know, not *too much—popular* of course." He was still, as ever, confidential, almost conspiratorial, in tone. But the air of gravity caused this to be rather of a hearty-to-hearty nature. Yes, a real hearty-to-hearty talk we were to have, he and I, that was the long and the short of it. "I never regard you *really* as a man of science Snoots. You mustn't be offended old chap but you know what I mean. You know however what I think. For me you are really *the artist*. And *what* an artist by Jove when you want to be! What an artist-in-words! I take my hat off to you old man, as *the artist*, every time! I wish I could write a bit of description a quarter as good as that account of *Mister X. Ten's* cashing the cheque at his club!" (Mister X. Ten!—the thing always chosen by the critics from my "People Behaving." *I take my hat off* as well—that was a favourite piece of heartiness, employed to clinch a dishonest puff, by the great fiction-review-king of the *Evening Mail*.)

This was very bad indeed! I had seen Humph pretty bad before but never quite so bad as this.—His lecture had only begun however: it was easy to see that some great purpose was informing it. I awaited with extreme resignation the appearance of the Big Idea.

"Something on the same lines as the book about the *fishes*—that is the sort of thing we want from you now old chap! That would wake them up—they need it! I say that *was* a good book Snooty, I was looking at it again only the other night! You know how I enjoyed it when I first read it—I couldn't put it down till I'd finished it and it was a pretty hefty book."

He had sprung up and began violently pacing the room. He was like an epileptic sentry. His hands were banged down into his expansive whipcord City bags. All this was to back up with the false pep of Action the cheaply trenchant, the humbuggingly hearty (which is more starkly apparent when the body is still).

He drew up in front of me after a storm-troop-rush down the room.—He glared down upon me, brown-eyed and massive-chinned. (What perfect brakes!—otherwise undoubtedly I should have been run over.)

" Do you mind if I say something to you " he panted (low-pitched to thrill).

" Intensely ! " I muttered. He did not hear.

" As your *agent* Snooty ! You mustn't mind if I tell you what I think—what's the use after all of having a bloody agent ! If he doesn't *tell* you. Well look ! I know the publishing world old boy, I'm not talking through my hat ! "

No he was not doing *that*. But he was talking through the top of his excalibur Chin, as never before ! I looked at him steadily for a moment. It was of no use. His peroration had the stiffening of some selfish purpose as yet undisclosed, it was perfectly evident. He sat down in front of me, I was invested. He took up his pipe from the table where he had put it down before his hurricane parade of the apartment.

" Your next book ought not to be about your *behaviorist* people, if you ask me."

I frowned. This was very bad indeed ! But how could I stop him ? His Chin still choked my brain. He levelled his eyes at me over it, took good aim, and spoke.

" I expect you won't agree with me—I can see you don't. Never mind that, I know what I'm talking about. People, you know, are a little tired of Behavior.—*I* am tired of Behavior myself ! "

He pooped off a defiant barking laugh at me at this, sprang up buoyantly, showing me his tail—his pipe horizontal, morticed in his jaw, smoke gushing from it as if his chin had been on fire.

Off he went in a frenzied rush : back and forth he marched and counter-marched, a half-dozen times both ways, before calm visited him once more and his excitement somewhat abated. Then he crashed down in front of me again, a little out of breath, his prominent chest rising and falling. His arm was thrown over the back of the chair, his pair of small-boy's leggies scarcely reached to the floor.

"It's no use" he went on passionately, talking in his nose (that he might articulate clear of the pipe-cum-chin combination) still heavily smoking, once in the upturned chimney there was a lurid flash. "I have to have this out with you first Snooty. I cede my place to no one in admiring—no one admires a lot of the stuff in 'People Behaving' more than I do!—*For instance.*" He paused, to allow his chin to relish something very much in its wooden way, and show that even if only a chin it was a great *book-lover*—and his mouth half-smacked itself to show how thoroughly it had appreciated etcetera. "Misses X. Fifty *Nine.—That* I consider was—that was simply marvellous Snooty —" (then he added under his breath in a rapid patter) "it-was-as-good-as-Proust." He paused and fixed me with his eye impressively. "*Proust could have signed that*—no I mean it!"

I always liked this expression about *signing*. He often had used the cutting for publicity purposes, in which the Big Gun on the *Sunday Monitor* had named Proust in writing of my book—"Proust might have signed" were the words employed by that illustrious reviewer. (Proust and "the *Douanier*" went well together, Humph considered. After all they were both Frenchmen!)

"All the same!" he exclaimed "I wish you'd let me advise you Snooty. I do *know*—on the practical side that's all I'm talking about."

The telephone bell rang, upon a desk beside the door. He charged across at it. I turned towards the window, but I heard him shouting angrily at once:

"Who is that! I can't hear! Who? Tell him I can't see him for a quarter of an hour. Ask him to come back! I am busy—I can see no one at the moment."

Busy indeed, thought I! And he returned swiftly to

his chair in front of me and took up his tale without taking breath.

" I'm talking to you as your *homme d'affaires*. But also as your *friend* ! "

I looked up at him with a shade of definite hostility this time, at the word *friend*.

" Is it as bad as that ? " I asked hoarsely.

" Don't be tiresome Snooty, you understand what I mean—with your next book we want to have something really decisive. Quite different to the last, it ought to be quite different. Of course that doesn't mean you should give up your research-work."

" Of course not " I said looking very hard at his chin.

" Why should you, of course not."

" I can see no harm."

Then he squinted at me as he believed craftily—upon the border line of what is " mischievous ".

" But you want Snooty " he said with an insinuating soft aggressiveness—he was being aggressive *for me* : " you want to put a stopper once and for all on that *Douanier Rousseau* business ! "

" Yes " I answered at once, imitating his tone " *also the Baronet*. We must hear no more of ' The Baronet ' Humph."

" Very well " said Humph, but without quite the same conviction.

As I was by this time perfectly aware that he was in fact in the act of providing a programme precisely for The Baronet (that he had enthusiastically accepted the theory that Baronets are expected to know a good deal about fishes, that *The Proper Study of Mankind is Fish*, if you are a Baronet, and that such a disreputably ' modern ' science as *Behavior* is not quite the sort of interest that goes with the heriditary rank) I was not therefore at all surprised that he should shy at mention of the dignitary I had bracketed with the Custom House Official.

"I regard The Baronet as especially abnoxious" I said very firmly indeed.

"Of course, of course—so do *I*!" he exclaimed evasively. "But look Snooty I have a scheme. I'm so glad you are here—I was afraid you wouldn't be back in time. To come to the point."

I laid a firm fist upon the solid arm of the chair in which I sat.

"I've got a pal in the Legation at Teheran, an awful good feller, Brian Hawkes. My holiday starts next week."

"So early?"

"Yes. I take a month's holiday, I can't be away longer than that.—I propose to go to Persia. And I want you to come too!"

"Why should I go to Persia?" I showed all my teeth, and cockrobined my head argumentatively on one side.

"Ah that's just it! It must be *you*. Only you could do it."

"My dear Humph—do what?"

He half-winked, or rather slyly and with coquetry blinked, what while he smiled and smiled.

"I will tell you" said he, easy and soft. "The cult of Mithras—you know the bull-god——"

"Very slightly."

"No but you know who I mean. The Spanish bull-fights are the last vestige, that is all that is left of the, of the religion of——"

"Of Mithras."

"I know nothing about it. You probably know far more than I do."

I made a rather violent gesture of deprecation—to superadd to utter ignorance desire for continuance of same.

"Mithraditism or whatever they call it was supposed to have been dead in Persia ages ago wasn't it?"

I shook my head and shrugged my shoulders.

" No but you know what I mean they're all Mohammedans there now—Shiahs they call it."

I yawned violently.

" Anyhow, no one ever supposed that the—the mithraditic beliefs were still—extant ! ! Did they ? "

" How should I know ! "

" Well they didn't."

" That's good."

" And they *are* ! "

" Are *what*—for Jesus' sake ! "

" Ex-tant ! " he bellowed.

" That's fine—that's peachy ! " I bellowed back.

After we'd laughed at the shindy we'd made, Humph cleared his throat (*extant* was a difficult word. He always wanted to say *extent*).

" How I do loathe the beastly american slang ! " he said. " *How* I hate it ! *Peachy !* Really ! Did you ever hear such an expression ! "

" It's pretty bad isn't it ! But it isn't the word—it's the lovely lips that use it."

" Ugh—that only makes it worse ! *Everything* American, without exception, makes me physically sick. They are an *awful* nation. Every time I go there I hate the country and the people worse ! "

" I like them."

" You can't. It's impossible ! "

" Indeed I can. I'd settle there if I were rich."

" Would you ? I'd pay half of anything I had not to."

His chin displaced itself two inches forward : he became " the Englishman " of american popular myth. I felt that Humph must be incessantly taken for a walking cartoon by the Newyorker.

" Well anyhow, among the Bakhtiaris " he said.

" Among the Bakhtiaris ! "

" The cult of Mithras is still alive ! "

I shrugged my shoulders.

" I think it's thrilling " he said: " no not thrilling. I think it's interesting, damned interesting. The cult out of which the Spanish bull-fights grew——"

" How does a bull-fight grow ? "

" I'm hanged if I know. But it is interesting to think the cult is still alive and kicking."

" How does a cult kick ? "

" How doesn't it kick, you ought to have said! But listen Snooty. The bull-cult——"

" Kicks."

" Is *alive*—is still alive. It's going on in Persia at this minute! *Now.* They're all busy worshipping away at their bulls—when the Mullah's are not looking. But aside from that altogether Snooty and *this* is the point my dear old boy I'm trying to impress on you." He leant forward, lantern-jawed and dour-chinned, his eye going lustreless with impressiveness, and he tapped me lightly upon my mechanical knee, I felt the vibration in my big-toe I had lost (but that is only a bit of one-legged blarney). " It would be of quite exceptional publicity value ! "

" What! For whom ? "

" For you you fool! Can't you *see*? Don't you see that ? "

" I can't say I do."

" But I'm making you a present of it man—can't you see! Why am I? Because I know you're the man to do it. Come with me to Persia! Come with me to Persia! We go to Teheran. You go north from Teheran. You investigate for yourself on the spot—among the Bakhtiaris."

" But I'm not interested in the Bakhtiaris."

" But you soon would be ! "

" Never."

" But the cult of Mithras ! "

" It bores me stiff."

" What nonsense. I'm sure it doesn't. Once you were there you'd be as keen as anything. Get captured if you like, while you're about it, by a brigand. There are lots of them there. Anything of that sort would go down well. It would help the book a lot."

" Which book ? "

" Why the book you would write about Mithras of course ! Why don't you come ? "

" Well in the first place I have promised only this morning to go to the Riviera."

" Who with ? "

" A woman."

He stared at me for a second or two, rebuffed. (Ladies first !)

" What's that matter ? " he burst forth roughly, in full reaction against *The Ladies God Bless Them !*

" It does. There are special circumstances."

" Of what sort ! " he riposted hotly, with his best pistol-shot technique.

" Well if you want to know, I am to be her guest. The lady pays."

He stared at me again, this time a little uncertainly.

" What's she like ! " snapped the ruthless Humph.

" How do you mean ? "

" Is she pretty ? "

" Should I be the guest of a hag ? "

" Bring her to Persia ! "

(Bring the wench to Persia ! Oh la la !)

" Bring her along ! Or still better get her to take you ! "

" I couldn't allow that."

" I don't expect it'd be the first time you'd been kept by a woman you old ruffian ! "

" I daresay not. One has to pick one's keeper with some care."

" Is she rich ? I suppose she is. Tell her you must go to Persia instead of Monte Carlo ! "

" What's it cost ? "

" Oh it's quite cheap. It's ridiculously cheap.—But there's something else I wanted you to do."

" Oh dear, what's that ! "

" You know Rob McPhail."

" I do."

" Is he still at Faujas ? "

" As far as I know."

" He is very interested in bull-fighting. He's a bull-fighter isn't he ! "

" I believe he does some bull-fighting."

" He is a bull-fighter, it's well known."

" What do you want me to do about him ? "

" I want you to get him to come too ! "

I laughed.

" Are you organizing a circus ? "

" Never mind ! Can you get him to come ? "

I shook my head.

" You can't ? "

" He wouldn't come."

" *Why* not ! I believe he would."

I laughed again.

Humph's irrepressible telephone burst out again into a breathless alarum, with the spasm of a teething ten-monther. Raging, Humph jackintheboxed off his chair, wild-eyed he flew (upon his sturdy scampering stumps out-of-sight) to quiet it—to soothe it or to throttle it. He hissed into, ordering it to stop summoning him in that uncalled-for way in season and out of season.

Meantime I for my part secretly took counsel with myself. *When a Kell-Imrie says yes he means yes !* So a Kell-Imrie it followed from that must not say *yes* too flippantly. Else a Kell-Imrie would find himself, one of these fine days, in the kind of fix that no Kell-Imrie could circumvent, cudgel his brains (which were none of the brightest) as he might.

That absurd Kell-Imrie remark held me to Val for a month in a Villa. I should go to the South of France. Yes I should go—it was a grim prospect indeed! Never again must I say *yes*.

But if with such levity I accepted Val's, why not close with his? Let me travel to Persia. I might do worse than go to Persia. This was a day of invitations. Why not then accept the lot, and let the devil take the hindmost?

Softly Kell-Imrie! I whispered, and I shot over a panther-glance in all secrecy at the broad black stockbroker-back of my stooping agent, as he stood sprawled out double above his telephone. This man had annoyed me very much indeed.

My agent had annoyed me, then, more than I should care to say, he had shown his hand as I saw it, in his preposterous exordium. *The Baronet!* His policy was based upon the principle of The Baronet—this so-called agent of mine was altogether too friendly with the egregious Baronet, to be at all the man for me. Could the conduct of my affairs be any longer regarded as in safe keeping, this being the case? Emphatically not! With proper caution and by imperceptible degrees they must be removed and entrusted to some person less susceptible to Debrett. Of course with The Baronet he entirely missed the point, he misunderstood the issues in the World of Books so patently as to convince the least expert that his judgment was altogether faulty.

Already (slow, clumsy, but in absolute secrecy, after my scottish fashion) I was plotting against 'The Baronet'.

Here now under my very eyes (in the person of my accredited agent if you please) was one of that gentleman's notorious friends, that was plain enough. But a dark and beautiful thought insinuated itself into the most tortuous retreats of my rather *bluff* intelligence. There its full seductions (with extreme slowness) were borne in upon the uncouth counsels of my mind, discovered as it were in debate, in the interior of its cerebral interstices—plotting with a portentous deliberation worthy of a synod of Elders of the most benighted scottish Kirk.

The beautiful thought was this (and can you wonder that it lit up the whole interior of my travailing consciousness ?). The beautiful idea was as follows :—

What if I could bring together and somehow conjoin the future Lady Kell-Imrie (to give her the title conferred upon her in her own private soothsayings) and this particularly dangerous confederate (supposed to be my 'agent') this sworn crony (now present) of her future ladyship's emblazoned consort ?

It was a bonnie notion ! I grasped its full meaning with that extreme slowness of my snail-witted people—I daresay a half-dozen seconds had elapsed before my brain had taken fire, after the lovely spark had first pricked into the fathomless dullness of its native peat. Slow in combustion, ay, but sure and enduring, once the fire taketh hold ! (*Thomas Carlyle*) : so that still at the moment of writing I *glow* with the rapture of this little discovery.

When Humph returned, I was upon my feet, or upon my foot, I suppose I should say.

"I'm sorry old man. That beastly *tel*-e-phone !"

"I must leave you now" I said.

"Oh no *must* you, *not yet* Snooty. Look don't go for a moment must you ! You haven't told me if you'll come to *Per*-sia !"

He sang Persia as if it were part of a dawdling nursery couplet.

"I'll think it over" I said.

"Oh will you Snooty that's splendid—I am glad !

Will you really !—You *must* come Snooty. I'm sure you'll come ; I knew you would. It will be the most tremendous fun."

I said I would lunch with him in three days' time and give him my decision then.—Oh *and* McPhail ! McPhail oh yes !—I would not forget about Rob McPhail ! No I would not forget. I would bear in mind my friend McPhail.

What astonished me was his lack of interest in what he had given himself so much trouble about. Had I said *no* it would have been all the same. He did not care if I came or not, or if he went or no. The springs that make these dull facts, of going and of coming, of Persia or Pimlico, take on a significance, were with him dead or dummy ones perhaps. *Persia* was an idea his mind had not except in the most external fashion possessed. It handled it, it paraded it, without in the least caring what it was. He was like a hired advertising hack, who had been given *Persia* to trot round as his week's task. And trot it round, upon his diminutive trotters, he certainly did. *Persia* in a word was a shallow fetish. His imagination was quite nerveless, it had no power to *grasp* whatever it might numbly handle.—Humph was, as I have said, *not real.*

MITHRAS

I HAD ALWAYS been interested in Mithras. Ever since I read somewhere it had to do with battles against bulls I thought I'd like to know about it.

Naturally I prefer bulls to men. Myself I'd be a credit to any cattle-stud attached to a *Taurobolium*—in a loincloth I'm a bearcat! (as I've hinted as much as I could). So I'm for the horned end of the mix-up every time! The harpooners are fish-fighting matadors—you see the situation better when the animal's the size of an island, as with the great cetaceans. Then any bloody bonehead can discover for himself that it's the embattled manikin making war upon his Mother Earth. That is the gist of the matter.

Without knowing what it was about, more than just to know it's Bull versus *Homo Sapiens,* I was fairly full of interest for it. *Mithras* was a name to which I responded. Anything *against Us* causes me to sit up and take notice, I'm always on the half-lookout for something hostile of that order. So that was programmatic right away: and I never saw about the fall of a popular matador without a grim scottish chuckle. For Mithras (if that's who it was the castillian clown in plush tights stands for) to get it in his gilt-frogged guts, at the hands of the animal (and to be torn down socially, de-pigtailed, or nailed up in a wooden overcoat) that caused me such stolid satisfaction as a thoughtful young bull might get from hearing about it. But I never went into the Mithras-business beyond saying " Mithras " for " Matador ", in the sense indicated above. I had left it at that.

To put all this in a pea-nut, I was ever *agin that government*, (of Nature as coming under *meum* and *tuum*) and all for chaos in plain English. I was ever upon the side of any wild force. I had thrown in my lot for better or for worse with Mother Nature. I conducted with herself what could at a pinch have been represented as an incestuous intrigue. (I would sooner repose upon the hundred-mile-per-hour bosom of a destructive wind, or lay me down for a slight siesta upon the tail of a whirlwind, than confide my destiny to the tepid hands of a brother or sister mountebank of the same flesh, spirit, speech, genus and biology as myself—you get me, oh my brother or my sister ?)

I had not, as I think I have shown, betrayed my interest in Mithras at all when Humph startled me with that name purposely at first. No one could have guessed from my manner that, hidden at the heart of my bottomless yawns, the cult of Mithras cut a good deal of ice with me though I knew nothing about it. But upon stepping out into the Strand, upon my departure from Humph's riverside office, I went directly to the nearest book-shop of any size. It was the shop for what I wanted, Somerset House is its main big town neighbour and handy landmark. It took me five minutes to stalk there from the street leading to my agent. I reviewed our interview. Everything fell into place. I gave up Lilly for that day.

Without delay I told myself it was up to me to acquaint myself in more detail with this rude cult. I had been visited by a brain-wave—right away—though perhaps it was merely putting two and two together after all and making them come to four ! Yes, that was what it was after all. *Had D. H. Lawrence, I wondered, gone off the deep-end about Mithras ?* There was at least a sporting chance that he had, it was worth trying.

There sure enough, among the small library made up of his life's work, which I found *au grand complet* in the book-shop, was what I had come to look for. A big bloodshot design (all in Corrida saffron and hemoglobin vermilion) of a sadly over-sexed bull, pawing the dust-cover, at once drew my attention: it announced the fact that I had not placed my reliance in Lawrence in vain. A fountain of steam spurted from the distended nostril of the animal. Above the towering crescent of its horns were printed in bold black the four words—

SOL INVICTUS—BULL UNSEXED

Here was the cosy D. H. Lawrence atmosphere immediately! (If a spirit flung down in some other age and feeling very lonely, suddenly came upon such a super-sexed book-jacket, how *cosy* he would feel and back among the boys!) I felt at home upon the spot—I knew my champion would not fail me now and the merest glance proved that indeed such was the case. I purchased this "Sol Invictus—Bull Unsexed" my eyes shining like marbles of freshly polished glass in the window of a quack optician. I stamped snorting out of the place to the great amusement of the assistants of both sexes (a big peachy girl had served me, I made her lips blush with my knowing glances) who were all of course nourished beyond question upon this Savage Messiah and perfectly fathomed my excited condition—I made their book-store into a china-shop with my bullishness while I was there, flashing on all sides my two white ranks of reactionary tusks: for was I not in the eyes of these initiates upon the eve of a New Revelation?

I had just opened the book and looked inside it while one of the men assistants was making signals to me (I think he had a copy of Lady Chatterley—non-authorized—he wanted me to see *sub rosa* but I am not sure): my eye had fallen at once upon the following typical passage, which I greedily read from beginning to end.

Mithras got all hot and clammy about the Bull. So as he was so much in love with the Bull, when God ordered him to go in pursuit of it with a view to killing it, since it had broken jail and gone off on its own again (like the wild animal it of course was) he sat down and wept unrestrainedly in the opening of his cave—because he did not wish to kill the Bull at all, seeing that he loved it, passionately.

" Oh why must I kill Bullie-Woolie ! " Thus spake Zarathustra.

Whereupon the incorruptible Raven of God (who did all the aero-post work of the Divinity, *By Divine Appointment*, in perpetuity, office-boy of Zervan) and who had stayed behind a few minutes to see his Master's orders promptly executed or to know the reason why, croaked on a tree, where he sat watching Mithras narrowly.

" Don't be a cry-baby Mithie you silly white-livered ape !—Save me from these pale bipeds ! "

The Raven cast up his eyes in unfathomable contempt, for he hated this peculiar pale-faced, two-legged hybrid, which his Master had seen fit to fashion, and, out of mockery, to put him over all the rest of the animals, calling him Mithras.

" Suppose anyone caught you crying ! " the Raven scolded on. " It doesn't matter to *me*, but this cave is full of rats—if they saw what a baby you were they'd think to themselves *Here's a fine Lord and Master to have had put in authority over us ! What a farce of a boss !* They might rush you one of these days when you were off your guard and chew you up ! Always the Tearful Tim ! Don't you see how bad it must look ! Besides remember you're supposed to be the Saviour of the World ! You are ' the mediator ' (I don't think !). Blow your nose and wipe your eyes and *be a man* ! "

The Raven said *be a man* with an irony the depth of which it would be impossible to convey. But when he heard it say *be a man* Mithras puffed his chest out (though his lungs were still choked up with sob-stuff) and looked daggers at this over-quothing snooty Raven, just above his cavern door—who should by all rights have left ages ago for the Plutonian Shore where he belonged and was awaited (the bird was just being officious). An aeon is but a pulse-beat in the body of God as every good muslim knows but the Raven was already a good many aeons behind his time-table, and Mithras was after all, at that moment, in human shape, and told the time of day by sun and by fixed stars.

" All because you're soppy over a silly old Bull you great blubber-mouthed Cissy-man ! " crowed the redoutable Raven, messenger of Unending Time. " Go off at once and kill it ! Do you hear ! You haven't the guts of a louse !—Excuse me but you must admit it's a act.—What's the use of you if you get all balmy over all the males of the different species the Boss is planning up !—But I knew it would be that way ! I warned His Majesty all along of the danger of creating you first, and all on your own, as he did. It was a great mistake. I knew he'd make a Cissy of you. So it has turned out ! All the same, *orders are orders* Mithie ! It's no use ! You have got to do in that He-cow. You might as well make up your mind to that ! Besides let me tell you, you'll find what is snapped at by the scorpion full of toffee (flavoured with ant-eggs and snake-spittle) and its blood full of red nosegays, and red-blooded grog-blossoms, implicit in its thousand-over-proof world-beating booze ! A blood-red Brandy fit for Bacchus—let alone you, effeminate Persian ! Go ! Drink up its blood—it'll make a man of you ! If you do God will decorate you—he'll stick a bull's-eye in your cap and call you Maccaroni. So *Action !* (for God's sake remember that you symbolize *Action* in this Pantheon !) Attaboy ! "

Mithras fingered his phrygian bonnet (of which he was very proud —he foresaw it would make a good " Liberty-cap ") to feel where the Deity would probably stick the bull's-eye. He smiled sweetly at the incorruptible bird, thanking him for this hint.

" Attaboy ! " it screamed hoarsely in its parrot-voice. " Attaboy ! After the kill you can swank round as a little tin-god *yourself*—I shall have to call you ' Excellency ' ! Don't be afraid of it—it's quite easy to kill ! Pluck up such courage as you've got—this wild-bull hunting-trip will be your star-performance as a god. After all the old bull doesn't fight with its sex ! It's far and away the stupidest beast of the field imaginable, it just puts its head down and never looks where it's going ! "

After this fight-talk old Mithras felt much better and wiped his tears away from his eye-pits which were full of salt-water. He stood up, quivering from head to foot, with fear and excitement. As he stood up the world shook from pole to pole. (This was only natural —seeing it was but a few sizes bigger than the great wheel at Luna Park, as to its meridian, and Mithras was a heavy boy.)

I saw at a glance that Lawrence was on my side and all steamed-up over the Bull. He made Mithras in love with the Bull because he always put himself in the shoes of any god he got interested in. He'd have fallen himself head over ears in love with any Bull if he'd been shut up in a cave with one all alone. So he made out Mithras was, as I could see. I allowed for that—and to spare. Elbow-room one must have for one prophet's weakness, and I guessed that *bull* would get Lawrence all steamed up.

The Bull stops top-dog all through. From start to finish the Bull's on top. I mean of course in the gospel of Mithras according to St. Lawrence. D. H. Lawrence and Yours Truly however are on the same side of the argument —both of us are Nature-cranks, if you like to put it in that way—if it gives you any *pleasure* to put it in that way, do so!

I turned back some pages. There I found he quoted some 'high' authority and I read as follows (it accounted for bull-fighting, for instance in the pastoral parts of France).

> The most extraordinary of these epic adventures was Mithras' combat with the Bull, the first living creature created by Ormazd. This fable carries us back to the very beginnings of civilization. It could only have arisen among a people of shepherds and hunters with whom cattle, the source of all wealth, had become an object of religious veneration. In the eyes of such a people the capture of a wild bull was an achievement so highly fraught with honor as to be apparently no derogation even for a god.

This is how it is that a pastoral people, in Spain or in Provence, take to the mithraic rite, and tend to perpetuate it.

Near the book-shop there is an Aerated Bread Company. (The success of this concern as a teashop-octopus has been largely dependent upon the fact that the first three letters of the alphabet, namely A. B. and C., are the short for Aerated Bread Company. Try as Joseph Lyons would to knock it out, he could never get over that lucky coincidence.) I blew into the Aerated (you have seen me leave the book-shop so you can imagine how) and before I had quit its underground smoking-room I had read the book from cover to cover. It took about twenty minutes. It was not over two hundred pages long and in places fairly to the point—my second quotation shows that.

I suppose now I have to boil down for you what I read. I offer it in tabloid. It's difficult to compress all the facts. Never mind.—Read this of course if you like, if you don't do the other thing, you are not obliged to. It is of no great importance that you should know it. It was one of the stepping-stones in my translation to Persia.

All you want to know is this. First Mithraism was a *popular* religion. (Some religions are popular, some only for the few.) So of course it was a second-rate one. All that was good in it was the ancient magic. The North of Persia, the mountains south of the Black Desert (through which the Trans-Caspian runs—an immense desolate windy tract of dark and whirling sand)—east of the present Merv (in " Mourus, the strong and pure, the third land of profusion ") south of Turkestan (Bokhara and so on) is the homeland of aryan magic (though to-day it is only found among the Afghan tribes it seems).

> Mithraism was a vulgar hybrid [I quote from the " Sol Invictus—Bull Unsexed "]. It was one of the great *salvationist* creeds (at least on the surface). It was one of the two principal systems of religion invented by the East for the West—to rot the great house of cards run up overnight by the troublesome graeco-roman children, and stew them in their own fat with a novel hysteria. It was very successful.

It sprang up in Persia (or was concocted in Persia) a few centuries prior to the birth of Christ. As to detail of ritual etc., it was built up on the mazdean backgrounds. We may regard it as " a nasty little Christmas present, presented with its best compliments by the Persian Empire to its friend the Roman Empire ".—For several centuries it was the main religion of the simple-hearted roman legionaries. The roman " common soldier " was (eighty per cent) mithraist. All over Germany, Italy, Greece, Asia

Minor, are the remains of temples of this cult. It especially appealed to the military man, because of the bull-business. It exalted military heroism. It was a religion of *Action*.—That was its popular side.

But it also had an esoteric and a non-popular side. The "Sol Invictus—Bull Unsexed" quotes as follows, and I quote after it. "The rigorous logic of its deductions assured to this stupendous chimera a more complete dominion over reflecting minds than the belief in the infernal powers and in the invocation of spirits, although the latter commanded greater sway over popular credulity." It was *a stupendous chimera!* But all its "rigorous logic" came from the semitic lands, not from the aryan.

Mithraism was, for the initiate, a babylonian *Destiny-cult*: for the popular worshipper a very martial salvationism full of comforting nonsense about "the Good" getting the better of "the Evil". It reposed upon the one hand (on its esoteric side) upon the secular magical practices of the Magi (a northern mountain tribe—to put it shortly, the *Levites* of Persia). Upon its popular side it came from heaven knows where: but it made a liberal and highly sentimental use of the Good and the Bad—the Light and the Dark business—in which the Persians specialized. (Compare our friends the Parsees—a very irritating sect.) And of course its underground and its all-square-and-above-board doctrines contradicted each other flatly.

This natural confusion (which must result from a doctrine catering for both the stupid majority and the intelligent minority) was greatly increased by one highly important fact: namely that the Magi had got in the habit latterly of going and living in the mesopotamian plain. They kept their end up there, and did some execution, for they were past masters at magic. All semitic religions are full of persian fairy-tales for instance. (The Garden of Eden is one of them.)

But the Chaldean, he was a pretty hefty fellow too in that line. He was no novice in the Black Arts. And he put his astrology over, lock stock and barrel, into the old visiting Magi. So, when the Persian (the Magi) came, in the fullness of time, to invent Mithraism, his mind was in a state of the utmost confusion. The God of Light became the God of Time—and vice versa. All that he really brought into it that was quite Persian was the story of the Bull. And that was what caught the fancy of the mob. So really Mithraism *is* a Persian Religion all right, if you don't dig into it too far. With all the ritual of the *naturism* of the ancient iranian cult, the Magi were great religionists, though scarcely a match for the Semites of the Plain. In Babylon they really went to pot, and ceased to function as independent spell-binders. Their beliefs were removed from the terrestrial surface up into the starry vault. *All* Chaldeans were astrologers. They got the Magi looking up into the sky. They got them star-gazing—that was the end of them. They got lost in the mathematics of the Heavens. In the end they became so degenerate that they would rush off anywhere whenever they heard from their Chaldean friends that a new god was being born. (In this way we find them dashing off to Bethlehem, you remember.)

" Stupendous Chimera ! " Yes, if you mean by that the Chaldean background. The esoteric god of Mithraism is in fact not a philosopher's god, but an astrologer's. The Machine-god, the *Fate-god*, of Mohammed (stolen from the chums of his early days, the Maccabaean Jews) was the God of the Chaldean. To-day it is the god of the metaphysics of the *Finite Universe* of relativist physics. (Another astrologer's god, if you will. *Everything* rounded off, and packed into a sphere, as deterministic and fate-bound as the cosmos of the Babylonians. A great achievement !)

So the *God of Destiny* turned out to be, in the occult

doctrine of Mithras, a more important and all-embracing *Chronos*. It turned out to be a Chronologic Deity. It was an ultimate God of Time. *Zervan*—that is to say " Boundless Time ". It was *he* that was at the back of beyond—the source of everything. We were of temporal stuff. We were the children of time. It was to this hybrid that the combination of the wits of Chaldea and of Persia led.

All this I lift bodily out of the " Sol Invictus—Bull Unsexed ". I do this to show you that there were backgrounds to this Bull-business that at first sight—in merely looking at a toreador—you would perhaps scarcely suspect.

What seemed to attract D. H. Lawrence almost as much as the Bull was the thought of a Mithraic Europe, in place of Christendom.

Until the third century A.D. it appears to have been a toss-up which would come out on top, Mithras or Jesus. Jesus won. But by a much narrower margin than it is comfortable to contemplate (for the Christian). If Jesus had not, then we should have had giant *Tauroboliums* instead of cathedrals—in Manchester, Edinburgh, Belfast, and everywhere else to-day. Herds of fighting bulls would have grazed all over Salisbury Plain and at the foot of the Sussex Downs. England would have been rather like Spain—full of Toreadors! Bizet's famous song from Carmen would then have been *a hymn*. Imagine that! Instead of the rather sickly Christianity (that is the puritan evangelical variety) with its humanitarian sentimentalism always tripping it up—we should have had a red-blood gospel of *Action* with Mithras. Everywhere the Gladiator in short, instead of the ' Creeping Jesus '. And it might quite well have been that under these circumstances " the Baronet " would not have felt quite so gloomy-deanish about mankind!

All this Lawrence brought out beautifully clearly in his " Sol Invictus—Bull Unsexed ". I saw *distinctly* a Mithraic

Europe. I could not have seen it better if it had been there. SOL INVICTUS at Stonehenge, instead of the Archbishop of Canterbury at Canterbury. Delightful! The Magi officiating in a semi-mazdean temple where Westminster Abbey now stands (a big bull-ring between it and the Tate). And our Government next door (assembled in a very fine building of Persepolitan pattern) not forced as at present to apologize to the ridiculous Bengalee for having thought of the machine-gun first or of having invented electric light and airplanes! The King-Emperor would visit Delhi in great pomp every year or two, and a few thousand herds of traitors would be brought in bags from all parts of India and heaped up in a pyramid outside his residence, as if our George were Ashurbanipal! What a transformation don't you agree!

If you consider this too glowing an account, all I can do is to refer you to Lawrence's book. You will find that that *glows* very much more than my potted version. As a matter of fact it glowed so much I simply had to pot all of it for you, else had I used more of its highly coloured passages to quote from it would have made a sort of sunburst in the middle of these rather sober, unpretentious pages, which are after all not intended to be lit up in that way at all. They are merely designed to tell a plain unvarnished tale in as pleasant a way as possible—avoiding as far as may be all the more gross and disquieting aspects of life, and also those mixed up with foreign scenes or with times that are too far off to interest a man who must See Britain First. I fear perhaps as it is I may have overshot the mark a bit, in my account of how I became acquainted with the doctrine of the Mithraists—in my anxiety faithfully to put on record just how it was it came to pass that I decided so suddenly to go to Persia.

* * *

Having found out all there was to know regarding Mithras and a little more besides, I felt distinctly attracted by the idea of Persia. But that did not mean I need hardly add that I relished the idea of Humph as a fellow-tourist. (I should have to choose some other route—once in Persia I could lose him at once.)

However my plans for Humph if I went included Val. That third party was my safeguard. Val would blot out Humph in some measure. In the end, mutually they might blot each other out, with luck, if they could only be persuaded to coalesce—vanishing from my sight altogether, into the Bed!—Yes, if old Val could only manage to *get him in the Bed!* That would be too perfect—it would immediately clear the air. I should be able to proceed with my affairs (I thought I would drop down and look at Babylon) without further responsibility. (I rubbed my hands beneath the A.B.C. table at the idea of Humph in the Bed—for that alone it was worth while to go to Persia!)

First Val must be sounded. But that was a foregone conclusion—when she heard I was going to Persia with a celebrated Literary Agent she would not only jump at the idea, she would never look back, she would pack her things on the spot—so as not to be left behind!—I should call Humph "very attractive" and add that he was disgustingly rich. Her I should describe to Humph as "a peachy girl". I should keep them apart as long as possible. I should not let them come face to face if I could manage it until we got near our destination, or had at all events started. The excitement and bustle of travel would do the rest. Humph might even think to himself that she was "rather pretty"—say in the half-light of a railway-carriage during a bad rainstorm—we might all pick each other up at Lyon or Graz—how do I know where! —I would see. (Of course I did not work the thing out in any detail.) Old Val might smell his money at a glance—and think that his monster chin and nice brown eyes meant it was hers for the asking or something of that sort, and make up her mind *to get him in the Bed* at the first opportunity that offered. (When I wasn't looking, of course she would say to herself. And I would have my head turned away all the time, I'd see to that. No stone should be left unturned.)

This, I insist, is *exactly* the terms in which I represented this affair to myself. Nothing more, nothing less. I did not care if I went or not. But I said indifferently—*All right! I will go!*

But these people I regarded strictly as pure automatons, to be quite frank. It would be like going to Persia with a couple of rag-dolls. Only of course they would *talk*—incessantly, they could not be turned off, the mechanism was so contrived that over their chattering propensities I should have no adequate control. I would take some cotton-wool with me, to stick in my ears, for use in the railway-carriage, if they got too outrageously noisy.

McPhail I had totally forgotten about. That was because I was quite positive he would not come to Persia. Even if I told him that the persian toreadors were one of the seven wonders of the world, and the Bakhtiari Mountains chuckfull of bull-rings, he would not dream of coming to Persia. Why, he had not even gone to Spain! Much as he liked the bull-ring, he disliked travel even more. He was attached to the South of France in a peculiar way. To mention Persia to him would be a sheer waste of time.

I must *pot* this next part of my narrative too. Not in this instance because it is too highly coloured—it would not cause a sunburst-effect of dazzling brilliance or anything like that. Rather for the contrary reason! " Potted ", it boils down to this (none of the details are important, except for one).

I went from the Aerated Bread Company straight to the telephone-box—in the Temple Underground Station. Need I say that I did not have to wait? I got through almost as soon as I had lifted the receiver and called my number, Val's that is. Val cannot have been at the time above *a foot* away from the telephone. She must in fact have answered as she was unhooking the instrument, at the first uncertain ghost of a clamorous tinkle.

"TO *PERR*-sia!" her steep sing-song archly expostulated—but with that odd quality that you always get with people who are not very real, namely, that *she did not seem in the least astonished.* It all passed as though she had *foreseen* that Persia would be our destination. It gave me an uncanny sensation—a sensation I have often experienced in talking with persons of a low reality.—*Had* I said anything to her about Persia? I was induced to ask myself—and had of course to reply that at that time I knew nothing myself about Persia!—Although of course it may in fact merely have been that, squatting day in day out beside her silent telephone, she was prepared to accept at sight *anything* that was proposed to her however much *out of the blue*—whether it were a flight in a rocket to our satellite the Moon or a dinner at Lockhart's!

"Are you serious Snooty?"

"Perfectly serious."

"Look—what are you doing now Snoots—I expect you're very busy."

I had nothing whatever to do, but I could not bear to see old Val just then.

"Exceptionally" I replied. "I have to go—*everywhere!*"

"Well! What do you want me to say—that I'll come to Persia?"

"Of course—if you want to go. I mean if that suits you as well as going anywhere else. Is the Midi necessary?"

" It suits me as well as going to the *Meee*-deee ! " she screamed in her gamine-manner of picking to pieces a funnily punning word.

" Very well. We can call that off then. And you will come to Persia."

" Not so fast Snooty. Not these *seven league boots* my dear ! It's not quite so easy as all that ! When do you want to start ? "

" Seven o'clock—for seven-thirty."

" Yes I know but when ? Soon ? "

" Oh yes. Certainly soon. I don't know the date. Captain Cooper Carter said some time next week."

" Have you a moment to spare tomorrow ? "

" Not tomorrow——"

" Well. I'll write you tonight. Will that do ? "

" No—don't write."

" Yes I will write."

" No. Please don't write ! "

(How could I stop her from writing, unless I said I would go to see her ?)

" Yes I will. I will write tonight."

" *Soit !* "

(I speak French awfully well—this means *so be it* in Frog-talk.)

" Very well ! " I said, as she didn't answer—I suppose she thought I had coughed and was waiting for me to speak.

" I'll write you tonight Snooty."

There the matter rested. We separated, telephonically —I left the box : she on her side undoubtedly put down the telephone slowly (to make the call seem as long as possible) and moving herself a couple of feet away from it (at most) thought over what she had just heard.

My movements for the remainder of the evening had nothing to do with Mithras, Humph, or Val. I spent the evening and night with a model I was working on (a big peachy typist dummy, in a family way) and went to bed with it for purely shoppy reasons. (The condition of the subject made this feasible of course.) I got rid of it as soon as possible in the morning, and sat down to make up my technical journal (regarding its behavior that is).

By the second post came Val's letter. I looked at it fixedly—the long sarcophagus-shaped envelope. Then I opened my mouth very wide and bellowed with anticipated fatigue. I burst the envelope—the letter was luckily not at all long and said :

DARLING SNOOTS.

I will come to Persia. But on one condition. That you let me pay for the trip. I want very much to go. I might just as well spend my money in that way as go to Hermione's villa which I probably shouldn't like. And I want to be with you. Do you agree to the terms ? If so please send me a letter to that effect—please do not come yourself if it is inconvenient. I hope I shall hear from you in any case.—Does Captain Cooper Carter know I'm coming ?—I think it is terribly amusing about *Mithras* ! It must be a lovely religion ! I think I shall become a Mithratist (is that what you call it ?) Love.

VAL.

Here was a complication, if one cared to regard it as such. It mattered nothing to me. I threw down the letter and forgot all about it.—I did not want the old girl to pay naturally. But she would insist, I knew that. She had her reasons.—She was just dying to come—the thought of the Literary Agent, that in itself was far more than enough to decide her (if there had ever been any question of her hesitating, which of course there had not). I had noticed she had mentioned Humph. At present of course she was busy sorting out all her manuscripts and getting ready for what she was persuaded would be a highly lucrative business trip—pointing out to my agent all the fruity bits, in this novel and in that of her latest period (the one since her complete social eclipse).—What do you suppose Persia means to Val? I said to myself. Certainly it meant *Teheran* in the main. She represented it to herself as Bucharest or Madrid, only smaller. That no doubt was just about what it was. She did not see the Kasvin Gate, the waterless moat, the yellow sand-world outside —the perfect snow-pointed, almost japanese, cone of Demavend (Demavend! recalling Zendavesta) to the north, the green dome among the eastern roofs (the feminine overhead boulevard) in the south of the city, and the yellow steppe in every direction, stretching away to the mesopotamian horizon, at the opposite point of the compass to the towering yellow mountains. She saw in her mind's eye the Legations, Cafés, and Clubs. She had been six months prior to that in Spain. She had visited Madrid in the train (with another woman) of two Soviet officials from Paris—diplomats, I suppose, of the rather odd sort sent out by the bolsheviks. It was the only link with the Great World, even of a backstairs order, that remained to her—the (poorly paid) Soviet patronage. They were hard-headed guys the Muscovites—they did not waste much money on old Val. On the other hand they appreciated her good qualities as I did. How much did they pay her, *argent comptant*? I had not the foggiest! She never uttered a word regarding that, or indeed anything whatever to do with them, she was as silent as the grave—loquacious as she was upon all other questions. Sovietic amours! What discipline those blighters have—even in the Bed!

What Teheran might mean then, as seen from Val's special angle, was (if the worst came to the worst, and as a *pis-aller* of course) a grubby sovietic intrigue, but still a rent-paying one. Guatemala, Portugal, San Salvador, Mexico and all the other skirt-loving corps of diplomats would not be found in Persia—only probably the loftier sort, the Big Five.

Nevertheless, and as she must sum it up, Val knew that whenever she *moved* (and wherever she moved) she *made* something at all events. Evidently she was likelier to pick up a few shillings by moving about than by sitting all day long within arm's-reach of her Chelsea telephone.

However the main prize was the *ladyship*. That is how I understood it. And I thought (and I believe I was right) that her other additions and subtractions would wait upon that chimera—upon the possible ladyship—with great decorum, with great self-restraint, with considerable abnegation.

Once a thing's said it's said. How my subsequent plans had been dominated only that day by something said! Now *she* had spoken—and I damned the woman up hill and down dale for speaking! But I supposed she would consider her beastly *condition* as a sort of thing like the word of a Kell-Imrie. Since she was dealing with me—that was the trouble—her *condition* might have a good deal of the sublime rigour imported into it. I knew quite well I must be prepared for that. I knew I must make up my mind to be paid for. Hang it all, I said to myself once or twice, when the thing turned up in my mind, if she is bent on going to Persia after a ladyship, why not let her *pay* for her Big Idea!

I really do not see why I should linger over this episode. I did not seek the society of Val for any reason except that I have already explained. Even then (as I have shown) she succeeded by her foolish conversation in making the "Bed" impossible for me almost. If she held me to my promise, why then I must either take back my promise, or take her with me in the new direction for which I had been headed by implacable fate. If subsequently when I took her to Cook's to buy her ticket she insisted on buying mine as well, I cannot see that she overpaid for the privilege (and business advantages accruing) nor that I need have thought over much regarding this unpleasant bagatelle. But I will not waste any more ink over this. She paid the fare to Persia for herself and me. And if she wanted to come again (as she will not) she would have to pay it again. I would not take her for nothing and that's flat. But I wish I had not taken her at all.

LILY

In some respects I have the oriental character. I am for instance quite unlike a European in one particular. I refer to my capacity for disinterested devotion.

If that is the case, I can easily account for it. It is because I am an extremist. You follow what I mean by extremist I hope—in other words I am to a high degree logical. And by logical I understand a nature consistent with itself, organized upon a single-gauge track so to speak.

But from what does that track set out—what is its " terminus " ? That is also an essential part of *extremism.* In my case it starts from a nucleus of impulse and of passion. I do not reason—I *intuit.*

To *feel,* I take it, is to *live.* You cannot, however much you try, separate feeling and thinking. Hence what I feel is of great importance to me. What I feel to-day, I think tomorrow. The *Emile* of Rousseau is my *livre de chevet.*

Yes, I pursue the pattern set up by my powerfulest sensation to its ultimate conclusion, until it leaves no part of my organism untouched. Call me *a wholehogger*—in the jargon of the golf-club and seaside-boardinghouse—and you have described me, in your language.

Consider the vendetta—is that not an admirable instance of the temper of the God of Justice, and is not the God of Justice likewise the God of Love ? The reverse of the vendetta is all that is madly loyal—that is commonly overlooked.

Certainly I am remarkably unlike the average Occidental,

as I have been able to observe him, in this connection. I am far nearer to the oriental mind.

Count de Gobineau in one of the best of his stories, called " Nouvelles Asiatiques "—Asiatic Novels—insists quite rightly upon this cardinal difference. I do not know if I should turn this passage into English or not, but I may come back and do so later, I will see. For the present, I put it down as it stands, that is in French—it stuck very much in my mind when I read it (about the period to which these chronicles are related) as it carried out what I had noticed with astonishment in Asia. " Le cœur et l'imagination, mobiles uniques du dévouement, tiennent une place énorme dans l'organisation des Asiatiques ; susceptibles de beaucoup aimer, ces gens-là se sont de beaucoup sacrifiés à ce qu'ils aiment. Ainsi, du moment où Assanoff trouvait dans Don Juan une nature sympathique à la sienne, il l'aimait pour tout de bon et sans se défendre." —In " the organization ", or the make-up to use a more familiar word, of the European as we find him to-day, it would indeed be wide of the mark to say of him that those emotional values " play an enormous part ". In the majority of cases they play none, except as regards marriage. We are not *nous autres Occidentaux*, subject to these powerful personal impulses, that attach us for ever—or separate us, upon the same principle. That *capacity for sacrifice* is a feminine thing, traditionally. And I cannot understand why I have got it. It does not seem to belong in my " make-up ".

I feel that in having made use of the term *extremist* I may, if I leave it at that, incur the risk of misunderstanding. For what most people at this time term extremism is only one sort of violence, whereas there are in fact as many categories of extremity as there are colours and sub-tints in the spectrum. To give you an illustration from political life, Wat Tyler was an extremist, but so equally was Burke.

And if I had to pick out of our annals a figure to explain myself by, I could think of no better one than that of the famous disciple of Burke, namely William Windham, of whom one of his biographers has said " His prime quality was independence, at once the choicest and the least serviceable of all qualities in political life." For of course Windham was a politician. " He was on the other hand *excessive*, like his great master Burke ; excessive in enthusiasm, excessive in resentment." And the biographer goes on to illustrate from this particular quality : " To him, for example, when a manager of the great impeachment, Warren Hastings was the vilest of criminals. But to him also . . . Burke was among the gods. There was in truth a want of balance in this rare character which marred its great qualities. It was this, from a fanciful fear of deterioration in the British character, that made him preach bull-baiting." Yes, if the name of William Windham is familiar to you at all, and I daresay it is not, it will be almost certainly as that of a legendary BULL-BAITER : for " by the irony of events " as his biographer says of him " he is now best remembered as the successful advocate of bull-baiting." Yet (it is the Earl of Rosebery from whom I am quoting) this man was " the finest english gentleman of his or perhaps all time ". That is for obvious reasons to my way of thinking very high praise, however you may regard it.

Excessive in enthusiasm, excessive in resentment—and *excessive* for the noblest motives. Yet here—in this bull-baiting hero—yes this *mithraditic hero !*, whom I have just unearthed for you—you have a man who was denounced as an " apostate " (by the ridiculous Parr) : who was given the scurrillous nickname of the " Weathercock "—given that name (how typical a fact !) *because of his constancy* ! The party-weathercocks schooled to every ignoble accommodation, threw this epithet at him, because, throughout all *their* changes, *he* never changed! Indeed, as the Earl of Rosebery remarked in this connection—" the independent man in politics must accustom himself to harder knocks than nicknames. Windham was indeed the most consistent of politicians. He was neither Whig nor Tory, but *always* an anti-Jacobin, and *always* . . . a Burkite."

Upon the death of Pitt (in the midst of the national grief) he deemed it necessary " to stand up and oppose the national honours proposed—a course which brought him many enemies and which seemed in execrable taste ". Because, for the most noble reasons—namely in order to protest that distinctions denied to his great master Burke should not be offered to another, who had not even been successful—because he (contemptuously disregarding the vulgar sensationalism of a period of sickly mob-mourning) denounced an injustice, for that the *taste* of this scrupulous, loyal, and fastidious gentleman was called in question! " Most men who felt the same would at that tragic moment have held their peace. But such a decent compliance seemed cowardice to Windham; so he wound his melancholy horn." And the comment made upon this " scandal " by the same writer takes nothing away from what has just been said.—" But the mere fact of isolation was the same temptation to him that the company of an overwhelming majority is to meaner minds." In that rebuke is concealed an even finer variety of encomium!

These remarks, of a rather personal nature, have been called for by the fact that I have now reached a point in this unusual composition where it behoves me to go into the motive for the existence at all of such a narrative. This requires a very careful handling indeed. And it was not the Mithraic Windham—of bull-baiting renown—that recommended him to me, in the capacity in which you find me using him—namely to improve my own case, by a great illustration. Much more it was *Windham the Flirt!*

The same biographer who spoke of Windham in the exalted terms you have just found above, considered himself constrained to denounce him as " a flirt ". (His words are: " We are bound to hazard an opinion that Windham was a flirt.")

It would take far too long to provide even the barest sketch of the alleged contradictory conduct to be found in the " Windham Papers ". If we are to accept the verdict of the same distinguished critic, " it had been better for his fame had this heirloom [the Diary] disappeared with the others ". Again he says, " Countless are the caprices of these strange journals " : but he adds in extenuation that " conscientious diaries are apt to make men morbid ".—Well this is not a *diary* of course that I am writing: and again I have to face uglier charges than that of being " a flirt " I know. But I feel in a certain measure that I stand or fall with Windham—*Bull-baiter, Apostate, Weathercock,* and *Flirt!* That is all I have intended to say. It rests with you to turn to the " Papers " if you wish to.

* * *

This book then has been written to vindicate my name—but I admit that this is so only in a rather peculiar sense. I am not of course referring to " The Baronet ", but to my name as a man of science—as a ' servant of truth '. And what is after all the *name* of a Servant of Truth! He has in fact *no* proper name. So really I am defending Truth, in the last analysis.

My reason for choosing this strictly narrative form again, to present my case, is perhaps not self-evident. Yet what is a body of formal evidence often? A collection of facts from which the essential fact is omitted. For unless a person is put in possession not only of facts, but of the mood and chronologic functioning that accompanied this or that salient occurrence (thoughts as well as utterance, tone and look as well as words), how can he possibly reach a judgment of any finality upon what he is asked to pronounce?

The rehabilitation that I seek is not that of a court-of-honour, finally, but such as could be conferred by a tribunal of my peers alone. What do I understand by my peers? Any set of men qualified to appreciate "People Behaving". That is what I mean.—I claim, as a "Person Behaving", to have behaved myself with rigorous consistency. I make no claim to anything but that.

There are many people who are ready enough to make others "behave" and to call themselves Behaviorists in consequence. But when it comes to behaving themselves, they do not show so much alacrity as you have a right to expect!

But I am, I will not go so far as to say "the Perfect Behaviorist", but I at least am not a shirker. I do not hide behind the waving arms and nodding heads of my marionettes. Anything but—why, I will dance a *pas de quatre* with the worst of them, and I will pick myself to pieces for the benefit of the Public as soon as look at it! As readily as I would pick a member of the Public to pieces I will pick my own self, bit by bit. All I ask is fair play. And that I know I shall not get!—But enough of this! My destruction of "The Baronet" is not a Punch and Judy show, when all is said and done. If I bare my heart and my imagination—holding the one like a slickly-skinned blood-orange in the left paw, and the other like a prodigious glow-worm within the palm-hollow of the right—it is not for your *applause*. It is a demonstration for the Learned or the expert—the man of imagination—the *homme de cœur*! Nor lastly is it, certainly, in order to resuscitate the stricken "Baronet"!

These are exceedingly hard and heavy times—hard in

every sense. They are times of great and wonderful profusion and plenty and of technical powers of limitless production beyond man's dreams. But upon all that plenty, and that power to use it, is come a dark embargo. It is all locked away from us. By artificial systems of great cunning this land flowing with milk and honey has been transformed into a waterless desert. There all the nations of the earth come in tremendous masses as if afflicted with the pestilence that follows famine. From being skinned and fleeced, we shall at last have *nothing*. And it is not *nature* but it is *man* who is responsible for this. That is why I have thrown in my lot with nature—that is why I break the social contract, and the human pact. Yet when we, children of these conditions, in our turn show ourselves hard and insensible—ever armed to the teeth, never with our guard down, darkling and vigilant—we are loudly denounced as inhumane. But *pace pace*! We are only scouting upon the fringes of this! Here we do not embark upon those questions.

* * *

I have mentioned, I think, that there were *two* women whom Mr Butler (as acted by me) visited from time to time. One was old Val. The other was Lily.

Lily worked in a tobacco-kiosk at Victoria. But I did not like going to the kiosk because once when I went I think I disturbed Lily—I dropped in and I believe it was a midday over-the-counter tête-à-tête of which I was the accidental witness as I rolled up. I felt apologetic and she was very sorry too. I bought fifty Capstans and was going away, pretending I was a chance customer, but she wouldn't hear of it. She was anyhow, I could see, well enough, really put out a little—to have been surprised practising what of course must have been her daily habit—the making if possible of a profitable date is the very ABC of such a girl's life-business when any chance, however remote, offers. Heaven knows they must be few and far between! If the kiosk-sirens were in their knickers or nude for that matter there'd be few enough men with the inclination to drop in and buy a box of matches! Since women in the market-sense have turned from peaches into potatoes and are so plentiful and by-the-peck in the nature of things (and on-their-back-as-soon-as-look-at-you at that!) since the Armageddon-revolution released them all into the world to prey freely upon each other, in cut-throat competition for men, from cock-crow till midnight! Also of course seeing how harassed, bullied, depressed and penniless are all the men! Well a girl has to be pretty damned smart to get her engagement-book anywhere near chokker-block and that's a fact!—Lily knew how much I liked her. She was my favourite. Naturally she didn't want to displease a devoted boy-friend on account of some chance lunch-hour moss-back, who had probably contracted the habit nothing more of dropping in to chat in her kiosk—teasing and tantalizing the poor girl, holding forth the *possibility* that he might take her out one evening to the Pictures, if he had nothing better to do.—In future, at all events, out of delicacy, I avoided that method of getting in touch with Lily.

Lily as a friend was on a different establishment from Val. This was because I'd got to know Lily differently, in an omnibus as a matter of fact, and we were fast friends from the start—her brother an ex-marine had a wooden leg like me and so she had a footing as it were in the pensioned classes and was closer to the operating tables, where limbs fall like ninepins, than most girls. She offered to help me out of the bus—that's how I first noticed her.—Lily knew nothing about me as well except my names and was quite ignorant of The Baronet. I was Mr K.-I., a struggling engineer, for Lily Tayle, cooking my own breakfast-rasher on a gas-ring in a basement flat. If the shadow of The Baronet had never crossed our path, equally the shadow of the Custom House Officer had never disturbed our contraband caresses, our illicit still of bubbling free-love.

Upon this occasion I thought I would go straight to her lodgings—she lived in a two-room flat with another tobacco-seller, but I had never been there, partly out of delicacy, though I had been as far as the door once or twice. It was my intention to take her out *à l'improviste*, I knew she would be delighted. Generally she got back from the kiosk about eight-thirty. I timed the visit for the moment of her return.

When I reached Lily's house, behind Ebury Street, I went up the steps and pressed the bell that was marked Lily Tayle. Then I turned about upon the step, in the direction of the street—there would be a short delay I supposed before she came down. The flat was at the top, the fourth-floor I think.

But as I did so I discovered two people entering the gate and I heard Lily's voice. As I turned the voice stopped rather suddenly. I saw her catch a man sharply by the arm and say something. Then she came forward quickly, leaving him outside the gate. But he followed her inside I noticed, and I, for my part delighted, went down to meet her, all my teeth coming out at the snow-white salute, calling to her in a ringing tone

"Ah Fleur-de-Lys this is lucky!"

"Mike! how perfectly ripping!" is what Lily said. She is a sweet girl, I was delighted to see her and I was just about to take her off in an impulsive way (I scarcely saw where I was going I was so pleased) to a taxi for dinner in the Strand (I had run my arm into hers) when the man who had come inside the gate got in the way I thought. I could not pass at any rate.

" Oh Mike this is my uncle ! " Lily said.

I shook hands with him. He was an elderly man, he wore a smirk I thought and hung about in a peculiar way.

" Well let us be going Lily " I said and I tried to propel her towards the gate.

She hung back and I thought she seemed a little confused.

" Perhaps your uncle will come with us ? " I said. Then for Lily's ear alone but owing to the traffic in a substantial whisper I added : " We can get rid of the old boy afterwards ! Let's give him a square meal first—he may remember you in his will ! "

Her uncle did not seem to like this for he seemed to overhear it (I agree that the " square meal " was a little patronizing and tactless) and from having been a passive assistant he became I thought a little actively off-hand and if it had not been for the close relationship I should have been offended at the way he stuck to us, in a manner suggesting that he had no care to remember that two is company and the proverbial position of the third party. I would go so far as to say that there was no evidence that he had ever heard of one of the master adages by which the Briton is ruled—the adage assuring the function of pairing and couplement.

I drew Lily outside the gate, but with an indecent speed for one of his advancing years he followed us. I discovered him next upon my offside, somehow he had got round in front of us almost and I turned back, saying to the girl—

" Shall we cross the road ? "

When already in the roadway, I felt myself restrained, and she was holding me back I found, her uncle looming in the background.

" Mike " she said " I'm afraid I have to go up to the flat first ! "

" The flat ! Why ? Let us go to dinner. Isn't your uncle coming ? "

" No he can't come Mike. He's got an engagement."

" An engagement! Have you asked him?"

" No. But I know he can't Mike."

" The old fool doesn't know when he's well off" I muttered a little impatiently behind my teeth.

Lily laughed as if she were amused at something. Giving me a nip on the arm she whispered—

" You silly boy—hush don't talk so loud, my uncle might hear! He's just behind me!"

" I don't care—why doesn't he come with us?"

It tickles me to death to be called a silly boy as I am forty now, I should say thirty-nine and three-quarters, and I grinned from ear to ear over my shoulder at her relative.

" Shall I go up Fluff?" her uncle asked in a very snooty voice I thought.

" Will you wait here Mike?" she said. " You don't mind do you—I shan't be a moment."

" No I'll wait here" I said.

We had gone back, and I now lay down vertically upon the gate, while they went up into the house. Her uncle gave me rather an offensive grin I thought as he passed me. At first I took it to be a jolly grimace as if to say *Ah you young dogs you!* and grinned back in the same spirit, but later I was not so sure that her uncle wasn't a bit of a bore and might even entertain sentiments for his niece, unsuitable in such a close relative.

As I was waiting I did a little speculation about them—would Lily tolerate his incestuous advances if her uncle made them? I concluded in the affirmative. Lily was the kind of girl that might. She was an original girl. The incestuous relationship would recommend itself to her on account of its uncommonness—there was nothing common about Lily. I could not see her repulsing an advance on the ground that it was beastly (she had quite enough sense to see that *all* advances were beastly).—I thought there was probably incest, and this put my mind at rest. This completely accounted for the attitude of the uncle.

When they came out five minutes later there was somebody with them, a tall young man in a fawn overcoat.

I stood up, faced the house, and the three of them came down to the gate.

" This is my cousin, Mike, Mr Robert Tanner."

Cousin ! I thought—*Um Gottes Willen—Um Gottes Willen !* Soon we should have the entire family gathered about us.

The tall young fawn-overcoated man (of the clerkly kind, ticket-puncher, purser's assistant) came up to me briskly, in a very business-like social way, and before I knew what he was doing grasped me by my hand and wrung it twice.

" Very glad to meet you sir ! " he said heartily and very civilly.

Sir—why ' sir ', had I given any signs of noble birth to this honest son of the people, that, finding me with his girl-cousin at the garden-gate in a semi-slum he should find it necessary to sir me !

" I'm very glad to meet *you* ! " I said pointedly and I eyed him with astonishment, but civilly, from head to foot.

The cousin smiled discreetly as he withdrew a step, as if one of a crowd, having done what he apparently had come to do, namely to shake me by the hand and say Well-met and then stand back. He continued to smile, civilly but knowingly—how shall I describe it ? It had the appearance of a smile of occult intelligence—conveying that that was perfectly all right (whatever it was !) that he perfectly understood—that I need be under no apprehension that anyone else would share this intelligence with us.

But then I began to notice that the manner of Lily's uncle had undergone some subtle transformation. He looked far less agreeable I thought than when he had gone into the house with his niece. He looked at me this time I thought with an air of sullen resentment, and the fellow had a sort of sneering manner that I did not at all like.

Now I am the world's simpleton certainly, and I daresay you will have thought I accepted too readily Lily's word for the relationships existing between these people and herself. But the fact is I had never noticed in Lily formerly anything that would cause her to behave in such a foolish way as that would mean. To find it necessary to pass off an old beau as her 'uncle' for instance—that was unthinkable with Lily, whom I knew pretty well.

I will admit that when the house-door opened and yet *another* "relation", namely the cousin, stepped out beside the first one, that—for a fraction of a second no more—I certainly did look at Lily a little doubtfully. But next moment I banished that impulse to doubt her entirely from my mind. With *Lily* (I said) such things simply do not happen!

No no, this was a fortuitous encounter, between several closely related people, an uncommon occurrence certainly, but not impossible. It might be, even, that a family gathering of some importance had been arranged—to discuss a matter of vital moment to the Tayle clan. (She had not said they were Tayles but Tayles they all undoubtedly were.) There might be other members inside. Indeed that was almost certainly the case.

Evidently I had barged in and attempted to whisk her away inopportunely. I could see that. Now, because of her great affection for me, she had decided to abandon the family conclave and come away with me to dinner. Of such light stuff were women made! Very naturally the uncle (blood-brother to her own father)—the elder and more responsible member of the party—took a rather serious view of the occurrence. Hence his somewhat unexpected treatment of me. He was (not unnaturally) disgusted with his niece. Was there not some justification for this? That she should—at such a turning-point, as it well might be, of the family-history—abandon the people of her blood (and so quite likely disorganize in some measure their counsels), that she should now of all times elect to go off and dine and wine with a stranger (up till then unknown to them even by report) would seem to this excellent man deserving of some reprobation.—The younger clansman, on the other hand, would, as became his age, take a more lenient view of the matter. He would understand that Youth must be served, and that sometimes the *call of the blood* (powerful as that might and should be) must take a back-seat, when sex is on the carpet (on the *tapis*).—Hence his desire to make my acquaintance, as a suitor of his fair cousin, and perhaps (who could tell?) future kinsman and cousinly in-law?

It was thus and in no other way that I explained the whole affair to myself. I swear upon my dying oath that I never harboured so much as an unworthy suspicion that Lily was being stupid. And so, linking my arm with hers as I had done before, I cried—

"Now for a taxi!"

Her uncle came up to me—I thought (making every allowance for his quite comprehensible disappointment with his niece) with a rather unnecessary truculence towards myself (who after all was not responsible for the turn affairs had taken) and said with a very uncalled-for ugly sneer—

"Well good night er—er *Mister*—er *Mis*—ter——"

"Kell-Imrie" I said holding out my free hand, which happened to be my left, and giving him my gauntletted forefinger.

"Good night—*sir!*" he repeated slowly, his old poached blinkers blazing away at me forty-nine to the dozen. A very odd variety of insolence (however incestuous he might be by temperament, and however oddly that vice may distort behaviour) paraded at the bottom of them.

"Good night sir" I said grinning—amazed at his classishness and poor-but-proud punctilio. *Sir* again! Well well well!—what a strangely respectful family! (All gentlemen's servants born and bred I expect thought I—the uncle perhaps a butler, and cousin a gamekeeper very likely.)

I dragged her out of the gate, shouting at the top of my voice—"Taxi!" as I saw one approaching.

Lily waved her hand to her family over her shoulder as I was dragging her off, my mechanical leg thudding jubilantly over the pavement, and we got into and rushed away in a brand-new Beardmore.

When we were in the taxi and out of reach of her family it was evident Lily heaved a sigh of relief. She became herself—the Lily I knew—on the spot. I was not long in getting pretty fresh as you may imagine. Lily was my favourite girl in the world and I met her but seldom at that. I was beside myself with delight. It was always the same, whenever I saw her she was the dream-come-true that tumbled my heart about and shook my pulses in an idiotic tattoo!

"Mike darling!" she said between two sunbursts of intoxicated kiss-stuff, and close-ups screwed down like thermos-stoppers—"You do seem *strange* Mikey after all these months!"

"I am!"

"I wasn't expecting you just yet—I am glad you're here Mikey!"

"Lily!" I said.

"Mikey!" she cried.

"Lily!" I shouted.

The taximan joined in with his klaxon.

"You did seem a long way away Mikey!"

"I was Lily—far too far off but I've come through!"

"Do you love us Mike!"

How girls adore the name of Mike, second only to Pat—ranging foreshortened from Mickey Mouse to something at the same time 'mighty' and 'bright!'

Did I love Lily! With no misbegotten fumblings of the word-habit, did I show Lily Tayle how I loved her—but by the actions of a man-in-love in a taxi, a red-blooded wholehogger in a hired cab, as far as the cab will permit. We rolled on like two foaming cataracts of bliss, rushing irresistibly up one street and down another!

We went to Bogani's in Great Auckland Street. During the war-years I went there for preference. Whenever I was wounded or during leaves I was to be found upstairs, between the pilaster and the curtain—at that time the place was full of strange nonsense and wildness, of uniformed persons under sentence of death. Now there is a deathly quiet all over it. I find this very soothing. For me personally of course it is a little macabre—it is like dining upon tombstones—beneath each white sheet of stiff-laundered table-damask an Unknown Soldier is lying! (Surreptitiously I have toasted the dead.) I hear the Revally as I pick up the Wine List—and the scratching of the pens upon the parchments at Versailles as I put it down again! Even the waiters—they are the same waiters—seem lifeless and depressed, as they tear the evening papers to shreds in the corners with anguished eyes on the Stop Press, or hunting for tips in the Runners and Betting.

But I was feeling uncommonly sick as I sat down. My head was giving me a bad time. Ah that accursed plate! The leg is a bagatelle.—Lily saw this and was silent, of course she knew what it meant. She never forgot she was with a *grand blessé*, bless her little heart of gold!

(The only people of course who ever had occasion to know that Snooty was anything less than an A1-life were the girls and they soon found out in the nature of things his weak spot.)

We had four Sidecars and I felt better, though still very sick. I ordered a bottle of Richebourg (*Rosenheim*). Lily was fond of wine for a poor girl. As she drank the burgundy she became very jolly. Lily's twenty-fourth birthday had been two months before, that was when I was in America. I had remembered it. I never forget a girl's birthday. I had bought her a little present—it had only cost fifty cents but it was not the value, I knew it wasn't that counted. It was a small metal ring of mexican make (it was only tin) with a red pebble in the side of it. I now drew it forth—it was in a pellet of tissue paper. Lily was as pleased as possible and kept turning it over and over in her hand (I think she thought there was some catch in it). At last she put it on her finger. It wouldn't go on properly. It stuck just above the knuckle (it must have been meant for a child). She held her finger up to show me.

"Very nice" I said. "It suits you."

"It's lovely Mike—thank you so much for thinking of me!"

I knew she would be pleased at my thinking about her.

"You didn't pay too much for it I hope Mikey—they didn't see you coming I mean."

"Trust a Scot" I said and winked as all Scots are supposed to do at any reference to money.

"It's very pretty!" she said.

"I didn't pay much for it, it's of indian make."

"Indian!"

"Yes they work for nothing, so what they do costs next to nothing, but at least what they turn out is never vulgar."

"Vulgar! I should think not—it would have to be

something brighter as a matter of fact before it *could* be vulgar—but it isn't a bit."

"Not a bit" I said.

"I had one like this Christmas-time" she said taking it off—she could not keep it on of course as it would not go over the knuckle. "Just like this."

"Was it a Christmas present?" I asked.

"No. It came out of a cracker, as a matter of fact."

That astonished me. What comes out of crackers is commonly rather vulgar.

"It was quite a nice little ring as a matter of fact" she said. "I wore it once or twice. Nobody noticed it wasn't a proper ring."

"Of course they wouldn't" I said. "Everyone knows nobody wears real jewellery nowadays, there are too many purse-snatchers and finger-choppers about."

"How horrible!"

"Ah yes finger-chopping! It's very dangerous, I wouldn't like to wear a diamond-ring."

"Of course not."

"It's the same with pearl-necklaces. No one wears real pearls even if they've got them. They always wear paste ones."

"I know, of course they don't!" she said. "I know I wouldn't."

"Of course not."

"All the same I'd like to *have* the real ones!" She laughed, and we drank together, she was a sensitive girl.

"Of course that would be nice" I said: "but I think jewels are only suitable for old women."

"It's usually them that have them!"

"You're right. Still the majority of hags have not even got paste!" I said.

I must confess I was all the time conscious of some alteration in Lily. It would be difficult to say what it was.

She seemed to be looking at me from time to time in a peculiar way I thought. I put it down to family troubles. She was as jolly as ever, it was not that—especially after the wine she had got very lively. But she did not seem quite at her ease.

I considered it appropriate at this point to make some reference to her family difficulties.

" I hope your uncle won't mind my taking you away so suddenly " I said.

" My uncle ! " She laughed with much nervous energy and polite mockery. " Yes he will quite a lot I'm afraid ! But I can't help his troubles ! "

" Yes why should you after all ! " I argued. " Why should you—I suppose it was some boring family affair ? "

" What was ? "

" Why that your cousin and uncle had come to talk to you about."

Lily opened her eyes very wide at that and then burst into still louder laughter.

" You are a fool Mikey ! That wasn't my *uncle* ! "

" Not your uncle ! "

" No you didn't really believe that was my uncle did you ! "

" Of course."

Something severe I suppose must have crept into my face in spite of myself, for I saw her face fall as she looked at me in response—incredulously at first.

" You're kidding aren't you Mikey ! You didn't think that was my uncle ! "

" Why not ? Of course I did. Why after all should you tell me it was your uncle if it wasn't ! "

" Oh I don't know—habit I suppose ! "

I raised my eyebrows—it was my turn to be incredulous.

" That's a gentleman called Mr Willis " she said. " He's a tobacconist."

" But Mr Willis is your uncle ? "

" No !—my uncle ! No ! He's no relation at all ! "

" No relation at all ! " my voice echoed her, insinuating something vaguely horror-struck however into the mechanical repetition.

" None, no—no relation. He didn't like my calling him my ' uncle ' either ! " She laughed a great deal at that.

" Why not ? " I said.

" Why didn't he ? Oh I suppose he thought it made him out too old."

" Too old ! But he's old enough to be your grandfather ! "

" Not quite so bad as that " she said, I thought a little displeased. " How old would you think he was ? You wouldn't think it but he's not very old—he's nothing like so old as he looks. He's only forty-one—it's old of course but——"

" He ought to be ashamed of himself ! " I said hotly— " if he's not your uncle ! "

" I suppose he should ! " she said smiling demurely and then with a pleased laugh.

" And so should you ! " I said.

And so that passed off agreeably. But frankly I was worried. Why on earth had Lily behaved in a manner so unlike herself, I asked myself with extreme astonishment.

When we got back to my basement I did not feel well. I had to lie down for half-an-hour in the dark because of the beating in my eyes while Lily made some russian tea and the flat grew hot. I took some aspirins and fell asleep. When I woke up I felt much better for the sleep and called out to Lily to know if the tea was made or not. She came in and said it was. Then I got up.

" How do you feel now Mikey ? " Lily asked.

" Much better " grinning heavily I answered and ran a fresh forearm about her slinky hip, and walked her into the next room left-right! left-right!—like a mechanical dollie, where the fire was, until we stood in front of it, when I began undressing her and she was helping me. Lily soon was undressed and naked, she was the sweetest milk-white packet of flesh that ever chirped upon a hearth-rug or fed out of a he-man's hand. Last but not least she did just suggest the full-grown female, I think in something sultry about the joints. Maybe she'd pupped, I never asked her. I knew she'd tell me and I didn't want to know that. (In Africa and Texas I had seen faint tallow-stains they seemed, like hers, which meant nigger—beneath the nordic fleur-de-lys. That's why I called her Fleur-de-Lys—I pronounced it *Ferdaleece.* But now I come to think, there was something mulatto in her strong over-chiselled lips, and in her sky-gazing bosoms—but in colour as white as expensive parchment, they were proper ' hills of snow '.)

I was looking down at her, my left arm stuck out stiff and straight as if it had been a wooden one, and riveted to a shot-off shoulder-stump, and my hand stuck in stiff too, up under her right armpit, while the fire roared in the grate behind her as if it wished to devour her as well as me. And she, erect between us, was like a flame of snow! (I was fully dressed—the living image of a lofty scarecrow, tantalized by a dryad. I was motionless, I did not breathe at all, from the chest.)

My eye was flashing about all over her and then sweeping off into the apartment and swooping back top-speed, to dash itself against a cliff of peach-lit marble, or thud down upon a nipple, smack!

Upon a chair there was something white and as my eye flew off it rested upon it, and saw that it was an opened book. I never leave books open. In consequence it must have been Lily who had taken it from a shelf and opened it.

" What book is that ? " I asked in astonishment.

" Which book Mikey ? "

" That one on the chair " I said.

Lily had never I think removed a book from a shelf or so much as glanced at them when she had come to see me. Indeed she never read. That I suppose is how I came to be astonished.

Lily laughed boldly but awkwardly I thought. I moved my hand from her armpit. We stood looking at each other, as if measuring the distance represented by the withdrawn arm.

" That book's by a man I know Mike. I wonder if you've read it ? " she said, pointing to it with a quick poke of the hand. I walked over to the book. I saw at once the title of the page-head. It was " People Behaving ".

I at once turned round upon her. I cannot say why but I thought it strange she should have discovered this so promptly, while I slept, and I looked at her as who should enquire the cause of something unexpected.

" I think Mikey you must be a *bit of a philosopher* ! " she exclaimed in a jolly teasing way in reply. " You never told me Mikey—I didn't know you were an author."

" Ah " I said.

" Oh look what I've got, I'd forgotten—I've kept this to show you ! "

Fleur-de-Lys went up to the table and my favourite piece of nudity with her back to me rummaged in her hand-bag. Then she turned and held up a much-fingered newspaper-cutting.

" You didn't tell me you were all *this* either—Sir Michael ! " And as she uttered the ominous *sir*—the mocking *Sir Michael*—I heard again her pseudo-uncle's voice, and the voice of her pseudo-cousin, and registered in retrospect the ugly sneering manner of the one, and the brisk know-all affability of the other.

" What is that ? " I asked.

She came up to me and held out my photograph in the newspaper, the one Val had.

" It's just like you Mike " she said, " you look a little fatter. I knew it was you before I saw the name. I called over to Netta 'Here's a man I know!' She recognized it too."

I took it and looked at it.

" Yes. I haven't paid for them yet " I said.

" For what? Did you pay to have it put in? "

" No I mean the photographs. He's not a bad photographer but terribly expensive. I don't recommend you to go to him."

She was reading the cutting.

" Known to his friends as *Snooty* " she read out. "Why are you nicknamed Snooty? *Are* you snooty Mike! "

" Very snooty " I said shortly. " Very snooty indeed! "

" No you're not Mikey! " she said, seizing me foolhardily around the neck, while the room resounded with my Butler laugh—a sound that fell upon her ears for the first time. " You're not snooty to me! I shan't call you Snooty! "

This was very bad! It was touch and go with us for quite five minutes. I wrestled with my snootiness! But I have said that when I give my heart I do not give it like an Occidental, it is not easy to make me reverse that, once it is done.

Trembling from head to foot I sat down by the fire, my teeth chattering as if it had been really cold. Fleur-de-Lys sat trembling upon another chair, as if I had been an iceberg suddenly. She liked me, Lily, as well as I did her. In a dead silence she watched me wrestling with my snootiness. (I must, while the issue was still in doubt, have looked uncommonly snooty.) But she saw me beat off the snooty monster, she saw my brow clear. Then I got up. I went over to the table, I took up the cuttings, spat on them, and threw them into the fire. I had conquered The Baronet.

"Come Fleur-de-Lys!" I said. (I always say *come!* when I mean business—I call to my mate of the moment in the Imperative. The gallic *Viens donc!* is part of a good bedroom-guide—always translate from the french, when in doubt in the bedroom, or near it, is an excellent rule. So you may without impropriety or a vexatious pomp pronounce the one word *come*, to beckon again to Carthage whatever love may be at hand, like a stage-Dido waving a palm leaf.) But things have never been the same again between Lily and myself. I was in the end brought to confess it—I had not won the day.—My darling, my *Fleur-de-Lys*, had been blasted forever at this contact with "Snooty"—Baronet!

THE PERSIAN VISAS, for Val and self, were to be obtained for us by Cook's that afternoon. All that remained was to discover the routes and times—our showman must be consulted. To that end I went by appointment to Humph's office, unaccountably down in the mouth, very sorry for Snooty—very very low, feeling like giving the whole bloody circus the slip. Humph's schemes for me were maturing. He was arranging to have me captured (he had written yesterday), I did not learn how. He obligingly suggested that it would be well to make a will. Not that there was the slightest danger as regards the banditti, but in case we met with a railway accident. (We could unfortunately not go by air all the way.) The amount of ransom likely to be expected for a baronet had, it appeared, been fixed. All was in readiness in fact.

I was amazed at him. But I did not let him see this. Nevertheless he apologized after a fashion, that was when I telephoned. What was the use of employing a Literary Agent if he didn't do these little things for one (he argued)? Did I suppose that by *writing books* I should ever get a reputation as a writer? Surely I was not so simple as to suppose that? And good books, too, it wasn't as if I did cosy best-sellers—that would be another matter. No, I was thoroughly unreasonable—if I would not write what the cab-driver and his missus wanted, how could I expect my agent to get me on to every cab-driver's lips? If I committed murder, for instance, why there would be some sense in having a Literary Agent then, it would be giving one's agent a chance, and the Literary Critics too. I had a wooden leg, yes. That went for something. But when had I ever done anything with it except stalk about on it? Had I ever pretended to write my books with my wooden leg? No, of course not—not me! I seemed to think that the Literary Agent was a magician. Agenting was a *mystery* of some sort, it appeared! Anyone would think from the way I went on that I believed the "Literary Agent" had something to do with *literature*!—He was very facetious indeed, very awful. I held my peace, while he rattled on.

Well, he said finally, if I insisted upon that unreal principle (or words to that effect), all he could say was that he would be compelled to wash his hands of me—the only other thing for it that he could see was to fall back upon the *Douanier*: and that as I knew was no longer feasible, because of his majesty "The Baronet".—So there I was!

So there I was—in the midst of these maniacs, and shortly I must find myself in the heart of Asia, unless I did something to arrest my progress, the prisoner of some undesirable outlaw, languishing in his inclement cave.—I knew Humph would carry through his plans—the Chin stood for that. I was *his* prisoner, already, in reality!

It was not that I minded. I favoured bandits rather than not. I did not mind Persia—I might as well be in Persia as anywhere else. But Humph was determined to act upon "The Baronet" basis.—So, although I had not planned it out in detail, I had made up my mind to escape from Humph. I would go along with him: but, if I could, I would give him the slip just as he was going to have me caught.—I watched this great prognathous filibuster laying his plans therefore in absolute silence. I followed all his movements with an astonished attention. Nothing escaped me—but I said nothing. *He* was the bandit—I saw that quite well. I saw perfectly that I was in his power. No doubt he had something up his sleeve as well but he had not so far given any indication of what it might be. I was unnerved, I must confess, by his mechanical energy. Yes he *Had me in the Chin* it could be said, to paraphrase—just as old Val *Had me in the Bed.* That was the fact of the matter. He had me under lock and key in this monumental feature of his person, as if it had been a castle-keep. Heaven knows if I should ever get out sound in wind and limb! I would do my best, that is all I could promise myself.

So at the hour appointed, very dispirited, I went to Humph's office.

When I arrived (late of course to show my self-appointed keeper he was not my master entirely) the room was full of authors and Gossip Column touts, all touting and talking loudly together. The Fleet Street exchanges landed with a vulgar smack, the repartee rattled like a Tin Lizzie.

Humph broke away from them and rushed up to the door as if at all costs I must be prevented from entering. I must not be allowed to come in—he nearly knocked me over in his charge. My hand gripped in his granite paw, he pushed me back against the wall. I fought him off, it was no use—I was as you can imagine speechless with annoyance: and he never said a word either, for several minutes at least. So we stood, or rather danced or shuffled, up against the wall, he gradually edging and thrusting me back into the corner, which was also the jamb of the door, my hand imprisoned all the while in his fist of stone—wooden and dour and blank, his at once full and hollow face staring up into mine, with never a muscle moving upon its meat-flushed, tanned-hide, surface, with never the shadow of a smile. Meantime his bold brown eyes, his expressive auburn eyes, poured their nonsensical messages—all their open conspiracies and patent long-exploded mysteries—into mine, substituting themselves for his tongue.—In fine, his play-acting had never been of a more tiresome order. I was paralysed with repulsion, as I now shrank stiffly back. At last, in a croaking whisper, this preposterous Jack-in-the-Box stammered with an absurd intentness all of a sudden—

"I say I've got some—I say I've got some—I've g-g-g-g-*got* some!"

"Yes yes" I hissed. "You've got some."

With infinite precautions so that he should not be remarked, imperceptibly he turned his head, and glanced apprehensively over his shoulder into the room.

"I've g-g-g-g-ot some—I've *got* some!" he stuttered and panted in a still lower key.

Flattened against the wall, I grinned helplessly at him. He had his stocky hobo-pipe gripped in his masticators. It was injured, at least it was bandaged (I was not at all surprised), a strip of flannelette was wound round and round the centre of its stem, puttee-fashion. The sweater, under his jutting nautical blue-serge jacket, had its high collar up, and it swept like a ruff (of plover-egg blue) all round his gigantic chin.

"I've got some—I've got some—I've got some *peep*!" he whispered hoarsely in my face—as if he had been a character at some breathless *dénouement*, of some fantastic thriller-serial: and he cast a further anxious and surreptitious—but absurdly sturdy and competent—glance over his shoulder (I was in good hands with him, I could rely on his sang-froid in any emergency!). His hand was as firm as a rock, nay firmer, his chin stuck out a yard from his face, and his eyes betrayed no trace of fear—no reader could doubt that he (or rather she) was in the presence of the hero of the tale.

"I've got some *peep*!" he murmured almost sweetly.

I threw my head back and yawned with the utmost unrestraint.

" I've I've g-g-g-got some *peep*—pull ! " lowering his voice until it was in his boots in fact, he told me—opening his eyes extremely wide and staring as if in doubt and hesitation as to whether he should confide in me or not.

" So I see " I said. " I can see that—I thought you said you would be alone ? "

" I *know* ! " he exclaimed under his breath, flinging a menacing half-glance over his shoulder at the company. " I know old man—isn't it *sick*-en-ing ! Do you mind ? I'll get rid of them at once ! "

He released me, he fell back. I shook myself, and without looking at him I advanced. I passed down the room. The crowd was collected about the Adams fire-place—it was very cold, the damp cold of Old England that chills you to the bone. I passed on to a window and stood-up against it staring out at the River Thames.

I gazed down in horror at the cold and yellow Thames. But I reflected, as I must, that a half mile higher up it was flowing past my Fleur-de-Lys (more or less—it naturally did not encircle the kiosk—it was a good quarter of a mile away from it, but you know how you place things along the course of a river for the sake of convenience). That reflection gave me less satisfaction than it had when last I stood before that massive georgian plate-glass of Humph. The shadow of The Baronet had fallen across our path, our lovers'-walk, as I knew, for the present. Perhaps for some time to come. It made the everlasting autumn of London's river, in sickly movement beneath its dirty mist, still more disconsolate.—In Persia, I had heard, phenomenal blizzards rage for quite half the year—it is intensely cold : but I thought that perhaps as it was July we might expect a little sun now and then. For the first time that day there was an anti-cyclone over Snooty, I cheered slightly up. It was my Lily I confess had made this possible. For now England had not even its Fleur-de-Lys—it had *nothing*.

I was almost glad to be going to Persia with this extraordinary bandit at my back—depressing as that ruffian certainly could be when he really gave his mind to it.

After a time the authors went away and I turned round. There was old Humph behind the table, filling his pipe from his oilskin tobacco-pouch, which lay belly-up and sagging open, upon the back of a fat book, left there by an author, or forgotten by a news-and-gossip tout. He was looking at me. As he filled his pipe he observed his captive. I yawned heavily at him and sat down, sticking out my leg in his direction. Then I yawned again.

At last Humph addressed me from behind the table.

" Snooty ! " he exclaimed.

" What is it ? " I said very aggressively. " Speak out you son of a bitch ! What is it ! "

" You are a made man ! "

I yawned and gnashed my teeth up and down, as if devouring an invisible club-sandwich at one mouthful.

" I met a feller last night who was in Dunsterforce."

I snorted.

" He was captured by a turcoman bandit."

I groaned.

" But listen—by a bandit who used to wrestle with *bulls,* in order to keep in training ! What do you say to that ! "

I shrugged my shoulders and tapped my mouth.

" He's corresponded with the bandit-feller ever since."

I looked at his ceiling.

" He's an awful good feller ! " he exclaimed with a hearty throatiness, blinking one eye—" Pat Bostock ! "

At '*Bostock*' I exploded in an insulting cough.

" He can speak five persian dialects and he passed first out of the Staff-College in Arab and Copt too."

" In Copt too ? " I sneered.

" Snooty ! "

" Sir ! "

" Pat has cleared everything up for us—he knows Persia inside out ! "

" Ah, inside-out ! "

" He can speak, as I said——"

" Yes yes ! "

" He tells me there's only *one* bandit left in the whole of Persia ! "

" Thank God for that ! "

" That is to say *his* friend—the one who captured him. He's given me instructions how to find his lair. It sounds marvellous. The place is a sort of mediaeval castle. Pat says it's extremely comfortable and the guest-rooms are spotlessly clean. It is *far* superior to the hotels he says—at least any but those in the capital. When he was captured he always had bacon for breakfast and *asaki*."

" What is that for Heaven's sake ! "

" A light Japanese beer—they have it all over the East."

" Have you ever been to the East ? "

" No " he answered irritably " I haven't."

I looked over my shoulder out of the window.

" Anyway this bandit-feller——"

" Yes ? " I said.

" It appears he makes a point of offering his prisoners nothing but the best."

" It sounds like Sing-Sing."

" The feller believes in making his captives as comfortable as possible. He stints nothing. He has an excellent cellar—he has Irish whisky if you prefer that—Pat thinks Scotch a little on the oily side so he got a case of Irish up from Teheran by return of courier. In a word, he's *very* hospitable. He's a real white man Pat says."

" What did he mean by that ? "

" He's a gentleman."

" What an absurd bandit ! "

" Not at all ! "

" What does it cost all that ? " I asked.

" You don't have to bother about all that—I'll fix all that up. You see you'll have a topping time of it—you'll live like a fighting-cock."

He puffed hard at his disabled pipe—it had a split in it, and some of the smoke escaped through the bandage.

" Pat Bostock " he said slowly " tells me that the bandit-feller's very exclusive. But of course in your case it will be perfectly all right, there will be no difficulty at all."

" You think not ? "

" I'm positive there won't ! There can't be—Pat Bostock said he was sure the bandit-chap would jump at you——"

" Oh will he ? "

" He'll be delighted to have you you know—I told Pat what we're after, all about Mithras."

" Did that interest him ? "

" Pat's very much Army and Public School—he's a very keen soldier—I don't think that *Mith*-ras ! "

" No I suppose not."

I understood perfectly well what the bandit *jumping at me* meant. It meant all was being worked on Baronetish lines—the Baronet would be *persona grata* in the highwayman's lair, that was the idea.

" Who is going to foot the bill ? " I asked.

" I've told you you needn't worry your head about anything Snooty—leave it all to me. What's the use of having an agent ? I'll fix everything up—if necessary I'll pay a small ransom in persian dollars—it wouldn't be much. I could charge it up against you—we're going to make a haul on this book, don't you forget it ! It'll be another 'Trader Horn' or 'Good Companions'. We can afford a ransom—but it won't be necessary."

" Why not ? Will the brigand put me up for nothing ? "

" No. But if you're captured the government will damned well have to pay ! "

" Don't be absurd."

" Of course they will ! They can't allow the premier baronet of Scotland to rot in a persian bandit's lair ! "

I scowled at him. But a deep look of satisfaction came into Humph's face, while I sat staring at him in scowling astonishment.

" But it's better than that."

" What do you mean ? "

" I mean—well as a matter of fact, the old bandit *pays a commission.*"

My astonishment deepened.

" How is that ? " I said.

" For a—well you know for *a good subject*——"

" A rich prize ? "

" Exactly—he allows something on the ransom."

" That's marvellous isn't it ! " I said, scowling still more heavily at him. " Who does he pay the money to ? "

" Well he keeps you until he gets the money."

" Yes ? "

" Then he pays you your commission out of it, and supplies free of all charge an escort—he gives you a safe-conduct across the desert to the nearest town.—I've a damned good mind to get caught myself ! "

Humph laughed—starting very slowly and ending as if he never intended to leave off, he then stopped with unnecessary suddenness.

" Does Pat Bostock get a commission ? " I asked.

" Pat ? " He called out *Pat* as if no one with such an open devil-may-care name as Pat would be capable of touching a commission. " No, old Pat doesn't get anything—at least I don't think so. As far as I know he doesn't."

" I thought that might be why he kept up the correspondence."

" I don't think so. I think it's only because he took a fancy to the jolly old bandit and sort of keeps in touch with him—you know like that. In memory of a very jolly experience."

" I see."

" Being in the Army, Pat couldn't as a matter of fact."

" Haven't the British Government got wise to him ? "

" Apparently not."

" When I refuse the commission will the brigand be offended ? "

" But you *won't* refuse the commission I should hope ! "

" Oh. Am I to accept it ? "

" I thought you understood that."

" No."

" Of course."

" And I hand it on to you ? "

" You give me some of it—I think that's only fair ! "

" What percentage ? Usual agent's fee ? "

" No no. We're in on this on a fifty-fifty basis ! "

" Oh."

" Supposing the ransom is four hundred pounds for argument's sake."

" I see."

" It might be much more."

" I thought that didn't sound much—for *me* I mean."

" No it might be a pretty tidy sum. It will depend on the circumstances a good deal. He might for instance threaten to shoot you. I would work up the Consul-General over that."

I began almost to admire this bleak, this owlish moron, furnished expressly with a mammoth chin. I gave him a smile at that. This he very much appreciated, and he came round from behind the table, and stood up stiffly quite near to me. Smoke poured from his mouth, nose, and pipe all of a sudden, as if the rapid movement he had effected, in the displacement of his mass through the air, had fanned the smouldering fire within and it had burst forth in smoke.—But the Chin was putting up a smoke-screen only, that was what it was—his dung-brown eyes went disgustingly dreamy, in the heart of the tobacco-smoke cumulus.—What next am I in for, I thought with apprehension. I stood up.

" Have you your visa Snooty ? " he asked.

" No. But the visas are arranged for. We shall have them by tomorrow. When do we start ? "

" Well, could you get ready to start at once ? "

" What do you call at once ? "

" The day after tomorrow ? "

" All right."

" I shan't be able to come."

" No ? "

" I'm afraid not."

" I'm very sorry."

" I have to go down to Cornwall again. A girl has got stuck at her last chapter but one. The poor girl's under contract to finish her book by next Wednesday, and she can't move an inch forward, not an inch—she is in an absolute *jam*."

" I say."

" The words simply will not come ! "

" Ha ! " I said with considerable aspiration.

" I have to go down, there's nothing for it but that."

" You lucky dog ! Is she alone ? "

" Absolutely, in a cottage right up on the cliff. She only has one bedroom—I have to sleep in two armchairs—at least I *did* " (very archly) " the first night I was there ! "

" The *first* night ! "

His Chin burst into a peal of cromagnon laughter. He began pacing rapidly up and down the room.

" But she has got stuck " he said pulling himself up. " I know she's stuck."

" Mind you don't get stuck old boy ! "

He was delighted. The Chin broke into a volley of haha's.

" I'll see to that old man ! Trust me !—I've done it before ! "

" Oh well you slip in and out easily then of her little cottage—how long will you be ? "

" That depends—I have to hold her hands or something while she finishes. I often have to do that. I was down with another one of my clients last week, just when you turned up. She'd got stuck at the *opening* chapter."

" That was worse I suppose ? Did she take much shifting ? "

" As a matter of fact it's *better* when it occurs at the *beginning* of the book."

" Do they ever think better of writing it altogether ? "

" I've never known one to give up ! "

" I suppose not."

" But there's nothing so bad as the last lap, if you get a *panne* there——"

" Does the muse always return, upon your appearance on the scene ? "

" I seem to have some influence with the muse ! "

" I'll bet you have ! " I hollered, as roguish as he !

" But women are very stupid about it—they wire for me on the slightest provocation. The one I'm going to see tomorrow is very beautiful, she's really a very beautiful girl. She's only nineteen."

" Is she peachy ? "

" What you would call *peachy* ! She *is* like a peach as a matter of fact—a perfect complexion, and a little downy. —I've got a photograph of her."

He went quickly over to his desk and came back with

a photograph of a thin, apparently very dark, gossoon, in a loin-cloth, stretching in a graceful dislocation, upon a rocky shore. Humph, grinning from ear to ear, was squatting upon a boulder within easy reach, also in sun-bathing kit.

I held the photograph deferentially before me for a minute or two.

" Is she an author ? " I asked.

" She's a damned clever kid ! " he said. " I think she's a bit of a genius ! " he confided.

I put the photograph down upon the table near which I stood.

" Not so bad being a Literary Agent eh what ! " I exclaimed in a tone of very hearty flattery. " I suppose you get quite a fair amount of tail, first and last—one way and another ? "

Humph blinked (as if his place in the sun were pretty hot and dazzling if it came to that) and laughed stupidly over his jolly agenting, and he showed by his whole manner that if it were not for considerations of professional etiquette and a high level of discretion, he could tell me a thing or two about our Writing Girls !

" I suppose those who are not lesbians " I said and stopped.

" You don't think *she* looks like a lesbian do you ? " he asked a little taken aback. " I had my suspicions to start with."

" I should think lesbians would like you old chap " I said.

He discharged at me a displeased sort of look I thought and taking up the photograph returned it to the spot where it had originally lain.

" They're not all lesbians, by a long way " he exclaimed a little aggressively, unduly soberly.

" No."

" I could show you two or three who are not anyway ! "

" Oh but perhaps it is you have given them back their normal interests ! "

" I have a suggestion to make " said Humph very much sobered up, after a fairly sullen interval, during which I yawned at the carpet and aggressively stuck out my mechanical leg. I had driven him back to cover, he had returned and again taken up his position behind the table.

I nodded my head.

" I wonder if you would care to go down and see Rob *McPhail* ! "

I shrugged my shoulders with a slight circular movement, as if I had a parasite camping under my skin.

" And see if you can per-*suade* him ! "

I shook my head.

" To come a—*long* ! " He spoke in dragging nasal tones now, slower at each intermittent spasm, and he softened so much the nigger-brown of what he regarded as his velvet glances, that I turned my head away, feeling a little sick. (Humph's sweetbreads were too much for me !) " To come to *Persssh*—ya ! " again (after an insinuating pause that he had overdone so much that I had shuffled about like a restless audience) he negligently drawled.

There was another pause—to allow for the too-too soft impeachment of the persuasive nigger-brown—the seductions of the muted voice—to take effect I suppose. Then again there was a burst of speech.

" With *us* ! " dropping his voice down, to come to *us*, he almost whispered.

" McPhail won't come to Persia or anywhere else " I said abruptly, to put a stop at once to this sickly comedy.

" But have you *asked* him ? " he gasped in almost a breathless plaintive caress of the atmosphere (or of my ear-drums) by his silken vocal-cords.

" No. I tell you it's no use."

" But supposing I—supposing I—supposing I ! "

I looked him up and down, he slightly gasped.

" Supposing I com—*mission* him ! "

I did a tattoo with my mechanical foot during a further preposterous pause.

" To do a *perssh*—ian——*book* ! "

I shook my head, sitting beneath the eye of this over-mannered auctioneer.

" Has McPhail money?—I've been told——"

I shook my head.

" That's what I thought."

He stepped out from behind the table. I knew quite well why he stood behind the table—it was (when he wished to be impressive) in order to conceal the shortness of his legs. That also was why, as a rule, he moved up so close to one : or else dashed about—that had something to do with that too. But now he stood well off from me and said—

" It might *appeal* to him—how do you know ! It might after all are you sure ! "

I gave him such a withering look that he went back behind the table, and became a half-length once again.

" I should be delighted to see McPhail " I said, with a great deal of indifference (not to McPhail). " I would far rather go to McPhail than go to Persia for instance."

" No would you really ! "

I tapped with my artificial toe.

" I can understand that " he blurted, after one of his pauses. " Well why don't you go—you can I'm sure ! "

" Can what ? "

" He will come ! I *bet* he will ! I bet he——! "

" Of course I will go—give me my ticket, I will start at once. I ask nothing better ! "

" That's splendid ! "

I was next compelled to act as audience to Humph in " a brown study ". He gnawed the stem of his pipe.

" How about the tickets? Which way are we going?" I demanded rudely.

Humph came forward again from behind his table, almost squaring up to me I thought.

" I will tell you tomorrow!"

He turned on his heel, and continuing the " brown study", started to pace up and down, between the door and where I sat.

" Capital!" I nearly shouted.

I will tell you tomorrow!—I like that! I thought—he would give me my orders tomorrow. It was not *I* had put myself in his hands was it?—it was *he* had put me there, which was a very different matter. I had made no resistance—that is quite correct, none whatever. This strange agent was to dispose of me as he thought best—that we understood. I must adopt the status of a servant—all this was to defeat " The Baronet".

I smiled to myself—to be seen and not heard was it?—Certainly certainly! That suited *me*! *For the duration of the trip!*—was that it? He was " my officer". Right—eehoh; Captain Carter!—I enjoyed this immensely. I grinned up at him, as he bore down upon me, and he grinned back at me.

" Oh by the way Snooty—you haven't told me," he halted his rush (again, what first-class brakes!), " I have never asked you—who is your girl-friend—I mean what's her name—I may have to."

I rather squinted at this. I was not prepared for this. There was nothing against his knowing the name as far as I could see. Still I looked at him without speaking.

" Don't tell me if you'd rather *not*!" he said.

" What do you mean?"

" I only asked—I only thought!"

" Why not? Of course. Her name is——"

" Please don't trouble to say who she is if you'd sooner."

" Nothing of the sort. Why should I? Of course not ! "

" It doesn't matter in the least."

" Her name is Ritter—she is Mrs Ritter. Do you want her thumb-prints ? "

" Mrs Ritter ? "

" Yes Valerie Ritter."

" But I *have* her thumb-prints ! " he bellowed.

As I had said *Ritter* his face had undergone a violent change, as if a series of shutters of different sorts and sizes were being swiftly operated upon it—shutting off one expression after another, as soon as each flashed up. Finally he burst into a loud rude laugh.

" Valerie Ritter ! "

" Valerie Ritter—yes that's her name, as far as I know " I said savagely—I was in no mood to engage in badinage about old Val of all people. It was no laughing matter: whatever else it might be.

" Valerie Ritter ! " he repeated softly as if to himself.

" That's it. Why, do you know her ? "

He began pounding about the room again, delivering himself of salvos of robust guffaws, while I watched him with growing displeasure.

" I don't know her old boy—I don't *know* her ! " he said at last, in a half-choke of the most affected sort of spasm of fun.

" Why are you laughing then ? " I asked pointedly and indignantly. Had he *known* her, then indeed it would have been ridiculous to object to his laughter, or to expect anything else. But he did not know her. Therefore his indulgence in offensive peals of laughter was intolerable. It was *me* he must be laughing at.

He stopped in front of me, fixing me with an eye of rich amusement—an eye, as I have said, of nigger-brown, of all colours that I dislike most in eyes (all the dog-shades in fact, and the Down-in-Dixie varieties).

" Have you read her books ? " he enquired. " I suppose you have."

" I have " I said, with a sinking feeling.

" Look ! " he said, as he went over to his desk. " Look," he pulled open a huge drawer. " I've got a drawer full of them ! "

This was very bad ! He pulled out manuscript after manuscript. I recognized them only too well ! The foolish old girl had I knew been sending the stuff out broadcast in every direction, all over Paris and London. Here was doubtless the result of her industry of the last six months—a sort of sterile, bawdy flux—completely filling a substantial drawer.

He opened the first manuscript, pulling away in facetious puffs at his hospital-case of a pipe. He turned over a few pages, shaking with Army-and-Public-School mirth, until he came to something he was looking for. Then he burst out into a clap of that particular laughter which the Public School reserves for *sex* with its capital letter on. The fellow began stamping up and down upon his dwarfish agile stumps. A great increase in the characteristic *taken-short look* of which I think I have spoken was noticeable as he did this. Whether it was that he was indulging in the pantomime of a person glandularly affected, or whether he was in fact provoked (by the perusal of such literature as that of old Val) to wet his bags, I cannot say. I should not be at all surprised if it were the latter.

I pulled him up as best I could—I could not have this going on. He was approaching me, splitting his sides as he came, his finger upon some frolicsome passage.

" I know her books—you need not show me that ! "

" No but have you seen *this* ! "

(Again I am constrained to suppress some sentences full of expressive words, which at this point he spluttered out, since I refused to look at what he pressed me to read.

Val's manner of writing and subject-matter is of a nature as I have already indicated to bring a blush to the cheek of Elinor Glyn or put out of countenance a bagman accustomed to 'travel' Lady Chatterley.)

"Yes yes" I said very impatiently indeed "I know—they're terribly funny aren't they—are you her agent too then?"

"I? no—she sends these things to me, I don't know why."

"She sends them to everybody."

"I suppose so. I've heard she does."

"Have you? Does she come round?"

"No. I've never seen her. Once I wrote her a polite note, I suppose she thinks I might *place* them for her!"

"It is possible."

"It of course would be impossible."

"She's mad. But we all have our weaknesses."

"We certainly all *have*," he said, so pointedly that I yawned at him, very wide indeed.

"Is she pretty?" he asked. "I expect she's as ugly as sin—they always are. I mean those that do this kind of stuff."

"Is that so!"

"That's my experience."

"You ought to know."

"I always refuse to see them when they write like this. When I first began agenting it was different—but I soon found that out."

"It sounds to me a pretty useful rule."

"It really is. But she may be different of course. Is she—perhaps she's pretty! Is she?"

I fixed my eye upon him and said very deliberately—

"She's a very pretty girl indeed!"

"Is she? I don't believe a word of it—I believe she's hideous! No is she pretty really? She must be or you wouldn't know her of course!"

I had seen his eye wandering over my person and it had settled upon my mechanical leg. He did not trouble to disguise his opinion that the chances of a poor cripple having a very pretty girl for a friend were fairly slender, and did not impose a belief upon *his* mind at all events pointing to the great natural beauty of Valerie Ritter.

" She's peachy ! " I said.

" Is she ? " He flung the manuscript back into the drawer. " So much the better.—I suppose she *is* coming ? "

I sighed.

" I'm afraid so ! "

" Why *afraid*—don't you want her to ? "

" She's coming and that's the end of it."

" Excellent. She's very nice I'm sure " he said with hearty patronage.

" That's as it may be. But it was your suggestion in the first place."

" Was it ? "

" It was. So be it on your own head ! "

" Oh why ! It ought to be rather amusing ! "

" Do you think so ? "

" Of course. Is she like her books ? "

" She is the image of her books. Only of course nicer —everybody is ! "

" Thank God yes—what a world it would be if they weren't ! "

* * *

I went out of Humph's office far more depressed than I came into it. Now I was in their power, and this one showed it by the high-handed conduct of his stunt. His way of disposing of my person, as if I had been an agent's chattel all my life, made me feel quite sea-sick.—Sold into bondage for a Baronet—to my despotic Literary-Manager ! Such abstractions as *The Custom House Officer* and *The*

Baronet had overshadowed my personal life, that was the fact of the matter, to such a point that I could no longer call my soul my own. Had not my agent been brought in to rescue me from The Baronet? That was so, and he had sold me to that gentleman, that was the long and short of it. All his astonishing best-seller technique led back to Debrett. What resource! What originality!

On my side I had set my traps—one for Val, one for him. But I found myself badly checkmated. My chances of getting Val off on Humph had sunk to zero. There would be no *getting him in the Bed*—he would not go into the Bed—he had just said enough to show the unlikelihood so that was love's labours lost—no research-work of that order to enliven the proceedings! As to Val, I was not cross but the old girl had known all about my agent all the time. That was not very good. Why had she kept her counsel? But I on my side should say nothing. Holding my tongue was my only chance with them, I knew that—not a word would pass my lips, about agents, or whatever it was. I would redouble my simple precautions. In fact I would cease to talk at all, except to talk nonsense. As to that I had quite made up my mind. These disagreeable puppets should be given rope with which to hang themselves—separately if they refused to do it together.

As to me, in the charge of these machines, they should —up to the last moment—have their way with me. *Up to the last* grain of sand, when the sands *at last* ran out.

Bundled off to Persia by them I would veto nothing, they should have their way—I would go through with that, step by step (all but the *last* step) Okaying order after order, accepting all their stipulations—but always *snootily* of course, otherwise I should arouse their suspicions.

What was the latest? A nice little commission! I was to be sent down to collect McPhail—given my ticket, packed off the day after next, by this Lunn's Tour of a

Book-Agent and Bestseller-Expert. (Should I best-sell if I obeyed this booster? I would affect to think that I suffered all in order that I might best-sell!) But I would catch the train they told me, cross on the boat prescribed —all would be in applepie-order, throughout—the aggressive minutes of their time-table followed with gardee robot precision. McPhail was the oasis.—As far as I was concerned in the whole stretch of the proposed adventure the only bright spot at all. But that too I would treat as if under orders. *Duty First* should be written all over me when I got there!

They desired me to be their automaton! *I would in the end become their Frankenstein!* I said this loudly to myself —in these words I said it (against my custom—I am no talker, I do not allow my mind to chatter).

Stepping out heavily into the Strand (up from a flight of stone-stairs, which descended between greengrocers into Adelphi) I entered the traffic without stopping, and reached the north side with my hat in my hand. I give you this detail because of what next happened to me—something very odd indeed, though you may regard it as a common enough occurrence. Fate played me a little trick. Nothing could ever persuade me that what next took place was not a deliberate trap set by destiny. The natural and familiar scene had been tampered with, and who would deny that everything pointed to its being on my account? —Fate may, quite true, have been setting traps all down the Strand, for Tom, Dick and Harry. But however that may have been I distinctly came into her calculations.

I thought I would go to a basement-bar, it was not far down, opposite the shell of the Cecil. At that moment I was upon the safety-island which lies in the traffic at the feet of Charing Cross Hospital (full of smashed bodies from the machine-ridden streets) my hat in my hand, as I have said. It had been my intention to go up by Hachette's bookshop and so to the Piccadilly Underground. But I thought of the bar where I could get a good Club-sandwich and a goodish Gin-Fizz so I turned back and went eastward up the Strand. My intestines had thrown up the picture in bold plaster-cast relief of a big chicken-hearted Club-sandwich. My spittle-ducts had squirted with a will and all together at the sight of it : so with the above life-size model, in crisp yellow-crusted impasto, of a super-Club-sandwich swelling inside me (blocked out in wind in mid-stomach—a cave, a receptacle—my thunderous belly had modelled a cavity, with a contour of such an object as a monstrous Club-sandwich, to attract my attention) and with my hat hanging in my hand, I took the route my destiny had traced out.

I stare pretty hard at all the people I meet, as a rule I am not particular. More than once I've got an " Eer ! Oo do yoo fink yoo aint arf starin at ! " in response, I don't mind : but I never pass down a big shopping-street like this without stopping to look every once in a while into the shop-windows. I am susceptible to shoppers' fever but there is also my field-work to consider—that must never be lost sight of—therefore I stop, scenting out bargains or for research-purposes. When I was about to pass in front of an important Hatter's window on this occasion I observed a stationary crowd.

I seldom see a crowd without pushing firmly into it (if only to break it up—nothing gives me so much pleasure as to disintegrate a crowd). I drive my bulk which is considerable into the thick of it and once there am at no pains to keep still—in a crowd I am a *ferment*. But there were only three or four people really and I got in among them without creating too much disturbance (though they all turned round of course) to examine at short range what they were all staring at in such a stupid way. I just pushed forward and stared ahead at what they had under observation.

What the people were looking at was a puppet. It was a Hatter's show-window and the Hatter by means of this ceremonious mannikin was advertising a new straw hat. This little gentleman had been created for that purpose. He belonged to the personnel of the Hatter.

I approached, as I have said, and I placed my hat upon my head (it may have seemed as a retort) at the moment the puppet removed his, with a roguish civility darting his eye at me as a new-comer—just as I thrust my way in amongst his spellbound admirers.

The puppet was a good size. I have called him " a little gentleman " but his head at all events was at least of average human scale, I am not sure it was not over. He was not " little ". He was a sturdy well-kept puppet. He was fashionably-dressed, in a somewhat loud, I thought, summer-suiting. But in England, he might have argued, where the summer is such as it is, the *summer-suit* has to be a bit on the *loud* side, and over-summery if anything.

His character interested me at once. It is absurd to say these things (if you insist upon calling them *things*) have no character. Those that are made to-day are, like characters in books, often much more real than live people. Next I observed his movements.

He removed his hat with a well-timed flourish, brought it down in a suitable parabola, twisted it about once or twice, to show off its beauties to us—all this time his face working about in the most expressive dumb show—except that it was not dumb show either, for his lips were in constant movement—he was evidently speaking, in a rather mincing way, not loud, but with his lips, and reinforcing his words, with a consummate salesmanship, by a half-closing, seductive veiling, of his eyes. He slowly winked or blinked once or twice. Then suddenly he opened his eyes wide, in a blank but not uncivil stare, as he ceased his salesman's patter, and stuck his hat down jauntily upon his head. Bowing from the waist once more in our direction, he carried to his eye a monocle, and, turning swiftly, looked up into the ceiling of the shop, then slowly he turned back his head, and scrutinized the door upon his right, smiling slightly to himself.—Then once more he removed his hat, with the well-timed flourish, bowing from the waist and smiling at us, he swept it down—turned it hither and thither, delivering, in well-chosen words, his little lecture—moving his eyes from one to the other of us, seeking to read the effect of his words upon our faces—then straightening himself out, put on his hat again at a somewhat rakish angle in his particular, a little dandyish, manner: raised his eyebrows, to admit of the insertion of the monocle, parted his lips to show a well-kept set of teeth—his smile spoke volumes as to his feelings at his position in the window—his nose was wrinkled slightly as he smiled, and I could swear that his eyes lightened as he looked down for a moment in our direction.

But what struck me most was the enormous *chin* of this creature. It dominated all his appearance. It alone was non-mobile and lifeless. For the rest, the springs that actuated his lips, nose and cheeks were excellently thought out. It was impossible as one watched him not to feel that he was in some real sense *alive*. At certain moments of course the imperfections of the apparatus would betray him. But is not this the case, for the matter of that, with the best of us?—At other times, as I say, he really deceived us—or at least he deceived me. I stood looking in the deepest astonishment at him. And the illusion certainly had communicated itself to the other people who were there.

I know well enough how I look—no one can tell me anything about that. I have made a careful study of myself. (Externally I am perhaps not unlike Sir Walter Scott or Stendhal —I mean that, as to my cast of countenance, I am no oil-painting.) But *of all things*, I know *to perfection* that heavy puzzled look that comes into my face apropos of anything almost! When I am uncertain about something—when for instance my brain has some difficulty in establishing contact with something outside it. That's the time to catch the look I mention! I must look as like an utter simpleton as a man can well be, in the face. If you saw me you would take me for a nobody, a great big puzzled dunce.

But, I have said it, I have literally to drill holes in this sheep's-head of mine before it can get an at all difficult notion, or sometimes any at all, into it properly. In all but purely mechanical things, of an external order (that is my strong suit) I am a profoundly dense person, I cannot help it. Mine is anything but a quick mind.—This may be why I am a *behaviorist*. If there is such a thing as a "soul", I at all events have never been able to catch it on the hop. (But I doubt it.) Again, a notion goes *so far* in with me and not an inch farther. That is what is oddest of all. It seems to stick in the surface shell. It remains embedded in the bone, quite hard and fast. Nothing will budge it. I have often tried but never been able to.

I understand only too well the meaning of the american "bonehead". Someone—a bonehead I guess! —asked me once upon a time what "bonehead" meant, or how the expression had arisen, and abused the Americans for being *obscure* in their slang. Mine was certainly a dud answer—I had never thought about it—I had just said "bonehead" for "stupid" I guess, like any other expression. But the american chap who first used it may have been a bonehead (and so thought of it) but he was no fool. It was a good word. That chap meant *a head like mine*—just opaque and solid skull, or it feels like that if you happen to own one, as I do.

Ideas come out of the blue, fiercely to get us, like wasps, or like a bacillus or a weevil dropped on a cork. I can feel one *strike* me. Then I feel it get stuck, quite plainly —the thing can make no headway at all. This is my difficulty as a research-worker. Yet ideas like me, if one may say that—I am " susceptible to ideas ". But I keep them stuck on the outside of me. They will not penetrate it's no use.—I tell you all this to account for that painful baffled mask I have got. That in its turn affects people's behavior to me, as you can guess. They look at my frowning and puzzled stare and they act accordingly. That is only natural. And I act back—that's only good sense too. That's " Behavior ".

As for the puppet, he went through his evolutions over and over again—each cycle was quite elaborate. I watched him with a painful amazement, attempting to penetrate what he meant, by being what he was. I had replaced my hat—I again removed it, as it happened it was just as he was taking off his. The fellow who was standing at my elbow had been watching me in the plate-glass window I think—I suppose I had pushed him. He had I suppose remarked that I was *partly* mechanical myself. My leg had not escaped his attention in short as it seemed to me, and now something about my manner appeared to amuse him. I became conscious of this. He was looking at *me*, instead of at the puppet. Of course this must have been because of my expression. I was not surprised of course, nor do I mind such creatures examining me as if I were of another clay. That is all in the day's work—the day's *field-work*.

That dull and baffled look you would see if you came face to face with me—heaven avert the omen, you would find it a strange encounter! If I could come out of this paper at you, you would find me a manner of man such as you did not expect I think, you would burst your eyes in your effort to fix me, if I rose from the floor at your feet—terribly *real*, with a whiff of stale tobacco, rough, crippled, with my staring startled difficultly-focussed glances and corn-lemon hair—that tense-as-well-as-dense expression, which when it lifts leaves an empty face behind it—for me to grin with and yawn with. But in the ordinary commerce of life I am always a little astonished if not startled—often I am absolutely amazed.

So this Hatter's puppet was large, and in addition to his chin he possessed another characteristic belonging to Captain Carter. Namely, he was all trunk with practically no legs. This was of course in the case of the automaton done in order to give him more solidity and poise, essential in a puppet—also, to make him more startlingly grotesque. But was not that also perhaps the reason for Humph's appearance? It was highly probable, I was constrained to admit.

I had begun smiling to myself as I thought of Humph. And then the puppet turned to me, bowed from the waist, and, raising his hat, smiled in the most formal and agreeable way possible. The fellow was playacting—and what I resented in this comedy was the fact that I knew (or thought I knew) that he was not *real*. There was something abstruse and unfathomable in this automaton. Beside me a new arrival smiled back at the bowing Hatter's doll. I turned towards him in alarm. Was not perhaps this fellow who had come up beside me a puppet too? I could not swear that he was not! I turned my eyes away from him, back to the smiling phantom in the window, with intense uneasiness. For I thought to myself as I caught sight of him in the glass, smiling away in response to our mechanical friend, *certainly he is a puppet too!* Of course he was, but dogging that was the brother-thought, *but equally so am I!* And so I was (a very thoughtful and important puppet—wandering in this sinister thoroughfare, in search of an american Club-sandwich—a place in my bread-basket, scooped out in wind, the size of a small melon like a plaster mould).

Now next why exactly had this light-hearted new-comer, standing beside me, been so ready to smile up? The good man would not smile if an acquaintance raised his hat to himself and his wife as they were taking their sunday walk in their suburb. That would seem perfectly natural to him, quite solemnly he would return the salute. To me *nothing* seemed natural. Often I have smiled upon occasions of that sort. Every day I was smiling hard at such common or garden things. Everything that passed as natural with him, looked exceedingly odd to me. The most customary things in the world struck me continually as particularly ludicrous. *How* ludicrous—or how normal on the other hand—would depend upon how I was feeling at the moment.

I shifted uneasily up and down upon my real leg and my false leg—I had become almost as much a fixture before the Hatter's window as the puppet inside it. The puppet had begun to notice me. His chin grew larger and larger. And the Hatter himself came out to have a look at me on two occasions as I remarked.

There were six of us now. I regarded with a dark astonishment our uneasy superiority, insecure as everything else about us—we outside (wrapped in our thoughts, disturbed in the secret places of our consciousness) with someone there so profoundly of our kind exhibited for our amusement within the show-window. We stood in a contemplative group without on the pavement (rather an absurd collection), the puppet he stood within. He was on show, but we were not.

There was something *absolute* in this distinction, recognized by everybody there excepting myself. I alone did not see it. What essentially was the difference however? The situation was exactly the same, was it not, as that of the animals in their cages at the Zoo. The other animals (who catch them and keep them there) walking about outside the cages, gazing at them talking and laughing at them—that was us over against the puppet. How surprisingly small is the difference between a mandril and a man! Certainly—but still slenderer was the difference between this stiffly-bowing so-called automaton, and my literary agent, for example.

Obviously the mandril was a far more complex machine than was this Hatter's automaton, and men were still more complex than the mandril. But this automaton *looked*, was dressed and behaved itself, far more like a man than did a mandril. And that word *looked*, that was for me *everything*.

What was Humph, for instance, more than an appearance? For me he was a fixed apparition. I believed that this creature before me possessed intestines of sawdust. But I knew no more of Humph's intestines (except by hearsay and unwarrantable assumption) than I did of this chap's in the window.

While I watched this creature, who was so like a man, I was in spite of myself beneath the spell of his reality. I could have spoken to him as if he had been one of us outside on the pavement. He was *one of us*, as much as the people at my side, about whom I *knew* no more than I knew of him, indeed rather less.

Was I certain, for instance, that Humph still existed, now that I no longer had him beneath my eyes? No I was not. That would be indeed an absurd assumption. It was far *more* absurd to suppose him still moving about, and behaving as I expected him to behave, now that I was no longer there, than to suppose him blotted out or dropped out of existence. (When I next saw him he would tell me all the things he had done in my absence of course, but I should know that that was all the merest bluff, or that *quite likely* it was the merest bluff.)

But while Humph was beneath my eyes—how was that really so different? There was just what I *saw* there, with my eyes, nothing else. And often he seemed to creak, did he not, or to weaken, or slightly wobble, like a dummy suddenly out of its depth—a machine attempting something for which it was not quite fitted. (Constantly there was this sensation of *strain*, was there not?)

There is of course nothing metaphysical or mysterious about these matters. The contrary in fact. So please do not allow yourself to be rebuffed by such a topic, because you believe it to be 'over your head' or anything of that sort. The world that we imagine—that that we call the world of common sense—existing in independence of our senses, is a far odder one, about that there is no question at all, than that world to which we feel ourself constrained to deny reality, what we can neither see, smell, touch nor hear!

Now of course my coming across this particularly vivid dummy did not teach me to reflect after that fashion. Such modes of thinking were habitual with me. It was the teaching of "Behavior", and this had become so much a part of myself that I could with difficulty imagine the time when I saw the world with other eyes—when, in the grip of a complex inherited technique, I shut out illusion, and saw what I did not see, and heard what I did not hear! This little fellow in the shop window I was as much at home with as a keeper at the Zoo is at home with one of the imprisoned creatures delivered into his care.—It was not that at all.

I have told you that when I get ideas into my head, they only go *a certain distance*. But this is true I think of all of us. You are familiar I am sure with how some reasoning impresses you, to a *greater* or to a *less* extent. Far as it may go in, it could always go *farther*, and get a more convincing hold. Sometimes after remaining stationary for years, it will suddenly move a little deeper in. Do you know that sensation? When some idea with which you are perfectly familiar becomes charged all of a sudden with a far greater reality than before, or takes on other and more intensely coloured aspects?

This was what happened with me now. The inner meaning of " Behavior ", as a notion, *got in motion* within my consciousness, stimulated I can only suppose by all the circumstances of my pact with Val and Humph. It went in deeper, that is to say. It penetrated into my consciousness *deeper* than it had ever done before. But another thing that had happened was very curious. ' Behavior ' had as it were turned round upon me as well. As the man at my side observed me putting on my hat, I was for the first time placed in the position *of the dummy*! I saw all round Behavior as it were—for the first time. I knew that *I* was not always existing, either: in fact that I was a fitful appearance. That I was apt to *go out* at any moment, and turn up again, in some other place—like a light turned on by accident, or a figure upon a cinematographic screen.—And must I confess it? I was very slightly alarmed. I saw that I had to *compete* with these other creatures bursting up all over the imaginary landscape, and struggling against me to be *real*—like a passionate battle for necessary air, in a confined place. And as a result of all this I said to myself that, in my absurd conceit, I was giving Humph far too much rope. To hang himself—that was the idea. But would he not hang *me*, perhaps?

I turned away from the Hatter's window a dense scowl settling upon my face. As I looked up I saw, in great letters, posted across the façade of a Picture-theatre, the words—

THE MAN-MADE MONSTER.

Beneath this, in smaller letters, was the word Frankenstein.—Was this an accident? Had I not said, as I emerged from the Adelphi, "I will in the end become their Frankenstein?" And I looked back at the Hatter's window as if to extract an answer from the being inside. All chin, he was smiling sardonically at me, as he bowed from the waist and raised his hat with a well-trained civility. I raised my hat, with a certain sweep, bowed slightly, and—my stomach echoing with report after report, thundering for the Club-sandwich—I continued on my way to the Luncheon-bar. I had a double whisky as soon as I reached it. Immediately I thought of Lily, and in the light of all that had just occurred I understood why it was I so greatly preferred her, and I made out a telegram then and there. That night I insisted we should be together.

A LORD OF LANGUAGE AND HIS BOAT

THE MARSILLIAN DOCKS are fine places. Harbouring yachts and small steam-fishers, they give you the relaxed joy of canals and crowded backward cities mixed.—Along, that is understood, with solid seafaring sensations.

I love the solid sensations. I am too partial, perhaps, to the solid sensations you get from seafaring. I am the landsman right enough, in that respect. Therefore I looked down off the squalor of the fishing quays, upon the Young Salts popping in and out of their cubby-holes, with the keen outsider's relish.

Whenever I go down South to see McPhail, having reached this port, before going on to his village to see him, I tread the marsillian quaysides. Such is my rule. I tread them with a certain modest rolling gait. My mechanical limb makes this an easy matter, it is almost natural: but a distinct roll in my walk I inherited, as it happens (as a small boy I rocked on my pins—later I was at pains to correct it). This I do discreetly emphasize, for the occasion, till my shoulders move with a rhythm reminiscent of Seafare, and I do softly hoick and deftly spit. Having selected my quay, deliberately, up and down, I may be observed to oscillate.—Such is the rule of these encounters with McPhail, that is all. I get my sea-legs, you might call it. I come down for a practice spin to the marsillian docks, down from the inaccessible Terminus.

However all solid sensations mean much to me first to last. (It was that brought me out so strong at first upon the side of the *Pequod* and its mad master.)—To such sensations my taste runs, as to that I am at one with McPhail. He and I both love the four-square sensations, of things that are properly solid. Certainly seafaring does block out great solid feelings: at its contact it suggests a dense reality, as does no other craft. No *Yo-ho-ho* at all about this though, it is simply the solid sensations of the Sea, that is understood, when you are on land.

The marsillian docks are splendid. Nothing but blind canals, their waters lie within the circumference of the city proper. Boulevards, as they are, used for discharging, by small sea-going bottoms, of Africa and the Levant—by smacks, lighters, bamtam tramps, whitewashed and brass-burnished pleasure-yachts—in fine all the small ships that float in, are headed for a free spot, and clutch the sides of the shabby parapets, and so swim fastened in rows for a week or fortnight, they resemble a beautiful slum-boulevard split down the centre, its left and right pushed widely apart, to admit a broad avenue of water.

Marsillia was Roman—there is a Roman Peace over Marseilles, throughout the small shipping. Solid sensations come from the Roman too, that is a truism. And does not peace dwell in the Solid?

Land-loving I certainly am: and here is an Elysium out of Time but solidly installed in Space. Space-time that is of course, with big dashes of Space in the mixture, or *Time gone thick* we equally may say. Here are none luckily of the appurtenances of Big Business, when it Goes-Down-to-the-Sea-in-Ships (impersonal and over-big as ever, dwarfing the blue-jacket as it dwarfs the black-coated). Here we have a traffic, conducted with small manageable capitals, where a wax-vesta in short, a pin, a pen-knife, a plush suspender, anything, counts.

So, rolling up and down, and lurching in and out, I discovered the abstract Chinese. When in Japan I became accustomed to these people. Discussing Chang-kai-chek, and Chang-Hsueh-Lang, I flattered a lonely Celestial into some gentle pidgin-talk. This was upon politics, done with a Bock and a fag: but leaving the café, long before midday I was before the Terminus, at the top of a perfectly stupendous stair, to go to Faujas de Saint Riom to drop in on McPhail as promised, to talk business—*small*, rational and personal, business, that is, nothing Big whatever.

Her ladyship (if everything turned out according to plan —*her* plan of course!) awaited me upon the lawn belonging to the 'Terminus'. At her elbow, which was stiffly planted upon the metal disk of the table up at which high-schoolgirlishly alert and shortwaisted she simply sat, was a stack of picture-postcards, as thick as a card-pack, stamped and addressed. This Armada of sunlit messages was destined for London, England. The names upon it, if alphabetically listed, would have afforded a preliminary "Who's Who" of the minor *Gossip Column Class*—a "Who's Who" of the *Second Class* of the "Gossip" galaxy—those definitely not Top Drawer yet with a place *somewhere* in the social Tallboys so to speak—not initiates, but with a right to an *honourable mention*, but not mentioned yet (except once by accident)—those who *gossiped* but were not *gossiped of*—a gallery of the postulants, outsiders *technically* within the Metropolitan Gossip Area but not of the Gossip World—ex-Stars, impecunious poachers and brazen gate-crashers—hangers-on and dogs that are definitely *under*.

Old Val was in her element—within Big-Bertha-shot of Cannes and the exclusive sunburnt mirth of Cap d'Antibes. She sat bolt upright, in a short-skirted Vaudeville sailor-suit, of sombre design, starched-collared, all-but-monocled, prune-and-prism-lipped, sipping a gin-fizz out of a straw, looking every inch the cool mannish *also-ran* in a beach-scene—half the body out of the picture, smile cut in half, in a snapshot of a slimming beach (with a big Gossip-Star bang in the centre, revealing the freshly massaged muscles of her abdominal nudeness) or an after-the-dip café-photo for *Miss Modern* from a fashionable suburb of Cannes.

Cocking a prim-victorian eye up from her tumbler, she gave me a short, gruff, sensible, off-hand

" *Hallo* Snoots ! "

I yawned and sat down in front of her, watching some french officers and banging upon the table with my hand.

" Are we going to Faujas Snooty ? " Val enquired with obvious submissiveness.

" Yah-yah-yah ! " I yawned, drumming upon the tin table-disk and working my leg up and down.—I had oiled it that morning.

" Did you get what you wanted in the town ? " she ventured to enquire.

" No " I said very snootily indeed. And she asked no more questions just then.

She paid for her drink when the waiter came up to us. I rose and we went over to the station. What was that proverb—*There is a great difference between a good physician and a bad one, but very little difference between a good one and none at all ?* Well *no* manners is good manners in a certain sense, and with this cattle like Val I carried this amended precept to its logical conclusion. I scarcely spoke a word to her.—She bought the tickets while I waited yawning at the barrier. When she came up with them I passed in, and gravely mounted into the train—she, pulling her lips down in a prim grimace, and elevating one eyebrow, followed me into the carriage.

I sat in the corner—I was grave, I deliberated. I had said that *Duty First* would be written all over me, and it was. Business is business, it is " grave-making " as Bernard Shaw would say, whether Big or not. I was a sort of Literary Agent or his deputy at this moment.

Already in my port-stroll, away from Val, Rob and I

had been in contact. Long since I had, in fact, entered the McPhailian field of force. With McPhail you had action-at-a-distance. He lived in a universe as straight as a gun-barrel—a child-world, a Newtonian universe. His fist is upon this landscape. Stamped with his image is all of the small marine industry of the Bouches du Rhône. So still gravely composed, I drew out of the Terminus. Val sat primly composed in the opposite corner of the carriage.

Rattling along the mediterranean cliffs, past plage after plage (each a miniature beach between small grey volcanic headlands, a few shoddy villas for summering town-trash and a *débit-tabac*) we neared and then I reached the station-halt for Rob McPhail.

At Faujas de Saint Riom it blows for half the year with such great violence that all the telegraph poles have to be planted along the windward sides of the roads : then when they blow down they tumble in a field, the traffic is not stopped. This is the african wind, the pest of the provençal seaboard. But it was not the time of the sirocco : Faujas was, as I had seen it before, enjoying moderate sunshine and a peaceful breeze. Here was the perfect *back-water*, of indolent and sheltered life, the land of *no extremes* (neither human nor natural). And this was the heart of the McPhailian universe.

Except for the above-named bad seasonal wind, Faujas de Saint Riom would be an ideal spot for a poet, who is tired of Capitalism (the xviiith Century called it " le siècle "). He wants to catch fish quietly in a big windy pond, he wants to gossip with rough fellows (but not too rough) and polish a lovely verse, or pack with gun-cotton and poisoned epithets another one, that will knock a man down with its well-timed percussion, *knock-out* couplets, that is the idea, and then rig-out grand swaggering stanzas, stuffed with barbarous imagery. You cannot live too quietly for such pursuits. To register the roar of storms you must yourself be just beyond their deafening circles, you catch my drift? That *just* beyond is the word to fasten on. (I am tracking for you the Artist, the Spectator, as against the blinded and deafened participant. That is what I am about to do. No task perhaps for me but we shall see.)

The man I had come to meet could do this—all the repertory of the elements, gestures of violence, he had at his finger-tips. He was a powerful verse-craftsman—at the head of a towering vocabulary, at once up-to-date and barbaric—but you know his name, I am telling you what you already know. The name of McPhail spells all this. But I surprised as it were a technical secret of his upon this visit; for—how shall I describe it?—I caught the creature shadow-boxing, in the world about him, with the shadowy solids. I understood perhaps more fully what a most conscious artist was McPhail—I report that for posterity: McPhail will not mind your listening-in—I give it you in outline.

The village itself, or rather town (it has a half-score of well-fed cops for instance, it is a place able to take care of itself), is an undistinguished modern french *bourgade*. Uneasily attached to it is a large berber settlement. The berber and frankish populations had the previous afternoon to this met in a pitched battle. It was upon the suspension-bridge. The police were with drawn revolvers between—both columns of adversaries were dismayed, before long they dispersed, with volleys of hot-scented oaths.

But friction is frequent between these two sets of fine fellows—the mediterranean fishermen namely, and the wild berber colonists of France. Generally the row starts following upon some alleged indecorous gesture, of which a white girl has been the blushing victim at the hands (or at *the hand* to be more exact—it was *one* hand only upon this occasion, and *one* cheek only of a delicate gallic buttock, of the tender gender) of an amorous Moor.

McPhail, as may be imagined, sides entirely with his pals, who are the White fishermen. Emphatically so do I. I have not lived in Africa for nothing. The fishers, the French, are often darker-skinned I know than the members of the interloping african race.

I have no need to introduce Rob McPhail to you, that I have already said. Young, as you know, he is one of the few authentic poets now writing in English. A craftsman in the grand manner, Rob has the touch of a great international chef—his kitchen-work with words, little and big, but especially those massive winged ones that propel themselves like bats or wild water-fowl, is beyond praise or blame.

Rob McPhail is often mentioned in the Gossip Columns of the great Dailies. It is no uncommon thing for him to have a photograph of cabinet size in a big Weekly like *Vogue*, where he is seen quietly counting his catch, upon the quay at Faujas de Saint Riom. He is, in short, a man of Gossip Column calibre: and Val I could see was beside herself with anticipation of making the acquaintance of what she regarded as an authentic Gossip-Star—a great man in her world, or rather an august inhabitant of the world upon the frontier of which she languished.

I turned round and grinned at her as we left the bus and made our way to a taxi in the main square of Faujas.

"You've heard of McPhail haven't you?" I enquired.

"Don't be silly Snooty!" she replied with dignity.

"Do you know what he looks like?"

"I've seen photographs of him."

"Try not to talk too much. These great men don't like talkers."

"I'll do my best. Would you rather I stayed here?"

"No. But remember he's the cat's whiskers."

" I shan't come at all in a minute if you go on like that."

" I don't think we'll talk about your latest book."

Val affected to bite her lip. She may even actually *not* have liked the reference to her latest book.

I found a cab-driver who worked for McPhail.

Rob lives quite outside the town, in a rather elevated position, from which he surveys the lake, his happy-hunting-ground. He was not expecting me, I had no time to write. At the end of a long path I found his house empty and partly locked up, so after shouting the name that is whispered with awe and growled with misgiving across the tea-tables of the W.C. district to the birds in his trees, I left the solitary residence above the fish-infested lake, returning to the taxi. I had left Val of course in the taxi.

" He's not there " I said.

" Ah, he isn't there ? " said the driver, on the defensive, for he felt he should as a local man have produced McPhail at once.

" Not at all. The house is empty " I said gruffly.

" He's at his brother-in-law's maybe " he said, and we went down the hill to another house, by the side of the high road.

The driver called loudly " Vieuxchange ! Vieuxchange ! " as I had called " McPhail ! McPhail ! " And the name he called was a household-word in the French Fleet—because Vieuxchange was a sports-champion and his name woke as many echoes in battleships and submarines as McPhail's did in drawing-rooms and studios, of West Central London. A fierce dog in the court barred our way. After shouting and barking on the one side and the other for some minutes the driver said " He's not there."—" Ah he's not there ? " I said. And we returned to the taxi.

We ran down the hill into the town. I did not fear not finding him but time was limited. I had to acquit myself to the best of my ability of my commission—I hoped he was not too far away. *Duty First* was written all over me, though I longed to see my friend again. ('Duty' made me understand that all the more.)

"He ought to be there!" the driver said, everywhere that he looked, "he should be there!" and I got the impression that the driver felt that McPhail was under the obligation to produce himself, as much as any other member of a small community is understood to be at call, and, at a loud shout or two, to be bound to reply and appear. Hunting high and low I could not hear any true news of him all the same. Not quite everyone knew McPhail—the town was big, big enough for that: but the driver knew who to ask. McPhail had been seen: several could tell us they had spoken with McPhail or they had seen him pass. Directions for finding him were offered with a great show of assurance. We sped away in our spacious machine, but it turned out that he had either not been there, or had passed and said "Good morning", or his wife had stopped for a moment to give an order or exchange a remark.

The driver became amused. It struck him as absurd that we had not found McPhail: and this sensation was growing upon him. Then suddenly and with great simplicity, he pointed with a satisfied

"*Le voilà!*"

His finger showed me, in among the crowd, in a square we had twice passed, where Rob was. Rob and Vieux-change were with their wives, the party took logical shape, they were at lunch. We were some distance from them, I paid the driver, who was as satisfied as if he had taken me to an obscure back-street and he was smiling like a Marco Polo. I made my way with Val through the holiday crowd towards the unconscious party. There were low exclamations to each other and I was recognized.

McPhail put down a chicken bone and stiff with surprise, rose gradually to his feet—lips parted, his filmy eyes fixed upon my face. I glanced at the ground, I stood back some way. I stood in front of Val. I blotted her out as far as might be.

" Good Lord Snooty ! " he hooted thickly through his nose.

" Hallo ! "

" Good Lord I am glad you've come Michael ! "

" Good afternoon," addressing the family of course.

" Have you met my brother-in-law ? This is Vieux-change."

" *Bonjour !* "

" *Bonjour !* "

" I am glad. Good Lord ! " Rob stood with his head forward as though about to crow at me, in craning welcome.

Vieuxchange is the fisherman, as you may know, who is married to a sister of Mrs McPhail. I admired the leonine aspect of this big fishing man, who is an ex-marine—he had just left the fleet, his service ended. He is fawn-coloured, like a lion, with all the heaviness in the paws, shoulders and neck. Rob stood, partly draped waist-high by his napkin as he had slowly risen, his eyes still very moist and filmy and said again :

" Good Lord ! When did you get here Michael ? "

We sat down and all looked at each other. The others were silent and Rob and I looked at one another.

Val had remained standing where I had left her behind me. Now that I had sat down she was revealed, the others saw her. She was gazing away, wistful and decorous, in the direction of one of the arms of the fishing port, exaggerating her involuntary isolation and smiling to herself with an open-covertness, to put the best face on the fact that we had all sat down and she had stood apparently unnoticed in the midst of us. I rose and called to her.

" This is Mrs Ritter who is with me " I said.

Everyone looked over at Val and McPhail got once more upon his feet, smiling mistily.

" Oh is it ? " he hooted thickly. " You did not tell me Michael. I didn't know Mrs Ritter was with you."

" Mrs Valerie Ritter " I said.

With a phantom simper, to show how she understood from long experience my absent-mindedness and did not mind in the least (I was a half-mad " hearty ", was I not, who had not had the advantages of the intimacy of the polished heroines and heroes of Gossip, a titled backwoodsman who was admittedly rather sweet like a rough and ugly hunting-dog) she advanced to be introduced. Anyone could see from everything about her that she was at home in the very smartest Gossip-sets—she was the well-known Valerie Ritter.

When, as perfunctorily as possible, I had got her settled, I turned my back upon her and resumed my contemplation of Rob—attempting to blot out that hostile stretch of Time, since I had last encountered him, which as Time always does had attempted to estrange us, and rob each of us, for the other, of our reality. I could see that Rob was wrestling with the same spatio-temporal material. We peered at each other, a little near-sighted, as if we were meeting in the polar twilight, on the top of the world, instead of in the sunlight of Faujas de Saint Riom.

" I am glad Michael ! " Rob hooted again. " I'm sorry not to have been there."

Like all great word-spinners and architects, Rob was a man of few words really. Any old word would do if it was for common use, with Rob (Renan in his lectures had two exclamations only, to express all that Renan had to exclaim about ! Rob was like Renan).

So much in league with language was McPhail, that was the fact of the matter, that in the street, among the men in the street for the occasions of the mass-life of this deaf and dumb century, he would stammer, or otherwise use street words for the street. What more rational? Rob was a Lord of Language, was he not? His tongue for common use was dull, panting and muffled. *Good Lord*, then, was the customary muffled, panting cry of Rob McPhail. He strained his neck towards me. A little roosterish, and throat-muscle-bound he boomed tonelessly again:

"*Good Lord* Kell-Imrie I am glad to see you!"

His somewhat cat-like, prominent green eyes indicated gladness—self-conscious and abortive, misty and entranced. Eye, like tongue, was dimmed, in the head of this poet. (What is an eye, that it should pretend to paint the impulsive satisfactions of the word-king, unexpectedly called upon to salute a fellow?) There was a cloud, an obstruction. I was still at some psychic distance, my arrival had been too sudden: as I integrated, the poet strained his eyes—eager, like a cat's in the dark, the large ears drawn back against his head; panting and weak-lidded, he strained his head towards mine.

Bob heaved up a few remarks quite at chance out of the volcano of the verbal commonplace. I spewed a few well-used words or two, I indulged in a trite exclamation. He said "Good Lord!" and I with a sheepish manner, not to be out-goated, sighed "Not exactly", then shouted "I hope all the same!" But he would not hear of it. I said, in an apology, that I had found his doors all open, I had shouted his name.

"Go on!" he said.

While I refused some chicken I addressed the french sailor at my side in fluent French. Rob talked it badly—I found he differed from me regarding French. I never minded how fluent I got in the Parleyvous, but he sticks to his spiked guns, to his linguistic muzzle-loaders. Let it be in French as it is in British! He panted in bad French at his brother-in-law, and I toned down my too-idiomatic uses of that treacherous tongue to keep in step.

Soon we were at home and they talked on, and soon I could guess there was something a-foot, from what was said, though I did not catch the drift. So I asked Rob if he would go afterwards over to the lake and see his new boat with me. Last time I had missed seeing the new pirogue that they had bought. But he told me he had promised Juanito to take part in the bull-fight—it began at half-past two.

I thought they had been referring to some sport, though I had not been able to make out which. I said I would not for the world!—and he said he would not dream of it! —neither of us would give way: he *would* stick round with me, he protested, whereas I *would not* be a spoil-sport, so the matter became a perfect impasse. But Mrs McPhail said it would be all right: he was not very well and should not really fight. At first I did not understand that it was at Faujas. I thought it was out in the Camargue. They talked a bit and I wondered how far it might be. But Rob said:

"I'll get out of it. I'm glad of the excuse. I will go and tell Juanito."

I would not hear of that as I have said. By accident I had arrived within an hour of the first rush of the bull. My coming spelled a total change of plan, but of that I would hear nothing, as you may guess. Events must take their course, as if I were not there.

"I will see the bull-fight" I said with impetuosity.

"Of course—it won't be much" Rob said.

"Oh I don't think so!"

"No, it won't" said Mrs McPhail. "It won't be much."

" Still—let us go ! "

" Oh yes do let's go ! " said Val. " I've never seen a bull-fight."

" Certainly " she said.

" We shall go " said he.

" Have you seats ? I can get in certainly—you must not say you are not going—don't disappoint him ! Why shouldn't we go together ? "

" No he had better not to-day " said Mrs McPhail.

" Of course Snooty " said Rob. " Good Lord ! I wish I'd known earlier " said he. " No, I'll tell Juanito I can't do it, I'll say I'm sick. I am."

" Why not ? " I said. " I'm looking forward—we must see your veronicas. I've never seen a veronica of yours."

" I'm not up to it " Rob said. " I had thought of telling Juanito anyway. I'll tell him—I won't go in to-day. That's settled. I feel rotten. It was a fête here last night."

" All night—*toute la nuit !* " spluttered Vieuxchange very quickly.

We left the family circle and of course old Val (who seemed to get on all right with the women) in the square : we went across the bridge to a café to find Juanito.

" Where is it ? " I asked Rob.

When he understood what I meant he told me it was here. It was at Faujas. That was far better of course. We had a drink or two and waited for Juanito. We went across to the lake and there was a bull-ring, with the lake on two sides of it, before and behind, a small peninsula. Some handful of fight-fans were collected near the roped-in enclosure. McPhail was recognized, we passed in.

" Good Lord " Rob said. " They won't be here yet. —Juanito's not here " he panted. " Here they are."

There was a big box-van. This was Juanito's circus—within stood, I knew, the cows and bulls of the spanish showman, they would be closely packed in the big travelling show-box.

Two or three bull-baiting fans had climbed up and were staring over the top at the cattle in the well of the van. I and Rob got up beside them—I hauled myself up by my arms, Rob giving me a hand, between the biceps and the body. There were the animals. All their spines, the horned heads hung on the ends of them, occupied in close formation the space beneath us. They were the charging-machines of the spanish menagerist. The bulls were the worst spanish bulls obtainable. What a pack of bloodshot brutes! I said to myself (naturally with a secret hope that they might be more than a match for the bull-fighters). It was their first time in the arena, Rob told me huskily. But the cows were for the preliminary Charlotade, the pantomime that came off first. I brooded stupidly beside him down upon cows and bulls as you would stare at a park of artillery in peace-time, or a police-exhibit of sawed-off shot-guns. These fighting races of big ruminants! Cud-chewers and killers! More power to their symbolic pornography thought I! And upon this box loaded with deadly animals, to be shot off one by one, I clung and hung, turning over in my mind the matter I had come to discuss with Rob, considering how Mithras might best be brought up, and wondering if I should do it before the sport or after.

"Does Juanito take them round?" said I.

Rob said he did, at least the cows.

"The bulls" he said "are to go into the ring for the first time."

"The bulls?" I said. "Are we extremely early?"

"There'll only be two" said Rob.

"Follow the cows" I muttered.

"What?"

"They follow."

I knew that would be a picnic.

" It's their first fight " Rob panted.

I did not think that was so. It did not seem to me that that was probably true. He told me the name of the ducal bull-breeder. A castilian title. It would be touch and go it was clear enough, if in this man's-town a chap was found to try it out with one of the duke's beasts. I was glad my arrival had been the cause of Rob's refraining from pitting his sensitive limbs against the rushes of these bison. Yet nothing was decided. If Juanito had been counting on him! If this spanish impresario must not be let down—Rob I could see was in no fit state to fight bulls.

I have sufficiently explained the nature of my pact with Nature. My friends the bulls would I trusted rout these modern Mithrases. But in this instance I suffered from divided counsels, because of the part Rob was to play. Rob was my good friend. But some sixth sense I had told me in confidence that Rob's view of the matter was not at bottom so very different from my own. He was more like the original Mithras I felt certain, than he was like the modern matador. He had been ordered to kill the bull no doubt. Or he considered that he had been instructed to kill the bull. But it went very much against the grain, as in the case of Mithras, of that I was positive. *At heart*—I could have sworn it—he was *not* upon the side of Man! He was like me, a parent of Leviathan. But that he would, very naturally, make it his business to disguise.

As we got off the box, I thought I would touch upon Mithras. It was time I put out a feeler about Persia. At all events I might broach the subject. So I dropped a hint.

" Do you feed upon the bull's sex? " I asked him, quick and offhand—a *by-the-way I had forgotten to ask* sort of a question.

"No. Do you?" he answered at once, without a shadow of hesitation. He gave me a swimming side-glance as he hooted back at me. I looked at him keenly as I stalked along. But I was quite unable to penetrate this mist-screen he put up, or to get behind his struggling smile. Did he know or not?

"I am not a scorpion" I said, flashing a searching bull's-eye look at him, worthy of a better detective.

"I'm not one either!"

And that was all! That, as you see, did not get me very much farther! At that I left it for the present. It was impossible to say if he had genuine cult-interests or not. He might have them and keep them dark. He might of course take his orders from the sun (nothing he had said ruled that out). On the other hand it was quite on the cards that he didn't. (He pretended of course to be a free-lance—the reason for that was obvious. And it might quite well be that he was.)

We went back to the family in the square. Val observed out of her piglike sparklers (set so close to her snout) her ladyship's snooty consort-to-be, side by side with this quite respectable-sized Gossip-Star. A Star, granted, not all the heavens!—but well *on the map*, of the social *planetarium*—really *quite* worth writing home about. She watched us approach with a grim satisfaction. Things were shaping very nicely! At this very moment were we not all of us making history (for what is History after all but a lot of Gossip, and of course how much more so, vice-versa!).

Old Val did not venture to speak to me, lest *too* snooty a snub should seem to reflect upon her "Gossip" status adversely, and perhaps even make these people think she was in fact some penniless impostor I had just picked up. Her ladyship must walk warily as yet.

Rob was worrying lest Juanito should be depending on him all the time. So that he should not rely on him he ought to find him and let him know the situation. We got up from the table. Rob was worried. We left the square. We started hunting about between the two bridges and then beyond the second bridge. He said it would do if he told him when we went to the circus to take our seats. He would tell him then he must get a substitute—he would, he said, not go in to-day. But I felt he would if Juanito was counting on him. I did not really think Rob meant to go in but I wished we could have met Juanito, then the matter would have been settled at least.

Rob McPhail was lightly clad in white sports outfit. All he had on as a matter of fact was a white sports vest, white canvas trousers and espadrilles. Rob sticks out his chest when in sports or summer undress. Rob knows perfectly well what he's doing. If he sticks his chest out he knows he is sticking his chest out. If he would pass anywhere for a very business-like second to a boxer, as he would, or one of the crowd that 'walk on' in the bull-rings (as daring as the matador) *he* knows that—he has no pretentions to being a star or killer. He is "no Prince Hamlet" as another ultra-humble poet has disarmingly put it about himself early on.

Rob McPhail is of our scottish stock. That may go for something. But whether or no it is the *bred in the bone* business at the bottom of it, the likeness in our respective ways of feeling (on a number of points) is exceedingly marked. I am astonished at the likeness. It is on account of this I value him so much I think. I feel towards him as I should towards a brother.—Now like myself Rob is an actor—he is the artist in action. He purges himself daily in make-believe. I am the man-of-action incarnate. So is he. But I *act* at being in action. And he too! What man-of-action has not? Lord Nelson was a famous *actor*. Any ship's rating in his fleet was the common or garden 'man-of-action' was he not—such as *I* am not to be sure (not 'man-of-action' in that brutish sense). I am not a brute. I am *conscious* of my actions. In a word, I am a Behaviorist.

In order to secure continuity to one's actions (and intermittent violence is but the affair of a dumb animal) so that one's actions may not be the mere rush of the excited bull nothing more—so must cunning be brought into play. I have my share of that quality. Mine is the roughest of finesse. But it *is* finesse—admit that or not as you please. —Even that humble adage—*He who fights and runs away, lives to fight another day*—it describes the *science* of warfare, does it not, as opposed to its empty-headed heroics. One must *retire*, from time to time! One must continually *reculer* in order the better continually to *pounce*. One cannot just fight and fight and fight—that soon conducts to the cemetery. Yet to *fight* is as essential as the drawing of breath, to the man-of-action—that is what m.-of-a. means I conclude.

Fighting and running away are not here in question—neither Rob nor I are of the stuff that is ever likely to show a clean pair of heels. (We are not fugitives—we are *pursuers*.) Rather it is a question of the category of action selected (by the man-of-action become conscious, and therefore *actor*) and the terms upon which one engages in it. And in that we are nothing short of siamese twins, he and I. Our life is a permanent *mensur*. (Did I lose my leg, sir, in a *mensur*? No sir, I lost that in a *massacre*—that is another story.) In pursuit of the solid sensations, we have suddenly found ourselves engaged in Faujas—beginning in the great nearby port of Marseilles, though *Duty First* is still our watchword. We are now in the company of that famous opium-eater, the big word-workman, we are together with him, in quest for the Solid, we touch it with our finger-tips, we are actually *above the melée-to-be* inhaling the same cubic feet of atmosphere as the nostrils of the actors, or were just now, the dangerous quadrupeds. We are the togaed ones laughing (of the senatorial caste, the great Freed-men) above the death-pit of the circus—we are if anything Neros who go down into the Mortuary playground, hedged-in by gladiators, we are the ones whose thumbs are erected or depressed. *We* scorn the reality. *We* are not animal! In fine it is that. Whatever we may be, we are not one of the fools that bleed and die. Or if we bleed and die, we do not do so to childish ends—we do so to some lofty effect.—We do not succumb in football matches!

But we are far from any mortal combat: following Rob, we observe him to treat Action as if it were a bull. That is how Rob comes to be a filibuster, and he knows it. Still you can guess I did not want this man who was one of the best of poets to swap his laurel-crown under my nose for the oak-leaves of the gladiator and perhaps get a *cornada* for his pains. I should consider I had a malefic eye. That's why I said we'd go off and see if Juanito was in the other square. In this shadow-play it was my duty to draw him off the bull, not with a crimson cloak but with muffled calls. (What man can be sure there is no evil in his eye? No man can be certain that his eye is safe.) *Duty First* was the slogan of the hour.

A gladiator Rob looked every inch of him—and he is nearly as tall as me—he advanced with his chest stuck out pretty bonily, seeing all the alcohol (not too much for the health but for the athletics yes) he puts away and I asked him about his espadrilles, to distract his attention—he was too intent, it seemed to me, in his reverie of action (he had smelled the bull) and I disliked this dream.—Not that I avoid the drug-sniffer. *All* poets smell to me of ether!

"Do you like espadrilles?" I asked, while I scanned their frail canvas.

" What these ? " and he shuffled to show where they were.

" Haven't you to be born with espadrilles on your feet like the silver spoon in the mouth I feel. Else you never can count on—in the way that you must have to in the ring—would not shoes be better ? "

He looked down, over his white-vested prominent chest, at his espadrilles. He stalked forward, sure-footed.

" Don't they ever burst ? "

" No " in a soft muffled pant Rob softly responded, looking down over his chest again confidently at his feet. " I find them all right."

" I believe canvas and rubber shoes would be better."

" I like these."

" Or leather sandals. They are the best. You must have leather, to be quite safe."

He had another look over his chest at the espadrilles.

" No " he said " I prefer these. I think these are the best."

" I've had espadrilles burst." As I leapt off a sand-castle on the Bay of Biscay as a spade-and-bucket architect of eight—but I saw he could not help wondering what manner of foot had been left to me (on the surgical side) to so strain to the bursting-point a french espadrille !

At that moment we were entering the second square and Rob turned round and looked after three men who had passed us.

" That's Juanito " he said.

" Who ? "

I was frankly a bit surprised. I saw three very stout smart figures in city clothes waddling airily away. The one in the middle with the conspicuous rings and super-shiny spanish footwear, he was the showman. It had been Juanito.

I turned back, we halted a little.

" No I'll tell him at the ring " said Rob. " Let's have a drink."

I turned back again towards the second square. I suppose Rob hadn't seen him, I had noticed him only in passing, I caught the guttural rattle of Spanish. I looked back uncertain of what to do and Juanito disappeared round a corner, gesticulating with his enormous gilt-stomachered Corona.

So we went to the urinal ; it stood out in the square, which was packed full of great thick clusters of moving morons, as some people I am sorry to say would call these excellent folks. Over the tin waist-high urinating-shield we watched a dance. The dancers pivoted deftly round the urinal, taking some time to get round, which was badly placed for public dancing. At a wooden trestle-table beside the urinal we had a *Fine* or two.

Duty First ! I said to myself (I was Humph's envoy. I would carry out *my* side of the bargain).

" When one says a ' bull point ' in business parlance " said I " what made them choose the sign of Taurus do you suppose ? And the Bear ! Why *the Bear* ? "

I cast my eye up in the direction of the meridian, and fixed it upon Sol Invictus. That was a pretty broad hint ! All in vain ! However much he tried, Rob could not look so obtuse as I can, but he gave the blankest grin he *could*.

" Good Lord Michael ! " he said. " I don't know, is that the Stock Exchange ? "

I ordered a further *Fine*. Next I asked Rob if he could cash me a cheque as I needed five hundred francs until I got a letter from a bank, and he thought that could be done at another café, over the bridge. So we went there : the place was at the other end of the town, near the bull-ring.

We passed Berbers on the way. Afterwards I remarked that no Berbers came to the bull-play. If there had been any killing they would. But it was a decadent make-believe this show from their standpoint, of their French masters. There were none there at all, though there was a very large settlement.

" You are fixed in Faujas " said I " for the present."

Rob said " Yes."

" It's very nice " I said. " It's quite off the beaten track."

He did not gainsay that.

" I am going to Persia " I told him.

For Rob, coming from the East (he was born in China, where his father was a Customs Official in the service of the Chinese Government) that was merely taking coals to Newcastle. And of course I had at first to represent this as a purposeless trip. He looked at me dimly.

" The wildness of the Turcoman Mountains " I exclaimed " will recompense me for the years spent in London." I knew this was utter nonsense, but as one filibuster to another—well he could read between the lines, to use a bookish phrase.

Rob stuck his chest out, in its skin-tight white vesticule. He stuck it out and held it there.

" London is awful " he said. " Well, as you know Snoots I never go there any more than I can help. I have to go, now and then. I'm glad to get back here."

" You like this all right, that's the main thing."

" Yes, I've got my family and my boat."

He gave me some details as to his fishing arrangements. His brother-in-law and he worked together. He told me how they fished.

" How would you like to go to the Afghan Mountains ? "

" The Afghan Mountains ? Is that where you're going Snoots ? "

" I think so."

" Good Lord. I've never been there."

" Doesn't the great girth, height, the solitude of those great mountains, Rob, remote places for us, does not that make you wish to wake up in them as I am going to? To be out of the civilized routine for a spell—to have a giddy tête-à-tête with a thousand foot of precipice—what the balloonist would experience, if he could stop in the clouds a week, or the airman, if he could anchor upon his wings? "

Rob knew that I was talking through my hat—he joined in with a smile at the superb presence of the approaches to Pamir. He took stock nevertheless of the frowning clouds, in the mental distances, with a professional eye—an asiatic eye—a filibuster's eye.

" Good Lord the Afghan Mountains! I can understand Snoots you liking—when do you go? "

" Tomorrow."

" I've always lived there. Not the Afghan Mountains, I've always lived in places like."

" Yes."

" When I was a small boy I often stopped up in the ——" Rob mentioned a very big chain of chinese mountains evidently—their name was not familiar to me, I have forgotten it.

" They are just about like the Himalayas " he said. " They are very big."

I said I supposed they were, and I understood that he did not want to go to the persian mountains, of course.

" Good Lord " he said, " you know Snoots mountains are all the same to me." He beamed filmily sideways, out of his moist slant eyes of swimming green. " I like Downs " he whispered huskily.

" A down? Not Sussex. *The Downs!* "

He nodded filmy-eyed. His favourite mildly uplifted sheepwalks—I knew of course they were just his nonsense.

" Sussex. Or—Lincolnshire. It's green I like. A meadow—a field! I never saw a field till I was——"

" When? Hadn't you really?"

" Not properly. When I first came to England that was the same thing to me as what you are speaking about, the mountains."

" I see that. But height—girth—solitude!"

He nodded at solitude.

" Since I was a boy I'd seen nothing but!" he said. " Whereas *a blade of grass*! Mountains! I'd always seen them. The East is full—there are millions of mountains."

" How enormous Asia is! It is an enormous continent. It is the biggest I think."

" Very big." We laughed at the Dark Magical Giant I was going out to visit. " You know when I first came over, the *grass*," he said, he grinned at all the grass he'd seen. " Good Lord I couldn't believe my eyes! If I was going anywhere——!"

" You'd go right up on the Downs now. I can see that —the Himalayas are nothing. Grass! Having always known the Orient——"

" Always" and as an after-thought, a low rumble " Asia."

(Since a child, always to have been familiar with Asia!)

" Good Lord!" he said. " A little lawn!"

GOOD LORD A LITTLE LAWN!

" It's just the same with me!" I meant of course the opposite.

" It must be."

" Show me an eagle!" I cried.

" Ah!" he panted.

Muffled, he panted at *eagle*, the film on his eye.

" Transport me to a glacier!"

I lifted my arm towards the ice-caps—the White Hell of Piz Palü.

He stared stonily forward. He was remembering the

Dark Magical Giant perhaps. Upon whom he had turned his back. Let us hope so.

" There are the Himalayas " I said, and Rob nodded. There were the Himalayas it was perfectly true. I mentioned a british Daily—there had been a report of Himalaya research expeditions.

" The ice-peaks " I said " were curling like crests of dragons. They were twenty thousand feet above the world. The tongues of silver virgin rivers stammered and thundered—there were boiling mists ! "

" Go on ! " he smiled at me, we smiled together, at all these romantic misunderstandings of the status of the mists of those mountains, and the illusions of scale. I thought of the twenty-foot tank in which the marine engineers provoke a tiny tempest, testing the model of the super-liner, with a view to banishing sea-sickness.

" Thatch and meadow are not for me that's a fact " I shouted.

" No ! " He gave his low thick hoot.

" I'm not off with an old love and on with a new. My first love was a wilderness."

" I don't like them much " he said—he soon now would turn his back on the thatches.

" I wish I could always live in the company of the most magnificent objects."

" I understand that ! Good Lord ! " panted Rob husky and hurried, sticking his chest out an inch or so more—a magnificent object.

" Life by contrasts, that is one thing. All the same—to take at its proper value a palace, why have to be sitting in a pigsty ? Not for me at least."

" Good Lord of course not ! " Rob exclaimed. " You can dispense with that."

" A green english field ! " I laughed : " there is nothing I love so much as a Wiltshire meadow of course—but a

Wiltshire meadow in its prime—the Old Prints of such places." Rob's Far Eastern eye saw only the green grass growing.

"I like them."

"Besides McPhail you are here. Where are your british pastures ! "

"I don't know. Nowhere. I don't know Snoots."

He hung his head.

"This is neither the Vicarage Lawn—Sweet Auburn Loveliest Village of the Plain——"

"I know." He kept his eyes fixed steadily ahead but he was thinking *Auburn of Goldsmith was an Emerald Island Pasture.*

"Nor yet the snows of the mountains of Asia."

"Good Lord no ! "

"You—you will not have contrasts."

"No."

"You are perfectly right ! "

"Yes " he panted eagerly, affecting eagerness. "This suits me Snoots."

He looked out upon all he surveyed : we looked about us slowly together (I wished Defoe could have seen us) like cows abruptly endowed with consciousness.

"I can live here cheaper, it's much cheaper than I could anywhere else."

"You have been here for four years : or more."

"Good Lord, yes, more than four."

"You have your business " I raised my voice " and you have your business."

"Yes my little boat."

"You are satisfied."

"It's a little beauty—I have my boat."

"It's peachy is it ! You must show me."

He paused on the eve of a weighty remark.

"This is a compromise here " he said very quickly,

looking away " between civilization and what I was used to when I lived in China."

There was of course nothing more to say but I am a great incorrigible talker.

" It is a compromise here " I responded therefore.

" Yes I don't want to live in London or Paris " he replied. " This is a compromise."

" You don't feel the call of the wild any longer ! "

Rob panted out a husky laugh—this fisherman snapped his fingers at wild life : how right of him, how right of Rob !

" The Lawrence-Kipling sensations do not ever visit you ! "

" The great open spaces ? "

" The same."

" Never " the Veldt-dweller, the Tundra-man, laughed in his beard-that-was-not-there, very softly and muted by the imaginary hair. " The Open Spaces Good Lord never —that's because I've always lived in them it may be that."

" Why yes."

" Once you've seen as much of the Great Open Spaces as I have Snoots ! But the opposite, Good Lord the Bloomsbury Life is worse than all the rest ! Much worse."

At the word " Bloomsbury " I spat, and he spat—I to the left, he to the right. I knew his famous aversion for Bloomsbury, and I spat in sympathy.

" No Bloomsburies have ever shown up round this man's-town yet ? "

We both looked round, to spy a Bloomsbury, but there was absolutely no one in sight.

" I've never seen any " Rob said.

I saw none.

" The Riviera is not unknown to highbrow London. Is this Riviera ? "

" They never come here " Rob said: and he stuck his chest out, to give emphasis to the fact and we dropped that subject. In any case, *Delenda est Bloomsbury.*

What Rob McPhail said about this being *his compromise*, that made a big impression on me. I saw with a startling clarity the silhouette of Asia. And do not all those without exception who are not stupid, do they not wish for a compromise, one between the impulsive poles of their natures? Was it not the bull-fight typified Rob's? It could be said he compromised with spanish bulls. How sensible! The vast steppes of Persia might of course be mine. In fact however I understand that as to my poles they were not at all so fixed. And of course to hell with Persia!

Returning to the family circle in the square we found one of the two children (Rob's) holding a shred of india-rubber in its dejected hand: upon the floor, beneath the table, a burst balloon. This catastrophe did not involve a disgraceful orgy of grief: the children, even, of poets catch some of the severity—you are not a poet's child for nothing—they must have something about them of persons born and bred in the mountains. (Later no doubt they move away, seeking the compromise.) Val (childless as far as I know) had attempted to convert this typically simple occurrence into a rather more emotional one, in order to curry favour, but without success. She was being unsuccessful as we arrived, and I gave her a hard look, which soon made her leave the child alone.

We moved off to the bull-fight, two by two. A door of dangling reeds, in the corner of a one-cornered court, parted before Rob—who had stalked aside—this was mid-way to the bull-place—and I followed.

The cane-tendrils disparted tinkling—upon Rob's heels I passed suddenly into a cold dark medium, within which I found him crying like a sepulchral cock, " *Bonjour Madame Eugénie!* " After the bright street the café in which we stood, he rooster-necked, and tall shadows both (Rob like a filmy sports-ghost, filmy-eyed) was as black as a crypt. We sank down at a marble slab, quickly swallowing lemonades, tasteless sparklets. Meanwhile the five hundred francs I had asked for were forthcoming, Madame Eugénie had the sum in her drawers.

In this unexpected gloom, created by the shopkeeper against the provençal hot season, refreshed by the column of cold bubbles sinking down my heated body, I thought I would pop the question. Rob seemed quite prepared for me and looked up at me suddenly as I was on the point of speaking.

" Rob ", I said. " Does Mithras interest you ? "

McPhail heaved up his delicate head a little from its dejected droop, or *poke* as it is called : a trick of his, I think an acquired characteristic, suggestive of a head so ponderous that it tired him to hold it erect.

" Mithras. Yes " he hooted in an unearthly way, in the obscurity, and I cleared my throat as Captain Cooper Carter would have done before proceeding with this difficult operation, to lassoo a poet.

" Your interest in *bulls* " I stammered. " The patron of the torero."

" Yes but it's not in that way. That's not the reason."

" Don't you think so ? You know best."

" I'm only an amateur."

" Still you know that Mithras—it's a persian rite to which we are going."

He smiled with a discouraging indulgence, at these far-fetched visions of a scrap with a bull, for an afternoon's sport.

" Not exactly is it " he said, with that distinguished politeness, at least in his dealings with me, which is so marked a paradox in this great filibuster.

" Certainly ! " I answered very stoutly—that was my

commission. I would not have the persian claims, however politely, put aside. " Absolutely persian. Juanito simply would not exist if it were not for the God of Unending Time ! "

" Go on ! "

" Certainly not ! "

Rob croaked gently at my side, with a little malice, as he thought of Juanito, and the blast of rancid smoke of his gigantic Corona, waiting upon Chronos. I laughed too at that.

" I suppose it is " Rob said : " the Romans bred the bulls differently—so they say, have you read old De la Rieux ? I think he's a charlatan ! He was here last year."

" No. Some one like you ought to write a book of the origins. There is no good book."

" I ? "

" Why not ? "

" Nothing is known " he said, rolling himself a cigarette in the dark.

" On the contrary " I protested eagerly " a great deal ! You know ' Sol Invictus—Bull Unsexed ' by D. H. Lawrence ? "

Rob smiled broadly. He would not say he knew " Sol Invictus—Bull Unsexed ". He would not say he did not. He bit his lip, where there was a particle of the loose tobacco, and grinned.—He regarded research into his favourite sport with disfavour, that was evident. There was nothing doing.—But when a Kell-Imrie says yes he means yes. So on I went.

" I have been getting up all about Mithras " I told him. I yawned. He did not follow suit.

" Go on ! " he said, trying to look as obtuse as me.

" He was a sort of generalissimo."

" Good Lord ! "

" In the proto-iranian pantheon he was the generalissimo of the Lord of Light. He was a *military* angel."

" A military angel ? Good Lord Snoots ! "

" His cult was a glorification of Action ! "

Biting his lip, Rob nodded.

" Mussolini ! " I said. " Action ! "

Rob looked quite placid—as if he had expected *Mussolini*.

" But what is of particular interest " (I felt like an auctioneer—this was a grim duty I had taken on) " in Persia *even to-day* there is ritualistic bull-fighting ! Mithras. The solar myth ! "

McPhail upon this immediately took an interest, or affected to, I was of course not sure which. My sixth sense—very active in the artificial gloom—told me all the time that he took absolutely no more interest in bull-fighting than I did. Or if not anything so radical as that, his interest was of such an opposite nature from the romantics of the french gang of *literati*, that he could be said to be indifferent.

Rob would have been a ' Pater ' in the old Mysteries —the highest grade of all. But the cult changed as you went up. The uppermost hierarchies had another religion in fact. This bull-fighter I was with was like a ' Pater ' who had gone back to take a hand in the celebration of the exoteric or vulgar rites, and made a habit of it. The cause remained obscure to me, I could not fathom these practices. So I suppose I invented a framework to account for it, I have told you what I felt about him. I felt he was definitely *pro-bull*. This was in some way I could not define. I am certain he was an antichrist at the heart of the sport. I could see him as a horned priest of Ahriman, sacrificing, in the moonlight of the persian desert, some screaming human victim, to the great astronomical Bull of the Zodiac.

You will no doubt say that because I liked McPhail I attributed to him my own anti-human propensities, and conferred upon him a romantic complexity he does not possess. However that may be, I was inquisitive regarding this to me obscure point—whether McPhail was in fact a messenger of Darkness, crept into the fold of the *Taurobolium*: but at that time *Duty First* thought I—we will talk sense afterwards!

" One of the things that takes me to Persia " I said " is to investigate this cult."

He opened his eyes wide—when I clowned he clowned, it is as if I were opening a magic closet inch by inch, and he considered that he was required to express amazement.

" Go on! " He gave a routine-hoot.

" That is so. Why don't you come to Persia Rob and try your hand with the persian bulls? "

" I couldn't leave my boat."

" Why not? You could leave it for a month."

" I don't think I could. I should have to get some one —it would cost too much."

" I am the bearer of a business-offer."

" Who from? " He grinned.

" Captain Humphrey Cooper Carter, the Literary Agent."

And I gave him the figure mentioned by Humph, as an advance on royalties, for a Mithras-book, about persian bull-fighting.

" The boat would be the difficulty " said Rob.

" That could be easily got over " I said.

" I'm not sure " he said. " But I'll talk it over with Vieuxchange."

I was amazed. I had not expected this of all things. He might after all come to Persia! I did not know whether to be pleased or sorry.

He got up.

" Let's go " he said.

" I am delighted Rob! " I said getting up too. " Will you really come? "

" I'll talk it over with Vieuxchange."

He looked at me mistily and with a queer cock of the eye, as he tightened his belt up. He knew perfectly well I was not delighted at all. I suppose I showed I was taken aback. In his lack of all appearance of resistance he might almost have been taking a leaf out of my book.

BULL-FIGHT—BOUCHES DU RHÔNE

DOWN AT THE bull-ring the Faujassers were flocking up. Juanito was invisible. We went to our seats, climbing upwards, tier by tier, the lake blandly ruffled with a brisk breeze behind us (it was an open circus) the sun shining and wind blowing. Val was in great form, she had the orthodox ladyship-look already, she was extremely pleased with the way things were shaping. She sat bolt upright on the rough plank trestle, prepared for the bull-fight: she made the whole affair look on the spot like a scene in a Gossip Column. Madame Vieuxchange and she were chatting. She only looked once in my direction, when Rob and I first came up. She had decided no doubt to behave as much as if we were strangers as possible, and imply that that was just our way of going on!

Mrs McPhail talked about her brother's life in Leningrad (he is a great supporter of Communism) and bathing in the lake. I glanced into the bashful black violet of her eyes and saw her brother sitting there, a little threatening, a heavy-weight Saint John of Leonardo (too broad and high for beauty but with a perfect head) frowning sweetly upon a magical wilderness—I saw him as he was when I first knew him, at the wedding of McPhail, my first introduction into literary London. He is so much more sombre now. And I gave, to this bolshevik Saint John, Laura McPhail's pre-nuptial dimples. "Is he going back?" I asked—this was to Brazil, for his groin-trouble (I believe the scorpion had been after this bolshevik Bull of Bashan as a matter of fact).

Laura McPhail had no idea. I saw Brazil. Twice I asked if he was going back. (I saw the Andes—I thought of the Persian Ranges. I kept up my rôle instinctively of purposeless tripper.) The orchestra had been coming in but by this time the circus was full. The high planked palisade surrounding the sanded ring (which had a diameter of perhaps forty feet) became the inner limit of a *paséo* : the flappers of Faujas—whose bottoms proved so irresistible to Berbers, who made cataplasms of their palms for these sex-appealing swellings, even in the market-places—these budding mothers-of-men were somewhat insignificant at close range. As a race, of course, the French are not anything quite enough : as was so plainly seen by Stendhal. In that respect they are dwarfed by their more primitive neighbours. They are pulled through by their civilization. You do not have to be any one thing very intensely to be civilized—it is essential in fact *not* to be.

A procession entered the ring. In provençal folk-dresses, a troupe of young men and boys lined up, flanked by a band of pipes and tambours that came with them. These had played them in, in fact. Mediocre athletes of medium size, the dancers gave a mildly seductive exhibition : very vigorous they were, at the moment of a measured climax, but never jumped very high, and when they twirled like tops they lost their equipoise quite easily. Bland spirited and pleasant like the music, the dancers withdrew with their period-band. The deep and narrow tambours beat peacefully as they marched out.

The circus orchestra immediately struck up and Juanito entered dressed as Charlie Chaplin. With him was a young man in pale blue, with a pill-box to match upon his head, strapped beneath a mild fat chin, anything but a martial bull-fighting figure. He may have been an out-of-work folk-dancer. Juanito shuffled and stumbled jerkily forward, waggling the Chaplin moustache. Strutting and tripping, he made the tour of the ring and sent the children into fits with his farces. Good old 'Littlejohn'! After a short while a thin small cow was released from the gangway leading to the menagerie. Provided with a scarlet cape, Juanito strutted forward towards the scampering cowlet. To the strains of *Toreador*, the great bull-song of Carmen, he advanced with a ramshackle chaplinesque fanfaronade. The highly trained dwarf cow lowered its head and charged. Juanito executed an elegant veronica. This continued. As he warmed up to his work, Juanito tossed off Charlie's victorian black frock-coat. He kept up an uninterrupted waggle though, with his dicky and a cravat to match his postiche lip-tuft. So in vest and black clown's pantaloons, he provoked the cowlet and played the heavy matador. With all the grand airs of a Bombita Chica or a Montes he advanced to the assault. The dutiful cowlet gave a low. The little cow almost laughed to see such sport. —Juanito or Littlejohn's arms were fat and short. They wobbled as the veteran cow-puncher went through his serio-comics. He had for great staring landmarks two prominences about the axis of his person—one fore, one aft—emphatically advertised. When he strutted towards the cow, then it was the one in front that offered a tempting target. But often, when only a few feet off, he would face about, bend down, and plant himself on all fours. *Then* it was the backside one that would come into play, and be offered to the animal. At this impolite unveiling of its patron's poop, the puzzled little cow would stand at gaze for some minutes, quite at a loss. It was the nearer the better, as far as this cow-gazing interlude went—sometimes the cow's nostril touched almost the showman's huge feminine spanish stern.

This was the pantomime of the Rump and Horn. So it might have been catalogued. The nursery bellowed with obscene gusto. For of all God's solemn handiwork none convulses so utterly his laughing creatures as the *seats* that that Old Craftsman so quaintly thought out, when he contrived our bodies—as odd as the velocipede. Lust and laughter both pursue the tail-piece, that is so—so that Berbers forget themselves when close up behind White Ladies, and so that a spanish clown can grow fat upon the laughter his buttocks provoke.—But all this to the bovine world is a closed book. The little cow would hear the roar of the audience : and certainly he could see its master's face, reversed—observing it between the podgy arch, as he straddled, upside-down. But the animal was merely bewildered. For it obviously could have no clue to the sense of these mysterious practices. What mostly happened was that it would turn away, after a minute or two of stupid staring.

At first the audience thought, for perhaps ten minutes, that the showman might possibly be hurt. The responses of its laughter had a ring, a snarl, about them. There's many a slip 'twixt the cup and the lip. *The buttock that goes often to the horn at last is spiked!* Or *Never say live—while there's life there's hope of violent death.* Juanito might strut up to the little cow just *once* too often! Who could tell?

But when it had become perfectly evident that the cow was no more dangerous than a performing dog, Juanito proceeded to take the extremest liberties with his docile horned plaything. *Its* shrivelled and somewhat untidy little stern came into play as well! There is big money in bottoms—and then most animals have the double advantage, as jesters, accruing to that happy thought of Nature's—*the tail* in fact (so waggishly suspended upon the stern-piece). That is worth its weight in gold. The stout showman got every ounce out of this magic wand : forsaking the upright position, upon all fours he crawled beneath the cow's stomach : he chased it round the ring still on hands and feet, butting at it as if he were a little cow himself. He seized it by the horns, forced it to the earth, and rolled over with it in the sand. Then at last he mounted upon its back—but stretched at his full length, facing its hindparts. Then came the *pièce de résistance*: he would fan his perspiring face with its limp tail which served as a handful of mesquite grass or a palm-fan.—The squeals of the little Faujassers caused this so-called Charlotade to have all the air of a London pantomime matinée, transported of course under the posh skies of sunny Provence.

I do not care for spanish bull-fights. I prefer as I have put it in a nutshell the bull to the men. Gulliver to the Lilliputians—the lion to the horde of beaters—the badger to the pack of hounds—in brief the One to the Many (whatever be the condition of the One) in such cases by nature I plump for the first—and should have done even if the *Pequod* had not opened my eyes. It takes me back too far upon the road to the monkey. I should prefer a Lewis-gun to these lances and swords. The former gives better the measure of the genius of man—the Lewis-gun. (Of man the individual—I mean Lewis of course.)

But this mock bull-fight—this chaplinesque Charlotade, after the great mithraditic rite—can be (of course as the mood takes you) exceedingly grim. It's a " let down " both for the bull and for the bull-baiter. As all things of the " Charlie " order (" Charlie " and Charlemagne representing the two antagonistic extremities of the great White Millennium) in essence it is obscenely destructive. Two real horns of a real bull should be introduced one fine afternoon behind the insulting rump of this new quadruped. Mock-matador, upon all fours (in this instance the showman Juanito) this rump should be put in its place. A fine chiselled horn should be plunged into each offending cheek of it—at all events this is how I always feel when called upon to assist at the bull-pantomimes (the Children's Hour of this once religious circus) especially in Spain. And Rob feels the same.

" I don't like these Charlotades " said Rob in his gruff purr. " They oughtn't to have them."

Rob is enough of the true gladiator to resent it. He'd said it, it was what *I* have just written—as to the horns in Juanito's buttock, that is my personal gloss. It lets us all down, then you and I and all of us are let down!—But Rob and real *officionados* especially. All should boycott the Charlotade. Men should cold-shoulder the facetious showman. It is the last insult of man, that animal-gone-wrong, to the Great Master. I said that to Rob. He endorsed every word of it. Rob nodded, but he hooted in my ear—

" Juanito used to be a *banderillero*. He was one of the best. He was never a matador."

" I hope he was not " said I.

You had to admit a good deal of skill went to the Harlequinade. Even to play with a tame cow in that fashion must have puffed Juanito. He knew its right from its wrong end (*coma non!*) and how to dance away from its little horns.

However at last the thing ended. The folk-dancers filed in, and composed a banal frieze, such as might be encountered in the principal saloon of a luxury-liner. The pipes, as wistful and graceful as an elegant tapestry, filled the air with the old songs. The strengthless drums returned to their delicate beatings. The porcelain figures come-to-life performed their musical-box gavotte. There were several dances. After that they went off again, the drums faintly rolled; then there was a considerable interval.

Rob went off to speak to Juanito. It was all right he said when he came back. His brother-in-law said that Jaffa could be very hot in August, so a man had told him. Val and McPhail's wife had discovered several mutual friends who were pillars of the Bloomsbury Pubs. Rob's sister-in-law had a talk with me. A one-legged Englishman in the crowd waved a hand. I scowled at him. Rob went to talk with a cop. Soon the band started, and rather suddenly a large bull dashed into the arena. It had leather sheaths, I think they were, upon its horns. Several men went over the top, jumping down into the ring from the palisade. Some took up their position in the *burladores*, the shelters provided at regular intervals : some stood with their backs glued to the fence. Several made helter-skelter sorties, and the bull chased them back to the shelters.

This is a good game and quite different from the Charlotade (also from the Corrida of course). According to its rules the player has to run quickly across the arena, and as he passes the bull stick in the cockade. I have been told that there is no cockade, but only a piece of string, but this I simply do not believe. I am sure I saw cockades, though that does not matter at all. It is foul to stick in the cockade in any other way—the bull-baiter has to be running across the ring when he does it. It would be quite easy for instance to stick it in when the bull is hanging about and looking at you and you are a few feet away from him—quite easy for a good player certainly. Nothing is easy naturally with a real bull for the novice. But the dash across the ring is essential.

A half a dozen men were engaged in attempting to do this. With the first and second bulls they drew a blank. A third bull was brought out. So far the show had been a particularly poor one. A young bull-tender took a hand. He was one of the personnel from Spain. He removed his jacket, then advanced upon the bull, and used his jacket as a cloak. But from this moment the stalemate ended. All was soon in the utmost confusion. The bull was dashing about and a dozen people were after him in all directions : several caught him by the horns, three to a horn, and a serious wrestling-match took place. The prime-mover hung on to his head. Then the bull shook them off all at once, all but the latter. This was the signal for the climax. In a moment with a great shout from the audience the bovine young spanish stable-lad was flung down upon his back : the bull butted away, it hammered him with its padded horn, it put its head to his ribs and pushed, while all the others darted round the animal to rescue their champion.—The audience bellowed with delight —it distinctly heard ribs cracking, it had seen a smear of blood. Dust, thuds and shouts. It was the *rouée* of the Bosche at Mons for the french crowd, or else Verdun. This was too much for Rob. He and Vieuxchange were in the ring quicker than it takes me to write it, as the old novelists said. As they went over the top there was a great ovation. Very popular in Faujas both one and the other. It was a great shout of local welcome.

The critical rumpus which obtained when the bull was on top of the trampled stable-hand, with all the rest of the bull-baiters hanging on to the poor toro's tail, horns and ears, and handing him upper-cuts, pinches and scratches —this terminated when the bull withdrew. The young bull-expert rose, groggy and stiff, badly buffeted. He fumbled about as he tried to push a broken rib into position, limping to a *burlador*, and from there was assisted over the palisade by a score of eager hands—everyone was aching to get their hands on him and find out where he had been injured. Like a big doll he came back groaning over the top and limped off to make his apologies to his boss for his accident. But the dart was in the bull—which was dancing about, so a cow was sent in, and the bull and cow left together, side by side, hustling each other. The game was won.—One point up to mankind. I yawned my head off and Mrs McPhail apologized for the dullness of the sport.

When the next bull appeared Rob and Vieuxchange dashed at it, the latter roaring like a lion or perhaps a prehistoric ox. This puzzled the old bull. In Spain I suppose he had been accustomed to people speaking softly to him and calling him "Toro!" in a coaxing undertone—not bellowing like a Bull of Bashan, in short stealing the bovine thunders, as McPhail's partner did. He was at a loss how to take this new move on the part of mankind.

After a little sparring, with quick rushes here and there (Rob stalking it like a cat and offering it a frail fawn-like body to toss, but side-stepping its responsive attack, old hand that he is, and other sportsmen scuttling about, and causing it to be highly confused but not apparently very angry), two flying forms catapulted off from the sides of the arena simultaneously.—Both bodies had had the impulse to dash at the same time it appeared, both darted out from the opposite sides. In one of them I recognized Vieuxchange. They sped forward at a great allure: the bull gave way a pace or two, its eye on both at once. Both veered in their headlong course. They collided near the bull and tumbled upon their backs, rolling in all directions, stunned but as active as blindfolded eels—they saw stars I am sure, but the threat of the bull turned their night into day, or perhaps it was the Sol Invictus.

Both sprang to their feet, but both forgot the bull instanter (who looked on in suspicious astonishment, at these cryptical somersaults of a hostile species whose actions at the best of times were shrouded in considerable mystery as far as he was concerned). A violent altercation took place on the spot. Vieuxchange who was as much bigger than the other fellow as the bull was bigger than him, *he* was the more extreme. He was the biggest man on the field. He had the biggest neck in Faujas. I was convinced that an alteration in the nature of the spectacle was about to take place—that the bull, in fact, finding itself neglected, would probably walk off in a huff, not even waiting to be shepherded off by the cow, and that thereupon a boxing-match would begin, in place of the much-advertised bull-fight. Far more amusing! Already I had stopped yawning and followed with some attention what was going forward. Rob and the other assistants in the ring approached the two angry figures, Rob stealthily, as if still he had bulls before him—though the bull had gone to scratch sand sulkily in the far corner. No blows were exchanged. The bull began to assert itself again. Vieuxchange and the bull were left alone. The man whom he had knocked down pursued with impassioned argument by Vieuxchange, was retiring. Meanwhile the old bull with its tail on high, swept round the arena, driving everybody into the *burladores*, against which he crashed his horns and then passed on. Still flushed and menacing, Vieuxchange walked back to the palisade. There Rob joined him. Both scorned the bull—Vieuxchange merely roared when it approached him and the bull fled.

The other people in the ring were half-hearted. They moved restlessly upon its periphery, sticking to the palisade like flies upon a curved strip of fly-paper, and if they got unstuck their flights were short. Here and there some continued to scuttle no distance at all with darts clutched in their fingers (or was it in fact pieces of string? it does not matter) but they could do nothing with the bull. Everyone saw that, and it had to be returned to its pen without anyone having so much as scratched its neck with a dart.

Almost at once an undersized but frisky animal charged out in its place. Now Vieuxchange and Rob who had been talking together in isolation looked up. I saw them both look up and Rob made a remark to his big brother-in-law. Rob moved off stealthily to the left, his eye fixed upon the quadruped. There were several feeble rushes from different quarters. The bull started chasing the swiftly moving shapes and thundering with his head upon the stockade—upon spots he had marked down as being occupied, though of course by the time he got there there was nobody left to crush, there was nothing.

I could not tell you how it happened, but the next thing McPhail was running like a lamp-lighter, in an unexpected spurt, in his characteristic crouch, without looking to right or left.—Suddenly I remarked him, no one else was watching him it seemed to me. I suppose they had got used to this. Then I saw he was running towards the stationary bull. I knew in a moment what he was going to do. Would he reach it, thought I, before it moved? Because a moving bull cannot be as good as one standing still—I knew nothing whatever about the sport and to be frank it bored me more every moment. It was plain enough all the volunteers were duds. But McPhail got up to the bull and he seemed to tap it as he passed. The next thing I knew everyone was applauding and I noticed something waggling upon the bull's neck. Rob had actually popped in the regulation dart and it had stuck. I was astonished. After the poor performance of the rest how could one expect this to come off, seeing that Rob was out of sorts, but there it was. The bull was beaten—its neck bled and it charged. A swarm of crest-fallen bull-baiters came out of their holes. They scampered towards it, I suppose they meant to try and plant their darts in its neck on their own account, side by side with McPhail's. What he had done looked effortless and it may be it was, but nobody had a look in any more—for the bull, tossing its head angrily, let fly with its horns right and left, and inside a minute it had cleared the arena.

Rob and his brother-in-law at once climbed out of the ring together, in a slow-motion hurdling, neck and neck, and for me the bull-play was done. The delighted partisan Faujassers received them with open arms. Rob was the hero of the moment. A girl gave him a big red flower. He smelled it, then put it up behind his ear. A rain of hearty hands fell upon his shoulders. Rob, smiling mistily, ploughed his proud way through the handshakes, and Vieuxchange was voluble with several old fishing-chums, scowling back in the direction of the ring.

Vieuxchange and Rob climbed up beside us and I levelled a flat-handed blow at his spine and Rob tumbled smiling into the place beside me.

" That was a good piece of work ! " I said.

" Not bad " Rob panted.

" It looked to me first class."

Rob shrugged his heaving shoulders. He was congratulated with a velvet sparkle of softly smiling eye by Mrs M.

" Those people are from Mestique " said Rob, wiping his brow, which like a dirt-track-rider's used to the helmet was baldish, cropped and in a word masculine.

" Who ? " I asked.

" All of them " he hooted, panting and muffled. " They all came over together."

" They're all together."

" Yes " said he plucking the flower off his ear. " They are drovers, they come from Mestique. They've been here before. They divide the prize if they get one."

" How much is the prize ? "

" Not much. It's a hundred francs I think. They didn't like us butting in."

" When ? "

" They thought we oughtn't to have gone in."

" Is it open to anyone ? "

" Yes. Good Lord yes."

" What was the row ? "

"Did you see that? Good Lord yes! They were ten to one!"

"There are about a dozen."

"Vieuxchange ran into somebody."

"I saw that. Was that it?"

"They were always running into us. One got in my way—I kicked him. Yes."

"I'm not surprised."

"They wanted to keep us out. Old Vieuxchange was angry. That was one of them."

"The one he?"

"Yes. They say we're fishermen. We ought to mind our own business."

"I don't see that."

"No. But they are always like that. They say fishermen oughtn't to butt in—it would be the same if they came and entered themselves for water-sports."

"Don't they ever enter for water-sports?"

"They do as a matter of fact."

"Well!"

Both Rob and Rob's brother-in-law are star performers in all water-sports, and at the regatta of the fishermen. They are known as such for miles round. As far as Toulon Rob and he are household words. I myself have seen photographs of Rob with an immense water-spear, upon the prow of a periagua-of-state, fitted like a roman galley with a fighting-platform aft.—This was a natural objection. Was it not a question of calling?

"I shouldn't like to be knocked down with that lot" Rob told me. "They wouldn't help you." He eyed mistily and with detachment the drovers in the ring beneath us. "Good Lord I shouldn't like to have to depend on them if the bull was on top of me! They'd do nothing. They didn't like it when we got in."

"I'm not surprised. *Chacun son métier*. You fish."

" They didn't say anything."

Meantime the fresh bull went on riding roughshod over the contemptible drovers from Mestique whose paltry and ill-conceived efforts proved useless against the big bustling horned creature. There was racing and chasing certainly, but the bull's neck remained intact. Juanito must have been satisfied with Rob and it had been a good gate, that was the main thing. No wonder his shoes shone and rings glittered upon his muddy fists!

But I yawned unrestrainedly. I hit out at my yawning mouth in big bored buffets. Rob was silent. I know it sounds melodramatic but I could not help asking myself afterwards whether these big, pointed yawns of mine played any part (what I really asked myself was whether they were not *the whole thing*, at the causal end of the nexus) in the unfortunate occurrence which followed so closely upon them. Who can say? However that may be, Rob grew silent and restive: and as if upon a concerted signal (there must have been some semaphoring that I didn't see) Rob disappeared through the fissure at our feet (we were only sitting upon an open trestlework of horizontal planks). At the same moment Vieuxchange sank through the planking too. I looked down and saw them rushing through the forest of struts and piles.

" Are they going in again?" I asked his wife.

" I don't know " she said.

Then there was a loud acclamation. Over the top the two local hearties hurdled once more, back into the place of combat—to the great cantonal and municipal satisfaction of the patriotic Faujassers. I felt uneasy at once. I confess that it occurred to me that the retirement of Rob and his brother-in-law (as a protest against their treatment at the hands of the unworthy drovers of Mestique) and now their spectacular return, might have been planned. Afterwards I was assured that that had not been the case. When they left the arena the first time it was their intention to stop out for good, that seems established.—But Rob might be driven now into a showy action, in order to show up the ineffectual drovers. It might go further than the petty circumstances justified. Could it be possible that loud applause would go to his head? Frankly I did not feel certain enough to say *no—never!* at that moment. Whereas the bull looked competent, and bovinely bright. I yawned. But this time I yawned under the pressure of an unpleasant presentiment.—This was very bad indeed!

I never remember very clearly what happens in such cases as this. I am so bored by such things that I can scarcely bring myself to look at them. If I look, my eyes send me up on purpose the most stupid images. Pictures arrive all out of focus, and I just throw them back where they come from—and forget them the next minute. It is like listening to a lecture or after-dinner speech on Empire Free Trade, Birth Control, or the Progress of Missionary Work Among the Arabs. One cannot shut one's eyes it's too much trouble, but they just do their photographic business all wrong like an idiot with a camera—nothing adjusted, the shutter working slow into the bargain and giving a duplicate image. That is of course why it is that I cannot positively swear whether they use darts or pieces of string, though I'm pretty certain it's the former.

Everyone present except myself got something out of it. They hoped our two brave champions would at last get trodden on by the bull or get an eye poked out with a horn. I alone (and Rob's wife) had no interest in the matter. Really on my side this was for no sentimental reason. I simply am very bored at bull-fighting—at street-accidents and trench-warfare. My public spirit, after that (in sharp contrast with the *private* sensationalism of the average majority) rather snootily perhaps hoped that as fine a word-workman as ever stepped would be preserved intact to us to continue to versify.—Still a dark suspicion did, I will confess, visit my mind, to the effect that McPhail was not quite the great guy I had believed him to be. And I who had bestowed upon him every satanic advantage! I was depressed.

Having done far more than could be expected of him, as a foreigner and a fisherman, why put himself out to go in again? This last minute come-back to capture further applause—must I admit it?—irritated me a little. Yes, I yawned because I was *bored with McPhail*. His five minutes upon the sanded mock battle-field of man-versus-nature should have answered all the requirements of the case. At bottom I still felt perfectly confident that he really was a priest of Nature and only shamming antagonism to her horned representative. But my credulity was being strained a little. Therefore when he took a fall, in rather a risky attitude, I will confess that I laughed. I could not help myself. (This I passed off—his wife had heard me—by saying heartily "The old bull has missed him again!" or something like that. She accepted my explanation graciously, with velvety-violety good-sense and good nature.)

There was an almost interminable sprinting and counter-sprinting. I have no recollection of the details of all that, I paid no more attention than I should to the uneasy play of the shadows of leaves upon a whitewashed wall. (Either in a garden or indoors of course, wherever leaves can play.) I got so sick of it that I opened my mouth as far as it would go—it threw my nose up at right-angles to my forehead—shut fast my eyes, and began a long-drawn shattering yawn. *When* were they going to take this tiresome bull away and put it back in its travelling-box or Noah's Ark and play God Save the King?

The crowd roaring woke me out of this. It was a big *Ah* like the spectators' response to a cleverly-kicked goal in a football match but much more uneven. I opened my eyes quick and looked down into the circus. McPhail was alone. He was lying at the foot of the pallisade. The bull was standing over him or I think he was, the bull was there too, in any case. Even from where I sat I could see a dark blood-splash upon the wood of the *barrera* above his head.—I was amazed. So much so that for a moment I could do nothing but sit and look as if perfectly indifferent to what I saw. I was indifferent as a matter of fact.

I rose in my seat as did everyone else and yelled out fiercely at the drovers, who were not hurrying themselves to go to McPhail's assistance at all. (It was as he had said it would be in such a case.) Vieuxchange was trampling towards the bull and waving his arms—he had been gossiping over the circus-wall with a fishing pal when it happened I was told, on the hither side of the arena beneath us. The bull turned upon Vieuxchange and the latter lifted himself up on to the pallisade just clear of its stupid head-on rush. It crashed beneath him. In a gymnasium Prize-day-pose (a recumbent levitation) he clung on, high up, out of reach of the animal, his foot-palms flattened against the wood. Almost he was a colossal Titian Venus, or Danae awaiting the shower of sovereigns.

I got down as quickly as I could and amid a constant uproar made my way round the outside of the ring to the place where McPhail lay. As I came up he was being lifted back over the top. He was unconscious—it appears that the animal had dashed his head against the pallisade. His face was covered with blood, it looked swollen and disfigured. His usual pallor was horribly intensified. One eye seemed badly injured.—Everyone was shouting out at once, everyone was as pleased as possible at what had happened, all but me. I was in fact very angry indeed. I nearly knocked several of them over as I pushed in.

Vieuxchange was white, he was alarmed. He was roaring out for a doctor. McPhail was very badly hurt.

In the narrow lane behind the pallisade it was like a football scrum in a Marx Brothers pantomime, of clownishness for the big babies of Broadway—I have never seen anything like it—no one had really anticipated anything half as good as this—and that too right at the last moment, just as the band was tuning up for the finale. What a *soufflé en surprise!* What a ' Mystery Port ', at this indecent taurobolic communion! Every man-jack of the Faujassers wanted to have a good squint at the bleeding victim. I straddled in front of him at once, to block out their dirty view—when I was, in my turn, nearly knocked over by a new arrival, a whiskered burly angry person. I stood my ground but I was no match for him. As I staggered about I trod on something soft, it was the inanimate chest of Rob. I clutched Vieuxchange and saved myself from falling, but just as I was turning to knock down the fellow who had charged me in this way, he said he was the doctor and that if I didn't mind he'd have a look at Rob—*if I would be so good as to step off him!* I said hotly that I wasn't standing on him and that if I had been it was no business of the bloody doctor's—I pointed out further that it was him who had caused me to tread on him, and added a remark or two that never come amiss regarding the general run of the medical profession, and last but not least my private opinion of his face. Mrs McPhail who was now kneeling beside Rob (holding his head up from the ground), asked me to allow the doctor to have a look at him. Of course I stepped away. I fell back.

I cannot say that I stood back with anything but a bad grace. Indeed the attitude of *everyone* towards this ridiculous accident irritated me. The wife's kneeling figure (a fatuous Hollywood wax-work it seemed to my irritated senses), the physician's frowning fuss as he made his examination—I made *no* exceptions! One was as bad as the other. Seeing that beforehand they had all consented to it—seeing they had assisted to promote these pretty results—since they were part of a system of life committed to encourage such meaningless energies—their behavior (looked at from the standpoint of the profession of 'Behavior') was only calculated to induce contempt. —I am not ashamed to say that as I stood back *I yawned.* Frankly I was *bored!* I should not have been the man I am if I had been anything else.—This was very bad indeed.

As to McPhail, it is perhaps an odd thing, for which I cannot entirely account. But I experienced practically no trace of that human sympathy that was I suppose to be anticipated (in a European). The War accustomed me to death too much—that may be it. It is the first thing that occurs to one. I had seen too many bodies lying in that strange and rather irritating repose, mutilated but peaceful —the debris of attacks. Or I was too brutally indifferent *to myself.* Which? (How important the self is, upon that I need not insist.) I was very indifferent. Of course I understood that he was dangerously injured. But he was *the same* dangerously injured and lying at death's door perhaps, on his back (to all intents and purposes an absentee) as he was up and about, conscious and functioning.—That is perfectly good 'Behavior'. That is absolutely routine Watson.

There is another thing to be taken into account. My feeling as regards *men* does not allow of that kind of tender human sympathy. I should experience it for a dog, or for a woman: but as regards a man I felt a series of *other* things, quite inappropriate certainly to the gravity of the occasion—such as criticism of his action for instance. No more tenderness visited me than any of the rest of the onlookers. And yet I liked McPhail very much indeed—

I would have protected him from their sensational prying had I been able.

I leaned back against the *barrera* or whatever they call it at Faujas. I heard a voice at my elbow. I turned my head slowly, not at all relishing the sounds I heard, and at no pains to disguise that fact.

" Is he badly hurt ? "

Fresh, starch-collared and chappish, her sympathetic Ladyship was there, with discreetly-corrugated, pink-pigmented, brows, of ladylike concern.—This was the last straw—it was old Val put the finishing touch.

" How the hell should I know—go and look for yourself ! " I shouted almost. " Haven't you eyes in your head ! Am I the bloody doctor ! "

McPhail was taken back to his house outside the town. His driver with whom he had an account and drove with to bullfights inland, or into town at Marseilles, was sent for. He was taxied quietly up the hill and carried gingerly across the fields.

Leaving old Val at a café (with her lips compressed into a bitter-prunes-and-sour-prisms grimace of waspish resignation—she longed to be in at the death, of a Gossip Star, if gloriously-gossipish death there was to be) where I could find her again, I went out to McPhail's. The doctor seemed to think the internal injuries might be bad (he had to say that in case they were) and the shock had been very severe. Any fool could see that. I went in and looked at McPhail, dragging my noisy leg to deaden the thumping sound. His head was in a big swollen cocoon of clinical turbaning. It was an impromptu creation of the artistic physician. (The fellow could always get a job with an ornate ex-sultan as turbaner-in-chief to the coquettish exile.) I told Laura McPhail that we should stop down in Faujas for that night at a hotel. I would come up, alone I did not need to tell her, after dinner for news.

I was now far more concerned than at the time of the accident. In the heat of the moment I am one man, as a mere reflecting-machine I am another. But what I can say is that I felt sorry for *nobody*, unless it was myself. I was only very depressed indeed.

Was I not confronted with something like an amputation? Rob seemed pretty bad. I saw a friend—namely a talking-machine like myself, attuned to me in an exquisite manner—valued by me above most men for a number of years, slipping away into the inscrutable backgrounds of Time. The Dead Land—Proust's *Temps Perdu*—came up into sight upon the horizon, I saw its frowning ranges (not unlike the supposed outlines of those towards which I was moving, to the westward of Hindustan) and it began to make the afternoon which had just passed over our heads—or beneath our feet—*unreal*: to me the unforgivable thing. It made my yawns above the amphitheatre unreal, the sterile exercises of a tooth-proud puppet. It gave a spurious look of half-truth to the patterns of bulls and men, in the academic sanded taurobolic circle. The roar of the crowd took on a hollow sound as well, as it came back to me—like the unsubstantial vibrations in a shell. It tainted (for an instant only) everything, even the present, with its unnatural airs.

McPhail lay lifeless, secretive and urbane—alien to us, in full possession as we were of our external clock-work senses. He was growing accustomed to the spell of that cold and distant Universe of Absence, into which he had been hurled—as if lifted up in the leather socket of a magical catapult. He had a fever of course, and he was hooting away to himself under his clinical turban, his robot head-dress, as I awkwardly withdrew, heaving myself along. As the door was gently shut and I found mysel in the passage-way outside, I felt ridiculously depressed—as the door closed behind me, as I thought forever, upon that softly hooting voice. The last words that reached me as I got out of earshot were *Good Lord!* That left a nasty taste in my mouth. It suggested pathos.

" You can't get a nurse can you, it's a pity " I said, leaning back against the wall, putting on my hat.

" Yes."

Mrs McPhail it seemed to me had the unpleasant fatalism of the highbrow-lady. Why should I use this disgusting term of canaille abuse—' highbrow,' the moronesque sneer of the Babbitt—in connection with this delicately chiselled bedmate of Rob's! But I was incensed, I recognize, against the very thing that made her a worthy wife for Rob. Is it because I like a bit of straightforward *Behavior*! I suppose so, it was that. Certainly from the standpoint of *Behavior* Laura was not behaving at all well, but deliberately obstructing her reflexes. She allowed stimulus after stimulus to pass without response. She had put down shutters against the stimulating assaults of Fate. (We call that to be *fatalistic* for some reason—what we should say is to be *fate*. For it is usurping the indifference only appropriate to God.)

" Is there no one in Faujas, I suppose not " I said.

" Yes the doctor is sending somebody. Tomorrow he will telephone to Marseilles for a hospital nurse."

" And a doctor, I hope."

" If Rob isn't better."

I looked hard at the ground. What it was next my painful duty to refer to went much against the grain as you can imagine.

" That woman who came here with me " I muttered.

I stopped, wondering if it was really necessary to proceed.

" Mrs Ritter ? "

" Yes Mrs Ritter " I said, with a great visible reluctance to utter her name, and distaste, and an apologetic grin, to clinch the embarrassment.

" Oh yes " she said and waited.

" Valerie Ritter " I said—with what answers for a blush with me, a slow sheepish-blinking of the eyes.

Laura McPhail looked at me but said nothing, and my confusion turned into a professional curiosity as I gazed for a moment into the stoic depths behind her glances—whose eyes, monotonous, immobile, violet-velvet had that *pool-quality*—which it would take more than a dead hero (struck down in a fifth-rate bull-fight, defending the sportive honour of the Faujassers to whom he did not belong) to ruffle. I saw all this and my eyes stopped their winking and with a slight smile I said—

" If *she* can be of any use ! "

It seems *unlikely* doesn't it ? my eyes politely remarked, and hers, with a faint sarcasm—a sparkle in the violet-bed, so to speak—replied civilly that she thought so too, so why take the trouble to mention it ?

" No thank you Snooty " she said " it will be all right. We can manage I think, until tomorrow."

" She was a V.A.D." I felt myself in duty bound to insist. " During the War " I added (as if V.A.D.'s existed at any other period !).

I looked up as Laura's sister, a big blonde woman, with pale blue eyes, came out of the sickroom, with a sort of staring, strained and stormy look. This woman's lack of *fatalism* appeared to me at the moment I must confess as affected as her sister's mastery of same. These people can feel nothing, I thought, that is about the size of it. They can only mimic feeling, or control of feeling. (I agree that I had not the leisure or the presence of mind to examine myself. But we always examine ourselves last—is that not the case ?)

" Mrs Ritter probably knows " I said, looking after her sister, " better than anyone on the spot how to do what is required."

Laura McPhail shook her head, moving a little towards the front-door, and I followed her.

" We can send for the doctor if necessary " she said.

" You are quite right " I said.

She smiled, standing in the doorway, as I left, raising my hat.—Why did I raise my hat?

The café was in a state of the most robust animation. Everyone was talking about McPhail. Against all expectations, Great Britain had provided the *pièce de résistance* upon this day of festive excitements. The Bull-and-the-*Anglais* turn was by common consent the trump of the whole hand, held that afternoon by the hospitable Faujassers. All the drovers had left in a body in the omnibus for Mestique. They could not help thinking that it served fishermen right: they saw no reason to regard it as anything but poetic justice: if they went back with empty pockets it was because a lot of fishermen had got in their way.—The ring was obviously far too full! What with the Faujassers and the Angleesh, the Bull and the authentic bull-fighter never got a chance of getting near each other. And when one meddled with what didn't concern one, one was apt to get one's block knocked off! *Que-voulez-vousing* the Mestiquians rolled away in the coastal omnibus.

Meanwhile Mack-phi-eel I heard on all sides, especially on my arrival: for the crowds in the square, in and about the main café, knew that I was the Anglais, his friend with the wooden leg, who had been with him all day.

The patron rushed after me, as I painfully diminished the distance between Val and myself, and half the swollen holiday clientèle crowded after him craning their necks. I stopped and faced him.

" How is he—have you seen him! How is he at present? " shouted the patron.

" How is who? " I coldly enquired.

" Why *l'Anglais* " he said " how is he, who was injured at the bull-fight! "

" He? Oh he's fine! "

" *How!* Fine!—He can't be fine! "

" Can't he? If you know all about it why do you ask me? "

" He was very dangerously injured. How do you call him? Monsieur Mack-phi-eel."

" Did you think so? "

" Think so! I saw him poor fellow. I saw him. I was there. I saw you too."

" I thought I'd met you before."

" Yes. Is he better—have you seen him? "

" Oh yes " I said " I've seen him. He'll be down here in a minute."

" How! *Down in a minute!* It's impossible! Down *where?* "

" Here in the café. He said he wanted a drink."

" *Here!* "

" Yes. You are an extraordinary man! Don't you want him to come? "

" Yes but—— Of course I should like to see him. But no. He cannot have recovered as quickly as all that! "

" He has amazing vitality."

" Yes but look here! Hold on! I *saw.*"

" He was preparing to come down for a drink when I last saw him."

Scowling at me, the patron withdrew.

Val sat bolt upright—her interpretation of the correct pose for the best Lesbos *chic*, sipping (without straws) an

Après-le-dip, more or less. At her elbow was a pack of one dozen picture postcards of Faujas de Saint Riom, eight out of the twelve of a bull-fight scene.

" What was all that about ? " Val asked, cool and efficient.

" Nothing. Absolutely nothing at all " I said, sitting down.

" How is McPhail ? " she asked with a firmness I regarded as an insolence. " Didn't I hear you say he would be down here in a minute ? "

" You did."

" But that is not true is it Snooty ? "

" Of course it is not."

" I thought not."

" Mob hysterics bore me very much, that is why I answered that fellow in that manner—more especially when a friend of mine *en fait les frais.*"

" Of course."

" McPhail is very badly hurt."

She pricked her ears up and waited with a correctly morose expression for more.

" We shall have to stop here in Faujas tonight, it's a bore " I said.

" I took that for granted."

" Oh you did, did you ? Well *Duty First* is my motto."

She settled back a little on the chair, a little less a bird of passage. Her body was still starched up to match her collar, it would be a wild exaggeration to say she made herself *at home* : she did not *unbend*, she rather gave the chair-back the benefit of the doubt and lightly leant her spine against it like a walking-stick.—I could see that she was very pleased—things were shaping *very* nicely !

" Can't I be of some use Snoots ? "

Great minds think alike, thought I, but did not answer.

" I did work in a hospital during the War ! " She gazed

at me for a moment, and then very delicately dabbed her pussy-cat muzzle with a pocket handkerchief the size of a postage stamp.

"I know—I thought of that" I said.

"I am quite *ready*."

"I suggested it."

She looked pleased.

"But they don't seem to require help" I said. "They became particularly independent when I mentioned you."

I was glad to be able to tell her this. She bridled bolt upright, faint wrathful undulations disturbed her stiff profile. This was not so good, evidently! A frown gripped her upper face. She only possessed one frown, a *studious* frown, for all occasions. So she looked rather *studious*—as if face to face with a bad cross-word puzzle, and became slightly red in the face.—Silence, thank God, supervened.

After two *Sevillanas* we went over to the hotel. We looked over it, as if we wished to buy it, but the people insisted upon referring to Val as if she were my wife. I put a stop to that.

"Voyons, Madame" I said, "si Madame était ma maîtresse——"

"Oh Monsieur qu'est ce que vous dîtes là."

"Vous n'avez pas pourtant eu le toupet de prendre madame pour ma *femme*!"

"Eh quoi—comment saurais-je donc monsieur——"

"Allons donc, vous plaisantez Madame."

"Au contraire c'est Monsieur qui plaisante!"

"Si Madame était ma putaine à moi, je ne me gênerais pas vous savez, je vous le dirais bien! Madame est une dame Ritter, née MacAuliffe."

"Mais parfaitement Monsieur."

"Donc, puisque je ne la baise pas, il nous faut *deux* chambres à coucher!"

"C'est parfait Monsieur!"

"La meilleure sera pour moi. L'autre sera pour Madame Ritter."

"C'est entendu!"

"Je m'appelle le Baron Imrie."

"C'est parfait, je vous remercie Monsieur le Baron!"

"Je suis capitaine. Nous partons demain matin de bonne heure."

"Très bien mon Capitaine!"

"C'est à madame que vous présenterez la note demain matin. C'est madame qui paye."

"C'est entendu, c'est à madame que je ferai apporter la note, Monsieur le Baron!"

"Parfaitement! C'est toujours les femmes qui payent."

"Mais bien sûr, monsieur le capitaine a bien raison, n'est-ce pas Madame!"

"Madame ne cause pas le français—elle est Boche."

"Tiens, madame est——"

"En effet. Au revoir Madame!"

"Au revoir Monsieur le Baron et bon appétit! Au revoir Madame, au plaisir."

I never knew how much French Val understood. Now as we left the hotel she said—

"What were you saying Snoots?"

"Nothing."

"Did you say I was a whore? *Putaine* didn't you say?"

"I said *putaine*" I said "certainly."

She raised her eyebrows, and looked *studious*, as I admitted that. And she walked with a great missish daintiness over to the café, thoroughly pleased with me for the first time that day.

It was a pretty awful dinner that we had. Val was distinctly angry. It was about McPhail. I did not mind that. But her silence put me in rather an awkward position, or that was her idea. Few words fell from her lips, but they all tended to bolster up the suggestion, in word or manner, that I was deficient in feeling, if not actually heartless. Unable to defend herself, in fine, she addressed herself to the defence of the bull-tossed Rob.

At first I refused absolutely to speak about McPhail. She was of course dying to gossip, but I would not allow her to. At last however I had to say something, if only in order to drive the old girl off that lay. So when she mentioned Rob *directly* I closed with her.

" Mrs McPhail told me that you and Rob McPhail had been friends for a long time " she said.

" That is so " I replied " he is one of my best friends, and then ? "

" Nothing Snoots."

" Nothing ? "

" You'd never spoken much about him. I didn't know."

" There are lots of things you don't know."

She ate her rabbit with a finicky fixity.

" You will never know how much I like McPhail. You do not understand such things, so why talk about them ? "

As the result of the events of the day, my snootiness was greatly in the ascendant.

" Thank you Snoots. I don't know why you say such things to me."

" Much as I like him however, I came here upon an important mission, not just to see him."

" A mission ? "

" Yes. Captain Cooper Carter wished him as you know to come to Persia."

" Oh yes. I had forgotten."

" Yes and *I* should have forgotten I suppose—seeing how badly my friend has got himself smashed up ! "

" Don't quarrel with me Snooty, please darling."

" But my motto is *Duty First*."

" Don't be absurd Snoots."

" It is. Duty First. This accident is extremely unpleasant. But from the standpoint of Duty what it means is that McPhail cannot come to Persia, that is all. That point is settled. We have no further business here."

" But you knew he would not have come to Persia in any case ! "

" That's where you're wrong. He had consented."

" Had he really ? "

That was rather a blow to her. She was missing a Gossip-event of the first magnitude. *With McPhail in Persia !*

" Yes " I said " but as tomorrow is Friday, we have to meet Captain Cooper Carter——"

" Oh Humph ? "

" Yes, oh Humph. I won't trouble every time to say."

" I don't really see why you should."

It was required by the etiquette of ' gossip ' that a name should never be used if a slang-name was known, at first hand or hearsay, by the speaker. I had deliberately offended. I stopped a moment and grinned silently at her with my teeth.

" Well go on " she said.

" The air-service Naples-Athens-Damascus-Baghdad only functions on Saturdays."

" Oh is that the way we're going ? "

" Yes didn't I tell you—yes ! "

" No Snooty. I didn't know."

" If we miss it on Saturday, early in the morning, we have to wait till Saturday-week."

" Is there nothing in between ? "

" Nothing. That would be impossible."

" Of course, we mustn't miss it if we can help it."

" We have to leave here therefore tomorrow evening."

Val said nothing.

" Yes. Meanwhile do not let us have a competition as to who is the more capable of human emotion, you or I. That would be more than I could bear. *Duty First* is my motto. Recollect that Val old fruit ! "

So I shut her up on that subject. She went on being offended of course. I left her after dinner and went out again in a taxi to Rob's.

The stars were shining above the semi-venetian avenues : in Faujas de Saint Riom the port was everywhere. There were the masts of the painted pirogues beside the restaurants, every street almost was a sort of quay. But of course there were no houses of any importance or beauty, and the bridges were of metal, and painted slate-blue like a british cruiser.

The doctor was there when I arrived. McPhail was no better, but was in a high fever. I left at once and returned to Faujas. All that was left of the Fête was intoxicated by this time. Val and I drank a beer in silence. She asked no questions. I volunteered no information. After that we gloomily retired, as it is called, in indian file—I was first. On the landing when I turned round she looked at me particularly hard and I could not help giving my Butler laugh. I knew what that scrutiny meant. She was seeking to convince herself, however much appearances might be to the contrary, that she had ' Got me in The Bed '. I decided to humour her and followed her in. There I remained, with Madame la Baronne. She was very pleased, needless to say. And this did not tend to cheer things up in Faujas de Saint Riom.

Next morning I went up to McPhail's about ten o'clock. He was slightly better his wife said. He was sleeping. I explained to her in some detail how it was we were compelled to return to Marseilles immediately. The aeroplane that was to take us to Naples left on Saturday. We must go. At this news her fatalism attained the proportions of apathy. If I went or stayed it seemed all one, I could not make it out. It was quite impossible to gather if she was anxious about Rob or not, and I did not bother.

I shook her by the hand, I wished her sister a polite good-bye. I raised my hat. I hurried away, back to my taxi waiting at the end of the paths that crossed between the fields to the high road.

THE UNIVERSE OF ABSENCE

POSTSCRIPT TO BULL-FIGHT—BOUCHES DU RHÔNE

SINCE WRITING THE above account of my visit to Faujas de Saint Riom, I have received a telegram to inform me that McPhail is dead. I like McPhail—it would be absurd to alter the tense—I *like* Rob.—Yet *is* it entirely absurd? Is any dweller in the Universe of Absence in fact of the same status as if he were permanently settled at the other end of the Earth to ourselves (still writing us letters and even having a chat with us by radio-telephone)? Frankly I think not. I am a snob about life, it would be possible to say I suppose. I actually find, upon examining it, that I *do not like Rob so well* as when he was not dead. Is it possible to dislike the dead, because they are dead? I think so.—Therefore after all I will say "I *liked* Rob McPhail." I do not like him quite so much now, because he is dead.—There is nothing more to like! After all, I could not *marry* a dead person! So how could I *like* one, really? But once I *liked* him very much. That certainly is beyond question. To me that is valueless. But it is *true*.

Was I not sorry to hear that McPhail was dead? Certainly I was not. I experienced no emotion of that order whatever. Why should I? But I confess I was *annoyed* with him for dying, or, if anything, that was the only emotion that visited me upon the receipt of this news.—No, it did not in any way interfere with my enjoyment of my abundant persian breakfast (the telegram reached me while I was still in bed).

In re-reading my account of his fatal accident it has occurred to me that, in view of his subsequent death, it may seem a little 'unfeeling', as of course it is. But I can at least add that nothing I have said there is a reflection upon McPhail. He died rather stupidly—but who amongst us does not? Of course, my growing dislike, I was going to say, but I should perhaps rather describe it as the progressive cooling of my attachment for this now permanent absentee, would tend to make me harsher in retrospect. If I were writing the same report again, I should doubtless be more severe at certain points regarding Rob than if he were alive. Nevertheless, I should not have to alter anything bearing upon his secret motives.

I still firmly believe that McPhail was secretly upon the side of Nature. I am as positive that he was an anti-man as myself. He simply, in the course of pretending to fight Nature (in the form of a bull), met with a fatal accident, such as might happen to you or me—anywhere, in the street for that matter as we ran to board an omnibus.

All McPhail intended to do (and I see that there has been some futile discussion in the Press upon this very point of his quality as a bull-fighter—and far too little regarding his splendid achievements as a poet), all he meant to do was to annoy the incompetent representatives of the human race, namely the Mestique drovers, and, in showing *them* up, to show up *us*.

Rob McPhail said to himself, "I will occupy the old bull with feints and sham rushes for the last five minutes or so of the performance, and prevent Homo Sapiens from scoring"—In the pursuit of this laudable, and secret, task, he met with an unexpected accident. He slipped on something. That is all.

I am not perhaps a good friend. It may be I am not a

good companion. The Shan Van Vocht, the snooty sibyl of the Gael—I can hear her grinding out her ceaseless imprecations, against all that goes upright—it has come now to be that! Within the twilight of my race's days, the hostile silhouette (once that of tradition, of the hated next-door neighbour) grows vaster beneath our eyes—but also far more impersonal. No people are exempt. Not *someone*, but *everyone*, has blundered! The Shan Van Vocht squats there calling Chaos about her—*as Chaos comes!* It is the soul of a defeated race, that nothing can reconcile to its unhappy lot—but at last it sees that not its next-door neighbour merely (a nation *tel et tel*) but that ultimately all mankind is responsible for its misfortunes.—And that blood of the cantankerous is in my veins, I am very much afraid. Expect nothing out of my mouth, therefore, that has a pleasant sound. Look for nothing but descriptions out of a vision of a person who has given up hoping for Man, but who is scrupulous and just, if only out of contempt for those who are so much the contrary.

PERSIA

EXPERIENCE OF THE Land of the Chrysanthemum—Tokyo like a rainy London slum, as it always was—had prepared me for the land of Mithras and Omar Khayyám not being exactly an Arabian Night's Entertainment. It was not. 'Entertainment' is indeed the last word to use. In the vast persian deserts, a continuation of *Arabia Deserta,* there are a few monster oases. These are the cities so-called. There everything, down to the doors of the bakers' ovens —the scarecrows, the barrels (I believe the gun-barrels too even)—their children's dolls and money-boxes—are made simply of *mud.* It is a mud-pie existence really. In the city where I stayed longest the inhabitants even ate mud. They liked its taste. But not I.—The houses, they too are all made of just mud. A large house is a chain of mud boxes (each room is conceived as a separate architectural unit, they are all stuck together one behind the other, about the compounds) with a cesspool beneath the middle mud box. The size of the cesspool will depend upon the time the people intend to stop in the house. They obviously cannot stop very long. Twenty years is a long time. A forty-year house, for instance, has a pretty big cesspool. When the cesspool is full the family simply leaves the house. It then falls to pieces slowly. Half of any persian town or village consists of abandoned mud dwellings. So half is always in ruins.—In the salt-steppes outside the mud-built 'oasis' nothing grows. Everything is as precarious and impermanent (depending upon the mountain-water of the pipe-lines of the subterraneous *quanats*) as a raft-life, if you can imagine it, at the heart of a hot monotonous ocean.—They get european goods up from Bombay and down from Russia. These are the wooden or glass goods. The raw material for all home-industry is mud.—All the time I was there I never saw a bull that any self-respecting matador would touch or even a Mestique drover consent to play with. I saw ravens and jackals galore—also hordes of disgusted-looking camels. Indeed the latter animals wore expressions of such fathomless disgust upon their faces that it is quite certain I am afraid that *they* could never be persuaded to engage in any rite which Man, in his infinite wisdom, might devise. (I liked the camels. I believe that the camel is my favourite animal—after Man of course!)

From the french air-port to Baghdad took four days, we made it in five, stopping up a day at Damascus. Four days Baghdad to Teheran. How long it took to go from Teheran to Yes I don't know. But we got to Yes at last, and there we lived for I should say two weeks. Quite two weeks—there was some hitch over the brigand. He had no guest-room vacant it seemed. Humph was very annoyed. He hated Yes more than I did I believe. We had been given a house and a fair-sized bag round the corner. (The latter word is generally spelt *bagh*, but if you can do anything with the *h* once you have said *bag* I can't. So I will just write it *bag*, as I pronounce it.) A bag is a persian garden. You lie on a persian carpet all day in the bag under a tree.—No one can see you lying in your bag unless they happen to be thirteen feet high (and I assure that no one is—if there ever were Genii of the Lamp in those parts they must many centuries ago have beat it) for the bag-walls are as high as that. So you can do anything you like in your own bag—with your own body that is and anybody else's, if you are feeling Omarkhayyámish. (But you won't be, believe me.)

I only once felt Omarkhayyámish in our bag in the fair city of Yes: and (I am sorry to be depressing) it was with old Val! I was reading a book that had a Dookobor in it. It was about an excellent man, who possessed every human virtue—he was a giant in the matter of his stature, but as gentle as a gazelle—he was liberal and friendly, honest in all his dealings. But in accordance with his religious principles—which exhorted him to enlist himself upon all occasions *upon the side of the Flesh* as *against the Mind*—he acted as a sort of *procureur* and was an enthusiastic go-between in all the "white slavery" activities of the Eastern Caspian. He would in fact 'procure' whole families of eligible youngsters in the same spirit as the missionary. As the latter procures the souls, so he would procure the bodies, with the same proud glee, and it was a source of constant bewilderment to him that his activities were misconstrued by the authorities.—I read her a passage or two from it, as we were lying under an apricot tree.

> "The Enemies of the Mind" I read, translating as I went along "are of opinion that the healthy, the honourable, the innocent, the inoffensive part of poor old Man, is his *flesh*. The flesh, left to itself, has no evil instinct. It has no trace of perversity. *Eat, copulate, sleep!*—such are the functions proper to it!"

Need I say that at the enumeration of the *second* of the functions in this admirably simplified life-plan, old Val rolled over my way. She made a gesture as if to remove my mechanical leg. I shooed her off of course.

Then I continued:

> "The prime cause of all human corruption is the Mind. The Mind is of diabolic origin. The Mind is completely useless in the natural development of our species. The Mind alone invents passions —alleged needs, alleged duties—which, contradicting in every way the gist of those occupations to which Flesh is destined, is productive

of troubles without end. Was it not the Mind that introduced into the world the genius of contradiction?—Of controversy, of ambition, of hatred. The Mind is directly responsible for all murder and homicide: since the flesh is only concerned to preserve itself—in no way to destroy. The Mind is the father of stupidity, of hypocrisy, of exaggerations of all sorts, and in consequence, of abuses and excesses which are generally attributed to the flesh—yes to the good old flesh, who is an excellent fellow, but easy to lead astray, if only because of a perfect natural innocence. That is why *really* enlightened and religious men must combine to protect this unhappy child (namely the flesh) against the seductions of the Intellect.—But from this it follows, *no more dogmatic religion*, please!—lest we become intolerant and persecutory: no more marriage, so that we may have no more adultery: no more carnal restraints (upon any appetite whatever) so that we may stamp out and have done with all those revolts of the repressed senses. And, last, but not least, we must decree the immediate systematic abandonment of all and every form of intellectual culture—*Kultur!*—oh what a disgusting occupation after all that is —only conducting to the triumph of every horridness—up till the present used exclusively, or I am much mistaken, in the interests of the Devil!"

Val was almost on top of me as you may guess, by the time I had finished about the Dookoboretz! We should soon, I could see quite well, be ever so Dookoboring an Adam and Lilith unless I nipped this piece of blasphemy in the blood.

"How perfect that is Snooty! What book is it? I liked where it said how *the flesh* gets all the blame for the vices of *the intellect*! That is *so damned true*! Isn't it?"

"It is. Would you mind not coming quite so close to me and breathing on my neck, it's rather hot in this old bag this afternoon!"

"I'm so sorry Snoots, yes it is hot isn't it. Phew! Who were the Dookobors? Rather Quakerish. Don't you think so?"

"No not the Quakers at all."

"No p'r'aps not. No *the Flesh* is not like the Quakers is it? I did like that about *the Flesh*—getting the *b'laaame*!" she baaed—and as I looked, in the hard persian desert-light, I could see the great yawning pores in her mobile upper lip, operating downwards like a rabbit's—coquettishly shooting up and down (pulling the pig's nose with it) in the manner of an india-rubber shuttle.

I laughed very heartily at that—she scarcely realized *how damned true*, as she had called it, it in fact *was* (that the Mind stood for the diabolical principle in this partnership!). For if there ever had been a *Menschenkind* who could be said to be the *Enemy of the Flesh*—the opposite of the old Dookobor—why after her very humble fashion it was certainly old Val. She stood for the most minor and disagreeable victories of Mind over Matter—matter being of course the simple-hearted, sane, generous, unaffected *Flesh*. As I laughed she giggled madly at the corner of my ear, the sparkling pin-points of her rapidly flesh-submerging eyes riveted roguishly upon me, only awaiting the bugle-call to summon her to battle (to make a Bed of the bag), the signal to fall to and be horribly matey—flesh-to-flesh as *she* thought, the reverse as I knew it to be.

Whether it was the eloquence of the Dookobor—*L'Ennemi de l'Esprit*—whether the effort required to translate it lying on my back, my powers of resistance lessened as a consequence—or whether it was just an effect of the natural *perversity* of the Mind (of which the Dookobor spoke) carrying its point, in spite of my flesh, I cannot say. But I succumbed to old Val in the bag, not long subsequent to the reading of the Dookobor passage. I confirmed—or did I not confirm?—the teaching of the Flesh Supreme. She can certainly claim that she has GOT ME, or once got me, UNDER THE APRICOT TREE. What an Eve to have provided for a persian garden of Eden!—the uninstructed may snootily exclaim—but really if you could only see a *bag* you would not consider that Val was so out of the way as all that.—Dust to the dust!—but also *mud to the mud.*

Mud to the mud—that is maybe a bit hard on the bag, and not fair altogether. There is a ripple in it—there is a gutter with some quite fair water, warm water of course. It is brought from the great hills that wall the deserts, a hundred, or perhaps twenty miles, beneath the surface of that scurfy saline waste, in a passage they excavate with their fingers in the bowels of the earth. They drop a well shaft into it every twenty yards.—There is no grass of course (there are no weeds even). There is none of that emerald green that the miniaturists used in their *See Persia First* book-plates and cartoons (not less lying than our poster-versions of sun-splashed Tor Bay). The mogul miniatures are a testimonial to the good quality of the mineral pigments that can be found by digging deep enough anywhere—as much in Lappland as in Khorasan, nothing more of course.—Faded potsherds is what you are reminded of, not well-preserved paintings—ceramics very much blistered far rather than dazzling cameos. The carpets that are brought in to take the place of nature do not help, of course, towards a less barren effect. One knows they were invented because there was no grass. Oh Dookobor, how right you are! No flowers having any punch in them, no leaves having any spunk—all is as dead as blotting-paper—therefore a simulacrum of absent nature is cooked up by untruthful man.—Often I thought of McPhail, his words came back to me. *Good Lord,* A *Little Field!* I thought I heard his hooting voice, as I was smelling a rose (in vain!) in Shiraz, and squatting upon a patch of spurious sward, of a cheap tissue, of a depressing bottle-green, in our fly-blown bag!

To say that Persia was a nightmare to me would give a ridiculously inadequate impression of the annoyance and sheer snootiness that it provoked in me to be compelled to dwell in Persia.—Over Teheran I shall draw a big black veil of silence more or less—except that there is simply nothing to draw it over. I daresay however I should have liked it well enough if I hadn't brought my two big puppets with me—or (worse still) if they had not brought me. But they gave me so much trouble that in the end I could do nothing but hide from them. Half the time I was in hiding. One of the main brothels hid me up from the egregious Humph on more than one occasion. When I was concealed in this way on one particularly bad afternoon, and I was being closely hunted by my indefatigable man of business, the incarnated JOWL of Old England came bursting and blundering into the room like a brutish bull-dog in a hardware shop, where I was hidden, bawling out—

"I say *have* you *seen* Sir Michael Kell-Imrie?"

"No sir!" said all the tartlets in lisping chorus, stuffing their handkerchiefs in their mouthlets.

"Where on earth's he got to I wonder!" in an injured bellow he enquired, looking very suspiciously at my favourite Shushani (yes *Lily*—for such it is, translated into the tongue of Pimlico!). "I can't find him anywhere!"

"Can't you Sir!" asked Shushani, who had the face of a persian angel though god knows where she came from—probably she'd drifted up as a white-slave of six from Gujerat—they called her Georgian—she was half-caste.

"No I *can't*!" he crashed, stamping about and frowning provocatively at everybody.

Kāfi stepped out from the cluster of women. Kāfi means simply *Enough*. It is a christian name given to a girl-child when the father and mother wanted a boy and have had *enough* girls. 'Enough' looked at him as if she intended to melt him down on the spot (and perhaps afterwards run him into a less ridiculous mould of her own choosing—

fashion him nearer to the heart's desire). 'Enough' had spent the night before closeted with him.

"I saw the Michael sahib making his way down the main bazaar twenty minutes ago in the direction of the Police Station honey" she cooed up, attempting to melt the Chin with her hot-stuff looks and waggling her blatant buttocks about as she spoke and pretending that her fat red mouth was certainly a delicious plum that would drop to the floor like a big globule of blood if he did not pluck it and swallow it, there and then.

"It's no use Kāfi!" he blurted out, getting red in the face "I happen to know Sir Michael is *here*!"

Evidently his chin watered for the buttocks of 'Enough' and if she went on swaying seasickeningly much more before him, Humph *would* be melting and wilting in one big slobber and I should be delivered by the timely intervention of Venus.

"It's no use—er—Kāfi" he almost wailed—waggling off, resolved not to be shunted off the stern track of duty by the monotonous grinding of an asiatic buttock. He pronounced Kāfi *coffee*, to make it sound more persian. "It's no use darling! I *know*—it's no use!"

If Humph had ever had the *taken-short* look before, he sure had it to the *n*th degree now—his knees were flexed at an almost bladder-bursting angle as I noticed.

I could see all this from where I was concealed. I had got under an enormous Bokharan camel-rug and several divan coverlets, of which there are such quantities in all persian houses, for everyone lies or squats instead of sitting, as you probably know. He paced up and down, but of course noiselessly on the three-inch nap of the felt and carpet, shouting at the giggling native tarts—

"If you don't tell me where he is I shall go and wake up 'Peacock's Eyes'" (that was the manageress—it was an egyptian syndicate) "and you'll get it in the neck!"

" Where the chicken got the chopper ! " Shushani (whom I called Fleur-de-lys) spluttered, prostrated with amusement. It was quite dark, so a hand of mine stole out like a marauding crab and nipped her sitting-jellies and she sprang in the air with a piercing squeal. Humph plunging round to see what had happened, and noticing that it was my favourite, came slowly over, peering to right and left, consumed with suspicion. But he could detect nothing unusual anywhere.

" I believe you know where he is Shushani ! " he said loweringly. Shushani trembling with laughter and excitement, shook her head a thousand times.

" I'll bet you do ! "

" No sir, I don't sir really ! "

They none of them gave me away. He never had the least idea that I was there all the time, of all places, and soon he left—thoroughly unmanned, melted into a lamentable pulp, really and in literal fact upon his last legs, followed with swinging gait by the preposterous ' Enough ', to whom he had made a despairing signal (half S.O.S., half olympian *Verbot*) as he went out of the door—pushing at the heavy curtains as if they had been great blocks of seaweed and he a diver whose stock of air was running out.

* * *

The mad mechanics of this trip cannot be properly understood without a full grasp of the central fact—the bad terms on which my two puppets subsisted throughout its duration, never giving me a moment's peace. I flew to the bottle as a consequence of it. I called in hashish more than once to help me out. Val and Humph were awful throughout. I have never met two worse-behaved people. I have rewritten an entire chapter of my " People Behaving " since I left Persia, an account of all I learnt in the course of this ill-fated trip about *behavior* of the very worst sort.

To go back to the get-away, the first crack of the starting-pistol. At the start all went wrong. Friction was set up at once even at Marseilles. Immediately upon their introduction these two people appeared to bristle. As we were flying over Athens Humph leant over and began in a loud whisper to say in my ear—

" I say what an *aw*— I say what an *aw*— I say what an *aw* ! "

He peered over his shoulder at the profile of poor old Val, whose ears were pricked to catch every syllable.

" I say what an *aw*— I say what an *aw*— I say what an *aw*—ful—what an *awful* woman ! "

I laughed good-naturedly at this, but it was not a pleasant situation—about to fly into Asia Minor with two people at daggers drawn, behaving as if at any moment they might fly at each other's throats.

The friction-to-be was already there at the very moment of the introduction. It became at last so confoundedly pronounced such a short time afterwards, that looking back one could see it must have been. I would say that it was already extant when Humph showed me all her mad junk in the drawer of his writing-desk in his Strand bureau.

Humph was at no pains at all to disguise his feelings and for this I may have been partly to blame. I didn't set him much of an example, I agree. He quite openly developed this unreasoning objection to Val. He spent quite half his time avoiding her. Far from any of the successes the old girl had promised herself with this swagger agent, she never had a look in. This she was certainly quick to see. I could scarcely get them into the same aeroplane at Marseilles, they were already up on their hind-legs. But that was nothing to what followed.

It is easy to see what might be contributory causes. Humph I imagine would consider her too common. (A man like that is always difficult in such matters.) She would be apt to seem an unsuitable travelling companion, for The Baronet and himself. Evidently I should have known better than to bring her. Again she was not a rich woman, that, as he would look at it, reflected upon me, as poor women should not pay for Baronets to visit Persia. But that would in turn reflect upon him. He was certainly not best pleased with me, on account of Val.

As to Val's appearance, that too was very bad. For all his experience of the pornographic authoress, he may have been disappointed that her face wasn't better than it was. I couldn't help it of course, but he would blame me. Undoubtedly that made it worse for me. It made mine, an absurd, as well as an unsuitable action. This penniless, not attractive, nobody, who wrote scurrilous as well as obscene books—it took all the prestige of The Baronet to counterbalance it. I lost caste I think with Humph.

Old Val was ready enough to be friendly. It was him I could do nothing with. First of all McPhail was a great disappointment to him. He wanted to go over himself to Faujas de Saint Riom. It was with difficulty I dissuaded him. He did not seem to believe about the accident. He cast incredulous glances at both Val and myself.

It was in Damascus I first saw that this capital difficulty was destined to last as long as the trip lasted. I told him without beating about the bush that he must be more civil to our travelling companion.—He would come up, slip his arm in mine, draw me away, if we were at a café, and lead me off to see something, usually a woman—generally a long way off. Val would be left for hours together by herself—no new experience of course, for her, I know, and at least she was getting plenty of fresh air. It was rather the manner with which it was done. And that I warned him must stop at once.

Humph had the quite sensible habit of going to the nearest brothel as soon as he reached any unknown town of importance in Asia. As in France or Spain, these places answer the purpose of a club. Val was left with a book at the hotel. She went to bed usually at nine. She was quite used to this of course I knew. But *he* could not possibly know that. I suggested taking her along at first. It was where she belonged I argued—why not take her with us—it would divert the whores!

But no! Humph would not hear of it. He said he would not take it on himself to offend the whores, he was sure they wouldn't like it! He for his part did not blame them! He wouldn't like it himself! And so on. He was quite impossible.

"Noooo my dear old chap. You don't under-*stand*! They *don't* like it!"

"I can't help their troubles. I find it convenient, and appropriate."

"She's not one of them my dear old chap!"

"She's a highbrow counterfeit—it ought to interest them."

"It doesn't—you're wrong, it doesn't! Besides it makes one un—*comf*—table!"

"Why not put it to the test?"

"Look here Snooty I'm damned if I'm going to go round to places like that with *her*!"

"But we can't leave her alone all the time."

"Why not?"

"Can we do you think?"

"I'm bound to say I don't see why not."

"That had never occurred to me."

"She came with her eyes open didn't she?"

"I'm under the impression that she did."

"Well then! She knew what she was doing! What has she got to grumble at? She ought to think herself jolly lucky to be with us at all!"

That was the sort of tone the man had adopted! In short, he had become Snooty. He had usurped my snootiness. (And what was worse he was growing snooty with me too.)

We all shambled up to each other at Marseilles. I believe it would be true to say that I never properly introduced her to Humph at all. They had to pick each other's acquaintance. So what I suppose really occurred was that Humph remarked (I daresay with some surprise) what my attitude was to the third member of our party. As you have seen, it was pretty snooty. He must have marked, learnt and very rapidly digested it. And almost instantly he *adopted* it.—It was, I now recognize, a fatal mistake not to modify my private manner toward the old girl. It brought her into contempt automatically. His was automatic contempt.

At first, in a hearty, condescending way, he would bluster—

"Are you coming Val!"

When she replied "No I don't think I'll come Humph thank you!" he was plainly extremely relieved—he is not exactly one of those people who disguise their feelings, especially where a woman is concerned in whom they take no interest. Very rapidly (it took my breath away!) this hearty patronage wore thin, his good-natured condescension became less and less boisterous, then petered out, then became a rude silent stare, that *dared* her to propose herself. At the last indeed he went one better than me. He imitated me so well, as far as Val was concerned, that we changed places entirely. He really became *Snooty*.

But this brought about a state of affairs that presented serious difficulties to me. It was in vain that (as at first at Damascus) I said to him, to all intents and purposes, " Listen ! It is *I* who am *snooty*, not you ! You keep to *your* rôle, and leave *mine* to *me* ! "

Fatally, I was constrained to show *some* consideration to Val, I could not help myself. She could not be sent completely to Coventry ! The idea had been that I should speak very little (to say the least of it) but *he*, he would engage her in suitable small-talk.—But that had not been the view of the matter that he had cared to adopt ! So I became more outwardly polite to Val than I had been before, in the first days of this affair. It became a very knotty problem. I found myself treating her once or twice almost as a Ladyship.—But this was very bad indeed.

To commence with Val was pretty angry with my insolent agent. Soon however she realized how, ultimately, this must tell in her favour. She saw that she benefited by Humph's misbehaviour—since patently it was causing me to be more polite than I otherwise should have been. But that was all she wanted ! She even encouraged the wretched Humph to be offensive. In order to put me into the position of making up for it afterwards she entrapped him into additional incivility.

Meanwhile she now incessantly talked about Humph. She soon began writing fresh books of course : and she ' put ' Humph in all of them. (She put me in too.) She told me over and over again what a *cad* Humph was. How he was *not* a gentleman—of course he could not help *that* —but he was such a mean old bourgeois skunk. (How any self-respecting woman could ever bear to find herself undressed with such a fantastic object *she* could not understand—he once showed us his chest which was certainly particularly hairy, in a conversation about mosquito bites —Val left the table hurriedly and reported to me afterwards that she had been overcome with nausea at the sight and had been violently sick upstairs as soon as she reached her room.)

So Val was pleased, oddly enough. All the unpleasantness fell on *me*. The fix in which I found myself (as her guest I suppose one must call it) was mercilessly turned to account by the busy Val. She behaved as if we were a sort of engaged couple and that two was company and three was none. She manœuvred for me in competition with Humph. She was incessantly plotting to get me away from him. At last it came to this. However snooty I might be with her, it made no difference. (For I soon grew snooty again, under this régime, as you may suppose.) It was *Humph* all the time who was to blame. It was *he* put me up to it. No one could remain in any doubt, she saw to that, that I was under the influence of Captain Cooper Carter—I poor lamb was easily swayed. And a very bad influence it was! This big rude bully it was who made *me* so rude—as I undeniably was at times. I ought never to have associated with him—but once she had *got me in the Church* so to speak, she would see to it (anybody could predict that) that Captain Cooper Carter never darkened her doorstep with his objectionable person. —As you can see, that was very bad indeed. I could do nothing with either of them.

When I first seriously expostulated with Humph (that was at Baghdad) he said he was sorry.—He climbed down. If he had seemed a little unceremonious in the course of travelling it was only because he was so rushed, and surely she did not expect him to stand on ceremony. He had not supposed she wished *that!* Had she complained? Well it was very stupid of her. He would make it his best endeavour to improve his manners, which he knew were vile, while in the presence of her Ladyship. (He began deliberately referring to her in this way.) All that said, he turned round and fired a parthian shot or two at me. He had not realized—the bloody animal had the effrontery to drawl at me—that I took her so seriously. (I scowled at him.) Had he *known*, of course he might have observed a greater *deference*, regarding (and he smiled —it was *her Ladyship*).—Indeed old chap, come to that, added he with a most ruffianly grin, *you* are not so damned considerate as all that (he said) with your friend Val. *You* can't talk in point of fact!—and so forth.

What was I to say to that?—I replied that I did not expect him to be especially ceremonious, but it was preferable to pass her the salt when she asked for it, not invariably hustle her aside and enter a room first, nor belch in her face if you could without personal inconvenience belch anywhere else. He agreed entirely. All I asked was that he should *share* with me the burden of being civil to such a painfully unattractive woman. He laughed loudly —I smiled, I had to humour him. After all, I continued, the poor girl is alone, thousands of miles from home, in a particularly inhospitable (indeed as far as I was concerned a disgustingly uncomfortable) country! I rubbed it in pretty well.

He said he would share with me as far as he was able the duties of host and consoler of the Englishwoman in foreign parts, so long as I didn't ask him to sleep with her! But he could not, and would not, pretend that he found old Val rather attractive or violently intelligent. Nor could he pretend he desired her society as much as he desired mine. *Eventually* she would have to stay put. She must learn to stop when she was told. Those were after all the terms upon which she had come with us (to pay the trip for me, see a bit of the wild, have the advantage of the society of a Literary Agent, and be seen (to some extent) but not be overmuch heard).

As to Val's ripe sex-life, as regards that too there was absolutely nothing doing—she flatly refused to have affairs.

She seemed surprised, if not pained, when one suggested it. Nothing would persuade her to GET a talented native in the Bed, however eligible he might be (she said, when I referred to the matter, that they were all impotent at twenty-one) or anybody else for that matter—excepting always the accursed 'Baronet'. She was more orthodoxly *Ladyship* (of a very old and crusted school), more the Caesars-wife-to-be than I would have believed it possible. I was flabbergasted. And the position of contumely and disgraceful neglect for which she was marked down by Humph contributed naturally to that result. She had to demonstrate what a lady she was! It was a thoroughly bad business.

I tried in Teheran to get her off on minor members of the Diplomatic Corps. She refused to be drawn. She spent all her time apparently covering acres of foolscap with hideous word-pictures of Humph.

The more this policy patently enraged me, the more steadfast she became in its pursuit. She starched herself up in spite of the really tropical heat. It made me feel quite cool to see her enter the hotel-lounge. It was like a block of ice tripping in. She must have been bitten from head to foot with flies, we all were, but she never scratched.—She *would* not be animal!

In the morning she would come out of her room as fresh as paint, ready for battle with Humph. She composed her elegant word-mincer of a mouth into a prunes-and-prisms lockjaw-grip, her chin even thrust out to defy the Chin of Chins—an inverted Cupid's-Bow, loaded with the shafts of hate which she was ever ready to discharge should Coop attack. But she was very taciturn in fact. If left alone, and she was usually left alone, as Humph ignored her, her words were few and to the point.

Humph saw perfectly what was going on. It seemed to amuse him intensely. I informed him on several occasions that for my part I did not regard it as particularly funny. But that merely sent him off into great rich claps of clubman laughter. It seemed to him a capital piece of horseplay on the part of fate. In fact, *it served me damn well right* !

Meanwhile, very much the bustling agent-on-the-job, insufferably up-to-snuff, he pushed forward with his arrangements to have me captured by the bandit. Letters from his London Bank smoothed the way for us in many respects—in such places as this the banks are the Thomas Cook & Sons more or less. This gave us facilities denied to men of straw. I met many officials of the anglo-persian banking system, who of course had everyone in their pockets, and they gave him much valuable information regarding Mithras. He kept talking about Mithras. At last I gave him " Sol Invictus—Bull Unsexed " to read. This seemed to sober him a little. I think he felt it would be difficult to get anything as flamboyant as that out of the land we were in.

After a few days in the capital, I forget how many, Humph came to me and told me that the next step was to go to the city of YES. (Consonants that I can do nothing with only bore me. I dislike seeing them on the paper. So let us call the place Yes. *No* would sound better, and be a name more suggestive of the stark reality, but I wish to be as scrupulous as possible about the geography of Persia. It was in the middle east of the kingdom.)—What did I intend to do with Val, he desired to know ?

I had not thought this out at all carefully. A new situation had come into being, clearly. He suggested that she should stop at Teheran and finish her book. (*Finish her book*, he thought, would be a form of words that would appeal to the lady.)

I went to Val and asked her how she was getting on with her book.

" How is the book getting on Val ? " I asked her with a very coaxing grin, standing over her, tusked and staring, being very big, blank and puppetish.

" Oh I don't know. Why do you ask Snooty ? "

The old girl was very suspicious. She smelled a rat. It was not my habit exactly to ask after the welfare and progress of her literary compositions.

" Which book do you mean Snooty ? " she asked, pushing out her *studious* look—a moulding of wrinkles, surmounting a suddenly rather ' weary ' face.

But this was a poser.

" Oh the *second* one about old Humph was the one I had in mind ! " I said a little awkwardly.

" About whom Snooty ? "

" His Excellency Captain Humphrey Cooper Carter ! " I exclaimed. " You know the one you mentioned the day before yesterday ! "

" Oh *that* one " she said with great contempt, as if it had been the object *Humph* that I in fact had mentioned.

" Yah ! " I said, yawning heavily.

" I have discontinued that ! " she answered grandly.

" *Discontinued* it ! " I gasped, in well-simulated astonishment. " What on earth do you find to do with yourself then ?"

" Nothing much !" she said.

" I am surprised to hear—that once having put pen to *paper* ! "

" Are you Snooty ? "

(By all the female saints in the Calendar I swear that this counterfeit submission, these crossed and folded hands in the lap, tried me beyond endurance. But I did not retaliate *then*.)

" Well Val " I said " the time has come for me to go off."

I said this a little heartily—on *the-best-of-friends-must-part* principle.

" Has it Snooty ? " was all she said, still with her brows rolled up, into a fillet of studious wrinkles, and her eyes thrown down upon the table at which she sat.

" Yes, I have to go off with Humph tomorrow or the day after ! " I said in a jolly tone.

" Indeed."

" We're going to the Afghan frontier you know, where the bull-fighting tribes are to be found."

" Are they ? No I didn't know."

" Good Lord yes. Mithras is still their God. Just fancy ! "

She looked up at me, very hard, and said with great determination—

" What shall *I* do Snooty ? "

" You ? Well that's what we have to decide ! "

" No we don't ! " she said. " I shall come too ! "

" Oh you will come too will you ? " I asked with affected incredulity.

" Yes. Where you go I go."

" Well I never ! "

She stood up suddenly—I started back a pace, eyeing her with certain alarm.

" I will not leave you here Snooty with that man ! Whatever I have to put up with, I will not do that ! He has done his best to drive me away. Well, you tell him from me that he damned well won't succeed ! "

She left the table and walked away. Before passing into the next apartment (it was the gentlemen's lavatory, but I don't know if she had noticed this) she turned and said—

" Go and tell him that from me Snooty—that is my answer to *him* ! "

She turned to the door, she halted a moment as she remarked the unsuitable word *Messieurs* upon it, sniffed very delicately, and then with great dignity passed out of sight.

This left me so speechless with snootiness that I hurriedly

left the room by the other exit, lest I should pursue her and say something really unkind to her. I went back to the room where Humph was waiting for me.

" Well. What does she say ? " he asked.

" She says she wants to come too " I said, sitting down.

Humph laughed. He gave a short, bitter and rather offensive little laugh.

" I knew she'd say that " he said, tilting his puggaree over his eyes, its strap circumscribing his bronze-red cheek, in a slack loop,—with which his lower lip flirted. He gazed at me fixedly from under the blunt pagodaed brim of this Conrad headgear.

" Well ? " I said at last.

" Well indeed—what next ? "

" That's what I should like to know."

" I await your instructions Sir Michael ! Am I to make arrangements for the transport of her ladyship ? "

" How do I know ? "

" Well you can't expect me to decide for you, upon a matter of that sort. It's your business old man, not mine."

" I don't see that," I said.

" Well hang it all ! You brought her ! "

" No no ! She brought me."

Humph was very annoyed. I was annoyed too. But the more offensive he was, the more disposed I became to wash my hands of it, and allow them to fight it out between them.

" Supposing *you* try and persuade her—to do whatever you think is best she should do " I said.

This he refused point-blank—no it was not *his* business ! If I wasn't able to manage the woman, he was damned if he was going to interfere. Let her come by all means and bitch the whole expedition if I liked. We couldn't *all* be captured. That would be too expensive. As it was we should be down on the whole transactions, quite a jolly little sum.—Unless she would like to put up the ransom of course! But since she said she had only a hundred quid left in the wide, it was unlikely she'd be wanting to do that! It would be as much as she could manage to get herself back to England, let alone to go travelling about any more in one of the most expensive countries in the East.

Well I would do nothing about it. I said it did not matter to me what became of her. I was in his hands. Humph was the impresario! Humph must deal with other members of the company. He must not ask me to do so, I had no authority in any case.

"Well hang it all old man she's your *miss*-tress!" he protested flamboyantly, in his heartily-musical singsong.

"How do you know she is? I like that! Mistress! We're quite french. *Maîtresse!*"

"Well she *behaves* as though she were your *wife*!" he added in a somewhat lower key and less assured tone, as if afraid he might be going too far.

"That again I can't help" I said. "I can't help how she behaves, any more than I can help how *you* behave!"

"No but hang it all you might *try*. You might do your *best*!"

"I don't see that follows at all!"

"But you must have *some* say in the matter!"

"Not necessarily. I am a guest here only."

"But surely you can manage your hostess *a little* old man!"

"I'm not a manager like you Humphie!"

"But she's nothing to do with *me*. How can *I*!"

"Because (as you remarked just now) a woman *behaves* as though she were my wife (you were perfectly right, it's exactly what she does do) why should I be held responsible for her? I don't see it! Because a man *acted as though* he were your dearest friend, would that be any reason to lend him a thousand bucks, or jump into the Atlantic Ocean to save the fellow from drowning if he fell in—at personal risk to yourself? Why?"

"Of course not. But what's that got to do with it?"

"A lot it seems to me. I can exercise no control over Mrs Ritter. I am not Mrs Ritter's keeper. Indeed at the moment she happens to be *my* keeper."

Humph turned his head away frowning, as if to remove his eyes from a displeasing sight. References to my financial dependence upon Val was a sure method of depressing him. He turned back, with a sour grimace, as if something bitter had been forced between his lips.

"*Why* don't you give her the beastly money back for the *fare* Snooty? I would. How much was it she paid? I wish you would."

"Why?"

"Oh I don't know. It makes everything so jolly awkward."

"I don't see that that alters things a lot."

"Well what are we to do now? What do you propose?"

"I don't see what can be done frankly. The woman is free. She is responsible—she is of age."

"Of age is right!"

"She's not so *very* old, poor old girl—she's quite young as a matter of fact."

"I know of course! But this is all a great bore Snooty—can't we do anything? Won't you please like a good feller go and tell—go and tell!"

"Mrs Ritter."

"Yes Mrs *Ritt*-er—tell her she had better wait for us here old boy!"

"But I have once."

"Now that she's seen *Persia*, she might prefer to return to England—but tell her she must do one or the other—she is holding up our *plans*!"

"No. You go and tell her all that!"

He sprang up in a rage.

"Where is she?" he asked fiercely—if the thunder could wail, his *where art thou?* was a complaint—glaring round in every direction.

I pointed at a large door.

"In there" I said.

"Where? In the next room?"

"Not quite—in the next but one."

I smiled as I said this—seeing her in my mind's eye upon the threshold of what she had stood before when last I saw her, at the height of her dramatic withdrawal, confronted with an ironical *Messieurs*. Humph noticed my smile and paused a moment to see what it meant. —There were a lot of meaningless rooms in this persian Ritz however—we had been sitting in one (suitable perhaps for playing chess). It was a coffee-room I suppose, so was the next, and the one beyond that. That was the one with the Gentlemen's Lavatory. I hoped that if he started off at once, his arrival might find her still closeted within. I should like to have been present if that had occurred.

"In there?" he asked resentfully (because of the smile).

"No the next one to that" I said, pointing again towards that part of the house where I had interviewed Val just now.

His great chin preceding him, he charged the door, swept it back and disappeared into the next room, which I could hear him noisily traverse, and then burst into the one beyond.

"I say Val!" I could just hear him exclaim, in a tone of loud querulous command. Then the door banged.

Out of the french window at which we had been sitting, was a large court packed with sun-burnt trees. Doves caused the afternoon air to gurgle, fountains sent up a thin splash. There were glimpses beyond of ultra-iranian architecture—persepolitan columns, and fretwork ogival openings and arched doors, entrances to monastic colonnades. I slyly ordered out my entire garrison of teeth, out of the black trap where they stood all day in rows, and contributed my little bit of ornament to the scene. Observed from the dove-encumbered fountain in mid-court my giant toothipegs would look well in the gloom of the interior where I sat—just like a piece of native handiwork, whitewashed and outstanding, as an observer would guess it to be.

After a very few minutes I heard a formidable disturbance, in the next room. Humph's voice resounded in the hotel, laying down the law—the pulse of the atmosphere beat quicker as the doves heard it and were vaguely alarmed: and Val was screaming after him. He came stamping across the next apartment, and stamping into the one where I sat, redder in the face than ever, his eyes flashing like luminous dung.

" Val is *impossible* " he shouted. " I really think she is the most insufferable woman I have ever met ! "

" Oh no ! "

" If you ask me to go about with her any more I shall simply throw up the whole thing ! "

" Not go on ? "

" I will not be insulted by her ! "

" Insulted my dear feller ? "

" Insulted, yes ! "

" She *is* rather insulting.—Why don't you hit her ? "

" Insulting ! I have put up with her—vulgar old beast that she is—for your sake Snoots ! "

" She isn't terribly old. She's quite young as a matter of fact."

" Of course—what's that got to do with it ! It's for

your sake, nothing else would have *induced* me, believe me or not, to do—what I have ! "

" I understand you perfectly my dear old man ! "

" To take her about with us everywhere."

" Not everywhere Humph ! "

" What did you say Captain Cooper Carter ? " came the voice of Val from the door.

Turning round with a quick grin to myself at this, I saw Val standing there, taking Humph's measure I thought in a very businesslike way. She had followed him in. But obviously he had known this. Obviously too Val had waited for her cue, until he should deliver himself of some big stuff. *Vulgar old beast* (of course for her benefit) had answered the purpose—she was now inside the room a few feet.

" You heard what I said " he hotly retorted, keeping his back half-turned towards her, to cold-shoulder the intruder (looking at me as if to say " We won't turn round ! Don't let us take any notice of this ill-bred female, who has got rather above herself and pushed herself into our conversation ! I believe she will go away, if we show her we do not desire her presence ! ").

" Yes I did Captain Carter ! "

" I'm glad you did ! "

" It shows you are the cad you are, to insult a woman in that way—out in Persia—where there is nowhere to go ! "

At this I howled with laughter literally and stamped my feet up and down like a very appreciative audience at a vaudeville.

" Good old Val ! " I shouted. " *Good* old fruit ! "

But they paid no attention to me, any more than actors would, had I been the audience, and they playing their parts aloofly upon a stage.

" *Nowhere to go ?* " Humph sneered over to me. " What's

wrong with London? That's just my point—why don't you go back to London where you belong Mrs Ritter!"

"Thank you Captain Carter—I beg your pardon *Cooper* Carter—I know where I belong—it is *you* who do not know."

"Come, you're not comfortable here are you Mrs Ritter now! You have nothing to do with yourself, really, have you? Why *not* return to London! There's nothing to prevent your going *there*!"

"I beg your pardon, there is!"

"You've got the necessary *funds* I suppose! If not, perhaps *we*."

"Thank you—I have quite enough money—but to *stay here* you understand."

"You must enjoy hanging about this hotel, that's all I can say!"

"As long as Snooty stops here, Captain Carter, *I* stop here!"

I put my fingers in my ears at this.

"Stop here by all means!" sneered Humph. "There's no reason why you shouldn't so long as your *money* lasts!"

"Please try not to keep talking about money Captain Cooper Carter. We all know you are a cad. You needn't keep showing it, in case we should forget! We shall remember all right you needn't worry!"

Humph came round in front of me with his two hands thrown out in a violent appeal—Val following him, her sparkling pin-points scintillating above the pouting sneers.

"Look here Snooty you must do something and that *at* once about this beastly woman!"

"Yes Snooty you really must!" Val echoed him.

"It's bad enough" he protested "having *a vulgar adventuress* fastened on to one as I have had, without——!"

"Quite quite!" screamed Val, "you are so terribly top-drawer yourself *Cap*-tain——!"

" It's your fault Humph after all " I replied vigorously, " I didn't ask to be brought by her ! "

" She brought you—I mean you brought her——! "

" I didn't—I swear I didn't ! *You* suggested Humph she should bring me, you know you did ! "

" Don't be absurd Snooty ! You know you made it a condition of your coming that this woman should come too. If I had known the sort of person she was ! "

" *Really* Mr Coop ! " began Val, beginning to indulge in violent mimicry. " *Really* Mister—I beg your pardon —*Cap*-tain ! "

" I thought at least you'd have the tact old man not to bring some one who isn't even *a lady* ! "

" Snoots—Snoots ! " Val sprang round in front of me —they were now both side by side—stamping her foot. " *Are* you going to allow—this *agent-fellow here*—to insult me in this manner ? This beastly bounder Carter——! "

" Val ! *Will* you go away ! " I shouted at her. " I cannot be held responsible for what Captain Humphrey Cooper Carter says to you. I *will* not be made responsible for my agent by you or anybody else ! "

This was very bad discipline indeed. I should end by being torn in pieces by these two enraged puppets. Val was much the worse of the two of course because she had no excuse to follow him in in that way. After having insulted him very much, when he asked her to go back to England, as she had obviously done, she ought to have remained on her side of the house.

" If she stops, I go. That's flat. It's my ultimatum " said Coop retiring behind a table—in order to appear only as a handsome bust, as if he feared his legs might come under fire—and lighting a cigarette. He felt he had won the day, after my outburst.

" So long as Snooty stops in Persia " Val replied, withdrawing slightly as well, " *I* stop in Persia. That is *my* ultimatum! I will not leave him here—that's *flat* as you call it, too! *I have my reasons!*" she added darkly.

"I'll bet you have!" Humph barked. "I'll bet you have!"

"Yes I have—Mister *Coop*-er *Cart*-er" Val sneeringly drawled, rolling her lip right up at *Coop* and at *Cart*—"did anyone ever hear a more ridiculous name than *that*—like Robinson-Smith—I suppose a little *fish*-monger called Carter married a little *green*-grocer called Cooper!"

"That's the idea!" yelped Humph, very angry indeed. "I daresay that's why I know *bad greens* when I see them!"

"Yeeew!" cried Val. "*You* don't know a woman from a gelded guineapig!"

"Well I'll leave you now I think Snooty in the company of this foul-mouthed, mottle-faced Tyneside coal-heaver's *touch*!"

"Better than a Literary Agent's lollypop old thing!" shouted Val.

"Who I am *sure* will continue to *entertain* you Snooty with her North-Country Billingsgate, which you appear to relish so much!"

"Ya! *Mist*-er *Cooop*-er *Humph*—er—rie *Cart*—ugh!"

I put my fingers in my ears again.

"Turn it off Val for Jesus' sake! Will you take this woman away Humph! *You* attracted her here just now!"

"No thank you Snoots! Do your own dirty work old man! He who touches pitch!"

"You shite!" screamed Val. "You think you'll drive me away from Persia! I'll see you damned Mr Cooper before I leave Snooty here alone with *you*. *I* see through you!"

Going out of the door Humph shouted back at me.

"Let me know when you're through Snooty. I shall be in my room."

When Humph had left the stage Val flung herself down

immediately upon a sofa and burst into a tempest of sham sobs. If it had not been so hot I should have gone out into the garden to get a breath of air. As it was I sat and fanned myself hard, and attempted to drive the flies away from my ankle and neck.

How I have longed in Persia for the gentle british house-fly! To human eyes the two look absurdly alike. But what a profound difference there is between the nice decorous winged creature of the Middlesex kitchen, or of a farmyard of the Western Hundreds, and these venomous winged pests, in these eastern desert-lands.

"How can you find the energy in such a climate as this to go on as you do?" I said, shuddering.

"Why did you send him in to me Snooty?"

"I didn't send him in. He just rushed off—I can't stop him."

"I'm not going to be bullied by a great fat cad like him!"

"Quite right! I shouldn't if I were you!"

"Just because he's got a lot of money! I know I have nothing to boast of! But at least I'm as good as a *Cooper—Carter*!"

I fanned myself vigorously. In such weather as this where might not these passions of precedence end!

"What did he say?" I enquired politely. "I suppose he asked you to stop here in Teheran for a week or two?"

"You *know* Snoots it won't be *a week* or two! It will be —heaven knows how long!"

It was at this point that Val first touched upon a question to which she often recurred, during the ensuing weeks with ever-increasing emphasis.

I scratched myself, and drove off a particularly bad fly, offering it my mechanical leg to bite. But it knew better.

"Have you ever asked yourself Snoots what all this *brigand* stunt is about?"

" How do you mean? It's for advertisement."

She shook her head slowly. Her old bobbed crop of ash-pale yellow wisps waggled.

" There's more in it than that! It's all very well sending you off into the mountains to be the prisoner of a bandit —he doesn't go *himself* does he! What is he getting out of it?"

" Nothing, I should think. He imagines he's going to get something."

" You don't *believe* all that do you Snoots! You don't swallow all that!"

" Humph is a romantic, pure and simple."

" Oh is he?"

" Certainly."

" I should not have said that."

" *Nothing* is too absurd for him to imagine—and to carry out. We may regard ourselves as extremely lucky not to find ourselves on the way to the moon!"

" That's not how I see it."

I looked lazily at the old girl, with a flicker of curiosity. A new line with her this surely! What fertility! Now she was dabbling in mystery. Valerie—mystery-merchant!

I scratched myself and leaning towards her enquired, low and nasal to fit the new earnest mystery-mood:

" What is it Val you *suspect*?"

But this was going too far. Suspect was too strong an expression it seemed. As yet! She drew back into her prim lesbo-victorian shell.

" I suspect nothing Snoots. I only tell you my feeling about the whole business that's all."

" Are you sure you are right?" I breathed across at her.

" *Something* remains to be explained."

" That is always the case. *Everything* is *never* explained."

" I know. But I am talking about something different."

" It's not on the square you think? I'm not getting a square deal, what?" I insinuated.

She sniffed, discomfited.

" Very well!"

" Very well! I only say what I think. Everything sounds like nonsense you know until it proves to be true."

" There is *something then* however, is there?"

" Jeer away Snooty—you will discover I am right."

" But what is it you suggest, after all?"

" It's self-evident, Snoots, isn't it—no average person would they—no one you *told* about our being here and what we are supposed to be doing would believe a word of it. He would think we were all crazy."

" Ah *now* you're talking something like sense!" I said, getting up. " We are all crazy right enough. You and Humph have proved that just now, for your parts. And I'm as mad as a hatter, I'm a match for you both!"

And I retired to my own room and avoided them both for the rest of the day. When I returned, the last thing at night, I heard that Captain Cooper Carter had been hunting high and low for me, and also Mrs Ritter (separately of course—each on their own initiative). My eyes shone as I heard I was being hunted. I went to sleep that night inventing man-traps for my hunters, to catch them in next day. One big spectacular trap for Humph. On the whole I resented Humph most. It is one thing to be hunted by a woman. It is another thing to be hunted by a man! There was a note on my table when I got upstairs from Humph.—*Please* to make a point of going to him as early as possible in the morning! *Oh certainly!* thought I.—And I went to bed and slept very soundly under my mosquito-net indeed—except that I dreamed of hunting expeditions (my african backgrounds) in which it was *I* who was the hunted animal. And then I suppose it must have got cold in the night. For I became Leviathan. I felt myself to be a massive diving fish. It was in the high polar latitudes. And then I became conscious of my eye, quite a small affair in my prodigious head, which was levelled across the surface of the ocean, where the waves had a smooth icing as they broke—or their icing cracked that was it as they cascaded—until all the sea was still.—All the Moby Dick images, in fact. But I slept well—I knew that I was being hunted, but I knew how it would end—so I was at peace.

I was breakfasting—off *Kouss-kouss*, peach-omelette, pigeon and sweet potatoes—I asked for a native breakfast, I was not going to be fobbed off with a pot of Lyons tea and a sup of the scottish national staple diet, the first thing in the persian morning (though porridge turned up twice for lunch). I was reading Omar Khayyám. The actual verse I had got to was the little-known couplet

> " *A book of verses underneath the bow*
> *A jug of wine, a loaf of bread, and thou,*"

when Humph breezed stormily in, grievances stamped all over his brick-red countenance.

" I say are you all *right* ? "

" Fine ! "

" Whatever became of you last night Snooty ? I looked everywhere for you ! "

I ' motioned him to a seat ' (as I remarked that the novelist always says on such occasions when I was reading up a novel or two, prior to composing the present unorthodox treatise) and eyeing my breakfast obliquely, with a censorious dissatisfied eye, he reluctantly sat down.

" How did you spend the evening Humph ? Did you pay another visit to the ' Marvel of the Ages ' or did you rather choose to lie with the ' Beautiful Silk Benedictions of the Moon ! ' ? "

" Neither, I was looking for you."

" Oh ! A somewhat prosaic quest ! "

" I don't know about that—I wanted to know about that woman. We can't stop here forever Snooty."

" I hope not !—Have you arranged the matter with her ? Amicably I trust ? "

" I—no ! Have you ? "

" I ? Heavens no ! I'm in your hands—and Val's of course. Who pays the piper calls the tune."

Well we had a long wrangle, and once or twice I nearly threw him out of my room. He was very obstinate and difficult about Val. He would not give way. I agreed to see Val at last. I went to her and implored her to fly off to London at once, and said I would help her pack. She refused categorically. Nothing was farther from her thoughts than a return to London ! She fell into a violent vituperation of Humph. I agreed with her of course, but suggested that, as he was so awful, all the more reason to fly away ! I returned with her answer to Humph, who subsequently descended to the coarsest invective in expressing his considered opinion of Mrs Valerie Ritter. The upshot was that he refused to move her out of Teheran. I will not touch her ! he said. *I will not move her !* He went off, advertising his exasperation by means of bearish shrugs, telling me that he could do nothing until I had reduced to submission this refractory scribbling bitch—who (it now appeared) had had the bright idea of reading him a page or two about himself out of her latest and most scurrilous libretto !

* * *

For a couple of days I scarcely saw Humph or Val at all now. I left them to their own devices—we might not have been in the same country for all we saw of one another. Everything plainly was at a standstill so I made myself scarce not to incur further trouble. I slept out. My time was mostly spent sprawled upon two gigantic cushions, smoking a *Kalyān* (or is it *Kalioun*?) perhaps, in the most exclusive brothel of the persian capital: sometimes I sought forgetfulness in hashish, but that gave me such a terrible singing under my silver plate (like an orchestra of cracked brass and wind with a good deal of gratuitous percussion) that I indulged in it sparingly.

I have spoken already of the georgian girl (did I say georgian?) of about fourteen, whose name was *Lily* in Persian—namely Shushani. It was in the establishment where she was to be found that I hid. Lily assisted me to distract myself. She spoke a lot of English (I can't imagine *where* she picked it up—it must have been from highly placed english people) and she knew more limericks than any girl I have ever met. She really had an enormous aptitude for them, nothing was too idiomatic. She was a great kid. I told her the one about *The Young Lady of Lea*, and she told me the one about *The Old Man of Cape Cod*. And every time, rolling up into a ball with a spasm of asiatic delight, splitting her sides (her hands clasped between her *cuisses*—no Englishman can use the word *thigh* any more, Lawrence has made it sound so idiotic) she would tell me a limerick, she would so to speak suit actions to words. I of course would assist her. So, in a kaleidoscopic charade, playing sometimes the most difficult parts I and she would succeed in whiling away many a ridiculous hour, while the other members of the sodality were sleeping off the effects of long night-work and while the clientèle were of course, on their side, either prone in their respective siestas in their private pavillions, or busy amassing money enough to be able to continue indefinitely their *mondain* european existences—the ever-renewed delights of the public brothel, exchanged for the out-of-date monotony of a frowsty seraglio.

The Snooty-hunt was in full swing, for days on end it continued. But I lost all count of time. I have described one of the principal episodes of this hunting of the Snark, by this bad Bellman. But there were even more striking ones than that. On one occasion, for instance, getting on for the fourth evening I should say, about the hour of the european *Five-o'clock* Humph tracked me down (by means doubtless of my noticeable, exaggerated gait—by the simple method of enquiring of everybody " Have you seen my friend the *Ferangi* with the wooden leg ? " I suppose).

I had organized a few simple charades, based upon the more conventional limericks. All the girls and old women of the *boîte* in question were waking up about this time and taking the creases out of their necks. Shushani and myself had got them together to try out the " Young Man of Devizes " as a charade. Shushani was the Young Man of Devizes. I was the supreme Judge in this Beauty Contest for which the Young Man of Devizes had so lightheartedly entered, at the suggestion of his mother, who was very proud of him. It was I who finally bestowed upon him the " several prizes " involved in the terms of the doggerel.

As the Judge I had assumed the form and apparel of a bearded " Persian Notable ". I sat upon a tea-stool and harangued the committee of giggling beauty experts (most of them in the picturesque undress or *fatigue* dress of afternoon persian underwear)—a synod of whores in fact. At this very moment the door flew open—or rather the curtain fell down before his rush (rather like the walls of Jericho) and Humph trampled in, wild-eyed, haggard and with lowering brow, evidently out for blood this time and thoroughly worked up over my prolonged disappearance. It may even have shot across his mind, who can tell, that I had stolen a march on him, and got myself kidnapped on the sly !

Perceiving me—as he supposed an eminent Persian (perhaps of the princely or rich merchant class) squandering my imaginary substance upon this public harem, and at the moment palpably engaged in some lascivious conference or other (bearing no doubt upon some of the more recondite technical niceties of asiatic voluptuousness)—he hesitated. He muttered something in the nature of an apology and withdrew with every sign of deep mortification. But a moment later he returned. Standing in the open doorway, he addressed me as follows (I put my head on one side, lowered my eyes, and patiently heard him out):

" I say sir, I'm most awfully sorry but I wonder if you would mind terribly *if I asked* these *ladies* if they had seen *a friend* of mine—*with a wooden leg!* " Shushani pretended to translate all this to me, in the musical persian tongue, and in reply I delivered myself of some guttural remarks in volapuk, interspersed with whispered English.

Shushani then turned with great dignity to Coop and reported:

" No sir, his Excellency the Finance Minister of the Realm of Persia (for it is he whom you see before you) considers that you might find a more appropriate moment than the present to pursue your enquiries, regarding the whereabouts of your one-legged friend—and also, he has asked me to add, with all due respect to yourself, a more suitable *place!* We are, as you can see, engaged in a discussion of some moment. Finally, it is customary in Persia, his Excellency has requested me to point out to you, to knock before entering a room! "

Doubling himself in a sort of mock-salaam in my direction, but definitely abashed (by the rank of his fellow-visitor, and the stately terms of the rebuke), very crestfallen indeed, Humph backed out, and this time took himself off for good.—But I was never safe for a moment. Once he caught sight of my wooden leg where I had laid it aside, through the crack of a door. (The sleeping-cubicles of the women have doors, to ensure greater privacy.) I had heard him approaching. I slammed it to only just in time. As I was escaping through the window he was thundering upon the other side of the door, bellowing in an autocratic coax, of prodigious acoustical volume (I could see the fellow in my mind's-eye standing there, with his *taken-short* look about the legs, beating with his hands, and marking time with his feet).

" It's no use Snooty ! I saw your *leg* old man ! What ? No. I saw your *leg* ! *The game's up !* Yes—the *game's up* ! Let me in Snooty—I *know* you're there ! Let me in Snooty —I know you're there it's no use really—I know you're there Snooty ! I saw your *leg* old man, *through the crack of the door* ! "

At length Humph gave way. This could not go on, he said. There had to be an end to everything. Having come so far,—he would go through with it ! If I *must* have my Mrs Ritter, well he supposed I must of course—provided *he* wasn't asked to talk to her or be burdened with her vulgar and particularly unintelligent company.

I congratulated him heartily upon this. And I said in reply that we neither of us need be burdened with her unsuitable and pitiably stupid society. We could *both* simply treat Mrs Ritter as if she was not there ! That would settle the matter. Yes true—she *would* be there all the time—that however neither I nor he could avoid. There was nothing for it ! *Kismét*. God's ways were not ours—He sometimes makes use of peculiar means to the furtherance of His inscrutable purposes. He only is wise ! *Amen*.

Humph was distinctly mollified, as a result of this simple understanding we had come to. So next day we all bundled into the fore-part of a crowded omnibus—to avoid the movement, but my God how *much* movement in spite of that took place ! I sat by mutual consent between Val and Humph. Nobody spoke a bloody word. By stages we journeyed across desert after desert, with halts to take in petrol, and so reached, after several days, Ispahan. From there by car, God knows how, we arrived at last at the city of Yes—across the interminable salt and tufa steppe, always surrounded by barren yellow mountains, as bare as your hand. There we stopped, as I have said, an almost infinite period—I really have not the least idea how long it was.

I recollect very well our arrival in Yes. We had been going on and on for hours, my leg at every shock of the ill-sprung conveyance causing me considerable pain. I am positive that Humph had selected this route in order to inflict on me and Val the maximum of discomfort. The bus cushions or rather heavy upholstered seats—fixed at an angle of forty-five from the upright, came out of their sockets with every pronounced forward lurch of the bus, until our legs were clamped in before us, between the advancing seats and the back of the row ahead.—Coop and Val stared out of opposite windows, that is when they were not sleeping. At one time however I had both asleep on top of me. One was snoring upon my left shoulder and the other purring upon my right. I sat there between them—like some miserable showman, bursting with snootiness—with these two heavy animals slumbering on me as if I were a mechanical passenger, stuck there for the convenience of the others. What a brace of puppets truly, to be bouncing with across these remote plains! They were beyond question the most oppressive companions I could possibly have chosen, or rather who could possibly have chosen me.—But owing to the painful discomfort I was suffering I was glad as it happened of that. I welcomed the fact that the two offended and snoot-ridden dummies at least kept their mouths shut!

At last we saw something or other, of the same colour as the steppe, elevated a little from it, yet not a hill either, about five in the evening. Gradually this abominable oasis hove more definitely into sight. Everybody exclaimed *Yes.* And then at last—*there we were!* We sought out the British Agent, a Bahaī merchant, and he conducted us to the little house which had been put at our disposal. (Very little—Humph had been particularly mean, and we were given the smallest available, with a *bag* ten minutes' walk away.)

In Yes, as I shall call it, the upper classes washed once a week and we had just missed the day. So as soon as I had got a room assigned me I went out into the court of the house and sat among the gold fish in the fountain. I was travel-sore and bitten from head to foot and my leg was giving me a great deal of trouble. After that Humph produced a bottle of whisky from his suit-case. Val declined a drink, but I accepted two or three. Feeling considerably better, we all sat down on the floor, and were squirted with scent, Rose of Shiraz and bolshevik-eau-de-cologne mixed. Humph and I talked away fifty-nine to the dozen, we had a simple meal of chickens and partridges, *chilau,* big disks of wheaten bread, *Kabobs* on skewers (very choice meat-bits)—stewed mutton with plums and choppings of quince, and of course *fis-an-jem.* (This is a filthy dish of squashed nuts, butter, oil and I think chocolate.) After that we had a sultana *pilau* and fried eggs that tasted of offal. Honey that tasted like sweetened giblets. Nuts and pomegranates. I was sick on the roof afterwards, where I had gone to look at the desert moon, shining in the wilderness of salt, hoping to espy a moonlit jackal (an animal I like, by repute). After that we left Val, who said she had some letters to write. We stepped warily out into the street, which was an open sewer down the middle, with an uncovered well every twenty yards, and made our way to the chief Yes brothel.—There are no cafés of course in such a town to speak of, the brothel is like a café and club merely. There, after a few hurried remarks and interchange of summary caresses, with a half-dozen dirty old women of the lower orders (I have never seen such a bunch) we spent the night, assaulted by fleas. Then I was sick again. Next day I spent in bed, listening to the sportive splashing of the fountain, entrenched against a gathering army-corps of flies. Thus our life in Yes began.

Humph was very busy, he informed me that his agents were *at work*. All the details of my capture were plotted out and the affair was well-advanced. It might happen at any moment now. He was awaiting a messenger from the brigand. I took no notice at all of this. I yawned so much while he was telling me I nearly made myself cat. But I do remember he said he had definitely traced the mithraditic tribes. We were within striking-distance! But it would be better, probably, to be captured *first*. After that, I could, with the customary armed escort, go into the districts where the bull-baiting and bull-fighting was prevalent.—I did not listen. I made no pretence to listen. I would adhere to my programme to the letter. Up to the last moment (up to the beginning of the last time-beat) I would be a fully consenting party—to anything whatever that he might be pleased to arrange for me.

Val and he got on no better. They so seldom saw each other that it would have made no difference if they had. On the first night we slept there (the second after our arrival) Humph came into my room about two in the morning—in pyjamas, and with very much the *taken-short* look.

"I say old man are you all right?" he asked. "I believe there is a snake in my room!"

"What a bore!" I said. "Can't you drive it away?"

"I did try and frighten it, but it refused to move."

"Kill it!" I said. "I knew this house was verminous. Why didn't you pay a bit more and get us a better one?"

I got up and lighted my candle. We went out into the

court. The court in a persian house is three feet below the level of the rooms (rather an awkward arrangement). It is below the street level. You go down to it by a stone or mud stair.

" Women are awfully good with snakes " I said. " They *charm* them you know."

" Do they ? I never heard that."

" It's a fact. I'll get Val to see what she can do I think."

Before he could stop me, as he was going to do, I had called out—

" Val ! "

Val appeared almost immediately, slightly above us, in the opening of her bedroom window, in the most absurd of all her pyjamas, her *Bediest* ones. Humph looked the other way, very annoyed that I had called her in.

" What is it ? " she said. " Is there anything wrong ? "

" No it's only a snake—it's in Captain Cooper Carter's room " I said.

" Oh yes, I've got one in mine too. Haven't you got one Snooty ? "

" Not as far as I know " I said.

" No of course there are only *two*. It is not venemous Captain Carter. They are instead of a cat."

" Instead of a what ? " asked Humph angrily at once.

" A cat. They catch the mice Captain Carter " Val said coldly. " They are domestic animals in Persia. So I understand. I was rather frightened *myself* last night just at first. I was alone of course. But that is what I was told in the morning. Since then as a matter of fact I have seen the one in my room catch several rats and mice."

" Several ! Really ? Were they large ? " I said.

" Pretty damn big ! I saw one just now ! " Humph drawled peering into a rose bush. " Over there ! It was *a rat* I think ! "

"It really would have been nicer if we'd have had a better house" I said.

"Well anyway I'm damned if I want the beast in my room!" Coop exploded. "What do you say Snooty? I'm going to sleep out here in the court."

"You'll be attacked by rats, if you haven't got your snake with you to protect you" I said, "but God arranges things as He pleases—you may not be."

"Oh I'd prefer that" said the crestfallen Humph. "As a matter of fact I'll sleep on the roof."

We should all have been sleeping on the roof, actually, had it not been for the strained relations subsisting between the other two.

Val watched us from her door. Humph and I said good night and I went back to my room. Next morning I had a pigeon stuffed with plums and honey, and a glass of japanese beer, by the side of the fountain. I threw crumbs into the basin for the goldfish. A pretty scene I think. The roses made a nasty heavy smell, I am sorry to say, in the court. The blue mosaic of the fountain was agreeable however as far as it went, like a public lavatory you know. As yet it was not too hot. Val came out of her room, very spruce as regards her get-up, but looking very sallow I thought, this time.

"It's funny having a snake instead of a cat I think don't you?" she said, sitting down on the edge of the basin and alarming the goldfish.

"Not particularly" I said. "It's funnier having a cat."

"One of the snakes lives in a hole in the floor of my room" she said.

"Indeed? Much more efficient than a cat—it can get under the boards you see."

"Well it can't this morning. It's swallowed so many rats that it can't squeeze into the hole. It's lying beside the hole now, and attempting to digest them."

" Have you made a pet of it? We might take it with us."

She did not answer this question. She had got into the rather offensive habit of not answering everything that was said to her.—I wished naturally that Humph and she would behave differently. But I was not going on making up for Humph's rudeness by being more civil than ordinarily I should be, now any more than before, and I think I ended up, by and large, by being if anything *slightly* less agreeable than usual.

" When are we off again—do you know Snoots?" she asked.

" I haven't the faintest idea."

" Doesn't he tell you anything about it? Does he keep you in the dark?"

" Not at all."

I had no intention whatever of informing her that I kept *myself* in the dark—that in fact I deliberately shut my ears to all his shambling verbosities upon the subject of this absurd adventure. That if he talked about mules I showed no interest—if he chatted of camels, I affected to snooze—that if he touched on the impracticability in such a country of using a car, I simply walked away!—Not explaining this, I just stared at her. And she on her side irritated me very much by just staring back at me.

I wish to avoid giving the impression that I was rude to her—or, I should say, *unfriendly*. I was not. I did not shun her as did Humph. Often we had a quite long chat—upon one topic and another. Only once at Yes did I go into her room at night, I don't know why I did then, but undoubtedly it was out of kindness. I allowed her to Get me upon an enormous triangular cushion. I believe Humph heard us from the roof. He coughed a lot and seemed very distant and unpleasant next morning. We stopped and listened as he coughed.

"That beastly cad Carter!" Val hissed in my ear. "Do you hear him?"

"How do you mean?"

"*Cough*—hing! Can't you hear his filthy cough?"

"Coughing! That's *a goat!*"

"No darling—it's Humph!"

We listened again.

"Do be careful about him Snooty darling" she said. "Don't let him do just what he likes with you!"

"I won't" I said.

This reply seemed to surprise her very much. She said no more just then. But she never ceased whenever the opportunity arose to ply me with *safety-first* exhortations—mysterious warnings, veiled denunciations, prayers—regarding my Literary Agent's plans for me, destined to enable me to wake up one fine morning and find myself a famous best-seller.

I really had strange dreams in our bag at Yes. Whether it was that bit by bit the constant reiteration of the absurd warnings of Val became concrete in some way in my consciousness, and then began to be given dramatic form (mechanically and against all rhyme or reason) by the mind in sleep, I do not know. Also, it was always in the afternoon, as I was having my siesta beneath the apricot tree, that I dreamed in this fashion—which again deserves attention, but I cannot stop to analyse it now.

I would dream that I was being put in a sack and in that way I was carried for a great many days. Also I dreamed constantly of wells—which was natural enough, it is true, since in the middle of the streets in Yes (which are of course only uneven lanes) there are wells, every few steps, and many a Yesi has pitched down them. These wells when they dry up are covered over with a few planks. The dust collects above the planks and is trodden down, by the feet of the passers-by and their pack-animals. In time the shaft is no longer recognizable. It becomes part of the road. But the hidden planks, in due course, rot. If somebody treads too heavily, then he goes down into what was once the well. And that is of course the last anyone sees of him probably. In the bag I often dreamed of these street-shafts. When I fell I got to the bottom gently—by rolling about against the sides as I went down. But in the end I was down below, I had touched bottom. There I invariably met Humph—he was waiting for me. He was down there and as soon as I reached the bottom he would attack me. He was armed and I was not. But in my dreams I usually have both my legs again which is better than a pistol. Sometimes it turned out to be a dugout twenty feet beneath the Trench level. It made no difference. He was always there and as I went in he attacked me.

Once when I was wounded during an attack (during the War in Flanders) I crawled into a dugout to get out of the way of the shelling. A wounded boche officer was there. He attacked me. This episode got mixed up with the well in my slumbers in Yes.—But on the whole I went on pretty quietly and peacefully in Yes.

One day at first as I lay in the bag, under a tree, I was surprised and startled by seeing a man come out of the mud wall as it seemed. I got quickly to my feet. But it turned out to be only the gardener. He had come through a hole he had made in the mud as a short cut. I always came in at the hole after that, it was a short cut for me too.

Events in Yes were overshadowed by what followed. But of course many minor patterns of *behavior* (on the part of my *behaviorist* troupe of two) were sketched in by *Time's moving finger*, to use an Omarkhayyámish figure of speech, and incorporated in the main design: and once having *writ* or drawn same, nothing that Time subsequently did altered or rubbed out those influential sub-patterns, and potent smouldering spells, of the long days in the bag. Into that one capital Event (whose zero hour struck in Humph's horrid City office) these minor events are built. Perhaps more than I was aware, they were contributory to the particular shape possessed by the I think rather imposing Whole (looked at of course in retrospect).—These minor events you must mostly take on trust. I cannot help that —it is obviously impossible to enumerate all of them. The outlines of the situation during our long halt in Yes I have pretty well indicated and the sort of things that were liable to occur there, given the dispositions of the parties.

One evening—after we had been there so long that I felt we should never leave it—Humph came into the bag. This was as I was preparing to return to the house. I was alone, except for the gardener. The fact that Humph had come out to the bag (which he seldom came near, in point of fact, because of old Val) as good as meant that a big move was contemplated.

"It's all settled Snooty" he said at once, as he came towards me. "Everything's ready."

"Is it?" I said. "What? Which?" I sat down again on the carpet.

"Everything.—We start tomorrow morning at sunrise."

"Good Lord!" I said, becoming McPhail for the occasion. Good Lord! I heard myself saying—"*Good Lord!* A LITTLE FIELD!" Humph was chock-full of filibuster zest and piratic pep, swelling in great Peterpannish glee.

"We travel all day till we reach a point over there, in those mountains" he pointed northward (as I had waved my hand towards the Orient, in mockery, speaking to Rob of these beastly Highlands in Faujas de Saint Riom). I did not look of course. I yawned as usual. "We camp there and tomorrow we should be at Hamgah."

"Should we? Go on!" I said, still McPhailified for the occasion.

"Yes or the day after—or the day after that. You know what these people are! Hamgah is a mountain village. Soon after Hamgah our friend the old brigand will do the dirty on us. Forty-eight hours later the entire world will read of his bold act of high-handed brigandage!"

Of course I paid no attention to all this nonsense. And while he continued to instruct me in a thousand executive details of this childish adventure, I just lay in the centre of the carpet, my hands beneath my head, and gazed at the sky (the persian sky is the sky of the miniaturist, at least that is authentic) thinking of nothing in particular. I was listening to his voice, blotting out entirely the sense of the words, and imagining the sort of model of his sinuses that a singing-teacher might construct in plaster —supposing Humph were his favourite operatic pupil, and he had been cast for the part of Tristan. Certainly Humph was wagnerian. He would have been a Ring Star, if a singer. His was very much the tenor-figure too, as it happened, I thought as I watched him holding forth above me, stepping on and off of the carpet, as if rehearsing a part. It was no difficult matter to imagine him in hose and doublet, as broad as he was long, bellowing before the footlights—with no legs to speak of—all Caruso *Cabinet*, all *musical-box* as it were—upon tenoresque tip-toe. Each time my eye encountered his at present he wavered in his rehearsal—he would measure me in doubtful and resentful glances (with distinct aversion for my type of *behavior*, so opposite to his). He saw I was not listening —he could tell from my eye that his words caused no rational impact upon my consciousness. Though of course he did not express it in that way or understand what I was doing. He would merely say to himself as he stopped— *"I don't believe the blighter's listening to what I'm saying."*

Next morning at all events, out of the principal gate of Yes, issued a briskly moving (because not over heavily laden) cavalcade. We were mounted upon ponies (Humph and myself) and there were a couple of large white donkeys which are a special thing in Persia, very good indeed—they cover four miles an hour and are better than horses. Humph led the way. Beside him was a big flourishing bearded individual, rather fine-looking, fur-capped and absurdly bandoliered. I afterwards knew him to be an emissary of the brigand. Humph's pipe-man followed on a donkey (the bearer of our communal *Kalioun* or *Kalyan̄* —that is our persian water-pipe, with a good stock of *tambac*—that is an aromatic tobacco). Our tableman was next in order with the samovar. Val came after that upon an enormous snow-white ass. Then came our baggage upon mules and yet more mokes. I brought up the rear. We were all armed of course except the Persian from Yes. Even Val had a large revolver stuck in a belt. I thought at the time when I saw Humph handing it out to her from store, and her receiving it with a " Thank you Captain Carter ", that it was a risky present for an ugly girl. Val was far more likely to fire it off at Humph than at anybody else. But as I had a sporting rifle myself, an automatic of my own, a Smith-Wesson of the same type as Val's (all out of Humph's amazing schoolboy's dream of an armoury) and a huge Jack-knife, I did not feel that I was entitled to any more. Otherwise I should have suggested that Val's weapon might, with me, be in more experienced hands, and have wrested it from her.

I don't know if you like desert-travel. I can imagine nothing more awful. Nothing but the desire *to kill* would ever have taken me into the heart of Africa and here I had no such motive to allay its boresomeness. The Oriental makes his mind a complete blank. He can do that at any time he likes. Lucky Oriental! I wish I were an Oriental!

I am rather like an Oriental—I believe I have said that already—except for this really capital incapacity for making my mind into a blank. I can't make my mind into that.

If you like desert-travel I suppose I shall disappoint you, but, if you don't mind, we will blot out as much as possible of this part of the affair. Let us in fact make our minds into a complete blank! For ten minutes lie back in your chair and relax. Or if you are in bed, just go to sleep. It is the nearest that we Europeans can get to the oriental common or garden nirvana of everyday—the lowest of their nirvanas, which any eastern hobo can capture. After forty winks, come to your senses again, then imagine that we have all arrived at the opening of a sort of upland valley, up which the caravan tracks mount. Here we bivouac. A few eagles, or it might be more correct to call them vultures, are circling overhead. They spotted us I suppose at our start off, and will follow us in the hope of some accident occurring—until we are safely indoors again, at the other end of our journey. It may have been Humph that attracted them, thinking of good pink-coloured pickings and beef-fed delicatessen. If I were a vulture, I would not sniff at Humph.

We watched these beasts for some time, and then Humph took his rifle and determined to bring one down.

"I don't see why we should be followed by those animals do you?" he said.

I did not answer, but I took up my rifle too. I brought one down at once at the first bang. One of the other vultures circling swiftly, followed its body down, screaming, until it was very near indeed.—I am the best marksman I know. I put my rifle down. Humph blazed away and nothing happened, except that the animals at last disappeared. The handsome hillsman who was our guide looked at me with admiration. He looked at Humph with contempt. From that moment we got on like smoke, he and I. This aggravated Humph extremely—especially as Val appeared to be making Gossip-notes in a large pocket-book, and smiling to herself as she did so.

Haste is of the Devil the Persians say. And I seem to have heard a story of a White Man's grave in Hindustan, upon which was to be found the epitaph: "Here lies a European who died through trying to hustle the Orient." Well Humph tried to hustle the Orient. But in spite of this it took us a solid week to get to the brigand.

The muleteers were rather restless and dissatisfied I thought. The fact is that when they had been loading up at Yes one of them had sneezed. This sneeze upset them all very much. It cast a big superstitious shadow over all the journey. Should anything go wrong, immediately the *sneeze* was trotted out. We could not escape from this sneeze. And when at last the brigand hove in sight—as finally he did, to my intense relief—all th muleteers in chorus assured Humph that *this* was to be expected—having regard to the sneeze which had preceded our departure. And the man who had sneezed was the loudest of all in his *told-you-so's* from start to finish—for after all it was *his* sneeze which had been overlooked by the *Ferangis*!

The name of the man who sneezed was Hasan. His was in fact a potent, spell-weighted *atishoo*. But how he came to be delivered of it was, I understood, an effect of his intemperance. The evening before he had made himself drunk with *arak*. This is a very violent and peculiar intoxicant. It is manufactured by the Jews (the Moslems have to leave that industry in other hands, owing to the absurd injunctions of their pussyfoot prophet). In the morning (as invariably happens with *arak*, it was later explained to us—though Humph refused to believe it at first) Hasan woke up as sober as a judge, but with a diabolical hangover, of a particularly insidious order. Nothing showed on the surface. It was a bit cold in the mornings, prior to the desert-sunrise. He got a chill no doubt, the *arak* had not fortified him against colds-in-the-head. But what was odd (and this amused his pals in the highest degree) was that whenever, during the next day or two, he had a drink of water, he immediately became intoxicated. It is this that *arak* does. Then he would rush and stagger over in the direction of Humph, shamming a murderous sneeze—*crash crash* he went, for preference all over the indignant Humphrey—he would violently explain to my scandalized and astonished agent that his sneeze was no ordinary sneeze—*it was fatal!*—that better men than Humph had succumbed to it: that we should never have left Yes at all after such a sneeze as *that*—but that beyond question, for the ignoring of his sneeze, we should suffer! We should live to regret our foolhardiness, and learn to curse the day that he had sneezed.

Humph was very angry every time this happened. The big tribesman sat and smoked his *Kalyān*, curling his bearded lip contemptuously at the antics of the porter. But Humph would spring up cursing, and hurry over to where the muleteers squatted upon their naked heels. Pointing at them an angry finger, he would accuse them, mostly by signs, of secreting a bottle of *arak.*—Whenever Humph came rushing over at them they were tickled to death, the more Humph stormed the more funny it appeared to them—the more wildly they laughed—actually at last rolling over upon the ground and spinning and bumping in all directions like a pack of dervishes. One laughed so much at Humph that he had to come to us for medical treatment afterwards, for some internal lesion, and another suffered from nose-bleeding—he had broken a blood-vessel from laughing. They kept it up incessantly until the effects of the drug wore off. They would press water upon Hasan at every halt in order to provoke a recurrence of this scandal. When, purple in the face, Humph would return to our part of the encampment, he would find Val and myself, as well, convulsed with laughter. He would turn his back upon us, frowning and too annoyed to trust himself to speak. For a half-hour after he would sulk, going aside and cleaning his gun, or pretending to have forty winks.

In the heat of day of course we rested. Villages are generally some miles from the caravan routes (which is safer for them) and when that was practicable, we turned aside and spent the nights in them, at last reaching a large one, with a big romantic caravanserai (such as to be found all over Persia, the handiwork of a single Shah). There we spent two nights in smoke-blackened chambers. The rooms above a court blocked with camels and asses, bales crowded the middle upon a massive platform. Here we were met by a second tribesman, tall and stately like the first one who had come with us from Yes. But he soon disappeared. Upon the third day we resumed our journey. It was soon after this that we fell in with the brigand.

The second day out from the large village, we had just crossed an enormous and painfully empty plain, and we were preparing to pitch our tents at the foot of the mountains, when out of a very sinister yellow gorge rode a band of twenty or thirty suspicious-looking horsemen.

"Here he is!" hissed Humph, seizing me by the arm, his eyes gleaming with romantic satisfaction.

"Is this where we part?" I asked, taking up my rifle.

"Yes—here they are!—Remember, you can't mount quickly *because of your leg*!"

"I know. Of course not. I stand my ground."

"Pretend to put up a fight! Well good-bye old man—so-long rather! You'll be as safe as houses! These people are real gentlemen!"

"Pukka sahibs!"

" Real good fellers—White Men ! " he panted, automaton as he was, as if the epithets had got stuck, one on top of the other, and if he pulled one out they all came out.

" To the teeth ! " I growled.

" To the backbone ! "

" I shall be safe with *them* I feel sure " I said heartily.

" *Of course* you will old man ! Of course you will ! As safe as houses ! "

" I promise not to try and escape ! "

" No don't do that ! " He laughed boisterously at my joke. " Don't do that old boy ! That wouldn't go down at all well ! Wait patiently till the ransom arrives. It'll probably come by aeroplane."

" Will that take me back ? "

" No no. You go on to visit the bull-fighting tribes."

" Oh I go on ? "

" Yes, you go on—to smell out *Mith*-ras. You've got the pellicules ? I say you *have* got your pellicules ! "

" All O.K."

I had my Leike in my pocket.

" But as a matter of fact the old brigand will probably send you up country while you're waiting for the ransom, not to waste time."

" That will be jolly ! "

" Not to waste *time*."

" Of course ! Don't you wish you were coming old man ? "

" You bet I do ! "

" You won't change your mind and come along ? "

" No old boy I'm afraid not. I only wish I could ! It'd make the ransom too damn much ! "

" Of course it would—I hadn't thought of that."

" Also I've got to go and fix the publicity end of it now old man and bring pressure to bear with our jolly old government—' Baronet ' and all the rest of the blah ! "

" Rub in The Baronet! Don't forget *seventeenth* ! "

" Trust me for that old boy ! "

" Don't forget the ' Custom House Officer '."

" Rightyho ! " boomed Humph facetiously, full of sportive fun. " But I don't think we shall require him."

" Perhaps not."

" Ali Akbar over there's a damn good feller. I should give him a good tip."

Humph indicated the imperturbable picturesque hillsman, who sat with his rifle across his knees, smoking his *Kalyān*.

" Have you tipped him ? " I asked.

" No old chap—it'd come better from you—*afterwards* ! After he's finished his job of work ! *Afterwards* old man —afterwards ! "

" Isn't it finished ? "

" Not quite."

" Rightyho ! " I echoed his facctiousness. We both laughed toothily and clubmannishly and rocked about a bit as we excitedly chatted, prior to parting.

" Well tra-la-la old man " he baaed " and damn good luck ! "

He warmly shook my hand—I felt his heavy healthy unmoist palm. The band of horsemen were by this time out of the gorge. Soon they would be up with us or rather down upon us. Ali Akbar had risen to his feet. The muleteers and our two servants were in a state of great alarm, all except Hasan. The ponies had not been unsaddled.—They stood beside them, transfixed at the sight of the horsemen, chattering wildly together. What was a joke to us might be death to them, they were naturally a little upset.

" Good bye ! Good luck Humph old fruit ! " I exclaimed, aiming a slap at his back.

" To horse ! " roared Humph. " To horse ! "

Val was at my elbow.

" What has he been saying ! " she hissed. " What has the swine been saying ! "

" Mrs Ritter " Humph cried. " Mount at once or you'll be left behind ! "

" I'm damned if I will ! " said Val to me.

This was very boring.

" Come on Val old thing ! You must get on to your moke ! " I said, pretending to hobble towards my pony.

" Mrs Ritter—are you coming or not ! You must really mount at once ! " Humph bellowed.

Val lighted a cigarette, and started walking after me very much all-in-good-time.

" Wait a moment Snooty ! " she called.

" Come on then ! " I said in a cross staccato. " What are you dawdling about for ? You must go off with him you know ! You can't stop here ! I'm damned if I'm going to have you stop here."

" I say Mrs Ritter look sharp ! " Humph boomed from his pony. " There's no time to be lost ! Aren't you coming ! "

I reached Val's snow-white donkey, and held it by the bridle. Val came up, smoking in a manner suggestive of anything but expedition. The two muleteers that were left with us were gesticulating, pointing to our seats, and pointing after Humph, who had put his pony in motion. I frowned at Val and said to her as snootily as possible—

" That's quite enough heroics Mistress Val ! Oblige me now by jumping up upon this beautiful ass and riding away with Humph. I am sick of the sight of both of you ! "

Suddenly a fusillade broke out, the horsemen really appeared to be firing on us. Bullets whistled and the earth flew up not many yards from where we stood.

" What's this ! " I said. I was certainly under the impression, in spite of all that had been said, that this was an ambuscade. My first thought was of Ali Akbar. Immediately I swung round upon him and covered him with my rifle. He did not notice what I was doing. He lifted his own rifle, took aim at the mountain-side, and sent a bullet over the heads of the attacking party. Shots came in response, and the earth spat up upon either side of him. He laughed like a child at his pals' warlike joke and again levelled his rifle, this time it seemed straight at the leaders of the band.

Meanwhile the horsemen were scattering, and soon affected to pursue the fugitives, firing as they went. A *fantasia* developed—a savage musical-ride of desert horsemanship, a wheeling and galloping in all senses at once, a firing and shouting. I turned in the direction of Humph, who had halted his pony, pivoted in his saddle, every inch a Bedouin, every inch a Briton. He was aiming playfully in our direction, and the next minute I saw the flash. I cannot tell you upon what impulse I acted, but lifting my rifle I brought it down till it was trained just short of the rim of his white puggaree, and fired. In the general confusion my action went unnoticed. I saw Humph pitch forward upon his pony, he was hit. Then I fired a second shot, and you may believe me or not, but of all the shots I have ever fired, at all the game I have ever hunted (and this includes the hippopotamus) I don't believe that any shot ever gave me so much pleasure as that second one, at old Humph's shammyleathered, gussetted stern, before he rolled off his pony and bit the dust. (The first was not great fun—it was almost automatic. I scarcely knew I was doing it. But I knew all about the second.)

I lowered my rifle and as I turned to my left-hand side, I found the blazing eyes of Ali Akbar fixed upon me. It was a gaze it seemed of fierce astonishment that he levelled at me. I had captured his attention I should say very much indeed. So he stood for a moment or two, and I returning his stare. Then he began walking over towards me, walking up to me I should say rather. I thereupon turned about to face in the other direction, and there I found Val—her eyes were fixed upon me as fast as Ali's. Her expression too was one of astonishment, but with it was a good portion of intense alarm, gathering at the back of them, where her mind was at work. I gave her a slow and owlish, mirthless, clock-work wink.

"Well let's have another pot!" I said, cocking my cowboy Stetson at a jocular angle over my nose. And lifting my rifle again I let fly well over the head of a whirling horseman. Then I turned about once more, rather jauntily, and found myself face to face with Ali Akbar—tall, tanned, almost a nigger-black, armed like a porcupine. His handsome bloodshot eyes were fastened upon my face, as if he had come over to take a look at closer quarters at me—to gaze into the recesses of a european soul as close-up as possible, in his simple physical way. A thing he evidently did not feel at all competent to form a judgment upon—the White Consciousness. For with a kind of cool, unhurried fascinated curiosity he went on staring steadily into the depths of my eyes (and occasionally running over the rest of my face—scrutinizing my nose, mouth, and, I thought, not neglecting either my prominent *ears*) but all this with a dash of insolent fierceness as well—as if requiring of me an explanation of what was to be deciphered in the depths of my nordic headpiece with such difficulty by an oriental eye. *Explain yourself, North Man—to me Ali Akbar, the persian brigand—for generations without end we have been the lords of this desert!*

I gave him glance for glance. But suddenly I sent out all my teeth in gardee parade order (for him to count if he wished to) and slowly raised from where it had been pointing at the ground the muzzle of my rifle. As he saw it coming up he started back, like a horse that has suddenly been flicked or stung—jumping up in the air a little and starting back three or four paces nimbly, doubtfully and enquiringly backing away from my weapon. As I grinned I frowned, and I motioned with my rifle that he should stand back.

"Pop off!" I shouted. "Keep your distance Ali Akbar! Another step and I shall drill you Ali!"

It seemed to astonish him far more that I should threaten him than that I should do what he apparently had observed me do, namely polish off old Humph. He was *a man—a wild animal*—and *a child*—all at once. Abruptly I turned my back upon him, and grounded my rifle, scratching the back of my head.

Val was watching my behavior with a settled speechless alarm.

"Snooty" she said in what I took to be a more natural voice than it was her custom to employ.

"What is it Valkyrie?" I asked.

"What are you doing?"

"First-rate sport!" I said. "First-class. Best yet!" I was very Humphish and hearty.

"I wish you'd put that gun away!"

"Why? This is all just a joke, we're all just having a joke with one another. There's no occasion for alarm."

"Do you call it a joke?"

"Not I. Not particularly. But that was Humph's idea."

"It was, that's true."

She gazed down at the ground, succeeding in looking like a haggard child, with her arms hanging (in fact like a particularly blowsy pantomime Babe-in-the-Wood). But she said very distinctly, as if to herself—

"I saw what you did!"

It was the voice of a cloud of witnesses. She was announcing her status. (For future use perhaps!)

"You ought to have ridden away with poor old Humph!" I expostulated with her. "He will be lonely! —He'd be glad of even your company I expect!"

The firing had stopped. The horsemen were gathering. Several had sprung down and were approaching us. I looked round behind me—Ali Akbar was going to meet them half-way. As they advanced they gesticulated—a violent altercation it seemed was in progress among these barbarians, in their tatterdemalion outfits. A small man of mongol appearance in the midst was the most voluble. He spoke I thought with most authority. And as he spoke he carried his hands to his holsters and half drew out a pistol every few seconds, as he shook his fist first in one person, then another's, face.

As they reached Ali Akbar they all fell silent. The whole group, six in all (and as they talked a couple more came up) listened with stupefaction it seemed to me to their comrade Ali, in a sort of stupid silence—who, as he spoke, looked over in my direction, pointing several times and mimicking my shooting. He pointed into the sky also and looked towards me as he spoke—that was the eagle I had shot. I was a first-class shot who did not miss he was saying. I kept my eyes upon them while this was going forward.

"Our guide saw you Snooty" Val said in a low voice. "I saw him looking."

"How's that?" I said, grinning as I watched the confabulation of the Forty Thieves.

"I shall say you didn't do it" she said in the same tone, of reciting a lesson, and a little girl at that.

"I really don't know what you're talking about" I replied, with routine snooty fanfaronade.

"No. But I shall say that, if anything is said."

"I'm sure I'm very much obliged to you!" I sneered over at her, without removing my eyes from the group of desert-gunmen. " Very obliged ! How shall I ever be able to thank you enough ! That's what I should like to know."

The small man with the tartar face now stepped out from among the rest, and came over with rapid steps towards me, the others crowding after him.

" Good evening ! " he said as he reached me in perfectly if a little clipped chicagoan english.

" Good evening " I said. " How are you ! "

" Fine ! " he said.

" That's capital ! " I said.

He planted himself in front of me with his arms akimbo. His booted legs were wide apart, which made him even shorter—he was a very short man. The fellow's expression was certainly threatening, I could see he was extremely angry with me.

" What's the big idea ? " he asked me truculently.

" I don't understand you."

" You don't get me ? Think again ! "

" I can't say I do. Who are you anyway ? "

" I ? Oh I'm just the brigand, the chief ! "

" Is that all ! I thought you were the Shah of Persia ! "

" No sir, I'm only a poor brigand ! "

" That's too bad ! Well, what can I do for you ? You've behaved in a rather extraordinary way haven't you —coming and attacking a band of peaceable travellers ! "

" You behave sort of funny too, buddy ! "

" How do you make that out ? "

The ring of ruffians gazed at me darkly, uttering in every pause what sounded like a volley of asiatic oaths, nearly choked with their panting aspirates. They were doubtless calling upon their Saints and all the cohorts of the mithraic angels—perhaps who knows upon Mithras himself, the celestial *chef-de-bande* !

" Who are you ? " he asked. " Are you Baron Imrie ? Or who are you ! What is it ! Do they call you Imrie ? "

" Oh you do know me then. Yes they call me Imrie."

He looked me up and down with a sort of constipated suspicion. He spoke to Ali Akbar, who was standing at his elbow and Ali nodded with great vigour, and pointed at my leg. They all looked with curiosity at my leg. I grinned at them, and lifting up my artificial leg, worked it about a little.

" I'm the one-legged man you're looking for " I said.

He still did not seem satisfied that I was not a one-legged impostor.

" It's all right " I said. " I'm the man you're after ! "

The chief took a pace forward, and stood almost up against me, his face raised to mine, his jaw stuck out.

" If you Baron Imrie, what did you go to shoot your friend for ! That is funny thing to do. Answer me ! Why did you shoot ! "

I threw up my hands, in a gesture of extreme deprecation, as if giving him up as a bad job.

" You're a pretty smart guy I can see *that* " he said. " I know New York San Francisco—I'm not a savage, get me ? I see you are a guy knows how to play—only you can't behave in this desert as you would in your own country ! Understand that ! This is first time anything's happened in this desert. I see *nothing ever happens*—I am the chief ! "

" How dull, if you'll allow me to say so ! "

"Yes you are one smart guy all right I guess. Very well ! You want the money. That is good, that is very good for you, but not for *us* ! Not for me and my men here ! For us this is a bad business ! "

" I don't know what you're talking about. What money ? "

" You think you get all the dough ! I see that—oh swell idea ! You think the dough goes to you now ! Ha ha ! But perhaps we none of us shall get ! That will not be so good ! "

I laughed loudly all of a sudden, for I saw his meaning. The fellow believed that I had shot Humph to collar all the cash—our end of the ransom money.

Those horsemen who had gone after the fugitives began to come up, in ones and twos. One of these horsemen had Humph's body slung across his horse like a sack of meal, across his lap. He tumbled it off, and it fell in a compact heap not above fifteen feet from where we stood—flinging himself off after it. Stooping he picked up an arm, held it, then let it drop. It dropped limp. Humph was dead. The others crowded round it, examining the gunshot wounds with critical attention and falling into arguments evidently as to what type of bullet was responsible for the wounds.

The chief walked over to it, and looked down at the corpse of my agent. I followed. Old Humph was on his back. He was pretty badly marked—a bullet had come bursting out of the centre of his chin (that was the one I put in just under thé puggarree) and split it open like a gourd.

" This your friend ? " the chief asked. " This your friend ? " the chief enquired again. " This him Carter ? "

" It looks like him " I said. " Is he dead ? Is my poor friend dead ? "

" Dead ? Yep. He is dead good enough I guess ! He won't need breakfast tomorrow ! "

He kicked Humph over upon his face—the old boy rolled over like a soft log.

" So your men shot my friend ? " said I sternly.

The chief looked at me in I thought a nasty way. I could see that he admired me, but did not like me I think. He was inclined to cut up rough. I could tell that.

" I'm not ugly see, not like some guys I'm not ! " he said aggressively. " I don't shoot for nothing. But I got these—I'm not afraid to use ! I kill as well—not for *nothing* ! "

He struck his jewelled yellow hand upon an assortment of pistol-handles that crowded his Tom Gallon belt. His followers, now to the number of twenty or thirty, muttered and shouted, and handled their rifles, menacingly as regards me. Two of them brought in the muleteers and servants who had fled with Humph, their chief had sent them off to round these others up. Pushing them before them at the points of their rifles and prodding them to make them move faster, they came to a halt outside the circle of robber tribesmen gathered about Humph. The chief muttered a few words to the men next to him.

The whole party became electrified and all began shouting at the tops of their voices and the next moment the poor devils who had come with us from Yes, all except Hasan, were first chased away with blows and curses, and then as they ran, or sank to their knees imploring mercy, they were shot down by his passionate followers. As for me, I was powerless to stop their massacre. Val screamed —a low and unexpected scream. Of course I shouted and went on like anything—I took the little yellow beast of a snooty kurdish chiefling by the elbow, ordering him to call his lousy men off or it would be the worse for him! He only turned and glared at me, in disagreeable yellow-eyed irony I took it to be, protruding at me his ugly underlip. Evidently he regarded me as a hypocrite. My protesting against this wanton killing offended him still more.

When all the pack-animals, ponies, and asses, had been driven in and assembled, Val and I were told to mount. I helped her up on to the big white ass. Then with a sort of nervous precipitation, as if released by a trigger, set in motion in a spasm of meaningless unrest (the other side of the famous oriental contemplation I suppose) we left the scene of these events in a sort of *sauve-qui-peut*—I even thought at first that in truth we had been surprised, that they had sighted troops or something unexpected.

But it was not that. We just hurried quickly off into the mouth of the horrid yellow gorge for no particular reason, out of which this party of robber horsemen, my surly captors, had emerged. It was their road home, to their lair. Several rode behind Val and me, their rifles in readiness. But they had not attempted to disarm me for some reason. I took this to be an excellent sign.—I was glad we were leaving Humph behind. That gave me a great deal of pleasure. He was dead, he was of no more use to anyone than an old waterlogged hat. He had ceased his troubling. I had not got over my enjoyment as regards the second of those shots yet. Indeed it is fair to say I think that I shall never lose that pleasant feeling of immediate satisfaction—the sting of pleasure like the ping of a rifle, is as fresh as a daisy, at this moment. It will never lose that quality—*Time cannot dull, use cannot* whatever it is!—A thing of beauty is a joy forever! That second one was *a beauty*!

BANDIT-HOST

MIRZA AGA, MY aristocratic captor, had his headquarters in a powerful castle, with a largeish village outside its gates. He was a small tribal chief. Howitzers would have been necessary to rout him out. His fortress was one of the *nid d'aigle* sort, and impregnable without the use of artillery, or air-bombardment. I was in bad odour when we arrived. He passed in and disappeared: I was sent straight to my living-quarters in disgrace. These were a fine suite of rooms with bath in a lofty tower, with a view over a delectable ravine. Immediately beneath the windows was a *bag*, laid out with great gimcrack taste. Val was in the suite underneath—they seemed to lump us together for all practical purposes.

I did not see the fellow all the next day. He was away I think. I suppose he had gone to see about the ransom and perhaps to bury Humph and the servants and porters. Val and myself sat in the bag in deck-chairs, recovering from the enormous meals which were placed before us. I slept from lunch on and when I woke I discovered old Val keeping the flies away from my live ankle and hand-and-face flesh—quite the victorian odalisque!

"What are you supposed to be doing?" I said.

"The flies woke me up" she said.

"Well leave *my* flies alone in future" I told her "and keep your distance when I'm asleep!"

She withdrew to her chair, and began scribbling hard in her notebook.

"What are you doing there?" I asked.

" Nothing Snoots."

" What is it ? "

" I'm only trying to get things straight.—Also I thought if I wrote it all down I should remember it better."

" Wrote *what* down ? "

She closed the book, and put it away.

" Only our journey."

Val did not say much all day. But towards evening she spoke to me in the following strain.

" Snooty " she said " do you mind if I talk to you about —I've been thinking Snooty. We are rather in a hole."

" *Hole ?* I think it's most comfortable—I don't see what you've got to grumble at here."

" Would it bore you if I told you what I have been thinking ! "

" Very much indeed " I said, and I yawned in the most forbidding way I could.

" Well Snooty. It has occurred to me that since these people have shot Captain Cooper Carter——"

" What old Humph ? Did they do that do you think ? "

" Yes Snoots obviously—no one else would. Don't you think it's likely there will be trouble ? "

" Who with ? "

" With the British Authorities perhaps, or the Persian."

" Well I can't help it. They shouldn't go blazing away like that ! "

" I know."

" They were certain to hit *somebody* ! "

" And then there are the porters from Yes and servants. Our pipe-man was killed."

" I know poor fellow ! "

" And the table-man, and the porters. Won't enquiries be made ? "

" Perhaps. I tell you what. I suggest we say that Humph committed hara-kiri when he saw himself surrounded, and invited us to do the same but we stoutly refused—and that the baggage staff fled and probably perished of thirst in the desert. We are the only survivors ! "

Her studious look (the only possible form of frown for Val) was very much to the fore, furrowing her forehead, her eyes staring in a composed distraction into space.

" I have been thinking of the different things that we could say " she said.

" *We?* "

" You know what I mean. The best is to stick to the story of the brigands having done it—in the excitement of the moment, probably by accident. It was a stray shot. No one can prove the reverse."

I looked at her, grinning snootily. She leant towards me, as if to impart something of a more confidential nature. Staring at me impressively almost a full second she said—

" I think *you* should be *slightly* wounded Snooty ! "

" I've been wounded quite enough thank you ! " I said, tapping my leg. " I never heard such nonsense."

" Couldn't you possibly—tell me if you think I am being absurd—spare a *finger*—off your *left hand* ! "

I got up from the chair, looking her straight in the eyes with a full minute's steady contempt. This was very bad indeed ! The old girl was actually being *snooty*—just as Humph used to be, the insolent puppet ! She was stealing my thunders. She wished to convey (what else could it mean ?) that she had the whip hand ! I was in her power, as she saw it.

" If you ever speak to me like that again " I said to her balefully and very slowly " I will decoy you to the top of that high tower up there and push you off—and pretend that you *slipped* while you were taking a photograph ! "

I walked back into the tower in question, where our suites were. When I reached my apartment, I stood in the window and looked down at her severely, to bring my words home to her a little more. She saw me standing up there in the tower and glaring down at her, and she scribbled feverishly in her memorandum book. That was the last time she ventured to discuss ways and means of white-washing ourselves (coupling herself with me) when we got back to civilization.

The next morning we were notified that Mirza Aga would be pleased to give us dinner at his table, or rather on his floor—at his end of the castle, at eight punctually. I expressed myself as delighted and said we would come. At three minutes to eight his Chamberlain arrived to conduct us to our host's quarters. We followed this blossoming turbaned personage of chains and keys, through many passages, whispering galleries, across cyclopean courtyards (where great hounds lay sleeping, or asses stood, prepared for a sepulchral bray), skirted the stables (where we saw a heavily-armed patrol which had just come in noisily dismount) passing under several massive arches. We at length were brought to a coquettish court, where a large fountain of six jets played: and above the court was the verandah, where we were to dine with the Aga.

Mounting a half-dozen steps, behind the burly domestic official, I entered a large apartment. I stopped ceremoniously upon the threshold and bowing remarked—

"*Salaam—Alaikum!*"

My host, who stood stiffly in the middle of the room awaiting us in a costume that was a well-tailored wedding of the styles of the East and West, responded—

"*Alaikum—us—Salaam!*"

He bowed to Val.

"*Ahvale sharife shuma cheh torast?*"

I thought a moment and replied—

"*Alhamdulellah!*"

The fellow laughed and said—

"Well that's that!"

We all three had a good european laugh together, and shook our legs out and put our hands in our pockets—in an orgy of jaunty western *sans-façon*.

Going towards a table, where there were european bottles and glasses he said—

" Will you have a snort ? "

" What have you got ? " I went over and noticed Gordon's Gin, and Jameson's Whisky, also Black and White. I pointed to Gordon's.

" This ? " he said. " What will you have misses ? " he asked Val.

" The same please " Val said with her bloodcurdling demureness, quickly looking away, away from the Aga, as she spoke.

White cloths had been spread upon the verandah, and by electric light, sitting sideways upon the floor, we ate partridge livers grilled on skewers, caviar, wild ducks, pigeons, venison, an entire calf (brought in by four men, from the smoked and dripping carcass of which Mirza Aga cut me off little choice pieces), grapes, peaches, melons and nectarines, persian candies and turkish sweets, *and* pink still champagne. This was to show that we were welcome. It was in recognition of my rank. He felt I suppose that he had been rather rude the day before and he wished to correct the painful impression this must have made upon a man of my stamp. A good report must have been brought in from his agents regarding the ransom. During the party he did not talk business. He gossiped about the United States mostly, where he had served his apprenticeship in the bootlegging traffic. He had lived there before he succeeded to the title and family business which, he said, he had always tried to keep clean of blood-spilling—that was the *only* remark he had made all the evening that was in any sense tactless or unsuitable, and we parted excellent friends.

During the three weeks of my stay at Mirza Aga's I was not always treated as well as this. Things oscillated—there were ups and downs. For several days for instance we had armed guards posted at our doors, and were not allowed out of our suites. The food got very bad during that period. Then our host apologized and another calf was killed and served up whole and we *again* had pink champagne. He was very reserved and kept his own counsel as regards what was happening in the outside world. I had not the least idea if our capture had been publicly reported or not. My method with him was the same as with Humph—I knew it was useless with such a ruffian to ask questions as he would only lie, so I said nothing at all.

Many conversations occurred it is true between us on the subject of the Humph incident. I did not care, of course, what he thought. But I considered it wiser to adopt the attitude that there had been a great deal too much firing. He got very short-tempered at times. He swore on one occasion that he'd never take on a British job again. The British were more trouble than they were worth and paid less every day and took longer to cough up the cash. (Americans paid best of all though they were not what they used to be.) I agreed that there could not be much in it for him poor chap, and I commiserated with him regarding the British: but I complimented him upon his arrangements at the castle.

Once or twice I went down into the village, always with a guard or two at my side. Europeans have from the earliest days employed the art of medicine to ingratiate themselves with the eastern and african victims of their commercial enterprise. The result is that to-day any European is regarded as a *Hakkim* in such places as this, which can be a great bore and exposes one to many dangers. The last time I went into the village I took Val, she had asked to come. A very poor woman—who stank like a sewer and was really a very repulsive and untidy object—mistook old Val for a *Hakkim* and came whining up to her. (My wooden leg I think made them inclined to say to themselves that I was probably not a very competent *Hakkim*, on the old principal of *Physician heal thyself!*) As Val did not respond, the filthy wretch thought evidently that the next best thing would be to rub herself against Val, which she proceeded to do, performing a sort of shambling dance in old Val's rear, brushing against her and bumping lightly into her, muttering to herself as she did so.

" I wish that woman wouldn't rub against me ! " Val said, shaking herself at these undesirable contacts.

" Kick her ! " I suggested. " You'll get some vermin, and then you'll hand them on to me ! "

Turning to Mohammed Ali (an english-speaking bandit, who had lived in Hindustan), accompanying us to see we didn't escape, I said—

" What's the matter with this scarecrow Ali—can't you get rid of her ? "

He laughed and showed his gums (and a miserable set of little teeth, like a consumptive weasel) and said—

" All her children and her husband have got smallpox. She believes she can rub it off on you ! She is ridiculous ! "

Val shoved her away after that with her bottom and hips, as the hag came up for the next rub behind. But Val got smallpox.

As soon as the infection showed itself, she went to bed. I did not go near her. Why should I ? I have explained in considerable detail my relations with this woman. Why should I go in and catch her smallpox ? I don't suggest that you think I should, but there are people who are fond of saying (and they have said it about me in the Press) that one should share these complaints with one's fellow-men (especially if they are women). But as meanwhile the ransom did not arrive, I went to Mirza Aga and suggested that I had been there long enough. He seemed to think so too. He listened to me attentively. Why did he not escort me back to the confines of civilized life—I would tell them all that Humph had died of small-pox, which would settle that definitely—inform them that unfortunately Val had it still, and get them to send a ransom. Of course if they *didn't* send a ransom, he could keep Val. He grinned at this alternative, and shook his head and winked. Also I said I would give him a cheque for a hundred pounds, as some compensation for his hospitality. But I did not want to stop any longer.

At last he consented, and I left with a strong escort and reached Yes in record time. From thence I was brought back in an aeroplane to Teheran and made a great fuss of by the British colony there. (It was in Teheran that I first knew that I had been starred in two hemispheres as THE LOST BARONET. This was very bad, but I grinned and bore it—it was the hand of Humph, still heavy upon me, even in death!) So the persian end of the story terminates, there is nothing more to say about Persia. Bulls I am thankful to say were never mentioned between us, while I was with Mirza Aga—and certainly I never referred to one nor had the bad taste to talk about Mithras or any priggish matter that, being a Persian, might have made him feel small, as revealing a so-called ignorance. I never saw him fighting with a bull, as Pat Bostock had said he did. It was I believe a lie.

SNOOTY'S S.O.S.

LILY AND I—Shushani, persian lily—are at the Bosphorus. We lead a happy turkish existence in this europeanized Orient, I shall be sorry when it ends. The threat of cutting off my disability pension, which has been freely canvassed in the British Press, I snap my fingers at! The *Book of the Month Club* have taken up these papers, entitling them (about this there will be a lawsuit or two) " SNOOTY BARONET ", which secures for my ' human document ' —my fictionist essay on BEHAVIOR—a sale of a hundred thousand copies as a minimum. The *Book Society*, the english imitation of the american affair, also has given me the prize. Both these events (artistically discreditable as they may be) promises wads of ill-gotten dough to the author of these pages, and upon the proceeds it is my intention to settle, perhaps with my London Lily, who has written me the most charming of letters—I put this in at the suggestion of my new agent, Mr Stinker, as he says that Lily ought to be heard of again—that otherwise the book would not sound like " fiction " but would have too rebarbative and *scientific* an air.

All that you may read in the Popular Press regarding this obscure affair you can discount at once. Mistress Val's smallpox has not improved her tongue any more than (so I understand) it has improved her looks. But this is the first full and circumstantial account of my trip to Persia. Before this I have (stepping into Humph's shoes and acting as my own publicity agent) issued a statement which was a bare outline nothing more of the facts. But what is an *outline* of the facts—it can give the Public no idea really of the motives and circumstances that are the necessary backgrounds for such a tragedy. Those I have now, as completely as my poor command of the narrative form would allow, supplied, down to my encounter with the Hatter's Automaton, which was a turning-point.

I have freely been described as mad and as a liar. This book is my answer to that. If it is mad to be a *Behaviorist*, then certainly I am as mad as a hatter, as mad as a Hatter's Automaton if you like. As to *liar*, it is my word against that of such a person as Val.

What Mrs Valerie Ritter says is that I never shot Humph at all, but have invented that—her version is the one she proposed to me for publication while we were sitting in the persian guest-garden of Mirza Aga. The bandits got out of hand (according to her) and one of their bullets, by design or accident, laid Humph low. She has the effrontery to set herself up as my defender against myself. And she associates with these categorical refutations of what I say a crowd of fantastic remarks, throwing a false light upon me, and a false light upon the whole mechanics of our trip—as is only natural.—Mrs Ritter's version is, as you know, the version that is generally accepted as true. I have written to England to give up my baronetcy for instance, but have met with a refusal on behalf of His Majesty, who is pleased to consider that I would do well to go into a nursing-home for a month or so, and is persuaded that after suitable treatment I would emerge in my right senses and become once more a normal member of the caledonian aristocracy, against whose fair name no breath of suspicion had ever successfully blown—I have been *unhinged* (that is the expression, as if I were a door) by my experiences. I require *a rest*, that is the idea.—And meanwhile Val is getting much kudos out of her attitude. When she first was able to be moved and arrived at Teheran her first action was to send me a most snooty cable—

SNOOTY YOU DIRTY DOG!

That was all. Was this the action of a friend? She still seems to think that she will see me again. *What hopes* as Lily would say—or *And then you wake up!*

This postscript to my narrative is an S.O.S. It is a " cry from the heart " (if you must put things in that way) of a Behaviorist, demanding justice. It is clearly most unjust that I should publicly be whitewashed (as if I were an *object*, unable to give an account of myself) by such a person as Val Ritter. My book " People Behaving " has been brought out in a popular edition, and it is for the author of that treatise, and of " Blurbs for Humanity " that I claim justice. I behave as a *Behaviorist* and as such I claim I should be accepted, and if there is nothing else that I can do to prove it, I will at least continue *to behave* as you have seen me behaving throughout these pages, and as all true Behaviorists *must* behave. If you are a true behaviorist, and not merely a sham one, you behave as I have behaved! Put that in your pipe and smoke it, all you professors of this implacable doctrine!